MORTAL HEART

His Fair Assassin BOOK III

MORTAL HEART

By Robin LaFevers

Houghton Mifflin Harcourt
Boston New York

www.hmhco.com

The text of this book is set in Adobe Garamond

Book design by Scott Magoon

Map by Cara Llewellyn

Library of Congress Cataloging-in-Publication Data
LaFevers, Robin.
Mortal heart / by Robin LaFevers.
p. cm. — (His fair assassin ; book 3)
Summary: Annith's worst fears are realized when she discovers that, despite her lifelong training to be an assassin, she is being groomed by the abbess as a seeress, to be forever shut up in the convent of Saint Mortain.
ISBN 978-0-547-62840-0
[1. Convents — Fiction. 2. Nuns — Fiction. 3. Assassins — Fiction. 4. Death — Fiction.
5. Gods — Fiction. 6. Brittany (France) — History — 1341–1532 — Fiction.
7. France — History — Charles VIII, 1483–1498 — Fiction.] I. Title.
PZ7.L14142Mor 2014
[Fic] — dc23
2014001877

Manufactured in the United States of America
DOC 10 9 8 7 6 5 4 3

4500516075

For Mark,
Again.
And always.
But especially for the last two years.

DRAMATIS PERSONAE

At the Convent

ANNITH, a novitiate of Mortain
SYBELLA D'ALBRET, handmaiden to Death
ISMAE RIENNE, handmaiden to Death

ABBESS OF SAINT MORTAIN (formerly Sister Etienne)
SISTER EONETTE, convent historian and archivist
SISTER THOMINE, martial arts instructor
SISTER SERAFINA, poisons mistress
SISTER WIDONA, stable mistress
SISTER BEATRIZ, instructor in womanly arts
SISTER CLAUDE, sister in charge of the rookery
SISTER VEREDA, convent seeress
SISTER ARNETTE, arms mistress
DRAGONETTE, former abbess of Saint Mortain (deceased)
SISTER APPOLLONIA, former convent historian and archivist (deceased)
SISTER MAGDELENA, former poisons mistress (deceased)
SISTER DRUETTE, former seeress (deceased)

MATELAINE, a novitiate of Mortain
SARRA, a novitiate of Mortain
AVELINE, a novitiate of Mortain
LOISSE, a novitiate of Mortain
LISABET, a novitiate of Mortain
AUDRI, a novitiate of Mortain
FLORETTE, a novitiate of Mortain

The Hellequin

BALTHAZAAR
MISERERE
BEGARD
MALESTROIT
SAUVAGE
MALIGNE

Followers of Saint Arduinna
FLORIS, a priestess of Arduinna
AEVA
TOLA
ODILA

The Breton Court and Nobility
ANNE, duchess of Brittany, countess of Nantes, Montfort, and Richmont
ISABEAU, her sister
DUKE FRANCIS II, Anne's father (deceased)
GAVRIEL DUVAL, a Breton noble
BENEBIC DE WAROCH, the Beast of Waroch and knight of the realm
VISCOUNT MAURICE CRUNARD, former chancellor of Brittany
JEAN DE CHALON, Prince of Orange
CAPTAIN DUNOIS, captain of the Breton army
PHILLIPE MONTAUBAN, chancellor of Brittany
BISHOP OF RENNES
FATHER EFFRAM
CHARLES VIII, king of France
ANNE DE BEAUJEU, regent of France
NORBERT GISORS, French ambassador
MAXIMILIAN OF AUSTRIA, the Holy Roman emperor, Anne's husband

The Nine
MORTAIN, god of death
DEA MATRONA, mother goddess
ARDUINNA, goddess of love's sharp bite, daughter of Matrona, twin sister of
    Amourna
AMOURNA, goddess of love's first blush, daughter of Matrona
BRIGANTIA, goddess of knowledge and wisdom
CAMULOS, god of battle and war
MER, goddess of the sea
SALONIUS, god of mistakes
CISSONIUS, god of travel and crossroads

MORTAL HEART

Chapter One

FOR MOST, THE BLEAK DARK months when the black storms come howling out of the north is a time of grimness and sorrow as people await the arrival of winter, which brings death, hunger, and bitter cold in its wake. But we at the convent of Saint Mortain welcome winter with open arms and hearts, for it is Mortain's own season, when He is full upon us. In such a way does the Wheel of Life turn, with every ending but a new beginning; that is the promise Mortain has made us.

So while most people bar their doors and shut their windows tight, we have cause for celebration and go traipsing through the wood, gathering the sacred yew branches and collecting holly with its bright red berries that remind us of the three drops of blood spilled when Mortain was pierced by love and Arduinna's own arrow.

And while Mortain is a far more gentle god than most people give Him credit for, I do not think He would look kindly upon His youngest handmaidens jousting with the sacred branches that are intended for His holy fire.

"Audri! Aveline! Stop that!"

"She started it," Aveline says, peering out from under the pale red hair that has fallen across her eyes.

"No, I didn't! You did. You always do. Because you're good with swords and knives and fighting, you always want to fight."

"Girls!" I clap my hands, wincing at how very much I remind myself of Sister Beatriz when she loses control of the womanly-charms lessons. "Enough. Audri, go help Florette. Aveline, you come over here with me."

Thinking the other girl in trouble, Audri sticks her tongue out at Aveline, then hurries over to help Florette. Instead of scolding Aveline, I take her hand, lead her to a holly bush, and give her a knife. "You will fill that basket, and I will fill this one."

Pleased at being given a blade, something normally reserved for older girls or the training yard, Aveline turns to the bush and begins cutting.

I keep my eyes on the leaves in front of me as I speak to her. "You are the oldest of the group, Aveline. There is no honor in besting those younger than you."

She stops her cutting and turns her strange, solemn gaze on me. "Are you saying I should pretend to be weak so they can feel strong? Is that not telling a lie?" Before I can untangle her knotted logic, she shrugs. "Besides, she is nearly as old as I am and likes to show off by going without her cloak and shoes."

I hide a smile, for it is true that Audri is quite proud of her ability to withstand cold. Not only does she not feel the wintry chill, but she does not suffer chilblains or deadened limbs when exposed to it. That is her gift for being pulled from the womb of a woman who had frozen to death in one of winter's most savage storms. She is as impervious to the cold as one of the great white bears of the far north, and proud of it. "That may be true," I concede, "but you have gifts every bit as glorious as hers and you constantly pick fights so that you may show them off."

For a moment, the old familiar wave of loss and longing rears up and I catch my breath at the pain of it. Among the handmaidens of Death our birth stories are our most treasured possessions, marking us as they do as Death's true daughters. But on the day that I was born, no cuckolded husband paced nearby, no herbwitch pulled me from a cold, dead womb, nor did any hedge priest administer the last rites to a dying mother while I rooted futilely at her breast.

Or at least, I think not, for the truth is that I do not even know the day on which I was born. I do not know the manner of my birth, the name of my mother, or even if she still lives, although we think she must not, else I would not have ended up on the convent's doorstep when I was less than a week old. Of all the women whose feet have pattered along these stone floors, I am the only one to have no inkling of the circumstances of my own birth.

It is like an itching, festering wound I have trained myself not to scratch. But some days the pain and burn of it are nearly beyond bearing. Especially when I am confronted with a cocksure nine-year-old who is blessed with reflexes so fast she has been known to snatch arrows from their flight.

Aveline keeps her attention on the holly but watches me from the corner of her eye. "Does that mean you will let me fight you sometime?"

I cannot help it—I laugh. "You think you can best me?"

She lifts one shoulder. "I think I would like to know if I could or could not."

At her words, my smile wobbles and it is all I can do to keep from throwing my knife down in defeat. Even this *child* thinks I am no longer a match for her. I carefully avoid looking out at the ocean, just beyond the trees. It is too painful a reminder that both Ismae and Sybella have been sent to places I have not, have begun to fulfill their destinies while I am stuck here playing nursemaid to a gaggle of budding assassins.

I feel a tug at the corner of my gown and look down to find Florette standing there with wide eyes. "We did not mean to make you sad, Annith."

"Oh, you didn't, sweeting. I am just"—what? Feeling sorry for myself? Pining for my friends? Wishing fate had dealt me a different hand? —"eager to finish up with these branches so we can begin decorating."

Her small face clears and she goes back to her own work while I move on to the next branch. It is hard—so hard—not to feel wasted, like a new sword that has been allowed to rust before it has ever been used. I tighten my grip on my blade, reminding myself that the abbess has assured me it is just one of Mortain's many mysteries, why He has called the others first. If I ever come face to face with Him again, I shall ask why.

Politely, of course.

"Annith?" Aveline says.

"Hmmm?"

"Are we supposed to chop at our branches like that?"

I look down, appalled to see the gouges and scars where I have hacked my knife, again and again, against the pale silver bark of the yew. Saints! "No! Of course not. It is simply that this knife needs to be sharpened."

She arches one of her pale red brows at me, looking far older than her nine years.

"Annith! Look!" At the sound of Florette's shouting, I turn around to find her pointing through the small copse of trees. Is it a crow? For I have promised to pay Florette if she alerts me whenever she sees one approaching. It is our little secret. In exchange, I change the sheets on her bed when she wets it and I tell no one, although I think many of the others suspect.

I hurry to the trees, my eyes scanning the sky, but I see nothing.

"No, not in the sky, in the water. It's a *boat.*"

I jerk my gaze down to the horizon, where I see that Florette is correct: a boat is making its way to the island. There is a quick, sharp stab of fear in my gut until I see that the boat does not bear one of the ominous black sails that portend death. "Aveline, go find Sister Thomine and Sister Widona. Tell them a night rower has arrived. Audri, you stay here with the other girls and continue gathering the greenery."

I slip my knife into the sheath at my waist, lift my skirts, and hurry across the rocky beach to the landing. There are two men in the boat, the rower and one other—a hedge priest, I presume. A girl sits between them. She is small, small enough that I do not think she can be older than Audri or Florette. As the boat comes steadily closer, I see that her hands are tied, and a rope is around her waist, securing her to the boat.

The night rower meets my furious gaze. "You can quit yer glaring, missy. We tied 'er up only so she wouldn't jump into the water. Thinks she's a fish, she does." I blink in surprise and turn to the hedge priest for an explanation.

He nods in greeting. "It's true. The locals sent her to Saint Mer at first, thinking she was one of theirs. But the abbess took one look at her and knew she wasn't. Turns out, her mother drowned, but they found her in time to cut the child from her womb. Except then the father wanted nothing to do with her. Thought she'd caused the mother's death."

Her story, like most of the girls' stories, twists my heart. So many mothers dead, so many daughters blamed. It is almost enough to make me glad I do not know the circumstances of my own birth. What sort of death did my mother suffer? What sins were blamed on me for daring to come into this world?

"Well, you're ashore now, so untie her at once. What's her name?"

The hedge priest shoots an uneasy glance at the rower as he unties her. "Melusine," he says. The sailor lifts the sacred conch shell he wears around his neck to his lips.

When I roll my eyes, it is his turn to glare at me. "'Tis a bad-luck name, miss. Especially for us sailors."

"It is a foolish name," the hedge priest mutters.

Ignoring them both, I turn my attention to Melusine herself. "What do you think of your name?"

She looks up at me with eyes the exact color of the sea, and nearly as fathomless. "I like my name. I picked it myself."

I smile. "Then I like it too. The names we give ourselves are always the best. Now, come." I hold out my hand to her. The hedge priest carefully helps her to the bow, then over the side and onto the beach. The girl glances longingly over her shoulder to the sparkling blue water. I quickly grab her hand and pull her toward me. "You can go swimming later," I tell her. "When it is not so cold."

When I turn to escort Melusine back to the convent, I find a small knot of three girls watching us with large, curious eyes. Aveline arrives just then, breathless from her running. "Sister Thomine is teaching the others right now, and Sister Widona is tending to a mare who is foaling. They said you can see to the new arrival. You've done it often enough."

And so I have.

I shoo the younger girls on to their next lesson a little early — comportment with Sister Beatriz. She will be annoyed, but her petty annoyances are a lesser concern than getting this newest girl settled. I do not think Melusine is injured or ill, but it is customary to have new arrivals thoroughly examined, for many come to us malnourished, beaten, or in other ways physically abused.

As I lead her down the hall, I try not to think of all the other novitiates I have escorted this way, novitiates who are even now serving Mortain in a much more glorious manner than I. I try not to think of Ismae, ensconced at court with her finery and weapons, doing the work she was born to do. I push away thoughts of Sybella, currently on her fourth assignment, with no word for well over six months. Although *I* did not escort Sybella down the hall—it took four full-grown nuns, two on either side of her, to be certain she did not injure herself or bolt.

No, I will not think of that now. I will not indulge in the weakness of doubt and self-pity. Even though the infirmary door is open, I rap softly on it so that our presence will not startle Sister Serafina. She often becomes so absorbed in her work that she forgets to eat or sleep or even, sometimes, where she is. "Sister? We have a new arrival today."

Sister Serafina looks up from a long, complex series of tubing and flasks, a contraption of her own design she built in order to streamline her making of simples and tinctures. She peers over a coil of copper tube at us.

"Her name is Melusine, and she was mistakenly sent to the convent of Saint Mer. Apparently, she has an affinity for water." I smile down at the girl so she will know this is meant without judgment.

Sister Serafina sets down a glass flask, wipes her hands on a linen towel, and studies Melusine. "Fond of the sea, are you?"

"Yes, ma'am."

Once I have placed the girl in Sister Serafina's capable hands, I leave the infirmary to inform the abbess of our new addition.

As I draw near her chambers, I hear voices coming from within. Hoping they have gotten word of Sybella or, better yet, word of some new assignment for me, I stand near the door as if merely waiting my turn to see the abbess, then lean my ear close.

"That is dire news indeed." It is Sister Eonette who is speaking.

"It is most unwelcome," the abbess agrees. "And could not come at a worse time."

"Does it not worry you for *other* reasons?" Sister Eonette puts an odd emphasis on the word *other*, an emphasis that has me pressing my ear closer to the door.

"You mean other than Sister Vereda's illness leaving us Sightless at a time when our young duchess is fending off angry suitors and trying to keep the French from sweeping in and claiming our duchy as their own? When our country is threatened by civil war and risking outright invasion?" The reverend mother's voice is drier than the week-old bread we feed the pigs. My thoughts fly immediately to Ismae and Sybella and countless others out in the world. Without a seeress, how will we guide their hands? This will leave them exposed and instructionless when they can least afford to be.

"I should not have to point out to you that it is rare enough for one of Mortain's handmaidens to take ill, even one as old as Sister Vereda. Does that not hint at some—"

"Enough!" The abbess's voice slices through the air, cutting short the words I was so breathlessly waiting to hear. "You are not to share your doubts or concerns with anyone. Have Sister Thomine sent to my office immediately."

There is a long, heavy pause that is finally broken by Sister Eonette. "But of course, Reverend Mother." Her voice drips with sarcasm so sharp it is almost mockery. I expect the abbess to take her to task for it, to slap her or order her to do penance for showing such disrespect, but she does not.

The soft tread of Sister Eonette's footsteps approaching the chamber door spurs me to action. Quickly, before she exits, I scamper down the hall, then begin walking toward the office so I am a good six paces away when Sister Eonette steps out. She glances at me. "She has a meeting with Sister Thomine," she tells me.

"Is Sister Thomine in there already?" I ask innocently.

"No, I am to fetch her."

"I will only take a minute." I give her a quick, cheerful smile meant to appease her, but she simply jerks one shoulder in an annoyed shrug. "Very well, but I warn you, she is not in good humor this morning."

"Thank you for the warning, Sister."

She nods curtly, then brushes past me to fetch Sister Thomine. With my head swirling full of questions, I rap softly on the abbess's door.

"Come in."

It has taken me well over five years to be able to enter this office without my heart racing in fear. I am pleased that today all I must fear is that the abbess will sense my curiosity.

"Annith!" The abbess puts down her quill. Even though she smiles, it does not reach her eyes, and her skin is pulled tight with worry. "What a lovely surprise. Have we a meeting today that I forgot?"

"No, Reverend Mother," I say as I curtsy. "I just came to inform you that a new girl has arrived, sent from the abbess at Saint Mer."

"Ah, yes. The abbess had written to me of her." She reaches for a small pile of correspondence and removes a letter from the top. "Her father thought her cursed and wanted nothing to do with her, so she was raised by her mother's sister, until that woman died giving birth to her own child. Her name is Melusine." The abbess wrinkles her nose at that. "An altogether frivolous and silly name."

"The child chose it herself," I explain. "Perhaps an attempt to grasp the very things that others feared her for and remake them as something lovely and mysterious."

The abbess looks up at me. "You are most likely correct, and very kind to have thought of that. She may keep it, then." She leans back in her chair. "You have such a deft touch with newly arrived girls, I wonder if we should have you serve as our novice mistress. At least until you are called by Mortain."

We have not had a novice mistress in years, not since the abbess herself—then known as Sister Etienne—held that position under the former abbess, whom we called the Dragonette.

She arches her brow, her mouth quirking in rare humor. "Since you look as if you have just swallowed a cup full of verjuice, I gather that you are not much pleased by that idea."

"While I do enjoy helping with the new girls, I fear that if I were to focus solely on that, my other skills and reflexes could easily grow dull so that I would not be ready when Mortain's call did come."

It was the abbess who kept me from despair when Ismae was sent out and I was once more left behind. She assured me it could have nothing to do with my skills or dedication, for who was more skilled or dedicated than I? Clearly, it was some whim of the god. She was certain He was saving me for something extraordinary.

"Very well, then. But from what I hear, you have surpassed many of your teachers in their fields."

I cannot help but savor her praise. Not because she is stingy with it — she is not — but because I so desperately need it to fill the hole that opened up inside me the day Ismae was chosen over me.

Perhaps fearing the praise will go to my head, the abbess changes the subject. "And how are preparations for midwinter coming along?"

"Aveline and Loisse have both grown so much that they need new white cloaks, but Sister Beatriz is taking care of that. She has assured me they will be ready by the midwinter ceremony."

"And how does young Audri fare?"

"She is fine. The fumes from the mandrake root only made her sick. Sister Serafina says she will fully recover. Her appetite is good, her bodily humors are in balance, and she sleeps deeply, with no nightmares or other problems. She should be ready to join the others for lessons as soon as this afternoon, if you wish."

"Make it so, then. There is no reason to keep her idle. And Lisabet? How is she?"

I smile. "Also fine. Indeed, she has found a new way to mimic death and is much pleased with herself."

The abbess sighs, as if bracing for the worst. "And Loisse's arm?"

"As you suspected, the fall from her horse did not break her wrist, merely sprained it. She also will be well enough for the midwinter ceremony, although she will have to carry her torch with her left hand."

"That will ruin the symmetry."

I try to keep the surprise out of my voice. "You would rather she did not participate?"

She waves her hand. "No, no. It is just a minor annoyance, an imperfection that cannot be helped."

"She will not try riding her horse while standing up again, I assure you." I do not tell her that Loisse was doing it in an attempt to match my own skills, as there is no legitimate reason for an assassin to ride in that position, and I fear the abbess will recognize it as sinful pride.

"Very well. Thank you, Annith." She picks up her quill, my sign that I am dismissed. I curtsy once more, then turn to leave the chamber, but pause when I reach the door. A question hovers on my lips, but before I can ask it, the abbess speaks. "I will save you a trip to the rookery," she says without looking up from her work. "There has been no word from either Ismae or Sybella."

"Thank you, Reverend Mother," I say as I close the door behind me. I am touched by how well she knows me, that even with her own problems weighing so heavily upon her, she takes the time to reassure me. For her problems do weigh heavily upon her, I realize. It was clear in the tightness around her eyes, and the grim set to her mouth. She has always been the strongest among us. Even when the great tragedy struck our convent seven years ago, she was the one to keep her head and move us forward when others were wont to wail and wring their hands.

Sister Eonette's veiled insinuations have plucked at my long-held vigilance, and seeing the abbess's distress causes every muscle in my body to grow tight. The need to know what is afoot is like a small hungry creature yapping at my heels.

I quickly check the hallway to be certain no one is coming, then dart into the short corridor hidden behind a tapestry of Saint Arduinna pointing her silver arrow at the dark, cloaked figure of Mortain. It leads to the small, private chapel that opens into the abbess's office. Few know about it, and I only learned of it because once, when I was five years old and locked in the wine cellar as punishment, I had overheard Sister Appollonia and Sister Magdelena discussing it, neither of them realizing my big ears were merely one thick door away.

It is a habit I developed when young, collecting secrets like a miser collects coins. I would never have survived my years with the Dragonette if I had not read every scrap of paper that crossed my path, listened at every door, and peered through every keyhole, trying to determine what she expected of me so I could meet those expectations as soon as possible and avoid the painful consequences of disappointing her.

Even though the Dragonette has been dead these last seven years, I have not been able to cast the habit aside. But, just like a miser with his coins, I have no intention of ever parting with any of these secrets. Instead, I use them to soothe the raw and chafed places of my soul and remind myself that others at the convent, others with skills more remarkable than my own, also possess human flaws.

I push aside the tapestry that hides the chapel door, then carefully lift the latch and let myself in. I settle into position just as a sharp rap sounds on the abbess's office door. "Come in." The abbess's voice is faint but distinct.

Both Ismae and Sybella possess the ability to sense the presence of others, even when a door or a wall stands between them. It is yet one more gift that I lack. However, I have learned to compensate by growing adept at recognizing the nuns without seeing them. Sister Beatriz has a light tread, as if dancing on the balls of her feet, while Sister Widona moves so silently, one almost feels her movement rather than hears it. Sister Serafina drags her left foot every so slightly, and Sister Thomine is a great stomper, with loud, sturdy steps that can be heard four rooms away. Unless she is fighting—then she is as silent as the wind and as deadly as an arrow.

"You sent for me, Reverend Mother?" I hear Sister Thomine say.

"Close the door, please."

A faint click of the latch as it is closed, then quiet. "How are Matelaine and Sarra coming along in their training?"

There is a long pause that makes me think that whatever Sister Thomine was expecting, this was not it. "Well enough," she says at last. "Sarra is skilled and competent, but also lazy and unwilling to push herself. Matelaine has less natural talent, but is far more committed. Unfortunately, her unique skills do not aid her in her tasks. Why do you ask? They are young yet. Surely the next one to be sent out is Annith?" I wish to hug Sister Thomine for giving voice to the thoughts in my head.

"Sister Vereda has taken ill." The abbess's words are clipped. "She is too ill to See for us anymore. I think Annith may be called upon to take the seeress's place."

At first, the words do not make sense to me—it is as if the abbess has begun speaking in some foreign tongue I have never heard. Or as if the thick wall between us has inexplicably distorted her words. But a faint trembling begins in my gut and spreads throughout my limbs, as if my body understands the words before my mind does.

"But Annith is our most skilled novitiate in years. Frankly, I am surprised you sent Ismae out before her, as Ismae had been here only three years and Annith has trained her entire life. Why would we waste those skills by having her be seeress?"

I hold my breath, waiting to hear the answer.

"I do not remember putting you in charge of such decisions." The abbess's voice is as tight as a newly stretched drum skin. "Annith has excelled in every task we have set before her. There is no reason to think that augury will be any different."

There is a short pause before Sister Thomine speaks again, this time so softly I can barely make out the words. "But will she welcome that fate? Again, she has trained since she was a babe to be an instrument of Death. Indeed, I believe that is what allowed her to survive her years with the Dragonette—"

"Enough!" The abbess's voice cracks across the room like a whip. "She is obedient and accommodating and always has the convent's best interests at heart. She will do as she is told. See to it that Matelaine's and Sarra's training is increased so they will be ready if we must send them out. For too long we have focused on training the eldest novitiates and have not spent enough time training the others."

My heart pounds so loudly that I can scarce hear the abbess's dismissal of Sister Thomine, and the sound of the office door closing feels so distant it could have come from the bottom of the sea. I grasp for the solid wall behind me, then slowly lower myself to the ground. What does she mean? How can she possibly—I put my hands over my face and scrub it, trying to restore my wits.

In all my seventeen years at the convent, it has never occurred to me that being seeress was a path open to any of us. Although, thinking upon it now, I realize the seeresses must come from somewhere. But I'd always assumed it was a position given to a nun when she was too old to perform other duties. Or—well, the truth is, I have not thought about it much at all.

And why would I? I have never shown any skill or affinity for scrying or augury. Nor have I ever been taught such things. I look down at my hands, surprised to find that they are still shaking. I clench them into fists.

The abbess cannot be serious. She herself said that I was one of the most skilled novitiates ever to have walked the convent's halls. It cannot possibly be Mortain's will, for if so, why would He have given me these talents? These skills?

For the first time in over seven years, I find myself wondering what the Dragonette would think of this if she were still alive. No, I do not need to wonder. I know—she would never have considered such a thing. It would be like fashioning a weapon and using it to stir a pot.

I do not even know if the abbess means this to be a great honor or a punishment.

No, not a punishment, but a tempering. That is what the Dragonette would have called it, her voice ripe with her palpable desire to create of me a perfect weapon, one whose existence would glorify Mortain.

Only now it appears this weapon is to be locked away, never to be used for the purpose for which she was intended.

I slip out of the chapel and being walking down the hall. I must come up with a plan. Find some way to dissuade the abbess from acting on this notion of hers. As I turn the corner, I stumble upon a small clutch of the older girls huddling and whispering among themselves. At my approach, their gazes fix on me like hungry crows on a gobbet of meat.

Merde, but I do not wish to speak with them now. Not with the abbess's threat still buzzing in my head like angry hornets, for this news has upended me as thoroughly as one of the lay sisters empties a bucket of wash water.

My long years of training rise up and take over, and I shove my distress and confusion behind a veil of piety and obedience. "Girls," I murmur in a near perfect imitation of the abbess.

Sarra grits her teeth; she hates me most when I act thus, but Matelaine and Loisse greet me warmly.

"Do you know what all the furtive meetings with the abbess were about?" Matelaine asks as she and Sarra fall into step beside me.

It galls me to have to pretend that they know something I do not, but I smile brightly at her. "No, I missed the fuss. What was it about?"

Sarra lifts one eyebrow and places a mocking hand upon her chest. "Do not tell me that we know something that Saint Annith does not?"

In a movement that shocks me, my hand snakes out and grabs her wrist. "Call me saint again and you will see just how saintly I am *not*." My voice is low and filled with anger that has little to do with her.

The begrudging admiration I see in her eyes surprises me almost as much as my own actions. I let go of her hand and take a deep breath. Everyone thinks that my goodness comes easily to me, that it hardly counts because I do not struggle with it, but I *do*. Just like rosary beads run through a priest's fingers, so does a litany of goodness run constantly through my head: *Be strong, be certain all your actions glorify Mortain, show no weakness, allow your will to bend before others'.*

It is especially appalling to be called a saint when I fear that my being so obedient is the very trait that threatens to alter the entire course of my life. I force my voice back to cheerfulness. "Now, you'd best fill me in so that I may know it too."

Sarra's smugness disappears and is replaced by sullenness. "I do not know what it was about, only that there was a fuss. I was hoping you would have the details."

"No, but give me a day or two and I am certain I can ferret them out." And with that, we reach the refectory, where we put our spat aside lest the nuns notice it and get involved.

Chapter Two

ALONE AT LAST IN MY room, I give myself over to the thoughts I have held in check all through supper. There must be a way to convince the abbess I am not suited for the task she has in mind for me. That it is not the best use of my skills — skills I acquired through hard work and steel-willed determination, despite the cost to myself. Skills I was promised would be used to glorify Mortain and do His work, not be sent to fester in the dark, musty closeness of the seeress's chambers.

The abbess said nothing about Seeing being one of Mortain's blessings or gifts that He gives to us — she said only that it could be taught, and that I would not mind because I was obedient and biddable and had the convent's best interests at heart. But it is to Mortain that I owe my faith and dedication, not her, although she might well be forgiven for thinking that.

Ismae and Sybella have always thought that everything comes easily to me and that I enjoy a position as convent favorite. They do not know, for I never told them, how fine a razor's edge I have spent my entire life walking, ever since I took my first few toddling steps.

To be raised in a convent full of women who are devoted to spiritual matters is a barren life for any child. But when those women worship Death and have dedicated their lives to serving Him, learning His arts, and carrying out His will, it can be a bleak and joyless existence.

So, while for Sybella and Ismae, the convent was a refuge of sorts, an escape from the horrors of their past, for me it was something else entirely. My childhood was a time of frequent and unexpected tests, usually administered when I had been lulled into a false sense of complacency—something I had been warned against, so the tests themselves were simply punishments that I deserved.

Like the time I was six years old and walking with the Dragonette on the beach in order to see the older girls off on their trip to the mainland. As soon as they were out of sight, the Dragonette picked me up and tossed me into the ocean to see if perhaps swimming came naturally to me, as it does to some daughters of Mortain. Or the time she ordered a sack placed over my head to see how long I could hold my breath (not long at all—especially since my screams sucked up the remaining air most quickly), or when she slipped her hand around my shoulders, and I thought I had finally done something to earn a sign of affection from her —only to have that hand move up and wrap itself around my neck and squeeze, to see if I could withstand such pressure as those who are born with their birth cords wrapped around their necks are sometimes able to.

I grew to dread those sessions with her, for all that they meant I was her favorite. And I hated that I could not be strong enough to accept the special favor she bestowed upon me without ruining it with my fear. There were times, many times, when I believed it would kill me. Sometimes, I even wondered if that was her intent.

If so, the Dragonette had not counted on my sins of pride and stubbornness. She did not yet understand just how firmly I could plant my feet in the ground of rebellion to prove her wrong. Or perhaps she counted on precisely that. I soon learned to make sure that even my failures were ones she would have to—at least grudgingly—admire, that showed that even though I may be flawed, those flaws would honor Mortain. I threw myself so wholeheartedly into my lessons and so thoroughly mastered my tasks that soon the sisters could find no fault with me.

If one of the other girls was a better archer, then I would sneak out in secret and practice for hours, days, weeks, until my fingers bled and my wrist was bruised from the plucking and the twanging of the bowstring. But soon the raw fingertips hardened and grew calluses and I learned to ignore the sting of my wrist. Thus I not only became the best archer among all the girls, but grew impervious to pain as well.

Eventually, the Dragonette came to know my every flaw and fault line like a mason knows his stone, and learned just how stubborn I could be. But this abbess and I have not had that sort of relationship. When I was younger, she was often off on her own assignments and duties and so did not see the full measure of my determination.

I will have to show her—remind her—that there is more to me than mere obedience and docility.

In the morning, I awake as sharp and ready as one of Sister Arnette's finest blades and am nearly bouncing on my toes in impatience. We are to report to the archery field first thing, before the wind picks up. Perfect, for I am as skilled an archer as anyone at the convent—including Sister Arnette, who teaches us. Matelaine tries to speak with me, but I pretend I do not see her, as I have thoughts only for the challenge before us.

As we line up in front of the targets, I narrow my focus so that the world consists of only the target and the tip of my arrow. As easily as I cast Matelaine aside moments ago, I cast aside any doubts or hesitation. The time for subtlety has passed. It is a luxury I can no longer afford. My only recourse is to prove that there is no one else at the convent whose skills compare to mine. Then the abbess will have no choice but to pick me for the next assignment.

I breathe out, then release the bowstring. Even as the first arrow finds the bull's-eye, I am reaching for the next. I release again, and again, and within a handful of minutes, I have fired all my arrows, with all twelve in a three-inch grouping in the bull's-eye.

Breathless, I ease back to see all the other girls have ceased their practice and are watching me. "That is how you do it, girls," Sister Arnette says with a satisfied nod in my direction. "Now, quit gawking and fire."

And then I must wait for them to finish so I can retrieve my arrows. I repeat the performance with my second and third volley, but by the fourth volley, the wind has picked up. I misjudge its strength, and an arrow goes wide.

"That's it!" Sister Arnette calls out. "We won't be able to get much more practice in with this wind. Put down your bows and—"

I close my ears to her words, make some calculations in my head, then fire again. This one hits the bull's-eye, and the next and the next. The fourth goes wide again, but only because there was a lull in the wind after I released the bowstring.

"Enough." Sister Arnette's voice is right next to my ear. When I turn to look at her, we are nearly close enough to kiss. "It is too windy. We'll come back to it tomorrow." She gives my arm an affectionate pat to let me know I have excelled. Part of me welcomes that small gesture of recognition and wishes to smile back at her in gratitude, just as I would have yesterday or the day before that. Instead, I force myself to ignore it. I want her—all of them—to see just how obedient and pliable I am *not*. "Truly, Sister? Will assailants stop because the wind is too great? Will Mortain unmarque our targets when a breeze blows too strongly? Would not a true assassin be able to shoot under such conditions?"

Still holding my gaze, she calls out to the others. "When you are done here, report to the stables." There is a spark of anger in her eyes. Good, for anger is exactly what I need today to feed this hunger—this desperation—to prove myself.

"Are you trying to shame them?" she asks in a low, tight voice.

Aveline's words of yesterday—was it only yesterday?—come back to me. "No, but how does pretending to be weak make them stronger?" With that, I turn and leave. Even as I make my way toward the stables, a small, bitter worm of regret tries to climb up my throat, but I refuse to feel bad for pointing out the folly of not training in all conditions.

The next lesson of the day goes much the same, only this time I manage to anger the even-tempered Sister Widona, something I have not ever done in all my years at the convent. Her face is white and pinched as she scolds me for driving my horse too hard and jumping him in his exhausted state, thereby risking breaking his leg and my neck. When she orders me back to the stables, I want to put my heels to the horse's sides and canter in the opposite direction. I can feel him quivering beneath me, eager to be allowed to show his full strength and power. Like me, he has more in him, and Widona coddles him just as the abbess coddles me. It is only the threat of being barred from riding for an entire fortnight that causes me to comply, for my riding skills are one of my best arguments as to why I should be the next one sent out.

As I return to the stables—alone and under reprimand—it occurs to me that if I anger enough of the nuns, perhaps they will beg the abbess to send me out on assignment lest they be tempted to kill me themselves.

The next day, we report to the training yard for knife fighting, using wooden blades fashioned by Sister Arnette that have the look and heft of true knives. I have spent nearly the entire night going over and over the abbess's words until my heart is raw and my muscles twitch with a desperate need to do *some*thing to avert the fate she has in store for me.

I use that sense of desperation to quicken my reflexes and rack up seventeen kills in the first quarter-hour.

Sister Thomine orders a break, then calls me aside. "Your skill is as fine as anyone's I have ever seen," she tells me. "Novice and full initiate alike."

It is all I can do not to ask that she report this to the abbess at once. Instead, I bow my head meekly. "Thank you, Sister."

"However, you are not the only novitiate here. You need to begin holding back or else the other girls will never have a chance to learn *their* skills." Her words cause my head to jerk up in frustration, but she does not notice and gives me an awkward pat on the shoulder, motioning me back to the group.

My next opponent is Matelaine, who looks more than a little wary of me. Instead of giving her a reassuring smile, I narrow my eyes. I cannot go easy, especially not on Matelaine. Not when it appears that the abbess is contemplating sending her out so soon. In the real world, assailants will not hold back or soften their blows, so how will my doing so teach the others anything except how to be weak and die young?

I nod once to indicate I am ready. When she steps forward with a right-handed strike, I move in, and with three quick strikes I have her on the ground. I am not even breathing hard as she glares up at me.

After I beat Matelaine once more, and Sarra twice, Sister Thomine orders me out of the yard for the afternoon. I keep my head held high as I leave, and remind myself that strength is nothing to be ashamed of.

My redoubled efforts in my training lessons have borne rich fruit, for not only have I demonstrated that no one else is equal to my skill, I have rebelled openly enough that reports of my behavior should make their way back to the abbess and have her reconsidering whether I will be so compliant with her every wish.

While I feel certain that the abbess will quickly see the error of her decision once the nuns' accounts begin to trickle in, it is always best to approach a problem from two sides.

If Sister Vereda were not ill, they would not need me to be their new seeress. Therefore, I must do all in my power to ensure that Sister Vereda recovers.

Chapter Three

SISTER SERAFINA HAS BEEN OVERWORKED ever since Ismae left, as Ismae was the only other one here who was able to handle poisons with no ill effects. With the additional nursing duties she must perform for Vereda, Serafina will be truly buried by all her tasks. It is logical enough that she will need some help.

But if I simply show up and announce my willingness to help, word of it might get back to the abbess, which would not only raise her suspicions but confirm her belief that I am willing to do anything that is asked of me — no matter that it is not what I have trained for. The trick will be to provoke Sister Serafina into ordering me to help so it will not seem like my idea at all. I assure myself that is the reason for my subterfuge and not this overwhelming need that dogs my every step to be precisely the opposite of obedient and helpful.

I pause just outside the infirmary door. As I listen to the clink and tinkle of glass flasks and a lone voice muttering, my mind casts about for some demand that will trigger her ire so forcefully that she will be quick to punish me with extra chores.

I think of the older nun's dear face, her sallow skin and plain features, and the small vanity that has her paying young Florette to pluck the dark hairs that have begun to sprout from her chin, hairs that her aging eyes can no longer see.

And that is when I know what will annoy her the most.

I close my eyes and try to muster the callousness I will need for this, for I am loath to cause Sister Serafina any pain. But surely hers will be a small pain when weighed against an entire lifetime spent shut inside the seeress's chambers.

Besides, as the Dragonette used to work so hard to impress upon me, an assassin has no use for a soft heart. *Ruthless,* she always urged me. *You must be ruthless.* With that reminder, I rise up on my toes, make my steps light and dainty, and prance into the room. "Oh, there you are, Sister!"

Sister Serafina looks up from the herbs she is chopping and frowns at me. At her elbow, a kettle sits over a small flame, and faint beads of perspiration cover her upper lip. "Who is looking for me now?"

I pretend I do not notice her tone. "Just me." I lift a hand to my cheek and frown. "I have come to ask if you could make a special wash for my face. Sister Beatriz says my complexion is not as smooth as it should be to pass for a noble lady at court." Sister Beatriz has said no such thing to me, but she *has* said it to poor Loisse.

Sister Serafina shakes her head in disgust and keeps chopping. "I do not have time for such frivolities, and surely neither do you."

For a moment my resolve falters. Should I not just confide in her? Would she not sympathize with my plight? After all, it was she who first saw, then subsequently tended, the wounds on my body, even when she had been ordered to leave them alone so that Mortain's own will could guide the healing process. Her hands were gentle and her tongue mercifully silent of questions as she carefully cleansed and then treated the lacerations. Even more admirable, she has never once brought it up or presumed any special confidence between us, nor even allowed herself to glance toward the scars she once tended with so much compassion.

But it is too big a risk. Just because she did me a great kindness years ago does not mean she has sworn herself to secrecy on my behalf. "Is it frivolous to make myself perfect in Mortain's eyes so He will use me for His work?" I allow my true concern to show on my face.

"You are already perfect, child," she says, her voice flat.

I turn to an empty polished metal basin on her worktable and angle it so that I may see my own reflection. "Then why have I not yet been chosen?" The distress in my voice is no subterfuge—it comes straight from my heart.

"I know it is hard for you with both Sybella and Ismae having been sent out. But your time *will* come."

In spite of the old nun's words, a hot prickly feeling rises up in me and I want to shout at her that it might not come, it might *never* come if the reverend mother has her way. Terrified by this surge of unfamiliar anger, I bow my head and speak softly. "But surely I must do everything in my power to be ready for that moment."

Sister Serafina presses her lips together and chops faster. Acting as if I cannot sense her mounting annoyance—indeed, a great thick *ox* would be able to sense her mounting annoyance—I move closer and peer over her shoulder. "What are you mixing? Is that mallow and comfrey? Those make a fine wash to improve the complexion, do they not?"

The old nun stops chopping and slams her knife down on the table. "I do not have time to hold your hand, nor offer you pretty comfort or useless potions. Surely there is something better you can do with your time. Other skills you can perfect besides your vanity." She wipes her hands on her apron and pours more water into her small bubbling kettle.

I let my shoulders slump. "But what would you have me do? I am like a fifth wheel on a cart. I am skilled in the use of every weapon in Sister Arnette's armory; I can best Sister Thomine in a fight as often as she can best me; my archery skills are better than anyone else's here; and I can ride a horse bareback, backward, or standing up."

Sister Serafina cocks her head, eyes alight with curiosity. "Standing up? I thought only the followers of Arduinna knew how to do that trick."

"No. Sister Widona taught me." I let a plaintive whine creep into my voice. "There is nothing left for me to do. Even Sister Beatriz has taught me every dance, every means of seduction. Why, she has even taught me how to—"

"Enough!" Sister Serafina holds up her hand, halting my words. Surely it was a Mortain-inspired strategy, turning to the one subject that makes her most uncomfortable—the skills of seduction they teach us.

She dumps the handful of herbs she has chopped into the kettle of boiling water. "Very well," she says. "If you have mastered everything they have to teach you, I have some things you have yet to learn."

I take an eager step toward her. "You will give me more poison lessons?"

She snorts. "I have already taught you everything I can about poisons. To learn any more, you would have to be immune to them, and you have not acquired *that* skill, have you?" She turns and looks at me sharply, as if almost hoping it were true.

I shake my head and sigh, fighting down a familiar pang of jealousy at Ismae's most practical and rare of gifts. "Alas, no."

"So I will teach you my other skill. Nursing."

I look at the row of empty beds. "But we have no patient."

"Ah, but we do. Here." She shoves the empty metal basin at me, then picks up a tray covered with small pots of salves and piles of herbs. "Follow me."

Of all the duties the nuns perform here at the convent, those of the seeress are the ones I know the least about. Sister Vereda does not join us at meals, nor participate in our feasts or celebrations. She does not teach us any lessons or train us in any skills. It is as if she does not exist. The only time a handmaiden meets with her is if she is going on assignment and Sister Vereda has Seen it. Since I have not yet been sent out, I have never met with her.

Old Sister Druette, who was seeress before Vereda, was just as mysterious, although far more terrifying. She was known to stand at her door, peeking out into the hallway, ready to grab or pinch a passing novitiate when she wanted something. Most of us did everything we could to avoid walking down that corridor.

I follow Sister Serafina down the hall that leads to the inner recesses of the convent and struggle to keep my footsteps firm and brisk. Dread begins to seep into my bones, an awareness that when I step into Sister Vereda's chambers, I could be staring into the face of my own fate.

No. Surely as soon as the seeress can See again, the abbess will put away this idea of hers.

Once we reach the thick oaken door that leads to the seeress's chambers, Sister Serafina shifts the tray she carries, lifts the latch, and slips inside. I try to follow, but my feet will not obey. They are stuck fast, as if they have been entangled in some invisible web.

Sister Serafina turns and frowns at me over her shoulder. "What is it?"

"Nothing," I say, and force myself to step over the threshold.

Sister Vereda's chamber is dark and dim. The smells of a sickroom hang thick in the air: pungent herbs, a full chamber pot, old fevered sweat. It feels like every breath the seeress has ever drawn still sits here, trapped for all eternity. It is all I can do not to gag and run screaming from the room.

I take slow, deep breaths through my mouth and allow my eyes to grow accustomed to gloom. Once they have, the first thing I see is a pale orange glow from the four charcoal braziers set around the room.

As my vision adjusts further, I am able to make out the interior, a small, cramped place with no windows, only the one door, and not even a true fireplace.

Sister Serafina sets down her tray, then takes the basin from my hands. "How is she?" she asks the lay sister who sits by the bed.

"She is well enough, for now," the lay sister replies. "But she is fretful when awake, and her breathing grows even more shallow and labored."

"Not for long," Sister Serafina says with grim determination in her voice.

When the lay sister has left, I trail behind Sister Serafina as she draws near the bed. Even though Vereda is old, her cheeks are as smooth and plump as a babe's. I cannot help but wonder if this is because it has been years since she set foot outside this room and felt the sun or the wind against her face. She wears no wimple, but a small linen cap covers her hair with only white wisps escaping in a few places. Her body is a lump, obscured by layers of blankets to keep her warm. As I stare down at her, Sister Eonette's comment that Sister Vereda's illness hints at some sinister undercurrent comes back to me. "What is wrong with her?" I ask, keeping my voice low.

Sister Serafina sets her little kettle on one of the charcoal braziers in the room. "I do not yet know."

"I thought we who were born of Mortain did not get sick?"

Sister Serafina purses her lips and motions impatiently. "Bring me the dried coltsfoot, comfrey, and mallow root you have in the dish there."

I do as she asks and wonder why she will not answer me. Still silent, she takes the herbs and dumps them into the kettle and begins to stir. After a long moment, she finally speaks. "We do not get sick. Or not often, at least. And when we do, we heal quickly. Let us pray that Sister Vereda will heal quickly as well."

Since it is the prayer I have uttered with every breath I've taken since overhearing the abbess's plans for me, it is easy enough to agree. "Good. Now remove her blankets and unlace her shift. We're going to put this poultice on her chest and keep it there until the phlegm releases its hold on her lungs."

In this moment I realize I have no earthly idea what this sort of nursing entails. It sounds most vile. I am torn between laughter and tears. All my life, I have waited in breathless anticipation for my meeting with the seeress. It would be the culmination of seventeen years' hard work —a triumphant call to serve Mortain. But instead, I am here to empty her chamber pot and wipe up her spittle.

It is almost—almost—enough to make me wish the Dragonette were still alive. And even though she has been dead these seven years, my stomach clenches painfully at the thought.

Chapter Four

IT TAKES NEARLY THREE WEEKS, but just as winter solstice draws near, we are finally able to chase the illness from Sister Vereda's aging body. She is still weak and frail, but she will live.

I have never nursed anyone as vigorously or fervently as I did the old seeress. I slept on a cot next to hers; spooned rich broth through her thin, wrinkled lips; sponged her fevered brow with cool water mixed with herbs; and applied poultices to her shriveled chest with my own hands, desperate to chase the fever from her lungs.

She was not an easy patient, for though I have helped Sister Serafina with new girls when they arrive, the seeress was far more restless and fussy. Not to mention the unpleasantness of her foul, stale little room. I vow, not a whisper of fresh air has entered that room since she was first sealed in it all those years ago.

And so it was with great joy that I awoke two days ago to find her milky-white eyes open, her skin cool, and nothing but grumbling and complaints on her lips, for it takes no small amount of energy to gripe, and surely that is a good sign.

A gust of wind, sharp and salty from the surrounding sea, snatches at my cloak and sends a gray cloud swollen with rain scuttling across the sun. Even though it causes me to shiver, I lift my face and spread my arms wide, willing the brisk air to carry away all the vestiges of the sickroom.

As far as I know, nothing more has been said of me replacing Sister Vereda, at least not that I have been able to overhear. But even if it has, there is more joyous news this morning: Sister Vereda's visions have returned. Assuredly, they were small, unimportant ones, but they were visions nonetheless, and I cannot wait to report them to the abbess. Once I have confirmed that they are true.

That is what brings me to the rookery.

It is dark inside the small hut and reeks of crow droppings and faintly rancid meat. Sister Claude is settling a crow on its perch and crooning in a soothing, tuneless murmur. The old nun's disheveled black habit covers her shapeless form like a set of poorly groomed feathers. Her head, encased in her black veil, is scrawny and birdlike, her nose as long and sharp as any beak. She cocks her head at me. "Haven't seen you in a while. Wondered where you got to."

"I've been helping with poor Sister Vereda, but she is better now, so I should be resuming my regular duties."

She grunts. "Too bad no one told the abbess that. You just missed her."

That news stops me cold. "The abbess? What was she doing here?"

She sniffs. "Said she was taking a turn in the garden and saw the crow come in, but I can't fathom what she'd be doing in the garden on a day like this. Do you think she was checking up on me?"

"I can't imagine why she would be," I assure her. But it is most odd. In all my years here, I do not remember her ever coming to the rookery for messages. It is not like I am the only novitiate who can fetch and carry for her. I distract Sister Claude from her worries by handing her the small packet of sugared almonds I pilfered from the kitchens. "Here, I brought you something. Let me stoke the fire, and then I will heat some wine to go with it."

The old nun's face brightens and she clacks her teeth together in anticipation as she goes to take a seat. That is Sister Claude's secret: she has developed an overfondness for wine. Although who could fault her when she is so often excluded from the excitement and festivities that take place in the convent proper?

I tend the fire until it is burning brightly, then take one of the pokers from the hearth and wipe the ashes from it with my apron. "Who was the message from?" I ask as I thrust the poker into the fire. Pretending I am not overly interested in the answer, I pour wine into a heavy tankard.

"'Tweren't either of those friends of yours," the old nun says around a mouthful of nuts, "so don't be fretting."

I ignore the thin rebuke, grab the heated poker, and then thrust it into the tankard. There is a faint hiss as the hot metal warms the wine, and the scent of it fills the room.

"'Twas Chancellor Crunard," she says as I hand the wine to her. That is her other secret, that she will trade bits of information for creature comforts and kindness, things that I would give her anyway.

"And we only received the one?"

"Aye."

I bite back a sigh. It appears Sister Vereda was spouting nonsense this morning rather than true visions, for she had reported that there would be two messages. Hiding my disappointment, I turn my attention to the crow who is still pacing across the table, faintly agitated and fluffing out his feathers. Trying to decide how much more I can press her for answers — did she have time to read the message before the abbess arrived? — I reach for the thick heavy crock that holds the birds' rewards and snag a gobbet of meat to feed him.

Just as he snatches it from my fingers, the door to the rookery flies open and crashes into the wall. For a moment I fear that the abbess has returned and has been listening at the door, but no, it is merely the wind howling into the room, causing the crows to raise their voices in caws of annoyance.

"I'll get it," I tell Sister Claude. I hasten across the room to push the door shut when my eye is caught by a small, dark speck dizzily making its way through the gathering clouds. It takes me a moment to realize it is another crow.

My spirits lift; the old seeress was correct after all. "I'll be right back," I call over my shoulder, then hurry outside.

The poor creature struggles mightily against the wind, which seems to be playing with it much like a cat plays with a mouse. A gust flings the crow higher into the sky, only to have an invisible hand bat him back down so that it is all he can do to stay in the air. For a few seconds he can do nothing but hover, trapped by the force of the wind, before it releases him and he shoots forward.

I raise my arm and the crow lunges for it, grabbing hold with sharp eager claws. Quickly, I bring my other hand up around the bird and begin murmuring soothing noises as I smooth his feathers. I stare at the bulging packet on his right leg. I must make a decision, and quickly.

If Sister Claude knows there is a message, she will watch me closely to be certain I do not read it. And once I leave the rookery, I will not have access to the materials I need to reseal the message and hide evidence of my snooping. In different circumstances, I might have kept the message for a few hours until I found an opportunity to read it, but with the storm coming in, the timing of the crow's arrival will be well known and my trickery easily caught.

But what if it is from Ismae? Or Sybella? Although I have all but given up hope of ever hearing from them.

Cradling the crow close, I remove the message from his leg. A surge of triumph rises in my chest when I recognize Ismae's handwriting. Thus decided, I slip the message into one of the pouches of my apron, then slip the crow into one of the bigger pouches. Once I sneak him in, it will be easy enough to hide him among the other birds.

I hurry back to the rookery, an excuse at the ready. But when I let myself in I see that Sister Claude's head now rests gently on her chest, the tankard empty and loose in her hand.

I murmur a prayer of gratitude, then move to the table and pull the exhausted, bedraggled crow from my apron. Before he can even think about opening his beak to squawk or complain, I slip one of the gobbets of meat in to silence him. I give him two more as bribery, and when he has thoroughly calmed himself, I place him on an empty perch, where he begins grooming his feathers.

I glance at Sister Claude to assure myself she is still napping, then slip my thin-bladed knife from its sheath and pry the wax seal from the parchment. I move over to the light of the fire so I may read the message.

> *Dearest Reverend Mother,*
>
> *Much has happened in the last few days, and none of it good. Count d'Albret conspired to come upon the duchess alone and attempted to force himself on her. His attempt only failed because—warned by Sybella—I arrived before he could carry out his ill intent. Alas, there was no marque upon d'Albret's vile person, otherwise I would have gutted him like a fish.*
>
> *The duchess is fine, if a bit shaken, and is adamant in her refusal to consider d'Albret's offer of marriage, no matter the consequences, and she has issued an edict to this effect. Duval, Captain Dunois, and Chancellor Crunard support her fully in this. Indeed, of all her councilors, I fear those are the only ones she can trust.*
>
> *We all breathed easier when d'Albret and his retinue left*

the city but alas, our relief was short-lived. Last night, in front of the entire court during a mummers' play, an attempt was made on the duchess's life. The masked hellequin in the play leaped up onto the great table and pulled a knife. Luckily, Mortain guided my hand with His own, and my aim was quick and certain—I was able to bring the assassin down before he could strike.

Reverend Mother, I fear he may have been a true helle-quin, for there was something unnatural about him—some absence of soul that leads me to believe he was not human. Or at least, not fully so.

Ismae's words send a deep chill through me, for while most think hellequin no more than tales told to keep children from straying too far from home, we at the convent know that they are real, and that they too belong to Mortain, although they serve a different purpose than His handmaidens do. They are the tortured souls of the damned who have pledged themselves to serve Mortain in order to earn their redemption.

In the Privy Council meeting immediately after the at-tempt, Chancellor Crunard revealed my true identity to the others. There is much anger and confusion among the mem-bers of the court right now, along with much finger-pointing. Accusations are flying. I pray daily for Sister Vereda to See a way out of this mess. Or, at the very least, to See who is behind it so I may take action upon him.

Yours in Mortain,

Ismae Rienne

When I have finished reading, I hug the parchment to my chest and breathe deeply. Ismae is fine. She is better than fine—she has proven her worth and made the convent proud by saving our young duchess's life. And she has been in contact with Sybella.

Close on the heels of that sweet relief comes a spurt of bitter heartbreak. I should be there with Ismae, protecting our duchess, doing our god's work, not trapped on this island. I close my eyes and let the feeling pass through me. I have proof of the seeress's returning skills; surely that will put a stop to this idea of the abbess's.

I return to the table and remove the black sealing wax from the small cubbyhole where I keep it hidden. Holding it near the candle, I wait for it to melt, place two thin drops on the exact spot where Ismae's seal was, then press the original seal into that. When it cools, it looks whole and unbroken, with no hint of anyone having tampered with it.

I slip the resealed message into my pocket, then cross over to Sister Claude. I gently remove the empty tankard from her hand and tuck the blankets closely around her old, thin body. It is time to give the abbess the good news about Sister Vereda.

As I make my way to the abbess's chambers, a flutter of excitement rises in my chest and it is all I can do not to give a little twirl in the corridor, but I contain myself. Surely a handmaiden of Death should not feel so giddy with delight.

When I reach the abbess's office, the door is closed. At my knock, she calls out, "Who is it?" and some part of my mind cannot help but notice this is not her customary response.

"It is Annith, Reverend Mother. Another crow arrived just after you left and I have come to bring you the message."

"Very well, come in."

When I open the door and enter the chamber, the abbess is just taking a seat. I dip a small curtsy, then approach her desk, the sound of my footsteps nearly silent against the crackle and snap of the fire in the hearth, a fire that does little to warm the chill in the room.

When I reach the desk, I smile—a smile I fill with every ounce of affection I have ever felt for her over the years, no matter that her recent decision threatens to undermine that. "Sister Serafina said I should let you know that Sister Vereda had two small visions this morning. They were true ones, not simply ramblings. And I bring proof."

Her eyebrows shoot up in what she no doubt intends as surprise, but it seems to me that there is also a faint gleam of alarm in her eyes. "Indeed? And what were these visions?"

I hold out the note. "That we would receive two messages from the mainland today, and that it would be raining before noon. The first drops began to fall just as I came inside."

The abbess's face relaxes and she quirks her mouth. "The cook can predict the rain simply from the way her knees creak."

"But she cannot predict the number of messages we receive," I point out gently.

She nods her head in a reluctant gesture of agreement. Unnerved by the less-than-joyous reception of this news, I fold my hands before me. "Is that not a good thing, Reverend Mother? That in these most troubled times, our wise and experienced seeress is finally regaining her Sight? I would think that would be something worth rejoicing over tonight as we begin to celebrate midwinter's arrival."

"But of course, Annith. I am most delighted to hear this. I only wish that we had more than a report on the weather and a courier's tally as proof of her returning abilities, but it is a good sign, nevertheless." She takes up her quill from its stand and nods at me. "I imagine if you hurry, you will be able to help the others decorate the refectory. And Annith?"

"Yes, Reverend Mother?"

Her voice softens, filling with warmth. "That was well done of you, helping Sister Serafina nurse Vereda. It made both of their lives much easier, and I know it brought the old seeress much comfort."

"It did?" I thought she hardly noticed whose hand was tending her.

"It did. And it proves once again how invaluable you are to the convent—how perfect your obedience and dedication."

Words crowd up my throat—I did not do it out of dedication, I want to tell her, but because I wanted the seeress to get better so I would not have to take her place.

But I cannot say it. I cannot confess to the abbess that I overheard that conversation. My need to keep such transgressions secret drowns out the need to deny her words. "I am glad I was able to be of service," I say, "for now that she is well again, perhaps she will See an assignment for me."

The abbess smiles fondly. "Perhaps she will."

I hold her gaze, trying to discern if she truly means that or if she simply thinks it is what I wish to hear.

In the end, I leave her chamber none the wiser.

Chapter Five

WRAPPED IN OUR CEREMONIAL CLOAKS made of thick white wool, we file out of the courtyard just past midnight. Nearly all of us are in attendance, from the youngest to old Sister Claude, who shuffles along beside Sister Serafina, holding on to her arm so that she will not trip and break her aging, brittle bones. In our right hands we carry a lit torch so that we may see the path that lies ahead, and in our left, we hold our offerings to Mortain.

Many of the younger girls carry small cakes from the convent kitchen, ones they piously chose to offer to Mortain rather than eat. Little Audri plans to offer her shoes, which would be more impressive if we did not all know how much she hates to wear them. I suspect the abbess will have one of us collect the shoes after the ceremony. Melusine brings a pearly pink shell from the sea. Matelaine carries the letters her parents have sent her — letters she has read aloud to us a hundred times, as we are all jealous of her two living parents. She is an oddity among us, for her parents — even her false father — see her as a joy rather than a burden and have sent her here to the convent for the opportunities it affords her, not because she is feared or hated. In truth, I am impressed by the depth of her offering.

I have brought an arrow. One that I made with my own hands and the one that flies truest. I intend to aim tonight's offering directly at Mortain Himself so that my prayers will be certain to reach Him.

Midwinter is my favorite time of year, a time when Mortain feels closes to us. Once, when I was a child, He was this close to me always. Whether because of my youth, my dire need of Him, or because the terror of those years was simply so strong that it parted the veil between our worlds, I do not know. But I miss it. It is like a faint hunger that gnaws at my heart rather than my belly.

And while I am not terrified like I was as a child, I do feel lost and confused, afraid I will be pushed down a path I've no wish to take. Now more than ever, I need His guidance.

The dim light of the pale moon casts everything in shades of black and silver. Our processional is accompanied by the crashing of the waves against the rocky shore and the moaning of the wind, which whips at our cloaks so that they flap like the wings of the crow Sister Widona carries in a twig cage.

As we make our way through long-dead scrub grass and jagged boulders covered with lichen, I think upon the many tales of the ill-fated love between Mortain and Amourna and why winter comes to our land. Each of the nine bishoprics of Brittany has its own tale of how Mortain did — or did not — capture the fair Amourna. In the land where the patron saint of travelers was born, it is said that Death traveled far and wide looking for a love that would survive even His dark realm. He thought He'd found it in Amourna, but in the end, the love she bore Him was too fragile to survive Death, and thus He travels the land, mourning for her.

The followers of Saint Brigantia claim it was Mortain's quest for full knowledge of life that led Him to seek Amourna out and open His heart to her, for how can one truly understand life without knowing love?

Those who have dedicated themselves to Saint Mer say that Death gazed upon the goddess of the sea and was smitten, but He could not follow her to her realm, nor she to His, so He settled for Amourna, who mourns being a second choice for all eternity.

In those places where Saint Salonius, the god of mistakes, is well loved and worshiped, they say that it was all a mistake, some trick of fate. Some even claim that Salonius himself had a hand in it.

Those who still honor Dea Matrona claim that Death was once Matrona's consort, and life and death were one. But with the coming of the new god, she cast Death out in order to find a place in the new church. Thus scorned, Death turned to her daughter Amourna for comfort, and it is not Matrona's sorrow that causes winter to blow its harsh winds over the land but her jealous heart.

It is only the followers of Saint Arduinna who have nothing to say on the matter, for while their goddess was there and surely they know what truly happened, out of respect for both Arduinna's sister and her mother, they choose not to contradict either story.

The true story—the one we learn here at the convent—is that Death came upon Amourna and her twin sister, Arduinna, in a meadow, and that He was instantly taken with Amourna's loveliness. Mistrustful of the way Mortain was looking at her sister, Arduinna drew her bow and let fly one of her sharp arrows, which pierced Mortain's heart. But not even a goddess can kill the god of Death. He simply plucked the arrow from His chest, then bowed and thanked her for reminding Him that love never comes without cost. Surprised by His demeanor, she consented to let her sister ride with Him to His home.

The rest of the world believes that winter comes because either Dea Matrona or Amourna is mourning her loss. We who worship Mortain know that neither is true. We know that when the night is at its longest and darkness reigns, Mortain journeys back to our world from His own, and winter follows on His heels simply because it is His own true season.

Tonight's ceremony feels different from all the ones that have come before, as if I am walking along the edge of some knife I cannot see. On one side lies the future I have always dreamed of, serving Mortain as an instrument of Death in the world of men. If that comes to pass, I will never be part of our midwinter celebration again. None of the other initiates have ever returned for it, and that thought brings me great sadness.

On the other side of the blade lies the future I do not wish for myself —that of seeress. And even if that should come to pass and I must remain on this island all the rest of my days, I will still not ever take part in this ceremony again.

Either way, it is the last time I will make this walk, and the night is made bittersweet because of it.

At last we reach our destination—the door to the Underworld itself. The dark gaping mouth is capped by a large flat stone that stands upon other stones, each taller and wider than a man and each planted deep in the earth so that the chamber disappears into the small hill. Smaller stones mark the pathway leading to the entrance.

As the head of our order, the abbess goes first, planting her lit torch between two of the rocks, then kneeling at the opening to Mortain's realm. She places her offering there—I cannot see what it is, no matter how I crane my neck—then bows her head in prayer. When she rises, Sister Eonette goes next, followed by each of the other nuns. Sister Claude is last, and when she is finished with her prayer, it takes not only Sister Serafina but Sister Thomine as well to help her to her feet.

Then it is the novitiates' turn. As the oldest among us, I have the honor of going first. All my life, I have only ever wanted to serve as His handmaiden. Now more than ever, it is important He knows that. That He be reminded of that.

As I step forward, I press my fingers against the sharp point of the arrow, sucking in a breath as it bites into my flesh. When I feel the faint dampness of my own blood, I let it drip onto the arrowhead, careful not to let any of the older nuns see. Something tells me they would not approve.

As I kneel before the door to Mortain's realm, I bow my head. *Please,*

Mortain, I pray. *My life is Yours to command, but if it please You, I would use my skills and gifts in Your service rather than simply sitting in a small room.*

When my prayer is finished, I lay my arrow down atop the other gifts there. As I do, the night breeze shifts, bringing with it an eddy of cold air from the barrow that feels as if it reaches out to caress my face. In that moment, I am certain He has heard me.

Satisfied, I rise to my feet and join the others.

Chapter Six

AFTER THE MIDWINTER CELEBRATION, THE black storm clouds move in from the north and envelop our island, bringing with them howling winds and stinging rain. It feels as if Mortain has come forth from the Underworld with a year's worth of unshed tears.

I am feeling hopeful, but wary and nervous as well, for while I know Mortain received my offering, I also realize I have made a grave — perhaps even fatal — error in my strategy. In my desperation to get Sister Vereda well, I have managed to confirm the abbess's belief that I am willing to do whatever is needed to serve the convent, and I do not know how to undo that. I wish that I could unravel time and replace my actions with different ones, but that is not possible. And so I wait. And fret. I am filled with a nearly unbearable tension, as if my body is a bow being drawn taut by the hand of fate.

When the clouds clear long enough for a crow to get through with a message, I try to haunt the rookery. But the abbess is always there first, as if she is watching even more closely than I am. It cannot be an accident, this new habit of hers to collect the messages herself, and I cannot help but wonder what it means.

What I truly need are some days of vigorous training to shed some of my tension, but the weather does not allow for that. Instead, Sister Beatriz arranges a mock ball so we may practice our dancing, but I am distracted and clumsy and manage to step on Sarra's toes—twice—until she pinches me in retaliation.

This season, whose gifts have always calmed me and brought a renewed sense of purpose to my life, now holds only questions and uncertainty.

Sister Vereda is slowly growing stronger and some days I wish to storm into her chambers and pepper her with questions—on her visions, how she was chosen, and how she lost her sight. Finally, afraid I will go mad, I make my way to the armory. Sister Arnette is not only our weapons mistress but our smith as well. Surely she has something—anything—that needs the pounding of her smith's hammer. I would even settle for horseshoes or cooking pots.

That is where Matelaine finds me, one week after the midwinter ceremony. "Annith?"

I look up from the dented vambrace I am planishing. "Yes?"

"The abbess is asking for you."

Everything inside me grows still and I carefully set the vambrace and hammer down on the bench. "Did she say what she wanted?" Matelaine gives a quick shake of her head, and thoughts of Ismae and Sybella bring me to my feet. "Have there been any crows this morning?"

"No," she says, the word allowing my heart to calm somewhat.

Somewhat, but not altogether. "Has she met with Vereda?" I try to keep my voice casual, but it is of little use, for Matelaine knows what I am hoping for.

"Not that I have heard, but then, I would not necessarily know."

We exchange a glance, and she reaches out and squeezes my hand. "I will pray she has an assignment for you," she whispers, then leaves me to make my way to the abbess's office alone.

I stand outside the abbess's chambers and try to compose my features into an expression of calm. I remind myself that this means nothing; I am often called to her office. It is most likely some new task she needs help with—taking inventory of convent supplies or checking on the seeds we have stored for the early-spring plantings.

When I have both my hope and my worry well in hand, I reach out and knock.

"Come in."

The abbess sits at her desk, a pile of correspondence at one elbow, the large convent ledger in which she records all the assignments at the other. When I see that book, my heart gives another flutter of excitement. "You asked to see me, Reverend Mother?"

She looks up at me and sets aside the letter she was writing. "Ah, Annith. Yes, I did. Please come in. Sit down." I have not seen her much of late, as she has been busy in her office writing missives that she sends out at the merest lull in the winter storms.

"The midwinter ceremony went well. Thank you for arranging that."

"It was my pleasure to be of some small help, Reverend Mother."

"I know. That is one of your best qualities, Annith. Your willingness to step in and do what must be done, cheerfully and with great skill. Sister Serafina says that Sister Vereda continues to do much better, thanks in large part to your help in nursing her."

I clasp my hands in front of me to keep my desperation from showing. "She *is* doing much better, Reverend Mother. She is having visions daily now. She saw that Melusine would be swept into the sea and would swim out safely. She saw where the barn cat had her kittens, and she has predicted with great accuracy when the clouds will break and the crows get through, as well as precisely how many messages will arrive." Except once, when she missed her count by one, but I do not mention that.

The abbess slips her hands inside her wide sleeves and smiles at me with such fondness and pleasure that in that moment, I am certain —*certain*—she will finally grant me my heart's desire.

"That is why, after much thought and prayer and discussion with the other nuns, I have decided that you will begin training with Sister Vereda immediately so you may take her place as seeress when her aged body finally stops working once and for all."

Her words are like a physical blow, sending all the air whooshing painfully from my lungs. "Please, no!" I whisper.

Her smile evaporates as quickly as my hopes. "What do you mean, *no?*"

"I mean, Reverend Mother, while I am eager to serve Mortain, I do not think I can do it as seeress."

The abbess frowns at my words, but I cannot tell if it is in annoyance or simply puzzlement. "For a girl as dutiful and devout as yourself, I would think it the perfect existence."

"No, Reverend Mother. It would not be."

A brief flash of pain appears in her eyes, as if somehow my not wanting to be seeress has hurt her, but it goes so quickly I am hardly certain I have seen it. "Come, Annith. We always knew you were destined for something special—what is more special than being the seeress, the most unique among all the handmaidens? You will not be interacting with Mortain through intermediaries like the rest of us, but will instead be His voice in the world."

Every word she utters is like a long bony finger wrapping itself around my heart, squeezing until there is no hope left within it. "Reverend Mother, I have spent my entire life training for one thing—to be Death's handmaiden and carry out His will here on earth. At no time have I ever felt called to the duties that Sister Vereda performs."

Her lips thin and her nostrils flare with irritation. "You are young and do not yet know what Mortain truly desires of you."

I realize now, now that it has been taken away from me, that the only thing that kept me from despair all these years was the belief that one day I would finally be able to get off this island — this place where I have had to guard every thought, hide every true feeling, and weigh every gesture. It was the promise of having a life of my own — away from the convent — that fueled my determination to excel at everything they threw at me.

That gives me the courage to speak freely. Or foolishly. "How do you know this is what He wants? Surely, if Sister Vereda had Seen such a fate for me, she would have made some mention of it as I sat by her bed day after day for the last fortnight, would she not?"

"Are you questioning me?" The abbess's voice is so forbidding and full of steel that I am reminded of Sybella's insistence that she is not the kind paragon she appears but a cold ruthless adversary one should be wary of crossing.

"No, I am questioning Mortain's will." That suddenly seems far less frightening than questioning hers. "I cannot believe I am the best choice for this job. Does it not take a lifetime of training to be able to do what Sister Vereda does? I have only ever trained to kill."

"Except the god has other plans for you."

"Then why has He not allowed me to peer into the future as Sister Vereda does? For I assure you, He has not given me any such gifts."

Ismae and Sybella used to tease me and claim that I was able to see the future, for how else was I always able to block their blows and slip away seconds before a door was opened or a curtain pulled back? But having a good sense of timing and quick reflexes is a far cry from being able to See the future, let alone See Mortain's will — a cold trickle of dread seeps into my marrow, and goose flesh erupts along my arms. Unless . . . does this abbess know my secret? The Dragonette promised she would never speak of it, but what if she had and now this abbess knows and *that* is behind the plan to make me the new seeress?

When the abbess speaks again, her voice is quiet, gentle even. "Annith, you need to understand. This is Mortain's will for you. You must either obey or be cast out. Surely you're not saying you would rather leave us than serve in the manner that is asked of you?"

Once again, I cannot quite grasp what she is saying. "I cannot be sealed up in that room," I whisper. She of all people should know that. I do not wish to let her down, but I fear I will wither and die if I must do as she asks.

Her face is so full of poignant regret that it pierces my heart. "If that is how you feel on the matter, we can make other arrangements." Relief, giddy and sweet, fills me. Until she speaks again.

"There are any number of men who would be only too happy to take you to wife. You are so good with the younger girls, and I am certain there is a widowed farmer looking for someone to care for his children. There always is."

I stare at her in utter shock, and the ground underneath my feet feels as if it has shifted irrevocably. "Are those truly my only choices?"

"Yes." She stares back at me, daring me to choose the drab, colorless fate she has set out before me. She is no longer the firm, loving woman I have known all my life but the fierce, ruthless tyrant that Sybella struggled with all these years. Thinking quickly, I bow my head, as if subdued by her words.

She casts aside her sternness for a moment and leans forward. "Think, Annith! How many handmaidens do we have at the convent? And of those, only one is called to act as seeress, only one is deemed worthy of sitting at the very heart of the convent and being privy to Mortain's wishes. You are being offered this great honor, one bestowed upon a select few."

"Then it is not because I am flawed in some way? Or because I failed one of the Dragonette's tests?"

She appears stricken by my words. "No! It is only that you are more worthy than most. That all your years of training and hardship and endurance have paid off in ways you had not dared to dream of."

And even though her face is the very picture of loving concern, even though her need for me to believe her rolls off her in waves, it is impossible to trust her any longer. Not when she has just altered the shape and direction of my entire life.

Time. I must buy myself time to think.

I allow the overwhelming enormity of what has just transpired to show on my face. "This is all so much, Reverend Mother. So much more than I had ever even considered. I . . . I would like to spend some time in thought and prayer before I give you my answer. I want to be certain I can commit my full heart to what Mortain wants of me, for I will not shame the convent or myself by serving Him falsely."

There is a brief spark of irritation, but she quickly tamps it down. "Very well. But the time I can give you is not infinite. I must know in three days so I can make other arrangements if need be."

"I will have an answer for you by then," I assure her, and I hope that it is true.

Chapter Seven

ONCE I AM OUTSIDE IN the hallway, I stop and lean against the wall, trying to keep panic and desolation from weighing down on me. I press my fingers against my eyes and force myself to take slow, deep breaths, but it does not help. My whole body aches, as if my very bones will burst from my skin.

I have always believed that if I did everything the convent demanded of me, I would be rewarded with my only desire in life—to go forth from the convent and serve as Mortain's handmaiden. It is the guiding principle I have built my entire life on.

If, as the abbess has always claimed, she is my ally, then how can she foist this unwanted fate upon me?

Before anyone can see me, I make my way to the back of the convent, where the wine cellar is located. My footsteps slow as I draw near. Sybella used to laugh at me, thinking me too afraid to steal wine from the cellar. But the truth—the truth I worked so hard to conceal from both her and Ismae—was that it was not stealing, but the cellar itself that held so much terror for me. Terror born of long nights shut inside, with no scrap of blanket to warm myself or bite of food to eat. A confinement so solitary and harsh that it took me three days to find my tongue after my first night there.

Terror, I remind myself, that I used to make myself stronger, tougher. The idea that it might not have made me strong enough is unthinkable.

But in addition to all that terror, one of my moments of greatest joy occurred in that room, and I cannot help but wonder if that joy is in some way tied to the abbess's decision to groom me as seeress.

The Dragonette quickly and harshly dismissed the event, and I came to believe what she claimed: that I had merely imagined it. I put it aside, buried it with all the other small shames and mortifications of my childhood. But now, now I wonder if perhaps it was real after all. While I always held out some small shred of hope that it was true—that the Dragonette was wrong, and it hadn't been my fevered desire to please her that caused it—today for the first time, I want desperately to believe it was *not* true. Because if it was, then perhaps I am uniquely suited to act as seeress after all.

I stop in front of the rough wooden door and glance both ways to be certain no one is nearby. As my hand reaches out for the latch, my heart begins to beat too quickly and I must remind myself that there is nothing to fear. No one would dream of shutting me in there again.

But the mere idea that they think to shut me in the seeress's chambers for the rest of my life is just as bad.

Squaring my shoulders, I step into the cellar, letting the cold of the room—and a rush of painful memories—settle over me like a mantle.

The first time I was locked in here, I was but two years old, punished for daring to cry when Sister Etienne had been sent out on assignment and I missed her.

The second time was when I'd seen the cook butcher the hen for our evening meal and so refused to eat it. I was locked in the cellar with my bowl of chicken stew and not allowed to come out until I had finished every last drop.

When I was five, I was locked in the cellar yet again, this time for balking at butchering the hen we were to have for our supper. While the other girls closest to me in age were simply scattering feed in front of the hen house or collecting eggs, the Dragonette had decided that

I must begin practicing the art of killing. My hands were too small to get a decent hold on the large ax, and the lay sister who had to hold the hen still had no stomach for the task, wishing instead to do it quickly herself and be done with it. And so I faltered, whether through lack of strength or lack of will or simply because I did not understand what was required of me, I no longer remember. What I do remember was being locked in the wine cellar with the wounded chicken and forced to watch its slow painful march toward death, a much more painful death than would have been granted it had I been strong enough.

I spent the first hour sobbing in remorse-filled terror, afraid the chicken would drag itself over to me and peck out my eyes. When that did not come to pass I cried for the chicken itself, and for its obvious agony. At last my tears ran out and I simply sat with my back pressed against the cold stone wall, chilled and shivering as I watched the chicken die.

During that long, horrifying night, at some point I realized I was no longer alone. A tall, darkly cloaked man was there as well. That should have frightened me even more, seeing an unknown man in the heart of our womanly cloister, but I was so relieved at not being alone with the dead bird anymore that it never occurred to me to fear him.

He was long-limbed and graceful and dressed all in black. Even though he lowered himself to the floor next to me, there was something proud and stately in his manner. When I saw him, my hysterical dry sobbing hiccupped to a stop. He quietly took my hand in his, although my fingers were so cold I could not feel it, and sat next to me, saying nothing. But I was no longer alone, and that brought me great comfort.

I remember falling asleep eventually, leaning against his shoulder, and when the door opened in the morning, they found me sleeping soundly on the floor with my head gently pillowed by a rough hempen sack.

It wasn't until we went to church that morning and I saw the marble statue in the sanctuary that I recognized the hooded, cloaked figure. It was Mortain Himself whose arm I'd drooled on while drifting off to sleep.

Excited by this, I could not wait until the Dragonette summoned me to her office later that day. I told her all about my nocturnal visitor. I thought she would be overjoyed by this sign of His pleasure with me, but instead, the corners of her lovely mouth turned down with disapproval. "You are lying," she said.

"No!" I was distraught and more than a little terrified that she would think so.

"Ah, but you are, for you wish yourself to be special. I'd expected more from you than cheap lies." Her eyes—always so shrewd and piercing and full of her confidence in me—filled with tears, and I was shamed beyond measure that I had caused her such pain. Feeling lower than the grubs that root in the convent midden heap, I fell to my knees and begged her forgiveness.

Now I cross to the wall where I once thought I'd dozed with Death. It is blocked by a stack of small barrels and kegs so that I cannot sit down and lean against it like I did those many years ago. Instead, I reach out to touch the wall, trying to resurrect that moment in my life.

But nothing comes. There is no strong visceral reaction, no sudden clearing of memory, no true answers flaring to life at the touch, and I am left hoping it was nothing more than a child's overwrought imagination coupled with a desperate need to worm her way into a demanding abbess's good graces.

If it was not, then I am well and truly suited to being the seeress. And as much as I love Death, I do not think that I love Him enough to entomb myself in the convent before I have even lived.

Chapter Eight

I DO NOT SLEEP AT all that night and instead imagine that the walls of my room are drawing closer, pressing down on me, nearer and nearer until they threaten to force all the air from my lungs.

The morning brings little relief, for we are all trapped inside yet again. Today we are confined to the convent armory under the sharp-eyed supervision of Sister Arnette. Winter's storms and damp salt air will corrode the fine steel of our weapons, dulling the blades, and mildew the soft leather harnesses and sheaths if we do not tend to them, so today we sit with crocks of goose fat and bags of fine sand, polishing every metal surface in the armory.

It is the perfect task for me—a mindless activity that requires little thought but allows for my physical restlessness. Just as the rag in my hand circles over and over the fine steel of the knife blade, so too does my mind polish the few options available to me so that they are bright and sharp and clear.

I can acquiesce to the abbess's wishes, as I have always done. Or I can . . . What paths are truly open to me?

I try to think if I have ever heard tell of a handmaiden of Death refusing to serve or choosing to walk away. I have not, but with my newly awakened cynicism about the convent and its motives, I'm not sure the nuns would pass down such tales, even if they existed.

I could simply leave. Sneak off in the dead of night and run away.

Except I feel certain the abbess would use all the power at her disposal to bring me back.

Or perhaps, as old Sister Appollonia used to claim, Mortain Himself would send His horde of hellequin after any daughter of His who dared to defy Him. I think of Ismae's letter and shudder.

I set down the knife I have just finished polishing and pick up another. I swipe the rag in the yellow goose fat, then dip it into the dish of fine sand.

But *am* I defying Him? That is at the root of my uncertainty. Has He asked this of me, or is it the abbess's will?

If it is His will, am I willing to turn my back on Mortain and all He has meant to me? Forget all the times He has been there for me? My faith, my dedication to Him, is as much a part of me as my arm or my leg or my heart.

It is hard not to question my own motives, for I realize now that I have been trained since birth to blame myself as thoroughly as I have been trained to wield a blade. It is so easy for the sisters to imply that it is my obedience and willingness to surrender my will to Mortain that is being tested—but what if that is not what is being tested at all?

What if that is what they tell us so we will not question their own selfish motives?

As I set down the polished knife and pick up the next one, a wave of desire hits me, so strong that it causes my hands to tremble. I want to use this blade. All the blades here in this room. That this could be taken away from me leaves me nearly breathless.

Then an entirely new realization dawns on me, and the fingers clutching the slender stiletto's handle grow white. What if this is a test from Mortain Himself rather than from the convent? A test for me to prove my commitment to Him, prove my unwillingness to be diverted from His plans for me?

What if, instead of surrendering, I am supposed to fight for what I want? For surely Mortain does not fashion His handmaidens into such strong weapons and then expect them to topple in the first stiff breeze. And how am I to know which it is?

Next to me, Sarra rubs her nose with the back of her hand before reaching for another knife. "You look like you're planning to stab someone with that, not polish it."

Keeping the knife clenched in my hand, I look up at her and allow every bit of anger and frustration I am feeling to show in my eyes. She blinks and leans imperceptibly back. *Good,* I think, then smile, a movement so brittle it is a wonder my cheeks do not shatter.

The armory door opens just then, admitting a gust of frigid air and Sister Thomine. When she steps into the room, her gaze goes directly to Matelaine. "The abbess would like to see you in her office," she says.

Matelaine looks shocked, then worried, and I do not blame her, but something in the way that Sister Thomine will not look at me causes an alarm to begin clanging inside me like a distant bell.

Matelaine rises to her feet and brushes back her long, bright red hair. "But of course," she says in a contrite tone, already apologizing for any wrong she has done.

As she and Thomine leave the room, I carefully resume polishing the knife. I feel the other girls glance my way, curious that Matelaine is being called to attend the abbess. Even Sister Arnette's gaze lands upon me, but I carefully keep my head bent and do not look up. For some reason, I think of Sybella and how she was sent back out before she had fully healed. All of us, even the nuns, could see that she wasn't ready yet. For a while, I thought it was due to the innate skills she'd arrived with, and perhaps tinged somewhat by the fact that she and the abbess clashed from the very beginning, like an angry cat dropped amidst a pack of dogs.

And then I remember Ismae, who had no innate skill except for the thin veil of anger she wore and her resistance to poison, and I am filled with a sudden desperation. I glance over at Sister Arnette. She is helping Loisse, who has managed to cut herself on a blade in spite of knowing better. Like a single ray of sun forcing itself through the clouds, a realization dawns—I no longer care, at least today, if I anger Sister Arnette or any of the nuns. An urgent need to know what the abbess is discussing with Matelaine drives me to my feet and pushes me toward the door.

I stop where the corridor branches off into the short hall that leads to the abbess's private chapel, but no one is around to see, not with the bitter wind howling down the hallways like an angry wolf.

As I settle into position, I hear the murmur of voices. I recognize the abbess's low, calm tones and Sister Thomine's shorter, louder responses. It takes my ears a moment to adjust to the low cadences so that I can understand the actual words being said.

". . . tells me you have shown great improvement."

"I am honored that she thinks so, Reverend Mother."

"You should feel honored that Mortain has seen fit to bless you with such skill," the abbess says. The reproof in her voice is mild, but it is there.

Matelaine murmurs something I cannot hear, then the abbess speaks again, this time her voice soothing, as if comforting the wound her earlier words have just made. "Because of your great improvement and your renewed dedication to your studies, you are to be rewarded with your first assignment."

My heart slams against my rib cage like a bolting horse, driving all the air from my lungs so I cannot draw breath. When my breath finally returns, it brings with it a hot gush of anger. My ears fill with a great rushing sound and something inside me snaps. Or breaks. Or shatters. With no thought to the consequences of my actions, I throw open the door to the abbess's chambers and step into the room.

The voices stop abruptly, and three heads turn in my direction. Two mouths, Sister Thomine's and Matelaine's, are open in shock, but the abbess's is pressed into a firm, flat line. Spots of angry red appear on her pale cheeks. "What is the meaning of this?"

My entire body thrums with barely checked fury. "You cannot send Matelaine." I step farther into the room and slam the door behind me. "You cannot."

"Have you been listening at my door?" the abbess demands.

"This is not right. Matelaine is too young to be sent out. Too untrained. She is not ready yet."

The abbess rises from her chair, trying to use her height to intimidate me, but I am beyond caring. "You forget your place here, Annith. Remove yourself at once to your chambers and wait for me there."

But I have not forgotten anything. Indeed, it feels like I have finally remembered myself. Deep inside me, the alarm keeps clanging. "You cannot be serious about sending Matelaine out! She is only fifteen. She has not passed any of the tests required to be a full initiate, nor has she learned all the skills needed—"

"So are you now the novice mistress, and no one told me?"

The icy sarcasm in her voice is sharp enough to strip the flesh from my bones, but it doesn't matter. Instead, I say what we all know is true. "I have trained longer and passed all the tests."

"We have already spoken of this. Serving Mortain is not a right, but a privilege. A privilege *I* grant to you, not one you can march in here and demand for yourself."

"I thought it was a privilege granted by Mortain."

Her head rears back slightly, but before she can respond, I continue. "I can best Matelaine in a fight, and shoot ten bull's-eyes to her one. I can land a killing blow faster and more accurately than she can." In spite of how it might appear to the abbess, it is no longer about what I *want*.

I am well and truly afraid for Matelaine. "Would you send ten-year-old Lisabet next? Or Loisse? No one this young has ever been sent on assignment before, and you are surely risking her life."

"What of Margot or Genevieve? They were but twelve years old."

For a moment, I cannot fathom whom the abbess is talking about, and then I remember. "Are you merely placing Matelaine in the household of one of our enemies to act as spy, like you did them?" The panic in my chest lessens somewhat.

"What I do is none of your concern."

"It is if I am to be seeress."

I hear Sister Thomine's sharp intake of breath, and Matelaine whips her head around to stare at me. For one hugely satisfying moment, the abbess is speechless, for she knows I am right. If I am seeress, then I will be involved in all these decisions—I will be the one to See who is to stay and who is to go. She cannot deny it.

"But not until you have completed your proper training."

"Then Sister Vereda has Seen this?"

The silence in the room is thick and absolute. Sister Thomine turns to look at the abbess, and even Matelaine seems uncertain.

"Of course she hasn't. Since her illness, her visions have only been of small, pointless things."

"Then how can you send Matelaine out?"

The abbess's mouth snaps shut, and as we stare at each other, I feel the past seven years of my life unraveling like an old rope. "You think Mortain's business comes to a stop when one of us is ill?" she says at last.

"What if that is the very reason she has grown sick? Because Mortain wishes the convent business to cease for a while?"

"Mortain will protect Matelaine like He does all His daughters," the abbess says through clenched teeth. She turns to Matelaine. "Go to your chambers and pack your things. I will be there shortly to give you your final instructions."

As Thomine and Matelaine leave the room, the abbess thrusts her hands in her sleeves and strides over to the window. I flinch as she passes, her anger as palpable as a fist. But so is my own. "I have earned this," I tell her in a low, hard voice. "By right of all of the Dragonette's trials, I have earned my place as an instrument of Death."

She turns to look at me, her eyes blazing blue fire. "And what of me, Annith? What have I earned?"

"What?"

"You speak of the Dragonette, of your time with her. Who was it that snuck you food to eat when she would have had you go hungry? Who was always there, ready to free you from your confinement early, even at the cost of punishment to myself? Who soothed you when you cried, hid your crimes from her, and did everything possible to make your life bearable?"

"You did." Every word she says is true. While Sybella might feel the current abbess to be harsh and unfair, to me she could never be a true monster. Not like the Dragonette, who still gives me nightmares, even though she has been dead for seven years. And while this abbess was as much my rescuer as any knight from the tales of chivalry, I never expected her to use the affection between us like a merchant with a sack of coins, trying to bind my will to hers.

She takes a deep breath and visibly calms herself. "By rights, I should have you expelled from the convent for such insubordination and disobedience. However, because of the extreme fondness I hold for you, I am going to assume this is a one-time occurrence — brought on by the duress caused by the weighty choice before you. But make no mistake, Annith, if this happens again, I will throw you out."

And there it is. The threat I have lived with my entire life. If I am not good enough, kind enough, thoughtful enough, obedient enough, I will be cast from my home like a stunted fish from a fisherman's net.

The abbess takes a deep breath and folds away her anger like an unneeded blanket. "Now, I must have your answer, Annith, for I am leaving the convent to travel to Guérande in two days, as events are growing ever more serious. I need to know if this is settled before I leave, and more importantly, I need to know if I can trust you."

My heart leaps at the news that she is leaving, for if she is gone from here, then I will have more freedom to . . . what? Maneuver. Think. Strategize. Search for answers to the burning question of why she will not let me take my rightful place in Mortain's service. All that I do not know swirls inside me, like some foul storm, so strong it nearly makes me ill. But I know my chance of finding answers will be better with the abbess gone. I take a deep breath and put my hands up to my face, as if to scrub the tumult away. When I withdraw my hands, I see the abbess watching me carefully. "Yes, Reverend Mother." I permit a faint tremble of uncertainty to show and allow my shoulders to droop, as if in defeat. "If there is no other choice, I will stay at the convent to serve as seeress."

It is not the first lie I have ever told her, but it is the first one that I do not feel any guilt or remorse for having told.

Chapter Nine

I FIND MATELAINE IN HER room packing a small leather satchel. She is no longer dressed in her habit but in a traveling gown of forest green with her red hair unbound from its customary braid. She looks up when I enter. When she sees that it is me, the bright look on her face evaporates and she returns to her packing. "What do you want?"

"I have come to bid you farewell. And to explain, and perhaps apologize."

"You think you can explain away trying to humiliate me in front of the abbess?"

"Matelaine, I was not questioning your skill or devotion—I was questioning the abbess's decision. You are being sent out before you have even completed your training and I am truly concerned for your safety."

"Are you sure you are not simply jealous? We all know how much you've been longing for an assignment of your own."

"That is true—I won't deny it. But even if I were leaving on an assignment of my own this very minute, I would still be worried for you. Aren't you the least bit concerned? With all the lessons you haven't been exposed to and the tests you haven't taken yet?"

She snorts as she places two clean linen shifts in the satchel. "If I was, do you think I'd confess it to you so you could carry the tale straight to the abbess and attempt to keep me from going?"

A sense of helplessness and futility washes over me. I look out the window, wondering how to explain to her the complexity of what I am feeling when I can scarce explain it to myself.

"Is being the next seeress not enough of a prize that you must grab my tasks as well?" Although she keeps her voice pitched low, anger hums through it.

I turn from the window, hoping she will see the truth of my words writ clear upon my face. "I do not wish to be seeress and would gladly trade with you! It does not feel special. It feels like a trap—a trap that I will be stuck in until the day I die. But more importantly, I have no skill, no aptitude for it, and I cannot understand why the abbess has chosen me for such a role."

She shakes her head. "And now you act as if you know more than the abbess. Truly, Annith, you have let the nuns' praise go to your head."

She is the third friend of mine to be sent away, and I am terrified that I will not be so lucky as to have all three survive. I fear for Matelaine in a way that I did not for Ismae or even Sybella. She is so much younger and less experienced. "Matelaine, I do not wish to part—"

"After Ismae left, you and I were the closest in age, and I saw that you were lonely, and I was lonely, and I thought maybe we could be friends. Well, I understand now. We will never be friends. You need not worry that I will make that mistake again."

Her words cut me to the quick. I reach out and grab her hand, squeeze it. "We have always been friends. But Ismae—well, she was one of the first true friends I had ever had. Of course I was closer to her, just as you are closer to Sarra and Lisabet over Loisse and Audri. It does not mean that Loisse and Audri don't have a place in your heart."

There is a long moment of silence, then Matelaine wrinkles her nose. "Well, I'm not particularly fond of Sarra," she says, and I am filled with a giddy sense of relief. Then her face grows serious. "You always hold a piece of yourself back, Annith. For all your love and affection and kindness, there is always a part of yourself that you withhold from others."

And of course, she is right. For one sharp moment, I teeter on the edge of sharing my past with her, my awkward, painful childhood, but I cannot. Not now, when she must be preparing herself for the challenges ahead. I squeeze her hand again. "When you return," I tell her, "if I am not sealed away in that cursed room and unable to speak to anyone, I will tell you about that part of my life."

She smiles then and gives my hand a return squeeze. "I will look forward to hearing it."

I surprise her by throwing my arms around her and giving her a fierce hug. "Be safe, Matelaine. I will pray for you every day until your return." Tears sting at my eyes and try to crowd their way up my throat. With one last encouraging smile, I turn and leave before the abbess arrives.

Chapter Ten

FOR ALL THE TRAINING I have done, for all that I have practiced stealth and cunning and deceit, I never dreamed that my first true use of those skills would be against the very convent I serve.

Because I do not want the abbess to change her mind about leaving, I become as biddable as the sheep she wishes me to be. I do not even give in to the temptation of letting my mind stew over all the questions and issues that plague me, for fear that she will sense it somehow.

It is like putting a lid on a boiling pot.

My new role at the convent is announced that night at dinner amid much merrymaking and goblet-raising, as if the abbess is determined to show me just what a joyous occasion it is. I smile so much that my cheeks ache with it, and I look demure, as if slightly stunned that such an honor should be laid at my feet.

By the next day, as the abbess makes her final preparations to leave, the other girls have begun to look upon me with poorly hidden suspicion, as if I suddenly have the ability to snatch the very thoughts from their heads, and they withdraw from me. They edge away on the prayer bench, claiming to remember something they forgot, then choose different seats when they return. All these girls whose bruises I have tended, whose bodies I have trained, and whose secrets I have shared now act as if I have suddenly sprouted wings or a second head. They have started to separate me from their daily lives just as Sister Vereda is separate, and

I feel a lifetime of isolation stretching out before me, as endless as the sea.

Of course, it is too much to ask that the abbess should leave the island without one final meeting between us. I marshal every fiber of deceit and subterfuge I possess and weave them into a façade of calm acceptance to wear for our encounter.

"I have told all the other nuns of your new duties so they know you are not to participate in any further training exercises except as seeress." She is not sitting behind her desk but standing beside it, putting a few final things into her valise.

I smile cheerfully. "Very well, Reverend Mother."

"Sister Vereda will start with small daily lessons that you can then practice on your own." She pauses in her packing. "Annith, I cannot tell you how important it is that you apply your considerable talents to these tasks. The gathering political storm is bearing down on our country. From all reports, the duchess's court has splintered into factions, leaving her and our country even more weak and vulnerable than before. We must bring every skill and every resource we possess to her aid."

"But of course, Reverend Mother. I will use every talent at my disposal to serve Mortain and our country in this most dire time." I wait to see if she catches it, the way I have avoided promising to devote myself to my new seeress duties, but she is so distracted by her imminent departure that she does not appear to notice.

She rattles off a few more last-minute instructions. Apparently, just because I am to be seeress does not mean I am not to serve as her right hand as well. When the meeting is finally over, I wish her a warm farewell, then turn to leave.

"Annith?"

I pause with my hand on the door. "Yes, Reverend Mother?"

"Is everything all right between us?" The note of longing in her voice surprises me. After all that has transpired, after all her bullying and cajoling, can she believe things might ever be right between us again? I look over my shoulder and give her a smile so warm I almost manage to convince myself of its sincerity. "But of course, Reverend Mother. Everything is exactly as it should be. I will pray daily while you are gone."

I do not tell her that the nature of those prayers will involve asking Mortain to help me find a way to expose her actions for the lies and betrayals that I believe them to be.

Needing to be certain she is truly leaving, I follow her down the path to the beach. Hidden from view among the bushes that edge the rocky beach, I watch as the night rower helps her into the boat. She is taking two of the lay sisters with her as traveling attendants, and they will row themselves across in a second boat.

As the old sailor pushes off, she sits, stiff and straight, in the prow of the boat, her gaze firmly fixed on the mainland.

Why has she changed the very nature of my service to the convent? Is it something inside me, or inside her? And what options do I have, short of running away? For if I were to do that, it would leave her plots and machinations unchecked and unquestioned, and she might send Sarra or Lisabet out next.

Surely there are rules that abbesses must follow, and avenues of redress available when they do not. Or are we novitiates fully at the mercy of the convent?

That prospect is too grim to contemplate, so instead, I decide to do everything in my power to learn what is behind her decisions. Then I will see if that knowledge can be shaped into a weapon that can be used to force her to change her mind.

Chapter Eleven

WHEN IT IS TIME FOR me to meet with Sister Vereda for my first seeress lesson, it is all I can do not to run screaming in the opposite direction.

"You're late," she says when I let myself into her chambers.

"How can you say so when you cannot see the hourglass?"

She sniffs. "Monette brought my tray in some time ago."

"Perhaps Monette was early, Sister."

Her mouth twitches and I cannot tell if it is due to some faint hint of humor or she merely found a crumb of bread hidden in her cheek. I fold my hands in front of me and try to look contrite. "What shall you be teaching me today?"

"Punctuality, for one. And respect for your elders. If you happen to learn a bit about how to read Mortain's will in the flames of the sacred fire, that would be good too. Bring that empty brazier closer to the bed now. And be careful not to spill the ashes."

Once I have done that, she sends me to fetch the small bag of crow feathers we will need. Unable to see a thing in the gloom, I light a candle before I move toward the shelves. They are crowded with boxes and small caskets, piles of small bones, and a silver chafing dish. I grope carefully, hoping not to knock anything over. My hand bumps into something as cold as glass but far, far heavier. Even though it is clearly not the sack of feathers, I pick it up and bring it closer to the candlelight.

It is a small, dark vial, but so heavy that I know it is made out of crystal, although I did not know crystal could be as black as night. The surface is cut into facets, and the candlelight shimmering upon it gives the illusion of stars in the night sky. Carefully, I lift the stopper, which ends in a long, thin pointed wand. That is when I know precisely what I hold in my hand. It is the Tears of Mortain, administered to every novitiate who sets out on His path so that she can better discern His will for her.

My hand closes around the vial and I clutch it tight, as if I could absorb the knowledge and gifts the drops bestow through the crystal. It is just one of the mysteries of the convent that I have been denied.

"Annith?" comes the old voice. "Are you still there?"

"Yes, Sister. The feathers were buried under the bones. What sort of bones are they, anyway?"

As she prattles an answer, I reluctantly return the Tears of Mortain to their place. I cannot use them now, but it comforts me to know where I can find them should I ever need them.

Having no intention of spending all my days studying augury, I begin making plans to learn what is at the heart of the abbess's decisions, for it has become painfully clear that she is not using me simply to fill some general need of the convent. Her desire to have me be seeress is personal. If it is something about me that makes me uniquely suited for the position, then why not just tell me? And if she will not, then perhaps there is something in the convent records of my birth that will explain her decision. Now that I have been awakened to how thoroughly trained I am to accept lies as truth, I feel I must reexamine everything I have been told.

It is possible that I am not truly alone in the world. Perhaps I have some family—however distant—to go to should I decide to escape.

And there it is: *escape*, the word I have been avoiding since I first realized I had no choice but to pretend to accept the abbess's plans. She has changed the very nature of the bargain we made so long ago, when I pledged my undying loyalty and unwavering devotion in exchange for —what? For her to see me as unflawed? For her to allow me to pursue what I had dreamed of my entire life? Of course, I was too young to put all that into words, but she knew well enough. She has always played me like an instrument tuned to her hands, and this was no exception.

After a week of scouring the convent's scriptorium, I acquire only a small pile of information, but it is more than I had when I started. I learn that the seeress must be either a virgin or a woman beyond child-bearing years who has sworn an oath of celibacy. That is it—the only two requirements for the office. Those who are caul-born or whose eyes have been blessed with Mortain's gift of Seeing into a man's heart make the best seeresses, but nowhere does it say that either is required. So whatever is behind the abbess's desire to have me serve as seeress, it is not my having something that others here do not possess. I am not the only one—or even the best one—to take on those duties.

But that is the only fruit my search has borne. I have found nothing about my own past. While I did not have a surname or place of birth to go by, Annith is a rare enough name, and I had hoped it was used only by certain noble houses. However, although I have learned that the noble houses of Brittany contain three hundred Annes, four Mildreths, and two Annelises, there is no other Annith on record.

With so very little on which to hang my hopes, I find it ever harder to endure my lessons with Sister Vereda. Thoughts of escape dance around in my head like leaves in a windstorm, and I fear she will reach out with her gnarled hand and snatch one, then all my hopes will be lost.

It is two weeks before I find an opportunity to search the abbess's office. Sister Eonette appears to enjoy her time in there and lingers far past her morning hours. I wonder if she wishes to be abbess, and if so, would she welcome my exposure of the current abbess's lies? I remember her heated conversation with the abbess on the day I first overheard the plans to make me seeress and realize I may have an ally in this, if it comes to that.

I do not like the unsubtlety of having to pick the lock on the abbess's door, but it cannot be helped. I slip one of my nearly needle-thin blades into the lock, lift, turn, and sigh in relief at the satisfying *snick* as it unlocks.

Pale moonlight spills in from the two windows, illuminating the enormous cupboard that covers most of the wall behind the desk. It might well take me all night to search each of its hidden drawers and shelves. I push away from the door, eager to get to work. Although there is only a quarter-moon, it is bright enough for me to see by, so I do not need to risk lighting a candle.

The intricate scrollwork of the cabinet is carved with strange wild beasts cavorting among curves and arches, their polished wooden eyes watching me as I try to open one of the doors. It is locked. I cast about for a likely hiding place for the key. Hopefully it is not dangling from the ring Sister Eonette wears at her waist.

My luck holds and it is in the first place I look, the drawer of the abbess's desk, for who would dare breach the abbess's inner sanctum without invitation?

Me, that's who, and I will dare much more than that before I am done.

There are four keys, and one by one I try them. The third unlocks it. The first drawer coughs up nothing but bills and receipts for goods sold to the convent: bolts of dark blue samite for new habits and white wool for the midwinter cloaks, leather for shoes and grain from the local miller. In the second drawer is correspondence with Church officials about local matters, such as the leasing of fields on the mainland, and the letter from the abbess of Saint Mer just before she sent Melusine.

I turn my attention to the bottom cabinet. This one contains a number of small drawers and cubbies stuffed with more letters and old correspondence, some small coins, and half-used sticks of sealing wax. At the very bottom is a large drawer. I take a deep breath as I open the drawer, letting it out when I finally see the prize I have been looking for — the large leather-bound ledger that contains the record of every one of Mortain's handmaidens as far back as the first days of the convent.

I grasp the book with both hands, carry it over to the window, and set it on the sill.

The pages are old and yellowed and some so fragile I fear they will come apart under my fingers. Gingerly, I turn each page, marveling at the old script, so ornate as to be nearly unreadable.

I keep turning the pages, looking for dates that correspond to my arrival at the convent. Finally, nearly three-quarters of the way through, I see *July 1472* scrawled atop a page. I run my finger down, past entries for July, August, and September, then quickly turn the page, but the next one is dated January of 1473. That cannot be correct. I arrived in the fall of 1472, toward the end of October. I turn back a page, but the last date is still September 1472.

How can that be? According to the ledger, I have never existed at all.

Perhaps the dates are out of order. I bring the heavy book up closer to my face and tilt it toward the moonlight. A leaf is missing. It appears that the page that holds all the answers I seek has been carefully torn from the book.

My pulse quickens, for is not the fact that the page is missing a sort of answer in itself?

To be certain, I hurry back to the drawer, thinking perhaps the page had simply come loose and fallen out, but no, the drawer is empty except for a large flat box. It is of some dark, glossy black wood, and I turn it over and over in my hands but can find no lid, no seam, no catch, no way of opening it. But it is heavy, and something inside moves when I shake it.

My hands tingle with excitement, for it must be something truly important to be enclosed in a box that cannot be opened. As enticing as that is, the box likely does not hold the answers that I seek, so I put it aside and resume my search for some record of my arrival.

I move to the bottom right cupboard and give a small gasp of delight when I find a neat row of small, calfskin-bound black books. I pull one out, flip it open, and am pleased to see the abbess's elegant writing covering the vellum. As my eye moves across the words, I realize that it is a recording of the day-to-day operations of the convent. I turn a few more pages, and when my eye is caught by the name Melusine, I quickly read the abbess's summary of her arrival. Surely that means all our arrivals would be noted in these journals as well as in the main convent ledger.

I pluck the fifth one from the end, and when I open it I see that the handwriting is not that of the current abbess but a bolder, more precise script. I glance at the dates: 1470 to 1475. With trembling hands I turn the pages, skimming the words until my own name jumps out at me. Clutching the journal to my chest as if the words might disappear before I can read them, I hasten back to the window so I may have the full light of the moon.

1472

Today the night rower delivered a small babe, a tiny wrinkled thing that cannot be but a handful of days old. According to the hedge priest and the herbwife who delivered the child, the girl was sired by Mortain, but the priest and the herbwife did not know who the mother was or could even name her. The night rower's son's wife has recently lost a babe and will be glad for the work as wet nurse. Thus does our Lord Mortain provide for even the least and smallest of His creatures.

1474

The child called Annith grows apace and is apparently healthy. At two years of age, it is not too early to begin her training. Indeed, she will be most fortunate among us, for few are given the opportunity to begin walking in Mortain's path at such a tender age. Besides, the novice mistress coddles her too much and will make her soft. Best to train any softness out of her as early as possible so she may be as perfect for Mortain's service as we can make her.

1475

The child cried and sobbed and made a terrible fuss over being parted from Sister Etienne. As punishment, she has been locked in the cellar until she is willing to sleep in her own bed in the dormitory with the other girls without fussing. I will show her that she does not need anyone to survive and that it is unwise to form such attachments. I shall have to think of some punishment for Sister Etienne as well, for she is almost as distraught as the child.

1475

*It took three days to break the child, which,
were it not so inconvenient for us all, would
speak admirably of her will and spirit. We will
take that raw stuff and mold it into a truly
remarkable weapon for Mortain's use.*

1475

*The child cried inconsolably when two of the
barn cat's kittens died. We explained to her that
death was nothing to be afraid of, but when she
would not listen to reason, more extreme measures
were called for. She was locked in the wine cellar
again, with the two dead kittens, in order to
prove to her that she had nothing to fear from
death. When she was finally quiet, she was let
out. Sister Etienne said she did not speak for two
entire days. Let us hope that means this lesson
has been fully impressed upon her.*

A hot sickness churns in my stomach, then crawls up my throat and
spreads down through my arms. It is one thing to have such memories
locked away in one's head where they are subject to one's own doubts
and the softening of time. It is quite another to have them so coldly
recorded upon a page, with no regret or admiration or anything to indicate the true torment of what I suffered.

I swallow convulsively as a wave of old familiar fear rises up in my
throat. But I feel something new as well, something dark and unex-

pected. Anger. No, not anger, I realize as my heart hammers and my skin feels as if it will erupt into flames. Fury.

Outrage that the awful terror of my young life is laid out so casually, as if the abbess were reporting how many lambs the ewes dropped in the spring.

Fury at the sheer callousness and cruelty and harshness of the punishments doled out to me when I was younger even than little Florette.

I want to fling the book from me, throw it into a fire and burn it to ash, but I also want to clasp it tight as proof of what I have endured. What I have *survived*.

Proof of what is truly owed me.

The Dragonette's calm, passionless words drive home just how much was demanded of me as a child in order for me to earn my place at the convent. That feeling has chased me all my life—that I am a flawed and imperfect vessel.

My cooperation—no, my full and utter capitulation to their desires —was the price I *had* to pay for survival. It was a bargain as binding as any contract, for all that it was a silent one. I pledged to do all that she asked of me, agreed to rise to the challenge of all her bedamned tests— and in return, I would be allowed to serve as handmaiden to Mortain.

I have earned that destiny. By right of all that I have endured, I have earned this. Such was the silent contract between the Dragonette and me, sealed in my own blood and pain and terror, and no one, certainly not the current abbess, can change the terms of that bargain.

I slip the journal into the pocket of my apron and turn to the cabinet directly behind the abbess's desk. It is nearly morning, and I am out of time. My heart hammering in my chest, I return the convent ledger to the drawer. I lift the box to return it as well, then pause, weighing its heft in my hands. To someone who collects secrets, the box is too great a temptation to leave behind. Besides, perhaps whatever it holds is important enough that I can use it as some form of leverage.

Chapter Twelve

I AM NOT ABLE TO leave right away. There are preparations to make in order to ensure the nuns do not come after me, at least not until I have gotten well away from the coast and the main roads.

For a moment, a brief moment, I feel a pinch of uncertainty. Who will See for the convent when Vereda dies if not me? Would that not leave them as vulnerable and as blind as the seeress?

No. They can simply pick another virgin. Or better yet, one of the women past childbearing age. I have had well over a dozen lessons now and have not discerned so much as an approaching storm or what the cook will prepare for supper, let alone Mortain's will.

I do not lull myself into believing this will be easy. I have only rarely been outside the convent walls, and have never been allowed to roam free on the open roads or wander through towns and cities unsupervised. My only experiences were the few trips Sister Thomine took us older girls on, precisely so we would have such experiences.

However, in the weeks following my discovery of the journal, I manage to put aside a small supply of provisions — an empty water skin, some hard cheeses and purloined loaves of bread, as well as a heavy gown that does not mark me as a handmaiden of Mortain. Obtaining a supply of weapons is harder, for Sister Arnette is always in her armory and most of the weapons are larger than the cheeses, and they clatter far more loudly than the gown. Poisons, too, present a challenge, for I must slip into Sister Serafina's workshop in the dead of night and pray that there is nothing noxious brewing that could cause me harm.

Unable to decide if I am arming myself for defense or as the assassin I have trained to be, in the end, I prepare for both.

My last step is writing the letter I will pretend has come from the abbess to request my presence at her side in Guérande. Without such a message, a search party would likely be sent out as soon as my absence was discovered.

It has taken me a while to come up with a justification for the abbess's request, as it is a complete turnabout of her plans for me.

It has also required that I become even more skilled at forging her hand. I lean back and admire the carefully scripted note.

> *Dear Eonette,*
>
> *Now that I have seen firsthand the threats that our duchess faces, I have decided to have Annith join me at court. I believe that all of Mortain's resources need to be brought to bear on the challenges that face our duchess if we are to have any hope of prevailing. It makes no sense to leave one of our most skilled novitiates withering behind our walls when the duchess so clearly has need of her.*
>
> *I know that we must still address the issue of seeress soon, but with Vereda having made such an unexpected recovery, I cannot help but feel that Mortain Himself has bought us some time.*

I fold the parchment and seal it. As the wax hardens, I pull my saddlebag from its hiding place under Sybella's old bed. There is no one I must say goodbye to, for while I will miss the younger girls, it is not worth the risk of alerting them to my actions. I will better serve them by confronting the abbess and ensuring none of them is ever sent out before they are fully trained. If it is some misguided fondness for me that is at the heart of the abbess's unwillingness to send me out, it is wrong and must stop. It is too gross a betrayal of the others and I will not have it on my conscience.

I take the message, crack open the wax seal, then crumple the note, as if it has been read in great haste, before tossing it on my bed. When they come looking for me in the morning, they will see the abbess's request and assume that I was the first to read it and set out immediately. While some of the nuns might wonder why it came to me directly, others will know of my talent for ferreting out information and should not question such a thing.

Dressed in my heaviest gown, I slip into my winter cloak and take one last look around my room. The convent has yielded what few answers it had, which in turn have created only more questions. And the truth that the Dragonette's journal pounded home with the force of a fist is that I do not owe anyone here a thing.

I sling my pack over my shoulder, running through my list of supplies one more time. There are no items I have forgotten. My hand twitches with the memory of the faceted crystal vial in Sister Vereda's chambers, as black as night and densely heavy. Do not I have a greater need than others for such a thing if I am to be cut off from the convent's support? Surely I must try to use every means available to better see Mortain's will for me.

The entire convent is dark and quiet, so it is easy enough to slip unobserved to Sister Vereda's chambers. There is the risk that with her returning skills, she will See what I intend to do, but it is one I must take. Even if she discovers my plans, she cannot yet rise from the bed, nor would anyone hear her frail voice raise the alarm, buried as she is deep in her own chambers, far from everyone else. Even so, I hope it does not come to that.

I carefully crack open the door. The room is as dark as the Underworld itself, with naught but a faint red glow here and there from the charcoal in the braziers. The old seeress's breathing is deep and even, so I slip inside and quietly shut the door behind me. I pause a moment to let my eyes adjust.

Once I have gotten my bearings, I slowly move across the room, watching the floor carefully to be certain I do not trip or stumble or make any unexpected noise. It takes me but twelve silent steps to reach the shelf. I glance once more at the sleeping seeress, listening to the deep, sonorous rumble of her breathing, then turn and reach for the vial.

As my hand closes around the dark crystal, I am surprised once again at how heavy it is. I know little of the Tears of Mortain, for it is one of those mysteries that only true initiates are supposed to be privy to, but I have heard stories. Whispered tales and hints of rumors. The Tears are said to enhance our ability to see and experience life in order to better imitate how Mortain is able to see and experience life. They are supposed to correct for our human inadequacies, whether by making it easier to sense life behind closed doors or by allowing us to better see His marques. I lift the stopper to reveal the long, crystal wand that ends in a sharp point. A single drop of the Tears hovers on the tip. I take a deep breath and slowly lift the stopper to my face. I force my eye open, but before I can place the drop of Tears in it, Sister Vereda snorts in her sleep. The sound startles me so that my hand holding the stopper jerks and the drop splashes onto the bodice of my gown. I freeze, wondering if the old woman will wake. There is a long moment of silence, then her loud breathing resumes.

As I replace the stopper in the crystal bottle, I decide to take the Tears with me. Not only so that I may use them when needed, but also so that I can ensure that the nuns will not send anyone else out on assignment while I am gone. Surely they would not send one of the novitiates without the Tears of Mortain to aid her.

Once the Tears are secured in my pack, I take a deep breath, turn, and begin carefully making my way out of Sister Vereda's chambers. I shift my hips to avoid the corner of one table, then shift again to avoid the stand that holds a charcoal brazier. By the time I reach the door, I am damp with sweat and coiled tighter than one of Sister Thomine's whips. Out in the hallway, I lean against the wall and calm my thudding heart. It is not Sister Vereda's chambers that cause it to race, but the enormity of what I am about to do. But what other choice do I have?

The day I have dreamed of for as long as I can remember has finally come — I am leaving the convent. Not in a triumphant march to do Mortain's bidding, as I have always imagined, but on a determined search for answers. I will find the abbess in Guérande and make her tell me precisely why she insists I be seeress despite the many others who could fulfill those same duties. If it is not something personal, then it must be a flaw or lack of mine, and I will force her to tell me what it is, not hide behind half-truths and lies. Because once I know what that flaw is, I can fix it. I can change that part of myself, as I have so many times before.

Chapter Thirteen

It is a terrifying thing to cross the sea at night, but I tell myself it is exhilarating. There is nothing but the glimmer of moonlight to steer by, and the sharp salt-scented breeze from the sea whistles past my ears, bringing a faint spray to my face. And while my arms are strong from long hours spent at weapons training, they are not accustomed to rowing and so begin to ache after the second hour. Or what I judge to be the second hour, for it is hard to tell. Exhilarating, I remind myself. This is what freedom feels like, and it is exhilarating.

After a long while, I begin to worry that I have missed the mainland altogether and am merrily rowing out to the open sea. I wipe the sweat and salt spray from my eyes and peer into the darkness in front of me. There are no lights to guide me toward shore, no cooking fires or candles or torches. I stop rowing and tilt my head to the side. It is hard to hear over the thudding of my own heart and my ragged breathing, but I think I detect a faint sound of waves breaking. And where waves are breaking, there will be land. Hopefully, it will be the smooth beach I am aiming for and not the jagged rocks and shoals of the southernmost coastline. With a quick prayer to Mortain, I adjust my heading to the north and resume rowing.

Soon, the sound of the waves becomes different, more of a gentle lapping with a hollow ring to it — the sound of water against the wooden hull of a boat. A labored sigh of relief escapes me as I muster one more burst of energy.

When I finally feel the slight crunch of rocks under the hull, I fling the detested oars from me, only too happy to be done with them. If not for my leather gloves, my palms would be blistered and shredded from the bedamned things.

With the boat firmly on the beach, I stand on the seat and leap as far clear of the shallows as I can, then turn back and grab the prow of the boat to pull it up farther onto the beach so the tide will not carry it away. I cannot help but note that my arms are as weak and feeble as newborn lambs.

I could head for the stable, saddle one of the horses myself, and simply ride off, but I fear it would raise doubts as to the legitimacy of my summons to the abbess's side. It seems more convincing to wake the night rower and demand assistance, just as if I were on a genuine convent assignment. After all, I have saved him the hard work of rowing. The least he can do is saddle my horse. Besides, I don't wish to be mistaken for a horse thief.

I approach the small cottage and rap sharply at the door. It does not take long for the old caretaker to open it—he is accustomed to being awakened in the middle of the night to row boats across the sea. "Eh?" He peers up at me.

"I need you to saddle a horse."

He stares at me a long moment, and I force myself not to fidget. "Haven't seen you out alone before, have I?" he finally says.

Annoyed that he would notice such a thing, I merely arch a brow at him. "Is it part of your duties to question my comings and goings?" The truth is, I would not put it past the abbess to arrange such a thing.

"Eh, don't bite my head off, missy. Let me get my coat and a lantern." He disappears back into his cottage, and I turn and look out at the sea, relieved that there is no sign of pursuit, although surely the earliest they would notice my absence would be after the second morning bell.

The old man comes to the door wrapped up in his cloak and carrying a lantern to light the way to the stable. Not sure what I am supposed to do, I follow him. At least until he turns and arches one of his own thick, white eyebrows at me. Pretending I do not see it, I swing my travel bag off my shoulder, set it on the ground, and begin rummaging through it, looking for one of my small leather pouches.

When I find it, I draw out a pinch of salt to leave as an offering to Saint Cissonius. He is the patron saint of both travelers and crossroads, and I feel most assuredly as if I am staring at some sort of unseeable crossroad, unable to discern the true path ahead of me. As I sprinkle the salt onto the earth beneath my feet, I whisper a brief prayer and ask Mortain Himself to guide me on this journey.

The old man returns just then. When I see that he is leading my favorite horse, Fortuna, my impatience with him leaks away, and I smile. "She is my favorite." I run my hand down her silky black mane.

He shoots me a sideways glance. "Why d'you think I brought her?"

It occurs to me that all of us at the convent should pay closer attention to this man, who sees far more than he lets on. "And I thank you for it."

He grunts, then helps me secure my bag to the saddle before cupping his hands and holding them out for me. I accept the boost and, stepping lightly, throw my leg over Fortuna's back, then settle into the saddle and draw up the reins.

My bow is within easy reach and my quiver of arrows is at my back. I do not expect trouble, but neither am I afraid of it. In truth, I am eager for whatever the road may hold, knowing I am more than able to meet the challenge.

* * *

Once I am on a horse that can outrun pursuit, the tension across my shoulders eases and I realize I did not believe that I would be able to escape undetected. But I am not a child any longer, and am more than able to pit my wits against any of the older nuns'. Nor are they still able to easily frighten me with their tales of the dreaded hellequin pursuing any who dare to defy Mortain.

The clear sky holds, and the moon is just past its fullness, providing plenty of light for me to see by. Fortuna is well rested and fresh, prancing in the crisply cold night air, her breath coming out in small white clouds.

As we set out, I quickly become aware of how different the world is at night. For one thing, there are infinite shades of gray, from palest silver to nearly black. And while I have ventured onto the mainland before, it has always been with others from the convent. I have never been as utterly alone as I am in this moment. There is no one to order me about or tell me what to think or how to behave. There is no one to say I must turn this way or that. No one to cast me disappointed looks when I fail to do as they wish. Nor do I have to bear the weight of those unspoken wishes.

There is a sensation—a lightness—in my chest, something I have never felt before, and I cannot decide if it is disagreeable or pleasant. Part of me wishes to poke at it, examine and sift through its meaning. Instead, I urge Fortuna to a canter and look to my future rather than my past.

The nearest village is only three leagues from the coast, but traveling in the dark it takes me the rest of the night to reach it. Some jaunty cock crows to greet the morning, and smoke from a dozen chimneys rises up, pale smudges against the dawn. Even though my bones ache with fatigue and my eyes are gritty with the need for sleep, I decide to keep riding. Unreasonable as it is, my fear of being followed is so great that I could not sleep, or even rest, if I allowed myself to stop.

I see almost no one on the road other than a man hauling a wheelbarrow full of firewood. A woman sits with her spindle in a doorway, watching a young child feed the chickens. In the fields to either side of me, tillage has begun. One lucky man has two oxen yoked to his plow, but I pass many more farmers too poor to afford any such beasts. Instead, they simply strap the yokes to their own shoulders. With the recent storms, it is muddy, backbreaking work, and I do not envy them. I think of the widowed farmer the abbess threatened to give me to, and my blood simmers in anger all over again.

My mind keeps going back to the choices before me and how to honor both my own desires and Mortain's. I have always hoped to live in accordance with His will, but for the first time I begin to fear I will be forced to make a choice between His will and mine. If being seeress is truly His wish and not the abbess's, if He truly wants from me what I cannot bear to give, then I will have to choose one over the other. The mere thought of that makes my heart feel as if it is being ripped in two.

Besides, it is hard to reconcile that sort of Mortain with the one I have known all my life. The one who comforted me and encouraged me, the one who accepted every gift I offered Him, whether it was the small black moths and beetles I found or my childish attempts to master some new skill in His name. I cannot believe that He would reject the gifts I wish to place in His service and demand of me things that fill me with dread and foreboding.

But if it does turn out to be Mortain's will, what then?

Will I continue to dedicate my life to Him as I have always imagined — even if that service requires me to spend the rest of my days in a living death?

I do not know the answer to that question, and that frightens me nearly as much as the abbess's plots.

I make the town of Quimper just as night is falling and am one of the last allowed through the city's gates before they close. The guard takes one look at the attire that marks me as one of Mortain's and hastily waves me through. Quimper, while a large town, is close enough to the coast—and the convent—to keep faith with the old ways. Or at the very least to have a healthy respect for them. More importantly, it is easy to lose oneself in a town of this size, and it makes the job of those pursuing me just that much more difficult.

I stop at an inn, where the innkeeper's wife fusses over me like a mother hen. It is all I can do not to point out to her that I am an assassin trained, but the fire she sits me in front of is warm, the cup of wine she thrusts in my hand is spiced, and her ministrations are soothing. I am normally the one doing the fussing, so this is a novelty for me.

The next morning I sleep far later than I intend and do not wake until the sun is high in the pale wintry sky. Cursing myself for the lost time, I slip into the extra gown I brought, the one that does not mark me as Death's handmaiden. Thus dressed, it will be easy enough for me to blend in with the other townsfolk, and my passing through will be less easily remembered should anyone from the convent ask after me.

Once I leave the town of Quimper behind me, I alternate between galloping and walking Fortuna, wanting to put as much distance as possible between me and the convent without exhausting my horse.

It is bitterly cold this morning, but the dampness has left the air, and the mist rolled back out to sea. There are few birds that have braved this wintry chill and their music is sparse and forlorn. The wind is sharp and biting and causes the nearby trees to rustle and shake.

The doubts I so easily ignored back at the convent begin to swarm in earnest. My plan to hold up the abbess's half-truths and lies before her and use them to convince her to change her mind suddenly feels lacking. I now wonder if it wouldn't have been better to wait and confront her when she returned to the convent. At least at the convent, those who truly cared that she followed our rules could add their voices to mine. Or would they? I have begun to wonder if any of them even care, else surely someone would have pushed harder against her when she sent Matelaine out.

But the abbess has already been gone several weeks, with no word of when she plans to return, and in truth, I could not bear to stay on that island any longer for fear I would go mad.

As dusk begins to fall, it becomes increasingly clear that I will not make the next town by dark. I do not know if there are any inns outside the city. There could be a convent or a monastery in which I could find lodging for the night, but I do not *know* that there is. My hands on Fortuna's reins tighten in frustration, and I am suddenly beset by all that I do not know.

The only things I have seen on the road are small cottages and farms, but their occupants will no doubt question a maid traveling on her own and will likely already be sleeping six to a bed, with naught but a shriveled turnip from the last harvest to put in their soup pot.

Besides, I cannot help but notice that the farther I am from the coast, the fewer homes have the silver coins or willow twigs marking them as followers of the Nine.

Instead, I decide to camp. Up ahead, just off the side of the road, is a copse of trees that is sheltered from the worst of the cold wind. The sky above is clear, with no storm clouds threatening. Sister Thomine took us out many a night to teach us precisely such skills, so it is something that I know how to do rather than something I must simply guess at.

I pick a spot carefully, one sheltered from the road and the weather and where the ground is covered with more fallen leaves than rocks and twigs. There is even a small patch of tender grass shoots peeking up through the leaf mold—sweet grazing for Fortuna.

Once I have dried her off to be sure she will not catch a chill, I slip a rope halter on her, then tie it to a tree within easy reach of the new grass. I lay down my bedroll, then try to decide whether I should risk a small fire. While I am not afraid of drawing anyone's attention—I am utterly capable of defending myself—neither do I wish to act foolishly. I decide on caution and pull two strips of dried meat and a chunk of stale bread from my saddlebag. As I withdraw my hand, it bumps up against the smooth black box I found in the abbess's office.

I place my food in my lap, wipe my hands, then take out the box. As I run my fingers along the dark polished wood, I wonder once more what it might contain. At one point, I wondered if it might hold the missing ledger page, or perhaps other secrets concerning my birth. But upon reflection, I realize that makes no sense. In any case, that cannot be all it contains. I shake it gently, puzzling out the slight shift of its contents. I could break it open now, as I am well away from the convent and no one can hear me, but for some reason, I hesitate. If nothing else, a box such as this deserves to be opened with respect and ceremony, not by being smashed with a rock on the side of the road.

As I shove it back into the saddlebag, I consider taking out the small calfskin-bound journal and reading more of the Dragonette's entries, but once again, I hesitate. I am not sure I wish to taint the start of my journey with her presence, and so leave it safely tucked in the bottom of the pack.

* * *

The thundering of hooves wakes me. Scores of them, I think, my heart thudding nearly as loudly as the approaching riders. I open my eyes and sit up, trying to orient myself.

The riders are drawing closer, close enough for me to hear the blowing and heaving of their horses. Trying not to lose my bearings, I reach behind me for the tree. When my fingers connect with the trunk, I stand up, trying to discern just how many riders there are. A hound brays off to one side of me, followed by a second bray, this one closer to the riders. The unearthly sound raises every hair on my head. Fortuna whinnies, then stomps her foot. Before I can move to quiet her, the sound of the hooves changes, no longer a dull thudding on a dirt road, but muffled, accompanied by snapping twigs and the rustle of trampled leaves. They have left the road.

I glance over to where Fortuna is secured. There is a jingle of harness as she tosses her head, snorting and blowing in fear. *Merde.* She will give me away, but I dare not go to her and try to quiet her. My only hope of not being trampled in the dark is to cling to this tree like a vine. I pray to Mortain to make Fortuna and me invisible. To let the other horses make so much noise that they will not notice the small ones Fortuna makes.

Keeping my hand on the tree, I slip around to the back of it so I will not be in plain sight if they discover the clearing.

They are louder now, the sound of the hooves accompanied by the constant baying of the hounds. I am assailed with a feeling of hot breath and red eyes bearing down on me. It takes all of my training and every last scrap of my courage to keep from bolting like a rabbit flushed from its lair.

I take a deep breath and imagine that I am as solid and strong as the tree I cling to. Before I can draw a second breath, there is a whisper movement off to one side. I whip my head around, but a large, firm hand clamps down across my mouth, then a heavy body presses along the length of me, so close that I can feel the rough bite of chain mail against my back. "Shhh." A deep voice slithers across my ear with no more weight or substance than a shadow. "You don't want to risk drawing their attention."

Even as my heart lurches against my ribs in shock, I begin to assess his hold, where it will be easiest to break. Before I can make my move, one of the great hounds bays again. The howl sounds as if it comes all the way from the bowels of the earth, wrapping dark ribbons of terror around my heart and causing all the hairs along my arms to stand up. It is so close that I am certain I will feel the dog's sharp teeth on my flesh any moment. The man presses his hand — hard — against my mouth in a signal to stay quiet. And while I do not intend to suffer his presence a moment longer than I must, I judge him a safer bet than the oncoming riders. Once they have passed, I can easily deal with a single man.

Clasped together like two lovers, we wait, our hearts beating nearly as one as the riders break into the clearing. They stream past, dodging and weaving among the trees, tall, dark shapes on even darker horses, the thudding of their hooves causing the ground to shake, the heat of their lathered bodies like a warm summer wind.

Their passing seems to last forever as rider after rider gallops by, the sound of the dirt churned up by their horses' hooves pattering like rain.

And then, suddenly, they are past us, growing farther and farther away in the distance.

The tightness in my body lessens somewhat, but the stranger does not loosen his hold. He stays pressed tightly against me until we can no longer hear the riders. Indeed, it is so quiet you would not know they had been here at all.

When I finally feel the muscles of his hand across my mouth begin to relax, I ram both elbows behind me where I judge his stomach to be, ignoring the pain as they connect with the chain mail he wears. He grunts in surprise, and I whip my arms up behind my head, grab his arms, and, using my own body as a fulcrum, lever him up and over my shoulder. I feel him leave the ground, feel him become airborne as he flies over my shoulder, then hear a thud as he hits the forest floor.

Chapter Fourteen

To HIS CREDIT, BUT FOR a faint *oomph* as the air is forced from his lungs, he gives no cry of surprise or any other sound that might give us away. For one, two, three long heartbeats, I stare down at him.

The darkness does not allow me to see him clearly, so I am left mostly with impressions, and they are not overly comforting. A strong arched nose, a square jaw, and dark eyes beneath dark brows studying me just as intently as I study him.

After a long moment of silence, there comes a creak of leather and a faint jingle of well-oiled chain mail as he rises to his feet. "A simple 'Thank you for the rescue' would have sufficed."

I step back to give him room to rise but also to put additional distance between us. "Except I had no need of rescuing." I keep my voice pitched low like his, so as not to risk its carrying on the wind. "Indeed, your attempt to help nearly gave me away."

"It was not I who nearly gave you away, but that hair of yours. It fair shines like a beacon in the moonlight."

Annoyed, I reach up, grasp the hood of my cloak, and yank it over my head. "There. The threat has passed. You may be on your way."

"You are wrong if you think the threat has passed. The hunt will roam the area until dawn and could easily double back this way. You will not be safe until the sun is up."

"What have I to fear? They are not hunting *me*."

"Aren't they, demoiselle?" He takes a step closer and I force myself not to take a step back. "Can you be so very certain of that?"

I do not try to hide my growing annoyance. "Who are they? What manner of men hunt in such a way at night? Have French soldiers landed on our coast?"

"They are not French soldiers."

I do not know him well enough to tell if that is a smile in his voice, but for some reason I think that it is, which rankles me. It was not so very foolish a suggestion. Before I can come up with something to say to put him in his place, he asks, "Where are you traveling that you must be out on the road so late at night?"

I can think of no reason not to tell him. "Guérande. I have family there. And what of yourself?"

"I am traveling east, along the same road to Guérande. You are cold," he says. There is a crunch of leaves as he takes another step toward me.

I cross my arms so that the daggers at my wrists are within easy reach. "Yes, well, it is winter and the nights are cold."

"You cannot risk building a fire. The light and heat will call the hunt back this way."

"You will be pleased to learn I have no intention of doing anything so foolish."

"How, then, do you plan to keep warm through the night?"

Gods' wounds! Could he be any less subtle? Sister Beatriz warned us often of men of his ilk. "Shall I guess at what you will suggest? You think we should close this distance between us so we may share our body heat, no?"

"We would not be the first to do so," he says.

While I have spent many an hour wondering what it would feel like to lay pressed close against a man, all that curiosity has fled under the weight of my current predicament. I reach openly for my knives, letting my sleeves ride up so that the handles of my daggers show. "I think I will take my chances with the cold, for I am no lightskirt to warm your bedroll. If you attempt such a thing, you will find only the kiss of sharp steel to greet you."

"I have no intention of forcing you." He sounds faintly aggrieved. "I wanted only to point out that two are stronger than one and more able to guard against the unexpected, that is all."

"You would make your camp elsewhere if I ask it of you?" I say flatly, making no attempt to keep the disbelief from my voice.

"No," he says, and it is all I can do not to crow, but he continues before I can speak. "They will double back at least once before dawn. I cannot in good conscience leave you to fend for yourself until then."

"I do not need your help. I am well able to defend myself."

His head tilts to the side. "What manner of maid are you," he muses, "that you can defend yourself against an entire hunting party? Not to mention heave a man nearly twice your size over your shoulder?"

I open my mouth to proudly tell him of my lineage and use the reputation of Death's handmaidens to keep him from attempting any mischief, but then hesitate. I have no earthly idea who he is. And as strong and skilled as I am, he is at least twice so, for all that I was able to toss him over my shoulder. He will not be caught off-guard so easily again. I have no idea if Mortain's name will even be known to him, or known in such a way that he would take it as a deterrent. "I am someone who was raised to be the equal of any man and know well how to defend myself."

"Against a horde of fourscore or more?"

As many as that? I think, somewhat dismayed. "Of course not," I snap. "No man can defend against that many."

He leans back against the trunk of the tree and folds his arms across his chest. I cannot help but remember the rock-hardness of that same chest pressing into my back but moments ago. "Not even if that man is one of their own and therefore has the power to protect you?"

He is one of them? "Why would you do that? Protect me?"

He shrugs. "Let us just say I believe I know the manner of your upbringing and why you claim to be a match for any man. I have a . . . debt I owe to those who raised you, and I would pay some small part of it by seeing you safe."

His confession robs me of speech and all I can do is gape at him like a caught fish. Who is he that he would owe the convent such a debt? And how did he guess who I was? But I let none of my confusion show on my face. "What manner of men maraud through the countryside eager to do others harm? Surely there are other, better, targets for them to fight. I hear we are recently overrun with French troops. I would suggest they start with them."

He narrows his eyes, studying me anew. "How do you not know the nature of the hellequin's hunt? Have you sprouted from the earth wholly formed, like some miraculous cabbage?"

There is a faint clink of chain mail as he leans forward, eager to impress upon me the seriousness of the situation. "For that is who will be pursuing you if you do not come with me. Hellequin's hunt."

A sharp ribbon of unease snakes along my spine, and I must work hard to put a note of disdain in my voice, lest it tremble instead. "You must truly think me wool-witted to believe that, for they are otherworldly creatures, not fashioned of bone and blood. They ride steeds of smoke and moonlight, not the pounding horseflesh that horde was riding."

"Did they appear wraithlike to you? Did the force of their horses' hooves sound unearthly?"

"No," I say, my mind scrambling furiously. "They did not." The ribbon of unease turns into a cold trickle of fear as all of the nuns' scoldings and warnings come back to me. Who is to say the nuns' tales of the hellequin hunting down those who dare to defy Mortain are not real as well? Ismae's mention of the hellequin that appeared at the Yuletide festivities rises up in my mind.

Which means they could, in truth, be hunting me.

Could my absence at the convent already have been noted? Or in leaving, have I broken some sacred binding that has called the hunt upon me? And if I have, are they to return me to the convent or simply to hunt me down?

Almost as if my thoughts have called the hunt back, I feel a distant rumble that begins in the ground beneath my feet. I glance accusingly at the stranger. "I cry foul," I say softly.

He gives a single shake of his head as he pushes away from the tree. "I did not call them." He turns to peer out into the darkness, as if judging their distance. "But you'd best decide what to do swiftly."

"What are my choices?"

His head swivels around and he pierces me with his black gaze. "Come with me and allow me to protect you from the others, or be hunted."

"Why do you care what happens to me?"

"Let us just say that I have a good idea what awaits you out there on the open road alone, and I am not certain that you do. And remember"—he flashes a grin that could only be described as morose—"I am a hellequin. I am hunting for redemption as much as for prey. Perhaps saving you will bring me closer to that end. Besides, we are traveling in the same direction."

In games of politics and maneuvering, Sister Eonette has always claimed it is best to keep one's enemies close. If the hellequin are really such a threat, then it seems wise to do as he suggests and ride into their midst, keeping my true identity hidden from him, just as he tries to hide me from the hunt. Then, once I have become a part of their routine and earned some small measure of their trust, I can slip away when the opportunity presents itself.

He cocks his ear, listening, then holds out his hand to me. "Now, unless you wish to be caught . . ."

"Very well." I ignore his hand and turn to pick up my bedroll. While I hastily roll it up, the stranger plucks my saddle from the ground with no more effort than plucking a flower from a bush, then settles it onto Fortuna's back. She stomps briefly in unease, her ears twitching nervously, before she calms under his touch.

The sound of the approaching riders grows louder, and my heartbeat starts to match the pounding of their hoofbeats.

"We must hurry," he says.

I slip my quiver over my shoulder, then grab my bow. "I am only waiting for you to get out of my way so I may mount," I tell him. It is not wholly true, but it gives me some small sense of being in control of a rapidly crumbling situation.

He lifts one mocking brow, then steps away from Fortuna. I ignore his cupped hands and mount without his help, another small but important declaration of how I intend our relationship to progress. Fortuna catches the scent of the approaching riders just then and tosses her head. Before I can ask him what he plans to ride—he is not riding with me on Fortuna!—he moves to the edge of the copse, where his own mount is tied to a tree. He leaps gracefully onto his horse, then wheels the demented-looking beast toward me. In truth, the horse looks as if he has ridden straight from the Underworld itself. His eyes are wild, and his nostrils wide, as if he is taking in all the scents of the night around him. His neck arches proudly and he paws at the ground, eager to be on his way.

And then they are upon us: one of the great horses breaks through the edge of trees surrounding our clearing. Before I can react, the stranger reaches out and grabs my reins. I do not even have time to protest before the jolt forward forces me to grab hold of my saddle lest I tumble off, then both his horse and Fortuna leap forward as the rest of the riders emerge from the trees and surround us. Shadowy black hounds nearly as big as ponies lope along the edges of the pack.

The galloping horses are an unholy sight that raises goose flesh along my arms. They are the color of midnight with churning hooves, their lips and nostrils seeming to glow red with their efforts. They engulf us like a river, swirling around us like water around a boat. We join them, causing barely a ripple.

The riders are as unsettling as their horses. Some wear hooded cloaks, so I cannot see their features. Others are garbed in dark chain mail and boiled leather. One rider has spikes on his vambraces, and another wears a bandolier of knives across his chest. I have an impression of dark eyes and unshaven faces that are fierce with the thrill of the hunt. They do not react to my joining their ranks other than to shift slightly to make room for Fortuna.

I do not know how long we ride—hours, it seems, although time has taken on an almost ghostly form so it might have been only minutes that passed. Every once in a while, the group breaks into four sections and appears to quarter the countryside, looking for prey.

I cannot help but be grateful that they are not hunting me. Or if they are, that they do not yet know it.

Chapter Fifteen

WHEN WE FINALLY SLACKEN OUR pace, I realize that my rescuer and I have moved toward the front of the pack. He raises his hand in the air, and the hunt slows to a walk. A small knot of hellequin break off from the others to ride forward. "Why are we stopping?" a giant of a man asks. He wears a boiled-leather breastplate and his arms are bare except for long gauntlets that reach almost to his elbows. An ax is strapped to his back, and a long sword affixed to his saddle. His hair is long and flutters faintly in the night breeze. He is utterly terrifying.

"I'm calling a halt for the night," my rescuer says.

A faint grumble begins among the other riders, building into a growl of discontent.

"But there is at least another hour until dawn!" A tall, lanky youth speaks. He is loose-limbed and fairly bouncing in his saddle, so I assume he was not accustomed to riding before becoming a hellequin. His most riveting features are his easy smile—unusual enough in this group—and his eyes, which are like those of a child who is convinced that everyone has gotten a larger sweetmeat than he has.

A third man, who wears fine armor and is strikingly handsome but for the fact that his eyes seem to hold nothing but emptiness, shoots me an unreadable glance. "It is because of her, isn't it?"

Slowly, my rescuer turns and looks at the speaker, his manner so chilled that I am surprised frost does not appear on the ground beneath his horse. "It has nothing to do with her. It is because there is nothing out there. If you had not been so caught up in your riding, you would have realized the hounds have not brayed in hours."

That quiets most of them, although one lone voice in the back is still grumbling, reminding me of nothing so much as a petulant child. "Stay here, and do not speak to anyone," my rescuer orders me, then rides off to deal with the malcontent. That is when I realize he is not just one of the hellequin, but their leader.

As I wait, the nearest hellequin drift closer. I do not see them move, but become aware that there is less space between us than before. In addition to the giant, the armored knight, and the lanky youth, there is an elegant, sharp-featured man whose face is tinged with the unmistakable arrogance of nobility. He is an exceptional horseman and carries a well-wrought sword at his side and wears fine leather gloves.

To my other side is another truly terrifying figure. He is just as tall as the first giant, who now sits to my right, and even broader across the shoulders. He wears spiked vambraces and an armored breastplate, and in his left hand he carries a mace. His horse wears an armored faceplate, the only one of the hellequins' horses to do so. It gives him a most unnerving air. Just looking at him calls to mind the hacking of limbs and the scent of blood, and it is all I can do not to shudder.

They say nothing but study me intently, some with hunger and others with dispassion. I force myself not to fidget, but Fortuna, sensing my unease, grows restless beneath me.

Just as I decide it would be safer to move than to obey my order to stay put, the giant to my right, the one with the long hair, speaks. "You've nothing to fear. No one will harm you." He grunts in what can only be disgust. "Not with Balthazaar's scent all over you."

His words bring a hot flush of embarrassment to my face and I want to explain how his scent came to be all over me, but that desire wars with the command not to speak with any of the men. Then righteous indignation flares and I want to throw my true identity before them all like a gauntlet and tell them I am one of Mortain's own and they'd best treat me with respect.

Except, if they are hunting for me, it would be beyond foolish to dangle my identity in front of them like raw meat before a wolf. Instead, I swallow my pride—which burns mightily as it goes down—and try to look like the sort of woman who would allow a man (a hellequin!) to make her his. To distract myself, I turn my attention to the rest of the hunt. While dawn is still a way off, the sky has begun to lighten enough that I can see the whole of them somewhat better than before.

They number between sixty and eighty, all of them men. Some look like outlaws and brigands, unkempt and bearing every manner of weapon. Others are concealed in darkness, their black cloaks and hoods the only things giving them form and substance. A handful of the riders are striking in their beauty, looking almost like the fallen angels the Christian priests speak of. Some look like fallen warriors, rough, scarred, and gruff of manner.

My rescuer—Balthazaar, the giant called him—comes riding back to my side just then, and it is the first time I am able to get a good look at him. He is breathtakingly handsome in a dark, almost broken way. He wears his hair long, and his jaw and nose are strong and sharp, as if chiseled of the finest marble by a master stonemason. His eyes are deep-set and so dark they look like pools of night without so much as a star shining from within their depths. Even more intriguing, there is something vaguely familiar about him. Although I know I have never seen him before in my life, there is some thread of recognition, a hidden connection between us, as unwelcome as it is unnerving.

He looks up just then and catches me staring. I long to glance away, to hide the boldness of my perusal. Sister Beatriz says that is the first step in the complex dance of ensnaring a man with one's charms, but I do not wish to ensnare him—or even have him think that is my purpose—so I raise my chin in defiance and leave my gaze on his face.

"It is too late to turn back." The left corner of his mouth tightens in what could be either amusement or annoyance.

"I've no wish to turn back. I merely wished to see what manner of man I had thrown in my lot with."

Without even moving, he does something so that his great black horse takes a step toward me, then another, crowding Fortuna so that she must back up or be trampled. "And have you passed your judgment? Detected the reek of sin and evil and found us lacking? Condemned us all over again in the court of your mind?"

I meet his gaze steadily, doing nothing to hide my irritation. If he —if they—are hunting me, I cannot afford to show fear and act like prey. "No. I myself know something of darkness and sin and am not so very quick to judge others."

Balthazaar turns from me to the small crowd that has formed around us. "Be gone," he growls.

They all scatter except for the longhaired giant, who lingers a moment, giving the other man a long, hard look. "It is not fair. To the others." His voice is so deep, it seems as if it rises up from the ground beneath our horses' hooves. "She is too great a temptation to them."

Balthazaar does his thing with his horse so that it tries to crowd the other man, but it is like trying to crowd a mountain. "This is no country jaunt, Miserere. It is meant as penance and atonement. Being surrounded by temptation is part of the indenture."

The giant stares a beat longer. "There is temptation, and then there is taunting." His impersonal gaze flickers over me once more, then he turns and rides away, his horse managing to send a shower of dirt our way as they depart.

"And so you meet Miserere."

"He is an impressive greeting party. Are all the men as pleasant as he?"

"No, but there are others who will be more dangerous to you, so you will do well to stick by my side."

"Like a thorn," I say with false cheer.

"A long, sharp, inconvenient thorn," he mutters.

I gape at him. "This was your idea, not mine."

He shrugs that truth aside. "Now that you have seen them, do you really think you would have been better on your own?"

"No." Even so, I am already questioning the wisdom of my plan, for these are not merely servants of Mortain but dark, tortured men who reek of threat and danger. Once it is full light, I will slip away. None of the old tales speak of the hunt riding during daylight. Surely I will be able to escape then.

Balthazaar leans across his saddle, putting his face close to mine. "Do not even think it," he says. "They have your scent now and can hunt you anywhere. No matter how much of a head start you think you have, they will find you. And they will not stop until they do."

I am saved from replying when all around me, the hellequin begin dismounting. Eager to be out of my saddle, I remove my left foot from the stirrup. It takes me two tries to actually dismount, and then — at last — my feet are once again on solid ground. I cling to the saddle, waiting for my legs to remember how to unbend at the knees. Balthazaar looms over me like a specter of the night. "Are you all right?" His voice is brusque.

"Of course," I reply lightly. "If you would show me where to tether my horse, I would like to tend to her. She does not have as much practice with nocturnal hunting as your horses do."

I am fairly certain I see a pinch of regret cross his face, and it heartens me, even if it is for my horse. "I will have one of the others tend her —"

"No!" The force of my refusal surprises us both. "I would rather do it myself." I need something to focus on besides the strange group of men in whose midst I have found myself.

He nods, then motions to the right, where the other horses are being picketed.

I glance at them dubiously. "Will she be all right with the others, do you think?"

He arches an eyebrow. "They are only horses, demoiselle, and not even flesh-eating ones at that."

"I am not so sure," I mutter, then I lead Fortuna away, my body grateful to be moving again. Balthazaar follows me. In spite of his words, I am careful to choose a spot as far away from the others as I can. As I reach down to unbuckle Fortuna's saddle strap, he directs his gaze to the surrounding countryside, as if he cannot bear to look at me a moment longer.

In the ensuing silence, I quickly finish tending to Fortuna. When I am done, Balthazaar motions for me to follow the other hellequin, who are milling at the far end of the copse, where two great stones frame an opening that seems to lead into the earth. With a start, I realize it is a doorway to the Underworld, just like the one at the convent.

So that is where they go during the day, why no one ever sees them once the sun has risen: they return to the Underworld. Which means there must be many such passageways throughout all of Brittany.

Once inside, I see that it is not a narrow cave or a tunnel leading to the Underworld as I had always imagined, but something far more immense. An antechamber, is my first thought. It is hard to tell with the shadows and darkness that swallow up the contours of the place, but the cavern appears to be as large as the convent. The walls are carved out of raw earth, and the ceiling . . . I look up, but there is only darkness and shadows overhead.

At the far end of the chamber, it narrows again into a much smaller doorway than the one we entered through, one that seems to hold back a thick, almost living blackness.

"While you may move freely about the cromlech, do not cross that doorway." Balthazaar speaks from just behind me. "For once a mortal crosses the threshold of the Underworld, they may not return."

I study his face to see if this is a jest, but it does not appear to be.

Once they have gathered inside the cromlech, the hellequin sit and lean against the walls of the cave, stretch out on the floor, or huddle in groups of twos or threes. One or two even light a fire.

"I would not think that hellequin would need fires to warm themselves."

"They do not need them, precisely. It is more a source of comfort. And to remind themselves they were once human."

His words make me aware of how very much I do not know about these servants of Mortain, for all that they serve the same god that I do. I open my mouth to ask one of a dozen questions that crowds my head, but he holds up his hand. "You are hollow-eyed with fatigue. Your questions can wait until nightfall."

Nightfall. Their morning, when they begin their day.

Balthazaar chooses a spot near the front and drops my saddlebag on the floor. "You will be safe here. But if you do not feel safe, come find me. If you cannot find me, find Miserere, for he is to be trusted most of all of them."

"That does not comfort me as much as you think it should."

He grunts, then strides off to join the others, his black cloak rippling behind him like a piece of the Underworld itself. Unsettled, I turn my attention to my own needs. I am near the front, but there are over a score of hellequin between me and the exit. I do not think I will be escaping tonight—or this morning, I correct myself, adjusting to the upside-down rhythms of the hellequin.

I long to get up and explore. To be this close to the Underworld, to

Mortain, has me nearly restless with a longing to peer into His realm and see what mysteries I may discover. It is hard to be so close to answers and yet be unable to pursue them. But it is possible the answers might not be to my liking. Perhaps Mortain *has* sent the hellequin after me, and if I poke my nose in His domain, He might spot me Himself.

Besides, Balthazaar's warning still rings in my ears, and even if it did not, I am not foolish enough to go cavorting among all these rough men. Many of them still watch me—I can feel the weight of their gazes as they alight upon me, much like the wings of the small dark moths I use to chase as a child. There is a wildness here—everyone is a collection of hard broken edges and sharp prickly spines. Wholly bathed in sin, and still seeking redemption in spite of it. It puts my own smaller sins in perspective and makes me proud to serve a god who is so forgiving.

Then another thought comes to me—perhaps Mortain has answered my prayer. At the start of my journey, did I not pray for His guidance and protection? What if He has given it to me—in the form of His hellequin? It is a startling thought and makes me fully aware of just how hard it is to determine if one's prayers have been answered.

After my flight from the convent, the gallop through the night, and minimal sleep, I am well and truly exhausted. I do not even bother to eat but simply lay out my bedroll, then collapse upon it. Sleep overtakes me before I can so much as kick off my boots.

Some hours later, I come awake. Pale fingers of daylight penetrate the darkness of the cave, but I cannot tell what time it is. I blink in confusion, trying to get my bearings, and realize someone is next to me. I freeze. Every muscle in my body tenses—not in fear, but in anticipation. Moving as little as possible, I reach for the knives at my wrists.

When my hands are firmly wrapped around their handles, I turn and look.

It is Balthazaar, sitting on the floor with his back against the earthen wall. He is so close to me that his hip almost touches my shoulder. My grip on the knives loosens. Annoyed at the faint feeling of comfort his presence brings me, I allow myself a small, private defiance and roll my eyes in the darkness. "You're smothering me," I whisper under my breath.

"I'm guarding you."

My head whips around. He was not supposed to hear that; indeed, *I* barely heard it. "Can't you guard me from farther away?"

"No." Not so much as a muscle moves; he does not open his eyes, and I cannot even see his lips forming the word.

"I thought you said I'd be safe here."

"And so you are. Because I am guarding you. Go back to sleep—we don't ride for hours yet."

I struggle to get comfortable again, but the cave floor is hard and my bedroll thin. "Don't you need to sleep?"

"I was sleeping. Until you woke me. And if you'll stop talking, I will sleep some more."

For some reason I cannot explain, as I finally begin to drift off to sleep, I can feel a faint smile tugging at my mouth.

Chapter Sixteen

WHEN I WAKE, THE FIRST thing I notice is the growling of the hounds. I sit up quickly and turn toward the sound. The hellequin with the spiked vambraces is fighting — no, playing with? — the hellhounds. Either that or they are trying to kill him.

An older man with sorrowful eyes sits by one of the small fires next to the lanky youth I saw last night. The older man appears to be teaching the younger one how to do something with a knife. Many of the hellequin sit around such fires, oiling their harnesses or sharpening their weapons.

"It gives them something to do with their hands." I nearly jump at the deep voice behind me. When I turn, I find Balthazaar still leaning against the wall, watching me with a heavy-lidded gaze. "They do not use their weapons any longer. They are simply pieces of their past they carry with them."

"Do they not need sleep?" I ask.

"No."

Which means that, despite what he said, he does not either, yet still he chose to sit by me through the night. I pray that I did not drool or snore. To cover up my embarrassment, I speak, although rather more tartly than I intend to. "I am sorry if I delayed your departure."

"You did not. We won't leave until night has fallen, so we were stuck here whether you slept or not."

Unsure what to say to that, and acutely aware of his eyes on me, I pull my saddlebag closer. I reach inside, rummage for something to stick in my empty belly before it begins rumbling. My hand closes around one of the round, hard cheeses, and I pull it from the pack. I break it in two, then begin pulling the wax from one half. Like a ripple moving across a pond, the quiet hum and murmur around me ceases. When I look up, I see that nearly all the hellequin are watching me.

"Cheese," the lanky youth says, somewhat wistfully.

He is so very young that it is hard to imagine what he could have done to earn time with the hellequin. Discomfited, I glance at Balthazaar. "Do they not eat either?"

He shakes his head. "Hellequin do not require food, but we can eat it if we like. For many, it is either a painful or pleasant reminder of our mortal years."

Suddenly my throat closes up and my hunger evaporates. Not knowing what else to do, I take the second half of the cheese and hold it out to the boy. "Would you like some?"

He looks at me with equal parts disbelief and longing, then cuts a questioning glance to Balthazaar. Whatever he sees there reassures him. He leaps to his feet, crosses the distance between us, then reaches out hesitantly to take the cheese. I only wish I had enough to give all of them, for the face of every man here holds some measure of hunger, although what exactly they hunger for, I will likely never know. "Thank you," the boy says. He stares down at the cheese as if it were a sparkling jewel as he hurries back to his place by the fire. However, instead of shoving the cheese in his mouth as I expected, he breaks off a small piece and hands it to the older man who had been showing him how to carve wood. Other hellequin begin crowding near, and he breaks off more and more pieces, handing them out until all he has left is one bite of cheese. He pops it in his mouth, savoring it as he chews.

* * *

When we ride out that night, Balthazaar takes the van and the rest fall in behind him. The only exceptions are Miserere and two other hellequin who have been assigned to ride at my side. One is the lanky youth—Begard, he is called—and the other his companion of earlier, a former stonemason they call Malestroit. They are my protection, Balthazaar claims, but I cannot help but wonder if their true purpose is to prevent my escape.

Although he need not worry about that. Not yet. I am watched much too closely. Not only out of suspicion, but because I am something new. A diversion. Mayhap even a reminder of what they have lost. I see that in Malestroit's sorrowful eyes every time he looks at me.

However, not all hellequin feel that way. Some cast bitter glances in my direction, as if it pains them to have me in their midst. Still others wear expressions of awe and try to draw near, as if my presence offers them some hope or plucks some chord of fond memory.

It is all most disconcerting, frankly.

As Fortuna canters through the forest surrounded by the hunt, trees tower on either side of us, obscuring the moon. We ride so fast I dare not look up at the stars for fear I will fall off my horse and be trampled. Not to mention that the roads chosen by the hellequin are rough and little used, often barely more than wagon ruts.

When the path opens up again, I find that the cluster of hellequin around me has grown. Miserere keeps to my left and Malestroit to my right, but others press in close.

"You have drawn a crowd, milady." Begard's voice is cheerful, as if I should be proud of such an accomplishment.

"So it appears," I murmur, suddenly very glad for Balthazaar's caution.

"There is no need to fear. Most are not as terrifying as they seem. You've met Miserere." The boy glances to the giant who rides silently beside us and lowers his voice in an exaggerated manner. "He is not nearly so frightening as he looks."

Unable to help myself, I too glance at Miserere, who stares straight ahead and pretends we do not exist. "I fear I may need more than your word on that for me to believe it," I say.

Miserere's grim mouth twitches. I would like to believe it is in amusement, but it is most likely in annoyance. Or anger.

Begard ignores him and continues with his prattle. "Malestroit here used to be a stonemason. He's teaching me to whittle."

"Gives him something to do with his hands besides steal things from others," the stonemason explains. "A bad enough habit among the living, but especially stupid when surrounded by men such as these."

Begard looks sheepish. "I am—used to be—a thief," he says by way of explanation. While I am not surprised that he is a thief, I am surprised that such a small crime would earn him a place with the hellequin. To turn the subject from him—and his discomfort—I ask Begard who the second giant is.

"You must mean Sauvage." The boy gives a mock shudder. "He does frighten me. A little." He lowers his voice in earnest now. "He was a follower of Saint Camulos. He was called the Butcher of Quimper and became so overcome by battle lust that he destroyed entire villages. He has ridden with the hunt for at least two hundred years. Or so it is rumored. Mostly he keeps to himself."

"Or the hounds," Malestroit adds. "He does have a fondness for the hounds."

"Surely that speaks well of him," I say. "What of the man with the fancy armor and sharp features? Over there." I tilt my head in his general direction, unwilling to point and draw attention to myself.

Begard's young face is like a map, his expressions informing me just as thoroughly as his words how he feels about the men with whom he serves. "That is Maligne," he says sullenly. "I don't like him. He is cruel."

"Only because you tried to steal his knife," Malestroit points out. "He is not inclined to forgive that."

Begard ignores this and whispers to me instead. "He swore an oath to the duke of Brittany during the first war of succession, then broke it. He is one of the forsworn."

"Ah." I had always known it was a terrible thing to break an oath, and I cannot help but wonder if I have broken some similar oath—albeit unknowingly—in leaving the convent.

Beside me, Miserere shifts on his horse and leans forward to scowl at Begard. "If you're going to tattle on everyone else's sins, boy, be sure to tell your own."

Begard squirms in his saddle, then looks down to study the reins he holds in his hands. "I was a thief," he says.

"So you said. This seems hard penance for such a crime," I point out gently.

He grows even more miserable. "I . . . I lured a merchant and his wife to an isolated road so I could rob them. The merchant, he fought back, and I ended up killing him."

Perhaps to distract attention from the younger boy, or perhaps as part of his own personal vow of penance, the stonemason speaks quietly into Begard's melancholy silence. "As for me, I accidentally beat my only son to death in a fit of drunkenness." His face is haggard with the memory, and clearly his own guilt and regret are worse than the punishment of riding with the hunt.

Unable to look at his sorrow-ravaged face any longer, I glance over to Miserere and wonder what sins he has committed. To my surprise, I find him looking at me. "I was an executioner," he says, his gaze never wavering from my own. "With nearly a hundred deaths on my hands."

"That seems hardly fair, as they were deaths sanctioned by the law."

"They are still deaths," he says, looking away.

"Begone! All of you!"

I jerk my head around at the sound of Balthazaar's voice. He has left the lead and moved to my right, where Malestroit had been. "You are not nursemaids. You have duties to attend to."

I wonder if Miserere minds very much being called a nursemaid and sneak a glance at him. By the pained look on his face, I can see that he does.

The others fall back, but Balthazaar says nothing as we ride side by side. His gaze searches the trees, as if he suspects there are souls lurking just beyond his reach. "I suppose I should ask what you know of the hellequin," he finally says.

"Far more than I knew an hour ago," I murmur.

"The boy talks too much."

"On the contrary, I found it most helpful."

"You are not avoiding my question, are you?" The weight of his gaze presses heavily on me, like a pile of stones.

"I know they are the souls of the damned who have pledged themselves to serve Mortain in order to earn their redemption."

"You know more than most, it seems."

"It is also said that when they ride out at night, they bring the chill and despair of the Underworld with them."

"And do you feel the chill and despair of the Underworld, demoiselle?"

I glance around at the hellequin whose stories I have just heard. "Of a sort," I say quietly.

"What?" he scoffs. "No words of demon spawn, of ambassadors of Satan himself? No stories of our cavorting across the countryside leaving sin and destruction in our wake?"

I know he intends his sharp manner to drive a wedge between us, to push me away. But there is pain hiding behind his bitterness. It is hidden, deeply hidden, perhaps even from him, but it is there. I know because Sybella tried to keep us away in precisely the same manner when she first came to the convent. The comparison gives me pause. Is that why he feels familiar to me? "No, for I do not follow the new church, but keep to the old ways instead."

"What manner of maid is raised so steeped in the old faith that she is unafraid to ride with the hellequin's hunt?"

"Who says I am unafraid?" I counter.

"I saw you with my men. You shared your food with them, but more than that, you saw their humanity and offered them compassion. There was no fear."

My gaze drifts to the hellequin around us. "Some of them frighten me," I murmur. "Miserere, Sauvage, that hooded fellow."

"So how did you come to be raised in such a way that you can so easily overcome your own fears?"

I open my mouth to answer his question, then pause, all of my senses sharpening, just as they do when I step into the training yard with Sister Thomine. When he came upon me that first night, he said he knew the manner of my upbringing and owed a debt to those who raised me. But now he is acting as if he does *not* know the nature of my upbringing.

Or else he is trying to catch me in a lie.

While it had seemed possible that the hunt could actually be pursuing me, I did not give too much credence to the thought. But now, now I must consider that possibility once more. "I am from an old family, one of the oldest in Brittany," I tell him. "A remote branch that keeps to the westernmost regions, where many still honor the old ways. My family is one of those, that is all."

"But it is not." His words cause my heart to stutter with concern. "You easily accept what some believe exists only in myth and legend.

You are not only respectful of Mortain, but worshipful. Dedicated in a way that few are. Especially as the new church encroaches ever more on the old faith."

He is right—even those who respect the old ways are not so enamored of Mortain. I must answer him but also steer him away from any hint that I am one of Mortain's own handmaidens. "My mother's sister was an initiate at the convent of Saint Mortain and she has written to us often over the years, her words glorifying the work that they do there. Because of that, the members of my family more than most, have a deep connection to Him." I glance up at him to see if this will satisfy his curiosity.

His gaze grows heavy with intensity, as if he is trying to call forth all my secrets. "And you have never questioned your faith? Never doubted or turned your back on Him?"

It is not his question that gives me pause but the dark undercurrent in his words, which suggests something that I cannot fully discern. Anguish? Anger? "No," I say simply. "I have not." It is not a lie that I tell him, for it is only my faith in the abbess that has wavered.

We ride on, and the silence between us grows thick and weighted. Afraid he will ask more questions, I decide to ask some of my own. "Explain to me the nature of the hellequin and their duties so I may better understand them?"

He huffs out a breath of irritation. "I am no tutor."

"I have heard it said that because of the hellequin's own dark histories, they are easily corrupted by others' will, especially those that call them back to the darkness of their own past." I keep my voice low and fill it with all the sympathy I truly feel. "That once they stray, they are twice damned and thrust well beyond any chance of redemption or any afterlife at all."

"That is at the heart of it." He rolls his shoulders, as if he would shrug off the weight of this burden. It is a surprisingly human gesture. "We are broken and damned, the midden heap of Mortain's grace and mercy. We are tasked with collecting the souls of the wicked so they may be brought to their final judgment and wreak no more havoc upon the living." He pauses a moment before adding, "And we also collect the lost — those who cannot find their own way to the Underworld or simply refuse to leave the world of the living."

"So not only a hunt," I murmur. "But also a rescue mission."

His lips twist in scorn. "Do not decorate it with flowers and hang a ribbon on it, demoiselle. We are not noble or gallant men. We have sworn ourselves to this service, but the honor that binds us to it is a tenuous thing at best."

"Says the evil hellequin who saved me from his own men." I watch him closely to see if he has any reaction to being reminded of the deal he made with me.

He stares at me for a long moment, but there is no flash of remorse or recognition or, indeed, anything at all.

"How are you chosen?" I ask, unwilling to endure the silence any longer.

"We volunteer. It is one last chance to atone for the darkest of our sins." He looks up and squints through the trees as if he has spotted something fascinating up there. "We must move among the temptations of our mortal flesh each and every day. And each and every day, we must say yes to our continued penance, even as new temptations greet us with each setting sun. We must choose, not once, but again and again, in each hour that passes, to walk this path." He turns to look at me and I am struck by the brief glimpse of hunger I see in his gaze. "And there are many temptations."

Me, I realize dizzily. He considers me a temptation. And yet, he offered to hide me among his own men.

Or did he? What if, in truth, he suspects who I am and wishes to keep me close until he can find out for certain?

A short while later, the hounds begin to bay, and a ripple of excitement runs through the hellequin, as palpable as the night breeze on my face. Dark, feral grins break out as they kick their horses to a gallop. Their mounts seem to draw on some otherworldly reserves, and they surge forward, giant hooves pounding the earth beneath their feet until it sounds like a hailstorm.

Fortuna follows. Indeed, it is as if the wildness and ferocity of the other horses is some scent or eldritch sickness that she herself has caught. As I lift my face to the dark night, I wonder if I too might catch it.

The hounds bay again, this time sending a cascade of goose flesh down my arms. In front of me, the hunt splits into two, like water before a rock, spreading out, then encircling something. No—someone, I realize, as one of the riders shifts his position. Actually, several someones.

We have stopped in a small clearing surrounded by gnarled trees bent by the wind, their weighty branches drooping to the ground like long green beards. Now that the riders have stopped moving, my eyes are drawn to the three men inside the circle. Or rather, not men but something more otherworldly than that, for they do not seem solid or truly mortal—their edges are blurred somewhat and all the color leached from them, like a gown left to dry in the sun too long.

These cornered men show no defiance, only fear. Now that the men are surrounded and have no means of escape, the hellequin draw in close. But, much to my surprise, the hellequin are almost gentle with them, not so much pursuing them as herding them, urging them forward with their horses.

We continue on, but much more slowly, so that the men on foot may keep up.

It does not take long for us to reach a cromlech. It is not the same one we slept in last night, but another, even larger one, and I cannot help but wonder just how many there are. Balthazaar dismounts near the entrance, as do Malestroit and Begard. Once we are inside, the hellequin gently herd the souls to the threshold to the Underworld. The souls stand rigid and terrified. It is Malestroit who speaks first. "You do not wish to linger here on earth past your season."

The souls try to scramble back from the gaping darkness that seems to reach for them, but the hellequin press too close. "We're not going through there," one of them says. "We know what awaits."

"Do you?" Balthazaar asks gently.

"Hellfire and damnation. Demons gnawing on our flesh for centuries" is the soul's answer.

Begard steps forward, his cheerful face creased with earnestness. "No. It will not be like that. Let me show you."

The soul looks from Begard to Balthazaar. "And if I refuse?"

"Then we will let you go, and you will be free to wander, lost and alone. And after you have wandered some more, we will find you and bring you back to this place, where once again you will be given a choice."

"Here. I will go first," Begard says, and he steps through the doorway, the darkness in the opening so absolute that it appears to consume him.

One of the souls stares after Begard hungrily, and with no more words or arguments, he follows him through the door. The other two seem to lose their resistance and stumble forward, almost as if they welcome the pull of that which they feared was lost to them.

And then they are gone, swallowed up by the darkness. In the moment of stillness that follows, the mood around me shifts almost imperceptibly. It takes me a moment to recognize that it is a feeling of accomplishment. The hellequin are eager to do their task, not just because it earns them redemption, but because it affirms there is rest for all souls — eventually.

Chapter Seventeen

AFTER ONCE AGAIN STICKING to me like a leech as I slept, Balthazaar completely ignores me once I am awake. Indeed, it is as if I have somehow contracted the plague and he is afraid of catching it. Which leads me to wonder just how many physical ills hellequin are vulnerable to. I shall have to ask him. If he ever gets close enough for me to speak with him again.

After very little preparation — I am the only one who bothers with such comforts as a bedroll and food — we are off, moving out into the night like an undulating serpent across the grass. We ride, slowly at first but gaining speed with each moment that passes until we are galloping into the cold night air. For a moment — just a moment — I give myself over to the sheer pleasure of being out in the world once more, lift my face to the night breeze and simply enjoy the pleasure of being alive and moving to fill my skin. A part of me cannot help but admit to the thrill to be had in such unrestrained wildness, riding faster than the wind itself, the entire pack moving like one graceful entity.

Spending so much time in the antechamber of the Underworld gives one an entirely new appreciation of life.

Again Balthazaar rides in the van and assigns his minions to watch over me. Either we do not set as grueling a pace as last night or I have already grown accustomed to it. We ride in silence but for the pounding of the horses' hooves. There is a buoyancy, a rush of something akin to joy, for all that it is naught but joy's thin, darker cousin, that drives home for me why the hellequin relish these rides. Not only does it bring them that much closer to redemption, but it allows them the chance to be free from the confines of their daily prison.

I too am glad to be free of the cromlech, for it disturbs me as much as it fascinates me. It is easy to feel one's spirit become dampened, quiet, as if it is making ready for the final journey to the Underworld.

Besides, since I do not know if Mortain hunts me or not, it seems foolish to tarry on His doorstep.

And yet, what choice do I have? A lone woman, even one of Mortain's own, cannot go against so many any more than a leaf can swim upstream. So like a leaf in a stream, I will let myself be carried along in the hellequin's current and hope that it will take me where I wish to go. Eventually.

The trees on either side of us brush by, seeming to give way before our approach. The sharp bite of winter still hangs in the air and our breath comes out in puffs of small, white clouds, giving the riders an altogether otherworldly appearance.

Balthazaar falls back to ride beside me, and as if by some silent agreement or command, the others disperse. He says nothing. Does not so much as look at me, but simply rides at my side, his demonic horse crowding me and Fortuna.

As we journey in silence, his moodiness seems to fall away from him so that by the time we slow to give our horses a break, he looks far less forbidding. Relieved, I finally allow myself to ask one of the scores of questions clattering in my head. "How could you tell the souls you caught last night were only lost and not wicked? Do you see marques, like daughters of Mortain do?"

He brings his head around and pierces me with a fierce gaze. "How do you know of the marques? That is knowledge only those who serve Mortain should have."

Merde. In my eagerness for answers, I let my fool tongue run away with me. "Do not be angry. My mother's sister meant no harm in telling us. She was just awed by the gifts and mercy Mortain bestows upon the world and those who serve Him that she could not contain herself." I hold his stony gaze for a moment, and then another, to impress upon him that I am telling the truth.

When Balthazaar finally looks away, I allow myself a silent sigh of relief, then quickly change the subject. "Can you coax a soul to follow you while it is still in its mortal body?"

"Only Mortain can do that."

"Have you ever seen Mortain?"

His scowl deepens, and I cannot help but wonder what fault he finds with *this* question. "Yes. I have seen Him, but He is the god of Death, not some knight to be swooned over."

"I am not swooning over Him! I have heard stories all my life and want to know what is true and what is not."

We are saved from further arguing when the hounds begin to bay. Within moments, the entire hunt picks up its pace. Our path takes us darting between trees and leaping over streamlets, galloping past newly tilled fields and small stone cottages with the windows tightly shuttered and the doors barred.

The hounds' braying grows even more frantic and Sauvage takes the lead. I do not know if it is because he is the most terrifying or if it is simply his turn. Instead of going farther into the woods, the hunt veers to the left. That is when I see the two men — souls. They are racing toward the wayside cross that sits where our path intersects with the main road.

The hunt increases its speed, the hounds pulling ahead, teeth bared. Their manner is so different from last night that I can only assume that their prey is different as well. Not innocent, perhaps, but wicked.

The riders in the front of the pack, led by Sauvage, get out ahead of the souls, effectively blocking their path to the stone cross. Their hope of sanctuary cut off, the souls stop running and turn to face the arriving hellequin. The hounds do not lunge at them, as I feared they would, but instead hang back, milling about the horses' legs, growling as they keep their feral gazes fixed on their quarry.

While their eyes are wide with terror, they also exhibit a large helping of defiance. I look around, waiting to see which hellequin will talk to them, the way it was done last night, but none of them dismount. Instead, Sauvage takes a rope from his saddle, swings it out and around and then down over the two men, capturing them. He jerks hard, yanking them off their feet, then waits. After a moment, the two rise uncertainly, glaring at the hellequin. Sauvage jerks on the rope once more, but not so hard that the men fall again, only hard enough to get them moving. Thus roped and surrounded by grinning hellequin, they are escorted to the nearest cromlech.

It is not hard to wonder where rumors of demon spawn come from.

When we reach the cromlech, the hellequin dismount. Sauvage, with Balthazaar close on his heels, shoves the men through the entrance to the cromlech, and the rest of the hunt follows. They drive them toward the door to the Underworld, where the darkness waits, beating like a pulse.

Then, surprising both me and the souls, Sauvage removes the rope. They stand free once more. "It is time for you to pass from this world to the next," Balthazaar says.

One of the prisoners spits off to the side. "The Church says you will lead us to hell."

"The Church is wrong. Hell does not reside beyond that door."

"If you want me to go through there, you're going to have to carry me yourself."

"I will not. If you cross, you must do so by your own free choice."

"What if I do not?"

"Then we will hunt you again and again, until the end of time, if necessary, and each time, we will bring you back to the mouth of the Underworld until you grow tired of the hunt and surrender to what must be."

While the one man argues, the second one glances over at the blackness that fills the doorway. He must see something there that comforts him, for without so much as a word to his companion, he steps through the door.

Gaping in surprise, the other man stares after him, as if awaiting screams or cries for help. None come. The darkness that lurks in the narrow passageway seems to swell forward, almost as if reaching for him. Instead of fleeing in terror, the soul remains still, and something on his face shifts, the fear replaced by . . . wonder? Relief? He steps forward to greet the darkness willingly, even eagerly.

I look at the hellequin around me, yearning sitting heavy upon them, and for the first time, I understand the hunger I see on their faces. They cannot wait for their turn to be welcomed into their final resting place.

There are tears in my eyes when I turn and walk away, nearly ramming into Balthazaar. "I'm sorry," I murmur, keeping my gaze downcast. "I did not see you there." He is so close, I can feel the rise and fall of his breath. I hold myself still, waiting for him to say something.

Instead of speaking, he reaches out to capture one of the tears falling down my cheek. "Why are you crying?" His voice grows soft, intimate even, and I cannot help myself—I look up so I may see his face. "They will not be harmed," he says gently. "It was their own fear reflected back at them, not because of something we had done."

"I know," I whisper. "I am just overwhelmed by the immensity of Mortain's grace. That even if we are lost or wandering, He will find us —always, He will find us—and try to bring us home."

"Yes," Balthazaar says. "He will." His finger lingers against my cheek a moment before he turns and walks away.

As I watch him depart, I wonder if the hellequin are Mortain's way of ensuring I find my way home, wherever that may be, and if Balthazaar's words are a warning or a promise.

The next night is much the same, and I realize I have fallen into a routine with the hellequin. That unsettles me, for it speaks of acceptance, of resignation. I have become distracted by the wonder of Mortain's grace in action, by these inhabitants of the Underworld come to life before me, and by the men's own tragic histories.

So distracted that it takes me a full week before I wonder why we have not yet reached Guérande. That night, when Balthazaar falls back to ride beside me, I confront him. "What is taking so long? We should have reached Guérande by now."

"We *will* reach Guérande," Balthazaar says stubbornly. "We are just crisscrossing the countryside as we go. It is how we hunt, and I never said we would not hunt on the way."

"No, but you did not explain you would take over a week to make a three-day trip either."

He stares down at his hands holding the reins. "Is what you have waiting for you there so very important?" It is the faint, almost undetectable note of wistfulness in his voice that gives me pause. "A lover perhaps?" he continues.

"I have no lover." I am further intrigued when I see his grip on the reins loosen — in relief? "But I do have important business I must conduct there. I did not expect to linger on the road so long."

He looks up at my face then. "If there is one thing we hellequin have learned, demoiselle, it is that life is short and should be savored. It is best if you do not spend all your time wishing you were somewhere else.

We will reach Guérande when we reach it." And then he is gone, riding back to the front of the pack and motioning Miserere to take his place at my side.

As I watch him go, frustration and longing fill my chest, pressing heavily against my ribs. While I still want to get to Guérande and confront the abbess, the inner workings of Mortain and His world have appeared before me, almost as if He has willed it. Would it not be best to make the most of this short span of time when I am free? This is living without restraint like I have always dreamed of, even though the circumstances are far, far different then I ever imagined. Should I not just embrace this opportunity, accept that it may even be Mortain's own hand that brought me here? Would not this depth of experience and additional knowledge give me even more fodder for my confrontation with the abbess?

And it is not as if my meeting with the abbess will bear anything but bitter fruit. In fact, there is a good chance she will do everything in her power to send me back to the convent. Back to fulfill the very destiny I am running from. And I do not yet know if I will go.

As long as I keep my true identity hidden — no more slips such as the stupid question about the marques — I should be fine. Besides, Balthazaar does not seem to be in too big a hurry to be rid of me.

Surely these are the reasons I decide not to pursue the matter further. Not because of a pair of tortured dark eyes that feel as if they brush against my soul every time they look at me.

Chapter Eighteen

THE NEXT NIGHT'S HUNT PROVES fruitless, and the hellequin's disappointment is as heavy and ominous as an impending thunderstorm. Twice, the mood quickened, as if they had scented prey, but it came to naught. Indeed, this lack of success in finding so much as a rabbit to catch for my own small supper has cast a pall over the entire group. It is not yet dawn when we return, but none of the hellequin seem ready to retire for the night. Instead, they build a fire, a larger one than normal, and a dozen or so of them gather round. I start to slip away to leave them to their private misery, but Balthazaar calls out to me.

"Come," he says, holding out a hand. "You have said you honor the old ways and worship Mortain. Come tell us of your faith. Mayhap it will remind us of ours."

Unwilling to deny them this small comfort, I accept his hand. It is large and firm and feels wholly of this world, except for the faint chill that seeps through his glove. As he leads me to the fire, my mind scrambles for what to tell them of Mortain. Which words can I share without giving away my true identity?

The others make room for me, and though they are outlaws and sinners and have all manner of black hearts, their acceptance gladdens me, which is surely a hundred kinds of foolish.

I settle myself upon the hard rocky floor and stare into the flames, for they are easier to look at than the desolate faces around me. "What can I tell you? I was raised to see Mortain as the first among the Nine, for without Death, there could be no life. Just as the roots of living trees must reach down past the loam and soil to find sustenance from the Underworld, so too are we sustained by Death. Of a certainty, He has sustained me through many . . . trials." I look up at the hellequin, at their rough, broken faces. "Although my trials were much different from yours, they were hard enough in their own way, and I would have faltered without Mortain to lend me His strength."

Even though I am not looking at him, I can feel Balthazaar's nearness, much as a moth senses the heat of a flame. "People fear Him—wrongly. They see punishment and starkness in Death, yet there is beauty as well. The small black beetles that burrow deep in the earth to die every winter, only to be reborn in the spring. The tree branches that turn to barren bone, yet unfurl with new leaves. Those are the promises that reside in Death.

"The Mortain I believe in is not scary or terrifying. People's terror comes from their own fear, or tales told by the Church rather than from anything Mortain has done. People are afraid of what they do not understand, and since they have abandoned the old ways, they no longer understand Death and His true place—His true purpose—in this world."

Only when I am done talking do I allow myself to glance in Balthazaar's direction. His head is tilted to the side and he studies me intently, as if peering through my flesh and sinew to my soul. "You love Him," he says, his voice filled with wonder.

I duck my head, embarrassed. "He is a god, and I but honor Him." But Balthazaar is right: I do love Him. And in that moment, I know that I do not wish to leave His service. I want only to understand it —understand what He wants from me and trust that however I spend my life, it is His will coupled with mine, not simply the convent's. I lift my gaze back to Balthazaar. "If you do not see Him as I do, how do you come to pledge yourself to His service?" I ask.

The silence that follows my question is as thick and heavy as the stone upon which I sit, and I fear no one will answer until, at last, Begard speaks.

"Through true remorse," he says, staring into the flames. "In the moment of your death, the desire to redeem yourself becomes a physical thing, like a rope you can use to pull yourself back from the edge of drowning."

Miserere shakes his head, his eyes fixed on the flickering shadows on the cavern wall. "At the moment of your death, you are filled with a fierce need to claw your way back up the very sword that pierced you and bellow that it is not over. You are not finished yet. You still need time to atone for all that you have done."

Something at the edge of the group shifts, and I look up to find Sauvage standing there, his hand buried in the fur of one of the giant hound's neck. "It is all those you have killed, silently looking at you with their dead, haunted eyes, that chase you back into life, willing to pay any price to avoid looking at them for all eternity."

Silence descends upon us once more. I wish for Balthazaar to tell his tale, for I am desperate to know what sin he has committed to earn this penance. Almost as if hearing my wish, he looks up at me with a face that seems as if it were carved out of sorrow and despair. I want to reach across the distance between us and run a finger along one of his dark brows, as if in so doing I could wipe away the bleakness I see in his eyes. Instead, I pull my fingers tightly against my palm and turn my gaze to the fire.

Over the next few days, all the exhilaration and thrill of hunting gives way to the sobering fact that we have been five nights now with no luck. Balthazaar in particular takes it hard.

I am unsure as to what the absence of souls means, but the hellequin are unsettled by it. Their moods grow even darker, and the small bits of joking and camaraderie that they enjoyed have all but disappeared. Balthazaar, Miserere, and Sauvage spend long hours in conversation, conversation they are careful to keep from my ears.

Is the scarcity of souls some dire portent? A sign of the influence the new church has over our land? Or is it more personal than that — without souls to collect, the hellequin will not be able to earn their redemption?

The mood after tonight's hunt is the grimmest yet and I find myself wishing I had some way to ease their frustration. But I do not. Indeed, I barely have the ability to ease my own sense of futility, which bubbles through my veins like one of Sister Serafina's poisons.

While the hellequin busy themselves — somewhat morosely — with their meager evening rituals, it occurs to me how time must weigh heavily on them, with no sleep or chores or even pleasures to relieve the waiting. But I must do something to relieve the waiting or else I will twitch right out of my skin. Being surrounded by these strong, brutal men reminds me that I have skills I must keep up, skills I must keep honed as sharply as the edges of my blades.

With a renewed sense of purpose, I slip toward the back of the cromlech unobserved. While I want to be well away from the others so they cannot see — or mock — me, Balthazaar's warning against venturing too near the threshold to the Underworld is firmly etched in my mind.

When I judge that I am well out of the view of the others, I slip my bow and quiver off my back, then roll my shoulders to loosen the muscles and joints. I have not done anything but ride for nearly two weeks. Moving through my training exercises will not only help keep my skills sharp, but also relieve the pent-up frustration I am feeling.

As I begin the familiar movements, a sense of calm settles over me, as if the exercises themselves pull me back into myself, reminding me of who and what I am. I wonder if the abbess has been informed yet of my absence, and if so, what she has done about it. If nothing else, my current circumstances afford me a most excellent cover, for she would never in a thousand years think to look for me here.

I move on to the more complex set of exercises, the ones that take all my concentration.

"Does that not work better with an opponent?" The deep, gravelly voice pulls me from the sequence, causing me to stumble.

I glance over at Miserere, who watches me, face implacable, arms folded. I reply without thinking. "But I do not wish to hurt any of you."

Miserere's mouth twitches, and I hear a guffaw or two of laughter.

"If you need a rock or tree to batter yourself against, he is your man," Begard says cheerfully, almost as if he knows this from personal experience.

Miserere steps forward. There is no anticipation in his manner, or revulsion, or even resignation. He simply moves, like a boulder that has sprouted legs.

I eye him warily. I meant my words as a jest, not a challenge. However, I will not—cannot—back down. Not with all of them watching. At the very least, maybe when they see my level of skill, they will think twice before crossing me.

Just as I motion Miserere forward, a large, black glove appears on his arm and shoves him aside. "If the lady needs someone to spar with her, I will do it." Balthazaar looks not at me but at the other men, meeting each one's gaze and holding it for a long moment. His brows are drawn together in a thunderous ridge, and his mouth is set in a hard, unforgiving line. Unease snakes through me.

It is one thing to bash upon someone like Miserere, whom I have no hope of beating or even hurting. But fighting Balthazaar is far, far different. It feels too . . . intimate.

And then he is standing in front of me, arms relaxed at his sides. "They are all watching." He speaks quietly, and I cannot tell if that is resignation I hear in his voice or a taunt.

"Well, then, let's not disappoint them." Before I have finished my sentence, I launch forward, trying to catch him off-guard. In a rapid series of strikes, I come at him, but he blocks every blow, his eyes watching me intently the entire time. Indeed, the hunger that is always there is even more present, and it is more unsettling than his strength. I allow that feeling of unease to show upon my face, then use the moment of his surprise to spin myself around to bring a resounding kick to his legs, trying to knock him off balance.

He does not budge. But the hunger deepens and an almost feral smile appears on his face, as if he thinks some primal challenge is being offered and he has decided to accept.

We are just sparring, I remind myself. Nothing more.

I try every way I know to lever my body against his, to upset his balance or cause him to shift, even a bit. But every time we touch, it feels far too much like a caress. Every time our bodies slam into each other, it feels like an unspoken promise. Is this some hellequin trick? Some spell they are able to cast with their dark natures? If so, it is a most unfair way to fight. However, no matter how much I try or from what angle I come at him, I realize I will never catch him unaware as I did that first time, and that is the only way I can best him, by getting in under his guard.

Annoyed, I rush him again, then feint to the side and spin so that I am behind him. I push myself against his body—pressing myself against him precisely as he did against me that first night we met—and get a chokehold around his neck. I feel everything inside him still, then he relaxes so that he sags into me. I am so unnerved by the sensation of it that I pause. Only for a second, but it is enough.

The next moment I am flying over his shoulder in a dizzying rush.

I brace myself for my landing on the hard rock floor, knowing it will knock the wind out of me.

Except I never reach it. Instead, Balthazaar catches me and eases me back to my feet, almost as if we were dancing. My breath is coming fast now, but the bastard is not even breathing hard. And his arms are still around me. "If you wanted them watching you, they are," he whispers in my ear. "Every move, every breath that passes your lips, has their full attention."

I bring my arms up suddenly to break his hold, then leap away, annoyed that I am only able to do so because he let me. We are still close, too close, I realize, but before I can step back, he speaks once more. "What was your intent with this sparring of yours? To entice them? To entice *me?*"

At his accusation, a hot flush of mortification floods my body, for I was not trying to entice anyone. I reach out and shove him — hard — surprised when he gives way. "If that is the case, then it is their fault and not mine. I wished only to keep my own skills honed." I follow up with another shove, which he again allows. "Simply because your thoughts are base does not mean I must accept the taint you would lay at my feet." And then, realizing he is no longer as guarded as he was, I sweep my leg wide, knocking his out from under him, satisfied when he lands flat on his back in the dirt.

Holding my head high, I turn and begin walking to my bedroll. The other hellequin say nothing, but they move out of my way.

"If you so much as snicker, I will kill you all," I hear him tell the others.

None of them laugh, but my own lips twitch in satisfaction.

It takes me a long while to fall asleep, as fury and embarrassment simmer in my limbs. However, I must do so at last because the next thing I know, I come awake. Even though it is unseasonably cold, I am warm, blissfully warm. Someone must have built a fire nearby. Except there is no red glow or light flickering against the cave wall. That is when I realize there is something solid at my back. Slowly, I turn over to find Balthazaar stretched out on the floor beside me. He is lying flat, the entire length of his side pressed up against me, his hands propped under his head. "Go back to sleep," he mutters.

"You are making me too hot," I mutter back.

"I am keeping you from freezing."

"I do not need your help."

He does not respond, but he does not get up and leave either. Deciding I am too tired to insist, I force my mind away from the complex, infuriating man beside me. Just as I am drifting off to sleep, he speaks again, so softly I cannot be certain it is not a dream.

"I am sorry. You make me ashamed of what we are, of what little we can offer you, and I lashed out at you when what I really wanted was to punish my own dark thoughts."

Then, softer than a melting snowflake, something brushes against my cheek—his finger, I realize. It is a shockingly gentle gesture and dissolves what little anger I still harbored. I could not stay angry at him any more than I could stay angry with Sybella when she lashed out at us when the pain inside her became too great to bear. I do not know what personal demons Balthazaar struggles with, but I know pain when I see it.

When next I wake, two things occur to me with sudden clarity. Indeed, the ideas are so simple that I am sheepish I did not think of them before. Surely it was the shock of finding myself among the hellequin that so addled my wits.

But no longer.

I could take Balthazaar as a lover. If I am no longer a virgin, that will put an end to this seeress nonsense the abbess keeps insisting on.

Besides, I cannot help but feel as if riding with the hellequin is doing more to serve Mortain than sitting with Sister Vereda in some stone chamber. I could have a role here with these men. I am able to lighten their mood, to ease their despair just a tiny bit. What if I could be a glimmer of light on their long, dark quest for redemption?

Perhaps that is even why Mortain led me into their path.

The next night, when Balthazaar lies down next to me, I turn my entire body so that I am facing him. He grows so still, it is as if he has become part of the stone floor upon which we lie. I say nothing, hoping he will instinctively know what I want, but he makes no move, does not even, I think, breathe. *Merde.*

"Balthazaar?"

There is a faint sigh — a movement or exhalation, I cannot tell. Slowly, as if approaching some wild, untamed creature, I reach out and lay my hand upon his chest. His muscles bunch up beneath my fingers, and, almost as if against his will, his head turns toward mine. When our gazes meet through the darkness, it is as intimate as a touch and my heart begins to beat more deeply.

"What are you doing?" His voice is strained and hardly sounds like his own.

"I thought we could . . ." I stop and swallow. Now that the moment is upon me, I fear my nerve will fail. I close my eyes and remember the look on his face when we were sparring, remember the way his hands lingered on my body. "I know you desire me. I . . . I can see it when you look at me." For all of Sister Beatriz's lessons, I am doing this wrong, and a slow, hot flush of embarrassment washes over me.

He grabs my hand in his, and the feel of his naked fingers against mine sends a shock all the way down to my belly. We have rarely touched, and then only when he was wearing gloves. He brings my hand to his mouth and presses his lips upon it. A brief, fleeting gesture that is all too soon over. Then he tucks my hand under my chin. "This is not what you want. Not truly." His voice is gruff and filled with an aching loneliness, a loneliness that I know I can ease.

"But it is." I reach for him again, only this time I let my fingers drift up to his hair and touch the soft, dark strands of it. "I want to be with you," I whisper.

He closes his eyes for a long moment and leans into my touch. My heart lifts, thinking this means he will agree. But then he pulls himself away and puts an arm's length of distance between us. "That is not allowed." His voice is rough, as if the words are being dragged along shards of glass. "And even if it were, you are too young, too good, to pledge yourself to the road I must travel. To pledge yourself to *me*." Then, before I can argue further, he rises to his feet and strides away, leaving me cold and alone in the dark.

When I wake, Balthazaar is not at my side, and my heart plummets as I remember last night. Sitting up, I cast a casual glance around the cave, trying to locate him.

He sits toward the back, almost out of view, staring at something he holds in his lap. I glance away so he will not feel the weight of my gaze, but I am able to keep sight of him from the corner of my eye. As I stand, he hurriedly shoves whatever he is looking at back into his saddlebag and rises to his feet.

I avoid looking at him, or even acknowledging him, while we make ready to ride. Indeed, I manage to avoid him the entire night, my efforts greatly aided by his equal desire to avoid me. When the hunt returns to the cromlech, he still sleeps near me, but does not lie down until long after I am asleep, and he rises before I wake. He spends hours staring at whatever he keeps in his saddlebag, as if trying to coax an answer from it. After two days of this, my curiosity becomes piqued.

Perhaps he is holding some token of the sins he committed when he was human, something he is using to keep his resolve strong. Perhaps giving in to mortal temptation such as I offered him will only prolong his punishment or even remove his chance for redemption altogether.

Perhaps whatever he keeps in that saddlebag will answer all these questions that plague me.

Chapter Nineteen

As LUCK WOULD HAVE IT, the next night is a busy one, with lost and wandering souls so thick upon the ground that the hellequin are able to scoop them up like fishermen with a net. "Something is wrong," Balthazaar says when the men have captured their fourth soul. "There should not be so many in one place."

"Unless they have all been killed at once," Sauvage says. "Then it would make sense." He shrugs his massive shoulders. "Maybe there has been a battle. Or a fire."

A battle. "Where are we?" I ask.

Balthazaar barely spares me a glance. "About six leagues north of Vannes."

"Which means we are close to the port cities, a sure target if and when the French decide to make a move on Brittany."

He looks at me blankly.

"The impending war?" I remind him with impatience. "It is possible the French have decided to engage us, and some battle we have not yet heard of has taken place." Not that we would ever hear of it, seeing that we pass almost no one at night and those we do pass are not inclined to stop and share gossip.

"She is right," Sauvage says. I am so surprised I almost ask him to repeat himself, but silence my tongue before the words can escape.

Balthazaar nods in agreement as another shout goes up. The hellequin have found yet more souls. "Come," Balthazaar says. "Let us see if
we can ask one of them why there are so many." He puts his heels to his
horse and we all ride forward.

When we are close enough to the others, Balthazaar and Sauvage
rein in their horses and dismount. The souls must have been those of
soldiers, for they do not cower or shrink in fear from the approaching
hellequin.

Now, I think. Now is my chance, when everyone is busy with the
souls. I slip out of my saddle onto the ground, then wait, stomping my
feet as if to stay warm in case anyone should notice me.

As if I am merely stretching my legs, I saunter over to Balthazaar's
abandoned horse. The creature has grown used to my scent after our
weeks riding together. Even though he tosses his mane and blows loudly,
we both understand it is simply for show.

I carefully unlatch the strap that holds the saddlebag closed, glancing
around as I do to be certain none of the men are watching. I reach into
the saddlebag and grope blindly, certain my hands will recognize the
object, for I have seen enough of it from a distance to discern the shape
of it.

There! My hand closes around something long and thin. When I
draw it out, I see that it is an arrow. I frown. Balthazaar does not even
possess a bow.

Unease slithers across my shoulders. I turn to angle the arrow so the
light of the moon falls upon it. A jolt of recognition slams through me.

It is *my* arrow. There is no mistaking the supple yew wood of the
shaft, the black crow feathers I used for the fletching, and the single
dove feather that is my own signature mark.

My heart starts to race, and slowly I bring the tip up so I may see the
arrowhead itself.

It is stained dark with old blood.

My blood. Blood that I smeared upon it the night of the midwinter ceremony.

Every muscle in my body clenches. I shove the arrow into the saddlebag and begin backing away, struggling to keep my steps slow and measured.

I wait a beat, then another, before allowing myself to seek out Balthazaar's figure. When I see that he is still with the others, gently trying to coax answers from the confused souls they have captured, I allow myself to breathe again. I have time. My snooping was not spotted. I clench my hands into fists, then open them, trying to work some of the tension from my body.

I do not know what this means, except that nothing is as it seems and I now feel myself to be in grave peril. I can only assume the arrow means the hellequin *are* hunting me as I originally feared, although why Balthazaar has not made a move against me, I do not know. He must be playing some long game I do not yet recognize.

Or perhaps before he could send me on to the Underworld, he found himself drawn to me and thought to take his ease. For he *was* drawn to me — the sparks between us crackled and snapped from our first meeting.

But then why did he reject my offer? Was it a way to use my own sin of pride against me, to rub salt into the wound of wanting him? A punishment of his own before turning me over to the judgment of Mortain?

I shake my head, trying to disentangle myself from all the questions that threaten to cloud my wits. There will be plenty of time for me to ponder my foolish mistakes once I am free. For I must escape before he connects me to that arrow or, if he has already made that connection, before he decides to move.

The good news is that the hellequin have grown fully accustomed to my presence. They trust me now and are less inclined to watch my every move as they did when I first joined them.

Morning is almost here. It is the perfect time to make my escape. I need evade capture only until daybreak. Then they will have to return to one of their cromlechs and wait until nightfall again.

I glance up at the sky and try to determine how long until dawn. Less than an hour, I think. If I do not move soon, I will be forced to spend another night with them — with him — and I do not know if I can keep my newfound knowledge hidden.

To test if anyone is paying attention to me, I remount Fortuna, then urge her to take a few steps away from the group. No one spares me a glance; they are too intent on the conversation taking place between the others.

Now. The word flares up in my mind like a beacon, and I can only hope it is a sign from some god other than the god of mistakes. In slow and careful steps, I allow Fortuna to keep drifting farther and farther from the others. Still no one notices. I urge her to the right, into the trees, an excuse of needing to relieve my bladder ready at my lips, or a claim of spotting yet another wandering lost soul. Still no one follows.

Heartened now, I let Fortuna pick up her pace, threading through the thickest of the trees, which will slow down any pursuit.

The forest is quiet all around me, soaking up the sound of our passing like a thick blanket. I must put some serious distance between the hellequin and me, but to do that I will have to gallop. Once I do, there will be no way to hide that I am attempting to escape. My heart inches up into my throat.

After a moment's hesitation, I finally put my heels to Fortuna's flanks and urge her to fly. And fly she does. As if she can somehow sense my own urgency, she races through the trees, dodging them nimbly. Or perhaps it is all the nights she spent riding with the hunt that have given her such speed. Either way, I am heartened, as each step takes me farther and farther away from the hellequin. From the incrimination of my own arrow. From the pain of Balthazaar's rejection and lies.

We run for close to a quarter of an hour before I have the sense that I am being followed. I turn my head to the side, straining to hear, but my ears are full of the thudding of Fortuna's hooves and her heavy, rhythmic breathing.

She will need to rest soon.

I glance up at the eastern sky, which is just beginning to lighten. Sunrise is not far off.

I lean low over Fortuna's neck, grab hold of her mane, and whisper in her ear for her to run faster if she can, and if she can't, well, then may the gods themselves help us. I find I cannot pray to Mortain, not when He may have sent the hellequin to find me. At the very least, it is like pulling Him into some sordid family quarrel.

And then it reaches me: the distant thunder of horses' hooves. After spending weeks in the hellequin's company, I find the sound is nearly as familiar to me as that of my own breathing.

Fortuna has no more to give. Her sides are streaked in sweat, and her lungs are heaving like a blacksmith's bellows. I glance around, but there are no buildings, no houses, no convenient churches nearby in which to beg shelter. There is nothing but trees and forest as far as I can see. I glance up at the treetops, wondering . . .

Without pausing to think it through lest I lose my nerve, I kick my feet out of my stirrups and loop the reins loosely around the saddle horn. "Keep running," I whisper to Fortuna. "But slow down if you must. Just lead them away from me."

Then I reach down, grab hold of the saddle, and use it to steady myself as I slowly draw my legs up.

The ground below races by. I ignore it, and the sharp rocks and logs that lie in wait should I fail. I pull my legs under me, find my balance, and slowly begin to ease myself to a standing position, letting my body adjust to the rhythm of Fortuna's gait.

It has been months since I've done this, but the movements come back to me easily. I match my rhythm to that of the horse, finding my balance, and gripping tightly with my feet.

Then I wait for the perfect branch. One that will be low enough that I can reach out, grab it, then lever myself up onto it.

I remain in a half crouch while we pass scores of trees, but their branches are all too high or too narrow or not thick enough.

The sounds of the hunt are louder now. Soon they will be within sight, and once they are, my trick will not be of any use. I utter a quick, desperate prayer to Mortain: *I know they are Yours, but so am I. Please do not let me be chased down like a hunted deer.*

A dozen strides later, right after a slight bend on the path, I see a thick, low-hanging branch. I have no time to think, to consider, to judge if it will work. It *must* work. I straighten my legs, reach up, then brace myself as the jolt of the contact reverberates through my body. Then my legs are dangling in the air and I see Fortuna continue to run on without me.

There is no time to congratulate myself. I hoist myself up onto the branch, swing my legs sideways, then wrap them around the limb and shimmy toward the trunk. I reach it and pull myself to the far side just as the first of the hellequin come into view.

It is Sauvage, riding in the van, his face compressed in single-minded intent. I press my entire body flat against the tree and watch them stream beneath me, surprised to see Balthazaar bringing up the rear.

His hood is pulled close, so I cannot see his face. Even so, there is a grimness, a ferocity about his manner that makes my heart clutch painfully. *He is not your concern,* I tell myself. He has made that perfectly clear.

I wait, holding so still I scarcely allow myself to draw breath. Only when I can no longer hear even the echo of their hoofbeats do I let myself draw a lungful of air. They did not find me. There is a chance — a small one — that Fortuna will be able to outrun them without the weight of a rider on her back. And if not, well, they will not hurt her, for she is nothing to them. Even so, I will probably never see her again. Someone might find her, take her for his own. It is possible she might return to the night rower's stables; I have no idea how strong her homing instincts are.

Then I remember my saddlebag and the journal hidden deep inside, as well as the Tears, and the strange black box. I cringe to think of the convent learning what I took with me. Even worse is the idea of those things falling into some stranger's hands: the local prelate, a landed yeoman, or some random innkeeper who finds Fortuna nibbling at his oats. But it cannot be helped.

Slowly, I lower myself so that I am sitting on the base of the branch with my back to the tree's wide trunk. Now that the hellequin have passed, all my muscles are trembling, as if finally acknowledging the danger I was in. Or perhaps they are merely exhausted.

I glance once more at the eastern sky, which is now tinged with definite shades of gray and pink. Dawn has arrived. I make myself comfortable and settle in to wait.

I must doze, for a dream comes to me.

I dream of a great, white boar. In my dream I am lying on the forest floor in a bed of decaying leaves. I am cold and my body aches, and I am unable to sleep. At first, I hear a snuffling noise, as if some great creature has laid its snout near the ground to inhale all the ripe forest scents. But a moment later, I understand — the creature is searching for something.

It is searching for me.

A feral, gamy tang fills my nostrils, and my heart catches in my throat, for by the sound of it, it is a huge thing. I start to push myself up, meaning to run, but I realize I must grow still instead. I hug the ground, hoping the creature will not find me. But still it snuffles and searches. My heart beats so hard with fear that I am certain it will pound its way out of my chest. Or that the creature will hear it.

Boars this size are rare, and white boars rarer still, for they are sacred to Arduinna.

Closer it draws, and closer. I can feel the heat from its body now, feel the faint moisture of its breath as it leans closer, closer. Like a frightened child, I keep my eyes closed and shiver on the forest floor, unable to face my fate.

Then a coolness surrounds me, and before I can think to pull away, the press of lips upon my own shocks me into consciousness. A low, deep voice thrums near my ear, pulling me from the fog of sleep: "You will be safe now." I jerk awake, nearly toppling from my precarious shelter in the tree.

Chapter Twenty

I GRAB MY BRANCH and hold on tight until the fog of sleep clears. I blink my eyes and see that dawn has broken, sending long pale arms of sunlight streaming in all directions. My ears fill with the soft sounds around me: the rustling of small creatures in the underbrush and the faint beginning of birdsong. Day is well and truly here, and there are no signs of the hellequin.

I remember my dream and a shudder of misgiving moves through me. Were those the press of *his* lips I felt?

Dreamed, I correct, not *felt.* I lift my fingers to my mouth, remembering the distinct feel and weight of those lips. The voice said I would be safe now even as it filled my mind with visions of boars. Was it some trick? Some dark hellequin skill, an ability to insert dreams into their victims' minds?

Or only my own fevered imagination, awash in my fears?

I shove the disturbing thoughts away and rise to my feet, clutching a branch so I do not tumble to a painful death after I have worked so hard to escape.

The hellequin said we were only a few leagues north of Vannes, a large town with thick sturdy walls. But I have no horse. That makes it easily a two-day walk — if I'm lucky. I hold still for another moment, checking for the sound of galloping horses or snuffling boars, but hear nothing. I climb down the tree, careful not to tear my gown so that it will not be wearable, as it is now the only one I possess.

When my feet are firmly on the ground, I pause and find my bearings. If I keep the rising sun on my left, I will be heading south and should reconnect with the main road. I strike out quickly. With my lack of absolute certainty that the hellequin cannot ride during the day and my newfound fear of boars, I am determined to find the road as soon as possible.

I miss Fortuna already, not simply because riding her was faster than walking, but because she has been my one constant through these past few weeks. I hold on to half a hope that I might come upon her in the woods, that she might have run herself out and is now patiently waiting for me to find her. But there is no sign of her dappled gray bulk anywhere.

I have been walking nearly an hour when I hear it—a distinctive snuffling sound that is all too familiar from my recent dream. I glance behind me but see nothing. I cannot outrun a boar, but perhaps I can appear harmless enough that it will not charge. Just in case, I look to the surrounding trees for another branch I can use to pull myself to safety, but there is none within reach.

At the rustle of leaves just behind me, my heart begins beating so frantically I fear it will break one of my ribs. I quicken my pace, but if I go any faster, I will be running, and that will only inflame the creature.

In front of me, from what I estimate to be the direction of the road, I hear riders approaching. Judging from the sound, there are only four —no, three—of them, not an entire pack. And they *are* coming from the road. Not hellequin, then, but simple travelers. Travelers I may attach myself to until the next town.

I cannot help myself; I run, stumbling over roots, rocks, and my own feet so that I nearly tumble down the embankment to the road below.

I stop, breathless, in front of the riders. We all stare at one another in a long moment of surprise.

They are women, although it is hard to tell at first for they wear no traditional garb. Their arms and legs are encased in tight leather, and their overgowns are of rough brown fur. Each has a quiver of arrows at her shoulder and a knife in her belt. There are three of them, and they rein in their mounts. "Greetings," the middle rider says. She appears to be the oldest, as her light brown hair is shot through with gray. Her bearing is as erect and regal as if she were wearing a crown.

Before I can return the greeting, I see that they are leading a fourth horse—a dappled gray. "Fortuna!" I dodge around the others, deftly avoiding their horses' hooves, and reach Fortuna's side. I pat her neck and check her over for signs of injury.

"I take it you know each other?"

"She is my horse."

"It is poor thanks to such a noble creature, to let her wander loose and riderless so that she might trip on her reins." The speaker is tall, taller than the others and nearly as tall as Sister Thomine, who is the tallest woman I have ever met. She wears her hair in a long dark brown braid that swings as she dismounts. In that moment I realize they must be followers of Arduinna. And even though they are known to be protectors of women, this knowledge does not comfort me.

"I did not do that on purpose." I do not try to hide my indignation. "And I *did* tie her reins off so she wouldn't trip on them. But truly, I had no choice."

The tall woman tilts her head. "What happened to you that you must abandon your horse in such a way and travel on foot?"

I stare at her, trying to decide what to tell them. Arduinnites are scarcer than hen's teeth and I have seen one only once, and that was by accident. We'd been riding with Sister Widona on the mainland near a forest and caught a glimpse of a strange-looking woman—although we did not know it was a woman at first. Sister Widona nodded a curt greeting, then hurried us away. Once we were out of earshot, she explained that those who follow Arduinna bear no love for those of us who follow Mortain, since it was He who had robbed Arduinna of her sister.

Sister Widona's words clang in my head like a great loud bell and I mentally kick myself that I did not think to ask just how deep that animosity went.

So what, then, do I tell her? Which is worse, being a daughter of Mortain or being some headstrong maiden who has behaved in a foolish manner? The uncomfortable thought occurs to me that I could be both.

The youngest of them dismounts and begins to approach me. I am assailed by the smell of leather and fur, and the tang of blood. "Are you all right?" she asks. "Have you been hurt?"

"I . . . no."

The tallest one looks me over with haughty eyes. "You show no signs of a struggle."

Judgment drips heavily from her words, and at first I find myself wishing I had injured myself more thoroughly as I climbed out of that bedamned tree. But then a small spark of anger ignites within me. I do not deserve her censure. I shrug my cloak away from my body, flash my daggers at her. "Perhaps it is because my pursuers were put off by these."

The oldest one, still on her horse, speaks. "Do not take offense. It is our way, to help maids in distress or those who have been hurt or dishonored."

"I do not know that casting doubts upon their honor is a way to win their trust," I mutter, still ruffled by the tall one's manner.

"You expect us to believe that a lone maid held off pursuers with a handful of knives?"

"Well, that and I disappeared up a tree."

The eldest one's lips twitch, and the youngest one smiles outright. "How do you come to be traveling on the road alone?" she asks.

"I have business in Guérande."

"And you travel with no attendant or guard?" the tall one asks, disbelief still heavy in her voice.

The youngest one steps in front of me protectively. "Why don't we ensure she is unharmed before we begin questioning her." She is slighter than the others. Her voice sounds young to my ears, and I place her at a year or two younger than myself.

The tall one continues to study me with narrowed eyes and I wonder what I have done to raise her ire. "She has already said she was fine." She begins walking toward me. When she reaches my side, she stops walking, leans her head forward, and sniffs. "You reek of man."

"Aeva!" the younger one protests. Then, almost as if unable to help herself, she too sniffs, then frowns. "You smell of death as well," she says, puzzled.

"Death?" I ask, both annoyed and startled.

The tall one—Aeva, she was called—wrinkles her nose in distaste. "It is the stench of the hellequin that clings to her."

She can smell them? "That would be because it was the hellequin who were pursuing me."

The youngest one's lips part in surprise, but Aeva simply sneers. "Are you certain you were pursued and you are not simply a hellequin's lightskirt?"

Even if I could not hear the thick contempt in her voice, the worried look on the youngest girl's face would have alerted me that it was far better to be the victim of a hellequin than his lightskirt. It is not the least bit difficult to sound insulted, for I am sorely irked by their manner. "I am no one's lightskirt." Although not for want of trying, I realize, and I am suddenly ashamed by my actions. At the convent, we are not taught that it is wrong to lie with a man, but surely it is wrong to lie with one merely to avoid an unwanted fate.

"Then why do you reek of death?"

"I did not say I had not been close to one, only that I was not his lightskirt." At my words, the tension in her body relaxes somewhat. "But neither was I his victim, for I escaped just before dawn and waited high in a tree for daybreak. And then I found you."

"It was only the guidance of the Great White Boar herself that brought us here," the oldest one says.

"I dreamed of her," I tell them.

Aeva's head whips around. "You lie."

"I do *not* lie. I dreamed of a great boar, and that she was . . ." I cannot bring myself to say she kissed me with her great white snout, nor am I certain that is even what happened. "And she was protecting me."

The three women exchange glances and the youngest looks pointedly at Aeva. "That does match Floris's vision."

My interest sharpens. "Is Floris your seeress?"

"No," the oldest one says. "I am Floris, one of Arduinna's priestesses. I too saw the Great White Boar last night, and she led me to you."

Aeva studies me most skeptically, as if she is still trying to sort out how I came to be in their midst. "Did you make an offering to Arduinna?" she asks.

"No. The idea never occurred to me, as I have not been raised to be familiar with her ways."

"No matter." The youngest one reaches out and squeezes my arm. "It is a most auspicious omen. What is your name? I am called Tola."

She is so friendly and her blue eyes dance so cheerfully that I cannot help but smile back. "I am Annith."

"Well, Annith," Floris says, "we are pleased to hear that you are unharmed, and even more pleased to hear that the Great White Boar has taken you under her protection, for indeed, it will be perilous going from here. You will have to postpone your trip to Guérande, I'm afraid."

"What?" All the goodwill I had been feeling toward these women in the past few seconds evaporates. "You cannot stop me from traveling on my business."

"Well, that is a matter of dispute," she says, sounding faintly amused. "But it is not we who have caused the delay. The French troops have landed at Vannes and taken the city. These shores are crawling with them like fleas on a hound. In truth, that is who we thought to rescue you from — French soldiers."

Chapter Twenty-One

IT IS EASY ENOUGH to fall in with them. At least for now. They will offer me protection from the invading French, and although they dislike the daughters of Mortain, they despise the hellequin even more. That hatred of the hellequin makes them the perfect ones to offer me protection.

Surely the sudden appearance of Arduinna's followers on the road in my time of need is no accident. Indeed, it feels as if Mortain is placing small steppingstones at my feet, one at a time, so that I may have a chance to wrest my own fate out of the abbess's greedy hands.

Even so, I must resist the urge to keep looking over my shoulder. The hellequin do not hunt in the daylight, I remind myself at least a dozen times. The others make note of my unease but say nothing, and I hope that it gives the stamp of truth to my story.

We have not been on the road but two hours before we come upon a cart. Two hedge priests sit in the front, and it is draped in black. Our group moves to the side to give them room to pass. As they do, I cannot help but look into the back of it, wondering who has made their final journey into death. Perhaps it is the first of the French soldiers' victims.

But at the sight of the bright red hair spread out against the black sheeting, my stomach curls into a tight ball of dread. "Stop!" The word springs out of my mouth before I even realize I have spoken. Surprised by the command of my voice, the hedge priests reluctantly halt, then scowl at me while the Arduinnites shoot me curious glances. I dismount from Fortuna and toss the reins at Tola, who catches them easily.

As I draw near the bone cart, time seems to slow as if it is trapped in a thick slog of mud. *Please not Matelaine. Please, please, please.* The prayer hammers through my body with every heartbeat.

At last, I reach the side of the cart and look down. The girl's face is covered by a shroud. Slowly, I reach for the edge of the black linen.

"Don't touch her!" one of the hedge priests says in outrage, but I do not even pause. I grip the fine linen and pull it away from her face.

Matelaine's face.

At the sight of her, I feel as if a shard of glass has wedged itself into my heart. She is still and whiter than bone, her face stark against the black shroud and red hair. Her hands have been laid upon her chest, and in the right one she clutches an ivory chess piece. "Where are you taking her?" My voice sounds dull and hollow, even to my own ears.

"Back to the convent of Saint Mortain. Do you know her?" the second hedge priest asks more gently.

I nod, my eyes never leaving her face. "She is my sister." As I stare down at her, the pain from that shard of glass spreads out, filling my lungs, my chest, my arms with such a sense of wrongness that it is all I can do not to throw back my head and howl with rage and fury. She should never have been sent out.

And the abbess knew it. The abbess has betrayed the very tenets of the convent. The nuns are meant to foster and care for His daughters as they would their own, sending them out only when they are truly ready.

It is also, I realize with a sour sickness in my belly, my fault as well, for whatever the reason the abbess has held me back, it is at the root of her decision to send Matelaine. If I had been stronger, faster, more determined, argued my case better, I could have prevented this. I turn on the priest. "What happened?"

The kinder one answers. "We do not know. We were only given the body to transport back to the island."

I feel a hand on my shoulder and spin around in surprise. It is the oldest of the Arduinnites—Floris. "Is she your sister?" Her brown eyes are full of compassion.

"Yes," I whisper.

"What do you wish to do?"

Her question reminds me that I have choices. Part of me wishes to crawl into the cart and hold Matelaine close for the entire journey back to the convent. To whisper all the words of friendship in her ear that I was too busy to utter in real life. To present her body to the nuns who are still there and scream at them, *See what you have done? By your silence, your compliance?* The unspoken words in my throat are as hot and painful as red coals from a fire.

My own plans and ambitions crumble like winter's first frost under a heavy boot. A choking anger continues to build inside me, and rage spreads so quickly through my body that it is a wonder I do not erupt into flames.

Slowly, I turn to face Floris. "I wish to travel on and avenge her death by confronting those who have done this to her."

She holds my gaze for a long moment, and I see a measure of approval in them. "Are you also a daughter of Mortain?"

I look away. "Yes. I am sorry I did not tell you. I know there is a history of animosity between us. I will no longer travel with you if you'd prefer."

"If you are avenging this girl, then you are on Arduinna's business now, so you are welcome to travel with us. Plus, a lone woman is too easy to harass; a group of four women who are warriors and assassins, less so."

*   *   *

We make camp just before nightfall. I suggest we spend the night near a church so we can be assured of the protection of consecrated ground, but they refuse, and Aeva outright laughs. "We have no love of or use for the Church."

"But the hellequin claimed they would hunt me forever," I explain. "I do not wish to bring their vengeance down upon you as well." Not to mention incite some sort of civil war among the gods and their minions.

"They could not know you would find shelter with us," Floris says. "And even if they did, the hellequin will not dare approach the followers of Arduinna."

"But just to be certain, we will ward our camp," Tola adds cheerfully.

Aeva turns on her, eyes sparking with annoyance. "You talk too much of things that are for our ears only." When Tola simply shrugs, Aeva reaches for a handful of kindling and flings it onto the fire. "If you have so little care for the secrets that lie between her god and ours, why not simply get down at her feet and rub yourself against her ankles like an overfriendly cat?"

"Enough!" It is the first time I have heard Floris raise her voice. "It is Tola's choice who she makes friends with, not yours."

Unable to help myself, I glance over at the older woman. "You do not forbid it?"

She shakes her head at my question. "It is not ours to forbid. Every one of us must decide for herself."

After another long moment of silence, I speak again. "Why is there so much animosity between Mortain and Arduinna?" I ask. "As the old stories tell it, Arduinna gave her blessing to Mortain and Amourna's pairing."

Aeva shoots me a scornful glance, and my hand itches to slap the look off her face. "We who serve Arduinna are made, not chosen and showered with otherworldly gifts like the daughters of Mortain. Every skill we possess, every feat we master, we acquire through our own sweat and determination. Not because we were sired by a god."

I lean forward, wishing we were standing so I could back her up against a tree to shake her arrogance. "First, you will be comforted to learn that not all daughters of Mortain are blessed with His unique gifts and talents. I am one of those who have been given none, and have had to work hard for every skill I've acquired — often at great personal cost." Our gazes hold for a long moment, then she looks away. I take a deep breath to calm myself, then turn to Floris. "How do followers come to serve Arduinna if they are not her children?" Although as soon as I utter the words, I realize how foolish that sounds, for no woman, not even a goddess, can give birth to hundreds of daughters. Not to mention she is reported to be a virgin goddess at that.

Floris stands up to add another branch to the fire. "When a woman feels love's painful bite, that is when she prays to Arduinna. Every heart that has been broken, every lover who has been jilted, every soul that has been twisted by jealousy belongs to her. All girl children born of such a union — whether the jealous vindictive side of love or the heart-wrenching unrequited side — are Arduinna's own daughters. They may never know it, but *she* does, and she watches over them. If they choose to dedicate themselves to her service, they are welcomed with open arms.

"And to answer your original question on the animosity between our gods, it is because your god played our goddess false," she says softly.

The silence that follows grows thick, and they all exchange glances while I stare stupidly at her. Aeva looks smug. "Ah, you've not heard that story, have you?"

"No, I have not."

"Well, you will not hear it from us." Aeva sends the others such a searing gaze that even Floris does not contradict her. Then she rises to her feet in disgust. "I am going to do something useful, like hunt for our dinner, instead of huddling around and gossiping with our enemies."

I raise my eyebrows and turn to Floris. "I apologize. I did not realize I was an enemy. I have no desire to put any of you in an uncomfortable—"

Floris holds up her hands to halt my words. "You are not an enemy. Aeva simply sees things more rigidly than most. Now, here, if you would kindly clear a place for our bedrolls."

It is a simple task, even a mindless one, but I do not care, for my head is already overfull. As I pick up rocks and twigs from the ground, both Tola and Floris cut marks and sigils into the earth with their bone-handled knives. I am consumed with curiosity—we at the convent have no such magic, or at least none that I have heard of—but I do not wish to intrude on a private ritual that they are using in order to protect me, so I allow myself only occasional glances.

I finish my task before they finish theirs and look around for something else to do. Dusk is falling fast now, and a few squirrels and rabbits venture forth for a last forage before the night. The rabbits are thin, but thin is still better than nothing. Moving slowly so as not to startle them, I pick up my bow and two arrows. When they lift their heads, sniffing the air, I hold perfectly still so they will not sense me. As soon as they go back to their grazing, I fit an arrow to the bow and aim. There is an explosion of movement as the creatures take flight, but I am pleased to see that the largest of the rabbits lies still on the ground. I will much prefer eating a dinner that I have caught myself than relying on Aeva's bitter hospitality.

That night, as we eat, Tola keeps looking at me, and I know she wishes to ask me questions. I am grateful when she does not. Aeva, however, shows no such restraint. "So, you are a daughter of Mortain, and yet the hellequin pursued you?"

I keep my attention firmly on the rabbit haunch I am gnawing. "I did not tell them who I was."

"Why not?"

I should lie and turn her questions from me, but seeing Matelaine today reminded me that my reasons for leaving were justified. "Out of fear that it was me they were after."

The frankness of that answer silences even the belligerent Aeva. At least for a moment. She opens her mouth to ask something else, but Floris puts her hand on the other woman's arm. "Surely that is a convent matter and none of our concern."

Aeva swallows back whatever question she was considering. It might just be my imagination, but I think I discern a new measure of respect in her manner.

That night, I find it nearly impossible to sleep in spite of my exhaustion. Every time I close my eyes, I see Matelaine's cold, dead face, and I want to rail at myself for being so long detained by the hellequin. If I had gotten to Guérande earlier, could I have prevented her death?

Just as I finally start to fall asleep, the ground begins to rumble and I come fully awake.

The hunt.

I freeze, as if holding still will keep them from finding me. The rumble grows louder, and the ground trembles against my cheek as they draw closer. I turn to look at the others and find Tola's eyes open. "Do not worry," she whispers. "The wards will hold."

And they do. But I can see the dark ghostly figures riding just on the other side of them. One rider draws to a halt and stares at our camp. Even though I cannot see who it is from this distance, my skin recognizes the dark, brooding caress of his gaze, and I shiver.

The following day, we draw close enough to Vannes to see the spires of its churches. We also run into the first of the French soldiers. They have commandeered a local farmer's ox cart as well as what looks like the very last of his slim winter food stores. Since the new crops will not be in for weeks yet, they may well have just sentenced the family to death by starvation.

There are six of them, two on the driver's bench and four more flanking the cart to guard it. Luckily, we left the main road over an hour ago and have been traveling alongside it, hidden in the smattering of trees that rise up on either side of the road. The Arduinnites exchange a glance and draw their bows. Anticipation prickles along my skin as I realize what they intend to do. I draw my bow as well, for I will not stand idly by and hand Aeva an opportunity to question my skill or commitment.

Floris gives me a faint nod, then motions in silence to assign each of us a soldier. I am to take one of the men in the rear.

It is no different from the targets at the convent, I tell myself. But that is a lie. It is altogether different, for these men are flesh and blood, their bodies still pulsing with life.

I take a deep breath and sight along the arrow. The French soldier is thin and dirty and is boasting to his fellow Frenchmen about how the farmer nearly pissed himself in terror as he teased him with his sword. In that second, everything shifts, and it *is* precisely like shooting at the targets.

My vision narrows until the entire world is reduced to the French soldier. I squint against the pale winter sun, block out the soft chirping of the birds, and calculate the force of the light breeze.

But when I am ready to take the shot, for a brief moment my fingers refuse to let loose the arrow. I curse inwardly, then wrench my fingers from the bowstring and let the arrow fly. So no one will suspect that I hesitated, I quickly nock a second arrow and fire it as well. The air is filled with a brief series of thuds, and I watch as my arrow strikes the forward guard seconds before Aeva's does. She whips her head around and glares at me. "He was mine!"

I shrug. "He was going for his knife. I had no idea how accurate he would be at throwing it."

Aeva looks at me with a mixture of grudging admiration and annoyance.

Floris begins issuing orders. "Tola, turn the cart around and see if you can get it back to its owner. Aeva, go with her. You might suggest they hide their supplies better, unless they wish to eat nothing more than new grass and dirt clods." I avert my eyes, not wanting to watch as Aeva and Floris toss the bodies around like old sacks of grain, and I must fight to keep the sour churning in my belly from making me ill. It is the excitement, I tell myself. Excitement that I have finally made my first kill.

Even though this is what I have been trained to do, it does not feel nearly as joyous or righteous as I thought it would. I must remind myself that these are French soldiers who have killed any number of Bretons—and would do so again, even if only by confiscating all of their food.

Once Tola has the cart turned around, Aeva scrambles up onto the bench beside her. We arrange a place and time to meet later. As they head down the road, Floris sends me a sideways glance. "That was fine shooting."

"Thank you. I have had years of practice."

"You beat Aeva to her second shot," she points out.

An apology begins to form on my lips, but instead I say, "I thought the element of surprise was important."

Floris nods solemnly. "It was, but Aeva does not like being bested."

I turn and meet Floris's gaze head-on. "Neither do I."

She smiles widely, then changes the subject. "It could be hours before they return, so you and I are going to do a little scouting to see if the French have hunkered down in the city or spread themselves throughout the countryside."

We spend the better part of the afternoon riding through copses and crawling on our bellies through shrubs and brambles to get close enough to assess the enemy's position. More than once I find myself wishing for leather leggings and thick hide to armor myself against the sharp twigs, thorns, and brambles we encounter.

It is a most productive afternoon, even if it is a disheartening one. The French man the city gates as well as its walls. Additional guards have been set out along all three roads leading into the city. The largest of the farms and manor houses nearby have been seized, and I can only hope the soldiers were merciful to those whose homes they have stolen.

As the sun dips lower in the sky, we make our way back to the assigned meeting spot to see if Tola and Aeva have returned. They have, although they've been waiting for only minutes.

As Floris tells the others of what we found, I try to decide how best to get around Vannes and continue on to Guérande. Will the roads outside the city be blocked as well? And if so, how far north will I have to travel to avoid the French troops?

That night, we steer our horses well north of the city, toward a heavily wooded area. As we draw near, I hear the sounds of voices and movement and horses. I look questioningly at Floris. "It is our main encampment," she says. "For we are not here by accident, but by design. We are tasked with protecting the innocent, just as the hellequin are tasked with escorting souls from this world."

The road brings us upward in a series of switchbacks until we are at the top of a small rise. It is a good defensive spot, for we can see in all directions. As we clear the final switchback, the Arduinnites' camp comes into full view.

There are maybe a hundred Arduinnites in the camp, all of them dressed in tight leather leggings and rough-looking tunics. There are a scattering of tents set up, a handful of large ones and a number of smaller ones. To the south of the camp they have erected a fence around a large pastured area where they keep a herd of some of the most beautiful horses I have ever seen. I turn to Floris. "Aren't you afraid the French scouts will find you?"

Aeva smiles, fierce and chilling. "Let them. Not one of them will leave here alive."

Floris gives a small nod of agreement. "Tola, you will share your tent with Annith. Go fetch it from the supply wagons, and once you get it set up, find me." With that, she rides off to one of the larger tents. I watch as she dismounts, hands the reins to a waiting young Arduinnite who cannot be more than twelve years old, then enters the tent.

Before we do as Floris ordered, Tola and I take our horses to the paddock area and see them settled. I hoist my saddlebag over one shoulder, snag my bedroll, then grab my bow with my other hand before following Tola to where three large supply wagons have been parked. She rifles through one of them and then pulls out a rolled-up tent and a couple of blankets.

She picks out a spot that is halfway between the perimeter of the camp and the center. The tent is simple in its design and made of ox hide. It is not fancy and barely large enough for two, but it will keep out the wind and the moisture.

Even so, I do not intend to be in it for long.

When Floris and Aeva rejoin us, I tell them precisely that. "Thank you for allowing me to travel with you this far, but you have duties that keep you here, so I will leave in the morning and journey the rest of the way to Guérande on my own."

"How? You yourself saw that every road was watched by the French troops."

"I will travel due north far enough to avoid them, then give them wide berth before heading south again toward Guérande."

Floris tilts her head and studies me. "But the northern road is blocked."

"Then I will not use the road."

"But what of the hellequin?"

"I will not let them stop me. I shall look for walled cities and churches in which to pass the nights."

"Can you be so very certain there will be one on every leg of your journey?" Her voice is gentle as she points out how much I am leaving to chance.

"Of course not, but I will manage." I consider asking them to teach me how to draw those wards—Tola would, with a little persuasion.

Aeva folds her arms and looks at me in disgust. "You would abandon all these innocents and leave them to the French to avenge one who is already dead?"

"Aeva!" Floris's voice is sharp. "That is her choice to make, not yours."

I meet Aeva's gaze steadily. "All those innocents have the followers of Arduinna to see to their safety. Matelaine has only me to avenge her death and see that such a thing never happens to one of Mortain's daughters again."

Aeva barks out a laugh. "You would protect Mortain's daughters against death?"

"No. I would protect them against the betrayal that led to her death."

They all fall silent then, but Aeva's words have planted a small seed of guilt in me, and it begins growing, for there is truth in what she says. Confronting the abbess sooner rather than later will not bring Matelaine back from the dead. More importantly, I must think carefully about letting my own headstrong stubbornness propel me straight into the arms of the hellequin. Who will avenge Matelaine if they capture me?

"At least stay another night," Floris suggests, "so our scouts can report back on the French positions. That way, you'll be able to avoid them, if not the hellequin."

Impatiently, Tola tucks a stray strand of hair behind her ear. "Could we not show her the wards, so she could protect herself?"

Aeva's answer is fast and unequivocal. "No! She is not one of us and has no right to our secrets."

"Thank you," I tell her coolly, "but I do not wish anyone to betray their secrets. However, getting captured or killed in the attempt to avenge Matelaine will only ensure that the truth dies with me, so I will stay another day or two and think on other possible plans." I turn to Floris. "If you will have me."

"But of course. You are welcome to stay as long as you like." She flashes a quick smile. "You are also more than welcome to fight with us. It may help some of that pain you are feeling."

The suggestion startles me. "Is that allowed?"

Aeva snorts. "She will not sully herself by riding out with us. She will stay and cower in our camp while we do the hard work."

"I am getting tired of your constant slurs and insults," I tell her.

"Then do something about it. Something besides sitting secluded behind your thick stone walls, venturing out only when Death deigns to pay a visit, not understanding that dying is the easy part."

"The easy part?"

"Enough, Aeva! All of us who serve our gods have our own roles to play. And there are men who would argue with your belief that their deaths were easy." Floris's eyes grow dark with some remembered pain, and I look away to give her privacy.

I am being offered a chance. I do not know if it comes from Mortain or Arduinna—although why she would offer me such a thing, I cannot fathom. But no more can I reason out why Mortain would send hellequin to ride after me, then allow me to use my skills to evade them. But just because I cannot understand the reasoning of the gods does not mean I will pass up this opportunity. I wanted a life outside those stone walls that Aeva scorns; I scorned them myself in much the same way when I feared I would be imprisoned behind them all the rest of my days. This may be my only chance. I do not know how things will go with the abbess when I find her in Guérande, but I feel like a starving child who must eat all the sweets now, before they are taken away for good. "Yes." The word falls into the silence, causing everyone to look at me. "Yes, I will ride with you and aid your cause."

"Well." Aeva's eyes rake over my traveling gown. "You cannot fight with us in that."

"Of course not." Tola takes my hand and all but drags me away from the other women. "I will see to getting her properly equipped."

If fighting my way through the French soldiers is the only road to the abbess, then so be it. I will fight my way through them, soldier by bedamned soldier.

After pulling me back to the supply wagons, Tola rummages through their contents, then hands me a pair of leather leggings, a soft leather tunic, and a belt. I disappear into our small tent, slip out of my gown, and shimmy into my new clothes. The leggings fit like a second skin, and the leather tunic is both thicker and more supple than my gown. I cannot help but wish for a mirror to see what I look like in these strange new clothes, but of course there is none. Feeling self-conscious, I step out of the tent. Tola nods in approval. "See? You will move much more freely in those."

And so I do. Next, Tola offers to braid my hair. I sit on a nearby log and toss my hair over my shoulders so she can more easily reach it. As her fingers busy themselves making rows and rows of small braids, she chatters about which horse is her favorite and of her excitement about our mission. Suddenly, she stops and is quiet for a long moment. "What?" I finally ask. "What is it?"

She traces her finger down along the nape of my neck, just below the hairline. "Where did you get this mark?"

"What mark?"

"You did not know that you had it?"

"No. What does it look like?"

"It is nothing, never mind. It must just be a birthmark of some sort." And then she resumes braiding my hair.

Chapter Twenty-Two

EVEN WHEN THEY ARE in such a large encampment, the Arduinnites stick to small groups, or clans, as they call them, of anywhere from three women to a dozen. Campfires decorate the ground like the fireflies of summer, their flames twinkling yellow and orange in the encroaching night.

As I draw near our campfire, Tola and Floris stop their conversation and turn to me. Tola beams as proudly as a new mother, and I feel suddenly shy in my new attire. Floris smiles warmly, and even Aeva gives a begrudging grunt of—could it be?—approval. Four quail are on a spit over the fire, and my mouth waters at the scent of roasting meat.

Floris and Tola, while always friendly enough, seem especially relaxed in my presence tonight. Perhaps that is simply because they are surrounded by such a large number of their sisters. Whatever the reason, I welcome it, for I have questions I wish to ask, and it will be much easier if I do not have to wade through suspicion or hostility.

Once we are eating and all their attention is turned to their food, I begin. "Floris, you said that you are a priestess of Arduinna. How are her priestesses chosen?" I cut a quick glance at Aeva, bracing myself for a protest, but none comes.

"Followers of Arduinna can choose to be priestesses if they are willing to submit to the required nine years of training. Once they have mastered that, they take turns serving the goddess at different times of the year, then resume their normal duties when they are not." She tilts her head curiously. "Is that not how your convent does it?"

"No, we are fashioned more in accordance with the offices of the new church. We have an abbess who oversees all, and then a seeress who helps us interpret Mortain's will." Before she can think to wonder how our seeresses are chosen, I hurry to ask my next question. "Who rules over all of you? With so very many groups, surely you must need some way to settle disagreements."

Floris tosses the last of the quail bones into the fire and leans back, making herself comfortable. "Of course. If it cannot be settled by the clan leader, it is taken up with the high priestess and her council of priestesses on duty."

"And if that does not solve it? Say, if the priestesses could not all agree, or if they were overruled by the high priestess? What recourse would be available to the others?"

Floris studies me closely. "Then we would put it to a vote and all of us would have a voice in the matter." I ignore the dozen of questions shining in her eyes and turn my attention to my dinner. While I regret having to hint that there might be disagreement at our convent, it is most helpful to learn how others who follow the Nine solve such disputes.

Over fifty of us ride out to engage the French, but in small groups of four or five each. Arduinna's work is not about full-scale battle, but rather about protecting the innocents and the lowly that others are all too quick to destroy in the process of war.

My heart is heavy that I am not doing my own god's work, even as my spirits lift at the thought of finally putting my skills to use in the service of a god.

I am also pleased that I fit right in with the Arduinnites who ride at my side. An observer would never know I was not one of them, or even the newest among them. Floris is leading our group, and besides me it contains Aeva, Tola, and another Arduinnite, Odila, who is nearly as old as Floris. Fortuna too fits right in with these mounts, the only difference being in the style of saddles used.

We are not venturing into the city proper today. Instead, we are going to approach the outlying farms and homes in the hopes of protecting them from further scavenging and raids.

The farmer whose cart Tola and Aeva returned said that the French had arrived four days ago and that yesterday was the first time they had come in search of food. It is our hope that other farms have not yet been ransacked.

The first farm we pass is abandoned. Closest to the town, the family who lived here did not waste any time packing up all their belongings and livestock and moving on.

The second farm is inhabited by a more stubborn fellow; he greets us with a pitchfork in one hand and a club of wood in the other. "Peace," Floris says, holding up her hand. "We come only to be certain you are safe from the French."

"Just let them try and take my sheep. I didn't keep them all through the winter to feed a bunch of French pigs."

Floris manages, just barely, not to smile. "We are glad to hear it. However, there are hundreds of them and only one of you, so if you have family you can go stay wi—"

He spits off to the side. "I'll not be chased off my own land. Who sent you?"

"Arduinna, the patron saint of innocents."

"If that man is innocent, I'll eat my bow," mutters Aeva.

In the end, we cannot convince him to go elsewhere, but at least he has no wife or children who can be harmed.

As we draw closer to the French checkpoint, Floris motions Aeva and

Odila to dismount. They leave their horses with us and creep forward, quickly disappearing in the brush beside the road. Tola nearly quivers in anticipation. Floris glances her way. "It will be your turn next time."

We listen carefully but hear nothing. Good. That means the soldiers will not hear them either. Nearly a quarter of an hour later, two muffled thumps disturb the silence, and a host of birds takes panicked flight. When no more sounds follow, Floris gives a nod of approval.

It is not enjoyable, this crawling around in the brush, sneaking up on people unaware, and ambushing them. I much prefer how we who serve Mortain do it—by facing our victims and being certain they know full well they are being held to account. But this is war, and war has its own set of rules, for all that I did not study them.

The next day our mission proves harder, for word of our ambush has been reported back to the French, and they have tripled the manpower at their checkpoints. But they do more than increase their sentries— they begin pillaging the countryside in earnest. We spot four different groups riding out in all directions, eager to find whatever food and provender they can before we block off their access.

On this day I kill three more men, all of them French soldiers. I am grateful that the bow is Arduinna's favored weapon, for it is easier for me to kill from a distance than up close, and I am glad that the sour sickness does not return to my belly with each kill.

Well, not as strongly as the first time, anyway.

We harry the French at every turn, disrupting their supply chains and forays for food, protecting the innocent when they are threatened, and recruiting the able-bodied to our cause.

Floris is right: it is a good way to release some of the pain of Matelaine's death. It is hard work, not only physically but mentally, for it requires patience and cunning to wait out the enemy, anticipate their actions, then organize others to act, others who are undisciplined and afraid — afraid of both the French *and* the Arduinnites, for they are the stuff of legends.

In the following days, I kill seven more soldiers. None of them is marqued, but I do not feel the sick roiling in my gut like I did with the first one. While I never grow to love killing, I must admit that doing it before these men can harm others, whether by starving them or raping them or burning down their farms, feels justified, especially when there is no marque to guide me.

It makes it easier still when they rush to attack us, for then the killing becomes a mere reflex of self-protection.

On the tenth day, one of the Arduinnite scouts comes riding into camp and leaps from her horse before it has even come to a stop. "The Breton army has arrived!" she shouts, and a cheer goes up.

It takes them a week, but the Breton troops, flying Marshal Rieux's flag, are able to drive the French from Vannes. It is from those Breton troops that we learn that the duchess is no longer at Guérande. Indeed, she took her entire court with her to Rennes back in February.

"Rennes," I repeat stupidly. I could likely have reached Rennes simply by bearing directly north for three or four leagues, not even needing to worry about the bedamned French. Frustration at the futility of the wait fills me, and Floris and Tola look at me oddly.

"Then I must go to Rennes. I will leave today."

Floris nods. "It is time."

Seeing my surprise at her easy acquiescence, Tola leans close to murmur in my ear. "She had another vision," she explains.

Floris lifts her head and peers off to the north. "Someone at the duchess's palace has put out the sacred offering requesting Arduinna's help, and we must honor it. Therefore, we will be traveling with you to Rennes."

Chapter Twenty-Three

FLORIS, AEVA, AND TOLA ACCOMPANY me only as far as the bridge that leads to the Rennes city gates. "Tell the duchess we have heeded her call and will aid her in any way we can," Floris says. "We will await her instructions in our camp."

"You won't come with me to the palace?"

"No," Aeva says. "We avoid cities whenever possible. They are too confining."

"We will pitch our main camp over there." Floris points to the north, where the line of trees meets the valley. "The rest of our forces should be here in a few days."

"How will the duchess get a message to you?"

Floris smiles. "Through you, of course. It is not as if we will be in hiding. You may come find us whenever you like." She turns her gaze to the people entering and leaving the city, a great number of whom are soldiers. "Whenever there are this many troops around, there are sure to be innocents who need to be protected." Her lip curls faintly in disgust. "You may be certain we will have plenty to keep us busy."

I bid them farewell and thank them for all their help. I cannot find the words to tell them it has been so much more than simply allowing me to travel with them. I feel as if they have opened my eyes to an entirely new way of being, of existing in a group, and it has given me much to think upon.

I have grown accustomed to their company and feel nearly naked without them as I turn Fortuna toward the city. Her hooves thud hollowly across the wooden bridge.

The city's gray stone walls stretch out as far as the eye can see, like a mother's arms keeping her children safe. Sentries and lookouts patrol the catwalks atop the walls, and guards stand at the gate itself. They are not stopping people going in or out, but their eyes are sharp as they scan the crowd for trouble.

As well they should, for there are people everywhere. In truth, I never imagined so many could live in one place behind one set of walls. Or that they would want to.

And Floris was right—the city appears to be overrun by soldiers. They outnumber the townspeople by five to one, at least. Most do not seem to be on duty but merely wander the streets in groups. There is a bored, restless air to the men that makes me wonder if the sentries should not train their sights on the inside of their walls rather than outside of them.

I pull my thoughts away from the soldiers and take in Rennes itself. It is large and far grander than Vannes, although I saw little enough of that town, and in the poorest of circumstances. These cobbled streets are lined with shops and brightly painted two- and three-story timbered houses. The spire of a grand cathedral rises from the middle of the city like a beacon.

My ogling draws the notice of others—well, that and my strange attire, for while I have thrown a skirt over my leggings, I am still dressed mostly in the manner of the Arduinnites. Three soldiers lounging near a smithy eye me, and I urge Fortuna down a different street before they can think to create mischief. While I would not mind fighting them, the whole place has the feel of a pile of kindling, and I do not wish to be a spark.

* * *

When I approach the sentry at the palace, he gives me a lazy grin that I meet with a cool smile. "I am here to see the abbess of Saint Mortain."

I enjoy it more than I should when the grin drops from his face and he stands up straighter. "Your name?"

"Tell her that Annith is here."

He nods curtly, motions a page over from the small cluster of boys who linger just inside the door, and gives him instructions. The page, a bright-eyed boy whose mischievous grin reminds me of Audri, makes a perfunctory bow, then hurries off into the interior of the castle. I am sent to the antechamber to cool my heels, and I try not to gawk and gape as if I have just rolled off the turnip cart.

Sister Beatriz told us often of the grandeur we would encounter when our duties brought us to the ducal court, but, as I have learned again and again these past weeks, there is a difference between hearing about something and experiencing it. Sister Beatriz was no poet, so her words did not come close to painting the true picture.

The antechamber alone is as big as our chapel and chapter house combined, and it is richly appointed, with bright, colorful tapestries that do much to absorb the chill that comes in through the main doors. The wood paneling is intricately carved, and I long to run my fingers over it to feel the rich texture of the wood.

But even more dizzying is the number of people in the room, which is equal to the population of a small village. Over a dozen sentries and men-at-arms, a handful of pages, and clusters of well-dressed citizens and even more elegantly dressed nobles mingle about. This is the only thing Sister Beatriz did a fair job of preparing us for — the finery these nobles wear, for their garments are as brightly decorated and elaborate as she told us they would be. I also notice that most of them stand with their heads together, absorbed in tense conversation. Have they already heard of the French attack on Vannes? Or is there some other news that has them nervous?

I see the page scampering back to us before the sentry does, his eyes wide, his brows raised. "Her ladyship says to send Annith along immediately. I am to escort her myself." He says this last bit with no small amount of pride.

The sentry casts a curious glance at me before nodding his head and ushering me on. I hurry to catch up to the page, who apparently does not believe in walking when scampering will do.

Now that I am actually seconds away from facing the abbess, my palms grow clammy. I marvel that I have faced—and survived—the dangers of the hellequin and the French, and yet it is the thought of this conversation that makes my hands sweat. I will not give in to this fear.

I have been blooded in my first battle, and my second and my third.

I have lived now in the real world, with all its mess and turmoil, all its wildness and all its beauty, and I can never unsee what I have seen, I can never unknow what I now know. More importantly, something deep inside me has awakened, and now that I have moved through the world fully aware, it is impossible to let myself be lulled back to sleep. Perhaps that is why the abbess held me back. Perhaps, for some reason I cannot even begin to fathom, she was afraid of this very thing.

After leading me down one main corridor, then another, the page comes to a stop in front of a thick oak door and raps smartly upon it. "It's the Lady Annith, your ladyship."

"Send her in." The abbess's voice is clear as a bell, even through the door.

"It's *Reverend Mother*," I whisper at him.

He frowns at me. "What?"

"A woman in her position is not called your ladyship, but Reverend Mother."

His cheeks flare pink for a moment. "Why didn't anybody tell me?" With a snort of disgust, he shakes his head and trots off down the hall. I take a deep breath, put my hand to the door, and go in.

The abbess is waiting for me in the chair behind her desk, sitting stiff and upright. Her face is pale, her nostrils pinched, the skin drawn tight across her fine features. Indeed, her barely checked fury has the weight and substance of a living thing. "Reverend Mother." I execute a precise curtsy.

She does not bother with the formalities. "What is the meaning of this, Annith? What are you doing here in Rennes?"

"I have come to inform you that Matelaine is dead."

The pinched anger in her face does not soften. There is no flicker of surprise or remorse or sorrow. "While I am sorry to hear that, there was no reason for you to bring the news yourself. A message would have sufficed. You are simply using this as an excuse to avoid a duty you do not wish to perform."

The memory of Matelaine and her cold, still body lying on the hard wooden planks of the bone cart rises up, twisting my heart until it bleeds anew. My hands clench into fists and I shove them into my skirt so she will not see. "No. A simple message would *not* have sufficed, for I wanted to look you in the face when I accused you of being responsible for her death. It is because of your negligence and stubbornness that she is dead."

A gasp escapes her lips—one sharp intake of breath that lets me know my words have reached her. "What do you mean?"

As the raw wound of Matelaine's death reopens, all the hot, bitter pain comes flowing out. "You sent her out before she was ready. You knew it was too soon; Sister Thomine warned you. I warned you, but still you sent—"

"Silence!" Her voice cuts through my words like a knife. She places both hands flat on the desk and pushes herself to her feet. "How dare you? How dare you come in here screeching like a fishwife, berating me!"

I take a step toward the desk, enjoying the way her eyes widen in surprise. "I dare because Matelaine cannot do it herself. You have betrayed her, betrayed the sanctuary and trust between the convent and its novitiates, and I would know the reason why."

"Trust! Let us speak of trust and how you have disobeyed me outright. You have left the convent and your duties without permission. Have you given no thought to the others whom your actions might place in jeopardy? Have you given any thought at all to leaving the convent with no one to See Mortain's will? It is I who accuse you of betraying my trust."

I dismiss her accusations with a curt wave of my hand. "I have no gift for Seeing and you know it. Why did you send Matelaine when she was not ready? What is the true reason you held me back?"

The abbess closes her eyes for a moment and takes a deep breath. When she opens them again, she is calmer, less angry. She smiles then, a coaxing, beatific smile. It feels as if she is casting out a sticky net, hoping to entrap me with her beguiling ways. But it is poisoned bait she offers —I recognize that now. "Dear Annith. While I admire your loyalty to those you care about, you must understand that as abbess, I have duties far above any one individual's safety or comfort. I must use all the resources available in the best way possible to ensure Mortain's will is done. You know that. It is just your disappointment and envy talking." Her voice is gentle, sympathetic even, and it wraps itself around me in an attempt to lull me back to sleep.

For a sharp, painful moment, I miss a world where everything made sense. "I *was* disappointed, envious even, but now that is only a small part of what I feel. By not sending me out when I should have gone, you have given me a role in Matelaine's death, and to atone for that, I will see you held accountable for your deeds."

She is the first to look away. She tries to hide it in a gesture—she casts her hand wide, as if in exasperation, but her eyes shift, and I know this small victory is mine. "Do you truly think I treat the novitiates any differently than abbesses throughout the centuries have? Do you think the Dragonette would have flinched from using what tools were at hand?"

"Your methods may be kinder, but what you have done is a betrayal all the same. At least with the Dragonette, we would not have been fooled by a false sense of kindness and regard. We were not tricked into believing she had our best interests at heart."

Except for me. I *had* been that stupid and blind, and even now, I still don't know if the Dragonette cared for me more than the others or hated me beyond reason.

The abbess's lips press flat and her pupils grow small, two small black pinpricks in orbs of blue silk. "Is this how you thank me for all those years of kindness to you? For all that I have done on your behalf?"

"I do not want your kindness if the cost is others' lives. Even if you are willing to pay such a price, I am not." And that is at the heart of it. The rottenness at the core of her fondness for me.

She holds her hand up, as if warding off a blow. "Enough. I do not have time to bring a wayward novitiate to heel. There are too many real problems that threaten to destroy the very fabric of our country and our faith. I have half a mind to strap you to a cart and have you hauled back to the convent." She is quiet a long moment and I wonder if she sees something in my face that makes her reconsider such an action. "But for now," she continues, "I will have you escorted to chambers, where you will remain until I come for you."

She steps from behind her desk and brushes past me. I wonder what she would do if I reached out and grabbed her sleeve and demanded she answer me. My hand twitches, but I cannot bring myself to do it.

She jerks open the door to call for a page.

"Where are Ismae and Sybella?" I ask.

At my question, she freezes, then slowly turns to face me. "Ismae is here, attending the duchess. Sybella . . . Sybella is out on an assignment. In fact, I must prepare you—it is possible she will not return. Even if she were to survive the task Mortain has set for her, her own death wish has been heavy upon her of late, and I cannot vouch for what she might be thinking."

A new wave of fury swells up within me, but before I can act on it, the page arrives. Ignoring me, she turns to him. "See that Lady Annith is given a chamber in the western wing, then tell the maids to arrange a bath." She turns back to me and rakes her searing gaze over me. "You reek of poorly tanned leather and wood smoke."

Chapter Twenty-Four

ALONE IN THE CHAMBER AND feeling as boneless as an eel, I lower myself onto one of the short stools.

I did it. I faced the abbess and called her to account. The very core of my being is a-tremble with the ramifications of that.

Ever since I was a child, I knew in my marrow that if I did not wish to be cast from the only home I had ever known—to lose the only small crumbs of affection I had ever received—then I had to do and be exactly what the nuns wished.

And now I have sent everything tumbling madly into disarray.

The knock on the door nearly causes my heart to fly out of my chest. Gripping my skirt in my fists, I stand up, raise my chin, and hope that the tangle of emotions I am feeling will not show on my face. "Come in."

It is only two maidservants bearing a copper tub. I leave them to fill it and go to stare out the window, their gentle prattle falling over me like a soft rain.

The abbess may well try and force me to return to the convent, silent and in disgrace, but I will not go back. Not like that. Indeed, I can see no way I can ever return to the convent, for the abbess will not let me return in victory, and I refuse to do so in defeat.

"Does my lady wish assistance with her bath?" It takes me a bewildered moment to focus on the maid's voice.

"No, thank you. I can tend to it myself." Once I am alone, I step out of my skirt, then remove the leather leggings I wore under it, wrinkling my nose. The abbess is right; I do reek.

I slip out of my shift, check to make sure the linen towel and small pot of soap are within reach, then lower myself into the steaming water. I try to quiet my mind, to simply be satisfied that I am here. I have made it to Rennes and presented my grievances to the abbess. Considering all the dangers and detours I have faced on this journey, I have achieved far more than I had ever hoped for.

I turn to the business of scrubbing away weeks' worth of travel. When I am done, I step out of the tub and reach for the linen towel. I am nearly dry when I realize the only clean gown I have to wear has been wadded up in my satchel for well over a month. I grimace at the idea of donning the wilted, wrinkled thing—especially having seen all the finery worn at court—but there is nothing for it. I cannot prance about in naught but a linen towel.

I have just slipped my one clean shift over my head and tugged it into place when there is a small commotion at the door. Expecting the abbess to come in and resume her earlier argument, I whirl around just as it is thrown open. It is not the abbess, but—

"Ismae!" My entire body lights up like a candle, and before I know what I am doing, I cross the room and throw my arms around her.

She takes a moment to shut the door behind her with her foot, then hugs me back. "It *is* you. The page kept insisting he had escorted someone named Annith, and I kept insisting he must be mistaken."

Keeping her hands firmly clasped on my arms, she pulls back to study me. She is the same Ismae, but different too. There is an ease to her face and manner, but a new sharpness as well. "I take it by your warm greeting you are not angry with me?"

"No!" I hug her once more, savoring the warm, solid feel of her in my arms, safe and alive and unharmed, then force myself to release her lest she think I have turned into a clinging vine. "Angry with you? Why ever would I be angry with you?"

"When you did not answer my last two letters, I thought perhaps the abbess had told you of how I had veered from the course she had set for me."

"But I answered the last letter I received from you. It was the one asking about lovers. Were there more after that?"

"Yes. Did you not receive the message I wrote begging you to tell me the antidote to Arduinna's snare?"

Her question punches me like a fist, for it could only mean that the abbess confiscated the letters. "No, but surely you know the antidote? It is one of your gifts!"

Ismae looks down at her hands as if she still cannot believe it. "I do now, but I did not know until it was nearly too late."

"Too late for what?"

"Oh! We have so very much to catch up on! But first, what are you doing here? How did you get here? And does the abbess know?"

I roll my eyes and grimace. "Oh, she knows. And is most upset, which is not unexpected. As for the rest, it is a long and complicated story."

She studies me a moment longer, then gives my arms a squeeze. "Go. Sit. I will see some refreshment is brought and you can tell me your long and complicated story."

"I would like that," I say. As Ismae goes to the door and gives instructions to someone outside, I take my gown from the satchel and pull it over my head. Ismae turns around just then and grimaces. "You cannot wear that. Not in that state." As she yanks the door open once more and calls to the servant to bring a fresh gown from her chamber as well as the refreshments, I marvel at the changes in her. Not just the physical changes, although those are marked, but the changes in her very manner, how she moves though the world and talks to others. The hesitant girl who was always waiting for permission and unsure of her station now has the bearing and confidence of one of our most experienced initiates. She is a full-fledged handmaiden of Death and living the life I have always imagined for myself. The joy I feel at seeing her once more dims slightly at my own uncertain future with the convent. "You've changed," I say when she returns from the door.

She smiles. "As have you." We both sit, and her polished demeanor falls away as she leans forward, her eyes wide and incredulous. "Did you truly leave the convent against the abbess's wishes?"

"I did. Oh, Ismae. There is so much to tell you of, and very little of it good. Matelaine"—my voice gets stuck in my throat and I can hardly get the words out—"Matelaine is dead." Much to my surprise, I feel tears form, tears I have not been able to shed since I saw the younger girl's body. I swipe at my cheek, needing to get the rest of it out. "The abbess refused to send me out, refused to even consider it, and instead sent Matelaine, and now she is dead."

"But she was only fifteen!"

"I said as much to the abbess, but she closed her ears to my arguments and instead told me I was to be the convent's seeress."

"But that makes no sense! You have not shown any talent for visions, not since I've known you. Not to mention you are the most skilled of all of us."

I decide to say nothing just yet of my youthful visions, as I do not know if they are important. "It does not make any sense. It is a betrayal of the covenant the convent makes with the novitiates—that they will be properly trained and prepared before being sent out, or else they are just fodder." I take a deep breath, relieved immeasurably to have shared all this with someone I trust. "And that is why I am here—to insist she face the tragedy her actions have caused and hold her to account before she starts sending even younger girls out, because clearly she will not send me." I look down at my hands, which are twisted in my lap.

Ismae shakes her head. "I have never understood why I was sent to the Breton court and you were not."

"Perhaps Mortain knew that your poison gifts would be needed?" I am not certain I believe that, but it cannot be discounted as a possibility.

Ismae nods slowly. "Perhaps."

"When you met with the abbess, just before you left, could you tell if it was she who made the decision? Or had Sister Vereda Seen you at court?"

She shrugs helplessly. "The abbess informed me of the assignment after Duval burst into her office and confronted her. Whether Sister Vereda had seen it before then or not, I do not know."

"Well, if it was Mortain's decision, it is hard to argue with, but I still cannot help but wonder why. Have I displeased Him in some way? Failed in my devotion or obedience?"

"I cannot imagine that you have."

"And yet the abbess choosing not to send me makes no more sense."

"She has always been exceptionally fond of you," Ismae points out.

I cannot help it—I snort. "Only because I excelled at my duties and was extremely biddable. And"—honesty compels me to admit— "because I think she felt sorry for me."

"Felt sorry for you? Why on earth would she?" The disbelief is clear in Ismae's voice, disbelief that anything in my sheltered life at the convent could have earned me someone's pity.

I rise to my feet and busy myself with trying to smooth the wrinkles out of my gown. She deserves an answer, but it is so very hard to speak of those memories, to share them with anyone, that I am nearly overcome by a need to flee the room. "The previous abbess—the one our current abbess replaced—singled me out for special . . . attention."

Ismae's eyes narrow in concern. "What sort of attention?"

A faint hum of panic skips along my limbs, making me feel as if I have said too much already. "It is of no importance—it was a long time ago. But tell me, what of Sybella? The abbess said she was out on a dangerous mission and that I must prepare myself for the possibility that she might not return."

Ismae's face darkens. She pushes to her feet and begins pacing. "Oh, Annith. The abbess has done most poorly by Sybella. She has sent her back to the very family that nearly destroyed her."

All the blood drains from my face, and I must grasp the bedpost to steady myself. Even now, I had not suspected such a gross betrayal. I had assumed there was some assignment for which Sybella's unique skills would prove useful. But this? To return her to the source of her madness before she has fully healed?

"And her family—it is even worse than we had imagined. Annith, she is Count d'Albret's own daughter."

"Count d'Albret! The one who nearly raped the duchess?"

Ismae nods. "The very same. And he has a much darker history than even the most vile rumors about him reveal. Duval never trusted the man, which is why he was so against the match. But now that we have heard from Sybella's own lips how Count d'Albret has treated his wives . . ." She shudders, then meets my gaze, her eyes stark and filled with horror. "He has killed them. All of them."

"How many have there been?" I whisper.

"Six. The duchess would have been the seventh."

My knees suddenly weak, I lower myself onto the bed behind me. To think of Sybella growing up in such a household, with murders being committed throughout her young life. It is truly a miracle that she was not warped and damaged beyond recovery.

It also makes the abbess's decision to send her back all the more heinous, and anger surges through me once more. "And that's where she is now?"

"Yes and no. Three months ago, when the duchess faced d'Albret and Marshal Rieux before Nantes, d'Albret planned a trap. It was only through the valiant efforts of her small guard that she was able to get to safety. One of those guards was the Beast of Waroch."

"I know of him. He is rumored to be the fiercest warrior our country has ever known. And wasn't it he who rallied the duke's forces and allowed us to win the Mad War?"

"Yes. Precisely. And with the duchess's marshal turning against her, she had few troops left to her. Beast's ability to raise and motivate fighting men became even more critical to our mission. Under pressure, the abbess agreed to arrange for Sybella to free him. He was so wounded that she had to accompany him to Rennes herself."

"Then where is she now?"

"Annith, the abbess tried to send her back to d'Albret's household yet again! Even knowing her role in aiding Beast had been discovered, the abbess was determined to send her back." Ismae looks away. "So I took matters into my own hands and told Beast what was going to happen." She smiles faintly. "Then he took matters into his."

"I don't understand. Why would he intervene on her behalf? Because she had rescued him from the prison."

An amused smile plays about Ismae's lips. "Not only that. He has developed a great — fondness — for her, one that she returns, for all that she has tried to deny it. So he diverted her from that mission and took her with him when he went to give aid to the British troops at Morlaix, thus keeping her away from the abbess."

Her expression grows stricken again. "But we received word from Beast last week. Sybella's sisters have been threatened if she does not return to the family. She and Beast have gone back to Nantes to get them out, but so far we have heard nothing else." She looks up at me, tears glinting in her eyes. "Oh, Annith. I am so afraid for her, so afraid of what this will cost her."

It is all I can do not to go hunt the abbess down, and strangle her with my own hands. "What can we do? Can we send someone to help?"

She shakes her head. "There is nothing we can do that will not put her in greater danger, so now we must wait and pray." She takes a deep breath, then sits on the stool across from me. "From the moment I was first sent out, nothing was as I had been prepared for. There was none of the black and white that the convent had used to paint the world for us. The people, the politics, the world itself, were much more nuanced, with who was right and who was wrong often simply a matter of where one stood.

"I still do not know if she purposefully withheld Duval's identity from me when she sent me to court or if she thought I knew who he was. And Chancellor Crunard? Well, he is no longer chancellor. He now sits in a prison cell in the bowels of the palace at Guérande. Chancellor Crunard, the abbess's liaison, had been feeding her false information for at least as far back as my first assignment, and possibly longer."

I suddenly remember the abbess's new habit of visiting the rookery to collect her own messages. Could that be why?

We are interrupted by a knock on the door, and two maids bustle in carrying trays of food, the smell causing my mouth to water as I realize just how long it's been since I've eaten. While they set the food down on a small table, a third maid comes in carrying a dark blue gown. "Where shall I put this, my lady?"

"On the bed for now," Ismae tells her, and once again I marvel at her composure and comportment.

When we are alone again, Ismae busies herself cutting bread from the loaf and slicing the cheese. She lifts her shoulders in an apologetic gesture. "So what you tell me does not surprise me. As I say, I have learned much here in the outside world, and very little of it makes me inclined to trust the abbess." She sets the knife down, as if she has just made a decision. "Annith, I have come face to face with Mortain. I have seen Him as clearly as I see you now, and He spoke with me."

Even as her words send me reeling, they also fill me with hope. Not wanting Ismae to see my tumultuous feelings, I stand and slip the gown the maid brought over my head. For years I had thought I was the only one of His daughters to have seen Him. Even though the vision might have been a childhood fancy, it still held out the alluring promise that I was the only one to whom He had shown Himself. But if others have seen Him, then that means my own vision does not consign me to the position of seeress. "What did He say?" I finally ask.

"That He loves us." Her voice is soft and full of wonder. "No matter how we serve Him, the depth of His love, the fullness of His grace, is far bigger than anything we can imagine. Or, apparently," she adds dryly, "the convent."

Ismae's words wrap themselves around my heart, reminding me of the god I serve and my love for Him. As if embarrassed by her own words, Ismae picks up her knife and returns to slicing the bread. "Do you know the nature of Matelaine's assignment?" she asks. "Maybe some answers lie there."

"I was not able to overhear that part of it. All I know is that her target was in Guérande."

"Guérande?" Ismae looks up sharply. "When was she sent out?"

"At the end of January."

Abandoning the bread, Ismae begins pacing, stroking her chin while she thinks — a gesture I have never seen her use before. "That makes no sense," she says, stopping in front of the window. "By that time, the duchess and her party had left the city to go appeal to Marshal Rieux and Count d'Albret in Nantes and try and heal their break from her. The only person of any import left in the city was Chancellor Crunard, and surely he would have told her that — Oh!" Her head snaps up and she looks at me. "Chancellor Crunard."

"If, as you suggested earlier, he was feeding the convent false information, mayhap that was why Matelaine was sent to him. But, Ismae, I am not convinced that Matelaine's assignment was ordered by Mortain."

"What do you mean?"

"I mean that Sister Vereda had been too ill to See anything of true import for weeks."

"So you think the abbess ordered it of her own volition?"

"I fear so, yes. And from what you have told me, it makes even more sense now, for surely the abbess would want to punish someone who betrayed her."

"Or else she wished to silence him so he could not reveal the depth of her involvement with him and his politics."

Ismae's words cut through me with the force of a spear, for I had not thought about such a large-scale betrayal on the part of the abbess — I had thought only of how she had betrayed her sacred duty to her charges. But this, this would go against the very principles of her office. I shake my head, as if I can dislodge the thought. "No," I whisper. "That cannot be. She would not betray Mortain Himself."

"Mayhap it does not sound so far-fetched to me because I do not know her as well as you do. However, I have learned much from Duval on how to look at people unencumbered by our feelings for them. These are naught but the same suspicions I would have of anyone in her position." Ismae's mouth twists in a wry smile.

"And rightly so," I say, even though my heart is not in the words. I have known the abbess too long, known her when she was simply Sister Etienne, the nun who was kinder to me than most. She was one of the few decent people who inhabited my childhood; I am not sure if I can bear for her to turn into a true villain. Misguided, yes. Blinded by some emotion, yes. But to knowingly betray Mortain Himself? Unthinkable.

Sensing my distress, Ismae changes the subject. "But more importantly," she says, "in the short term, we must try to anticipate her next move and do whatever we can to block it."

"She will no doubt send me back to the convent, although I do not intend to go willingly."

Ismae cocks her head, her eyes twinkling. "You would make her tie you to a cart?"

Unsmiling, I look up and meet her gaze. "I would."

The twinkle fades from her eyes, and her lips purse slightly. "You have changed," she says at last. "Far more than I would have guessed."

While I do not know if she means her words as a compliment, I find that they please me all the same. "I have."

"Well." She pushes away from the window and comes to finish lacing up my gown for me. "We shall simply have to see to it that she does not send you packing."

"How can we stop her?"

The grin that lights up Ismae's face is full of cheerful disobedience. "I have been at court for months and serve as close attendant to the duchess. I have connections of my own now." She gives one final tug upon the laces, then ties them off. "Do not worry. We will get to the bottom of this. For now, you should rest. Or go explore the palace, if you'd rather."

"Thank you, I may do that."

She gives me a quick kiss on the cheek, then hurries from the room.

I wish I could find the same confidence she has gotten hold of, for in truth, I cannot imagine what she plans will be so easy.

Aware of the exhaustion coursing through my limbs, I stretch out on the bed and try to get some much needed rest, but my mind is too full of all the possible disastrous futures that lie before me. Unbidden, my thoughts turn to Balthazaar and I am appalled to realize I miss him. No—I do not miss him. Or if I do, it is only in the same way I miss not having Sister Thomine handy for sparring practice. I enjoyed our banter. When I was with him, I did not have even the slightest inclination to mince my words or pretend to be something I was not, and that is incredibly freeing. *That* is what I enjoy. Nothing more.

With a sigh of frustration, I get up from the bed and begin pacing in front of the dwindling fire. It does nothing to lessen my restlessness. Now that I have experienced the sweet taste of rebellion, it chafes me to sit here in my chambers doing precisely what the abbess ordered me to.

I do not *want* to obey her orders anymore—not even in the simplest of ways. If she told me to leap out of the path of a rushing cart, I would be tempted to stay rooted to the spot, simply to defy her. No matter how exhausted I am, I cannot sit quietly in my room simply because she has ordered it. I grab my cloak, wrap it around my shoulders, and slip from the room.

Chapter Twenty-Five

I ACCOST THE FIRST SENTRY I find and ask if the palace has a chapel.

"The new chapel is in the north wing. If you follow this hallway—"

"You said *new* chapel. Does that mean there is an old one as well?" An older chapel is far more likely to honor the Nine.

The guard squints at me as if puzzled by my question. "Well, yes, my lady, but hardly anyone uses it anymore. And the new chapel is every bit as fine as the cathedral in town."

I bow my head. "That may be true, but I am convent-raised and prefer to do my praying in more humble surroundings."

He looks almost put out, as if I have somehow insulted him by de-clining to view his fine new chapel. However, in the end, he gives me the directions I seek, if a bit reluctantly.

The moment I step through the chapel doors, I can feel how very old it is. Close upon the sense of the chapel's age comes the peace I have been hoping for. It descends upon me like gently falling snow, soft and cool, and I wish to roll in it in sheer gratitude. I know that when I look, I will find the nine niches just below the altar, because it is ever thus —when I am in Mortain's presence, I find a peace and contentment I can find nowhere else.

The chapel is dimly lit by a handful of candles and much of the room is in shadow, but I appear to be the only one here. Moving forward, I sink gratefully onto one of the kneeling benches. My gaze goes immediately to the first niche, and I am pleased to find the small carving of Death residing there. But I am distracted by a small lump in the third recess, Arduinna's niche. It is a small loaf or cake of some sort. The Arduinnites were correct — someone has made an offering, calling upon Arduinna's protection here in Rennes. The duchess? Or perhaps it is some poor beleaguered maid who is beset by unwanted suitors.

I will puzzle that out later. For now, I allow myself to close my eyes. Before even a whisper of prayer can pass my lips, a vision of poor Matelaine's face fills my mind. The sorrow and outrage I feel anew is like a kick to my chest.

It may have been my selfish desire to lead my own life that propelled me from the convent, but Matelaine's fate has taken this far beyond my own differences and disagreements with the abbess and turned it into something far more serious.

I do not have a specific prayer I wish to recite to Mortain. I never do. It has always been my custom to simply open my heart to Him so He may see and know all that I am feeling — the good along with the bad, my grand thoughts as well as my small ones. I do that now, and peace washes through me, clearing me of my doubts and renewing my sense of purpose.

For all that I am physically strong and skilled, I have always doubted my own heart. How could I not? It is what the nuns trained us to do, part of the way they broke down our will so they could sort through the pieces like a broken jug and reshape it to their own needs. All of us have let them — but me more than most. Indeed, once I realized what they were attempting to do, I wrenched the task from their hands and set about it myself — all in my desire to be the best novitiate who had ever walked those halls.

That desire now seems a shallow one, something that I have been taught to want rather than something that sprang from my own heart.

196

MORTAL HEART

I now realize I do not even know what it is that my own heart yearns for. Once that would have terrified me—to be so formless and shapeless—but now I find it freeing. I have removed the convent's chosen desire from my heart, like plucking a long-embedded splinter from my flesh. I have rejected the path they told me Mortain wants of me. Instead of fear, I feel . . . hunger. Hunger to fill my heart once again, but this time with what I want. I now recognize that my wants are not selfish simply because they are mine. Indeed, many of my wants are worthy ones, even noble: justice for Matelaine, safety for the other girls, honesty from the abbess, and to restore the integrity of the convent.

Ismae has managed to forge her own path between the convent and her duty to Mortain. No, not duty, but devotion, for she serves Him now with much more than simple duty. It gives me great hope that I may be able to find such a path for myself.

Thus encouraged, I murmur my gratitude to Mortain and rise to my feet. As I straighten my skirt, I hear a faint rustling off to my right. Startled, I whirl around and peer into the flickering shadows. A man stirs. Was he there all along? Or did he come in while I was deep in prayer?

He crosses himself and rises creakily to his feet. He wears a humble brown robe and a hempen rope at his waist with the nine wooden beads that mark him as a follower of the old saints. He is shorter than I. His hair is fluffy and white and dances about his head like a halo in the warm candlelight. He brings his hands together in front of his chest and bows his head in my direction. "Greetings, daughter. I did not mean to startle you."

"I was not startled."

The glimmer of amusement in his blue eyes gives me to believe he recognizes my small lie for what it is.

"You were completely lost in prayer," he murmurs. "I could not bring myself to interrupt."

For some reason I feel awkward and tongue-tied in his presence, although I cannot name why and it seems a most ridiculous reaction. It is not as if he could discern my thoughts and prayers. "It matters not, Father—"

"Effram. I am Father Effram." He takes a step toward me. "Have you a heavy heart, child?"

I sense curiosity rather than concern in his question. "No, Father. I pray so that I may better understand my own thoughts."

His face breaks into a smile, as if my answer has pleased him greatly. I wonder if that means he will try to tell me what he thinks my thoughts should be, and I think better of him when he does not. He continues to smile, letting the silence grow, and I cannot tell if it is meant to be a comfortable silence or an awkward one he thinks I will try to fill. If it's the latter, he will lose at that game, for I have had far too much practice at it.

In the end, he is the first to speak. "I've never seen one of Arduinna's followers dressed so . . . elegantly," he says.

I stare blankly at him for a moment before understanding dawns. "Oh, but I'm not one of Arduinna's followers!"

His white eyebrows draw together in puzzlement. "You aren't? My mistake, then."

But my curiosity it piqued. "Why did you think that I was?"

His eyes flicker to the small offering in the niche.

"I did not leave that," I hasten to assure him.

"I know. I thought perhaps you'd come in answer to it. You have the look of one of Arduinna's. A certain ferocity of expression."

Well, I am feeling fierce enough, I suppose. "I do not serve Arduinna. I serve Mortain."

He grows very still, his head tilted to the side, studying me even more intently, if that is possible. "Do you, now?" he mutters. "Well, that is truly interesting." He smiles once more, puts his hands together, bows again, then takes his leave.

Once he has left, I sneak a furtive sniff at my arm, just to be certain the scents of wood smoke and poorly tanned leather do not cling to me still.

Chapter Twenty-Six

THE NEXT DAY, DRESSED IN another one of Ismae's gowns, I am taken to the solar to meet the duchess. I have not seen the abbess since my arrival, and have done nothing but explore the palace and talk with Ismae. A part of me itches with impatience, while another part of me has always known any challenge to the abbess would be as long and slow and drawn-out as a protracted game of chess.

But this morning, my stomach is in knots over my meeting with the duchess, for in truth, I deserve no such honor. I half fear the abbess will have already informed her of all my transgressions and laid a pall of disgrace over me.

The young page who has led me to the duchess's quarters tells the sentry at the door who I am, then tears off down the hall to whatever duty awaits him next.

When I enter the solar, it is every bit as grand as I have been led to believe, and I am pleased that I do not stare and point like a small child. Carved oak paneling with thick velvet drapes and elaborate tapestries decorate the wall. Clear, mullioned windows sparkle in the morning sun, filling the room with cheerful light. But it is the ladies in waiting who draw my full attention, for they are not sitting at their embroidery but instead are clustered together, their heads bowed in concern. At my approach, they all look up. One of them gives me a halfhearted smile. "The duchess is not available right now," she tells me.

I frown in puzzlement. "My apologies. I thought the page said that she'd sent for me."

One of them looks me over with open curiosity. "Are you called Annith?" A woman gives her a quelling look. "What? She did say that if the Lady Annith arrived, we were to show her into the young princess's chambers."

By the poisonous looks the others are giving her, I am guessing that this sign of favor makes them uneasy. "Thank you," I say pointedly. "I look forward to serving both the duchess and the princess in any way I can."

"This way," the helpful one says, then leads me toward a door that opens off the main room. "Ignore the others," she whispers. "They are merely out of sorts because they have nothing they can offer to help."

"To help with what?" I ask.

The girl's face settles into sadness. "The princess Isabeau. She has taken a turn for the worse, I'm afraid, and even Ismae's famous tinctures are not helping." When we reach the door, she raps once, then calls out, "Lady Annith is here, Your Grace." She smiles at me, then returns to the group of waiting women.

The door opens and I find myself staring down at a small young woman, younger even than Matelaine was. She has intelligent brown eyes, rich sable-colored hair, and a high wide brow that is at the moment creased in worry. With a start, I realize that I am staring at the duchess herself. I sink into a low curtsy. "Your Grace," I murmur.

"Lady Annith." She offers her hand for me to kiss, which I do, then she bids me rise. "I am glad to make your acquaintance, especially after all that Ismae has told me, although I am sorry to have to do it in this way."

I glance over to where Ismae sits by the bed, then back at the duchess. "And what way is that, Your Grace?"

"I'm afraid I have invited you here for the most selfish of reasons. My young sister is gravely ill, and Ismae thought you might have some new ideas on cures to try. She said you successfully nursed one of the elder nuns at your convent." The desperate hope shining in her face nearly breaks my heart, for such desperation exists only when the outcome appears truly bleak.

"But of course, Your Grace. I am happy to offer any aid or comfort I can, although I think you will find Ismae is as much a master of tinctures and simples as anyone."

"Maybe so," she says. "But she also said you have sleeves full of tricks and charms to keep young children entertained, and those talents would be most welcome as well."

A part of me wants to laugh. Here I am, at the right hand of the ruler of all Brittany, free of the convent's walls at last, and it is my ability to charm young children that she is most interested in.

As she leads me to the bed where her sister and Ismae are, I try to reconcile this poised woman in front of me with the picture of the thirteen-year-old duchess I have carried in my head for so long. This girl is no child. She is unlike any thirteen-year-old I have ever known, although in truth, the thirteen-year-olds I have known are nothing like normal girls, either peasants or nobles. They—*we*—cannot be. We are not trained for normal—we are trained to be assassins and spies and rulers of kingdoms. To serve our god and serve our country with every shred of skill and intelligence we possess. There is little time for childhood in lives such as ours. With a sharp pang in my heart, I recognize that this is wrong somehow—that too much is asked of those we demand such sacrifices from.

The duchess reaches the bed, and Ismae stands up to make room for her. "Isabeau? Are you awake? There is someone here I think you would like to meet."

The pale girl lying on the bed *is* a child, but it is easy to see that her illness has robbed her of much of her childhood. Her face lights up at the duchess's words and her eyes move in my direction, the excitement in them dimming somewhat when she sees me.

I curtsy deeply and give her my warmest smile, the one I use to coax Loisse out of the sulks. "Hello, Princess."

Before the duchess can continue the introduction, the princess asks, "Did Arduinna send you?"

I blink in surprise. "No." As her hopeful expression disappears altogether, I wonder if I may have found the person responsible for the offering in the chapel. Although how she could have gotten it down there in her state is a mystery. "I serve at the convent of Saint Mortain, like Ismae," I tell her, but that does not revive her interest.

She turns to her sister. "I am tired," she whispers.

The duchess leans over and smoothes a stray hair from the child's brow. "I know, dear heart. Sleep now, and we will play more later."

She gives a faint nod, and her eyes flutter closed. The three of us slip quietly from the room, and the duchess herself closes the door, careful to leave it open just a crack.

"What is the nature of her illness?" I ask.

"She has been beset with lung fever since she was young. It comes and goes in bouts, sometimes severe. It has been getting worse these past few months, and there is little that brings her relief." When the duchess looks away to compose herself, I glance over at Ismae. She gives a brief shake of her head. The young princess is dying, albeit slowly.

"I will think back on all that we did for Sister Vereda," I assure both of them. "And see if there is anything Ismae has not yet tried. If nothing else, I should have some stories and games I can entertain her with."

"Any of that would be most appreciated, demoiselle."

Isabeau's question if I was sent by Arduinna reminds me of the message I bear. "Your Grace, I traveled to Rennes among a group of the followers of Arduinna. They asked that I bring you a message from them."

She blinks in surprise, then looks at Ismae, who shrugs in ignorance. "I would be pleased to hear it."

"They wanted you to know that they have responded to your summons and are here in the city, ready to offer you whatever support they can."

The duchess frowns. "But I have not summoned them. In truth, I did not know that I *could* summon them."

"I do not think they came as subjects to a ruler, or even as a religious order, but because a sacred offering was made asking Arduinna's help."

The duchess looks at Ismae. "Did you make such an offering?"

Ismae shakes her head. "No."

"Nor have I," says the duchess.

I look back toward the sleeping Isabeau. Now I am nearly certain it is the young princess who has requested Arduinna's aid, although I do not wish to expose her secret just yet. At least, not until I better understand what is going on here. "Either way, they have much to offer. While their numbers are not great, one hundred or so at the outside, they are strong and fierce warriors with a special fondness for the innocent. Perhaps there is some service they can perform for you."

"I am sure there is, or will be soon enough. I am not in a position to turn down even the smallest offer of help at this point."

In the quiet that follows, the sound of rapidly approaching footsteps thuds in the hallway beyond, just before a sharp knock on the solar door. Ismae and I exchange a glance. "Is it the abbess?" I murmur.

She shrugs. "Mayhap. If so, let me be the one to talk."

For a brief moment I am dizzy with how completely our positions have changed. In the past, Ismae always insisted that I be the one to run interference with the abbess, and now she is doing so for me.

One of the ladies in waiting goes to open the door, and relief flutters in my belly. Not the abbess, but a nobleman. He is tall and broad of shoulder with gray eyes that glow with intelligence and . . . glee? The glee has so transformed his face that it takes me a moment to recognize him as the man Ismae left with all those months ago.

"Duval?" Ismae takes a step toward him. "Is everything all right?"

He gives a vague nod of greeting—or perhaps it is an apology for interrupting. "Beast and Sybella have returned. They have just arrived in the courtyard."

Only the decorum of the duchess's chamber keeps Ismae from emitting a joyous whoop. The duchess clasps her hands together and closes her eyes, as if in brief prayer. "Praise God and His Nine saints," she whispers.

"If you will excuse us, Your Grace?" Duval asks.

She quickly waves us away. "Of course. And hurry back, for I want a full report!"

"Come!" Ismae reaches out to grab my arm as she follows Duval out of the chamber.

As we rush through the hallway, I cannot imagine three less dignified-looking individuals. It is clear Duval wishes to break into a run, and Ismae and I have both hiked up our skirts so that we may keep up with him. He checks himself slightly so that when we reach the exit, at least we do not gallop out the door.

Once outside in the courtyard, I see no sign of Sybella. The yard is a-bustle with ostlers and grooms and footmen making ready to unload a cart holding a passel of charcoal-burners and their children. A groom is talking to one of the charcoal-burners on horseback. Considering the horseman's size and bulk, I am surprised the sentries have allowed him to pass through the gate. He is at least a head taller than most of the guards and half again as broad in the shoulder. His face is battered and scarred. Indeed, he looks like one of the ancient, weathered standing stones come to life.

I hang back, but Ismae keeps running forward, and one of the mounted charbonnerie—a woman—leaps off her horse. She is dressed in a drab gown somewhere between brown and gray, and her hair is caught up in a linen coif. Even with the charcoal smudged on her face, she is beautiful—it is Sybella!

The fear that has been gnawing at my heart since the moment I heard of her whereabouts leaves my body with such a sickening rush that I must pause and take a deep breath to steady myself.

Ismae throws her arms around Sybella, and I am surprised at the ferocity with which Sybella returns the hug. I have never known her to be free with affectionate gestures. Of a sudden, I feel shy around her, around both of them, for they have changed so much, and I feel as if I have been left behind to calcify and harden like a barnacle on the hull of one of the convent's boats.

When Ismae turns and motions me forward, Sybella's eyes widen in recognition, her entire manner shifting like quicksilver. Her face grows white, making her dark eyes stark in her lovely face. She strides toward me, grasps my shoulders, and gives me a little shake. "Why are you here?"

A thick knot rises up in my throat, choking back my joyous greeting. "It is a long story," I finally manage to get out. "One I would rather not share in the courtyard in front of a score of people."

She studies me closely, the fierce look still on her face. "Did the abbess order you here?"

"Saints, no! I have traveled here on my own, and she is much angered by it."

Sybella's entire body relaxes, and then she smiles and throws her arms around me in a hug that near cracks my ribs. "Good. Although it does not matter—even if she had called you here, the reason for the assignment no longer exists."

"It is done?" Ismae asks.

A dark, triumphant smile twists Sybella's shapely mouth, accompanied by a shadow of pain. "It is done."

I look from one to the other, and suddenly it is as if no time at all has passed and they are sharing some worldly knowledge or joke that I cannot fathom. Sybella turns to me. "Count d'Albret, traitor to the duchy, is dead. Or as good as." No hint of the hand she may have played in his death or the full implications of that shows on her face. "Now we must make arrangements for my sisters, for the journey was not an easy one and Louise in particular is in poor health."

Ismae studies the two younger girls in the wagon, her lips pursed in thought. "The palace is growing more crowded every day as more and more Breton barons rally to the duchess's side. We may end up needing to share a room at some point, so I think your sisters would be safest at the Brigantian convent. In truth, young Isabeau should have been moved there as well, but the duchess cannot bear to be parted from her side."

"That will be fine. They would probably be most at ease there, anyway. And Tephanie will stay with them."

Ismae blinks and I am selfishly pleased that one of Sybella's revelations has managed to surprise her, as I am tired of being the only one reeling in shock. "Tephanie?"

"A dear and loyal friend who has attached herself to my sisters."

I find the idea that Sybella has found a dear and loyal friend almost as hard to believe as the idea that she has sisters, but Ismae is not daunted. "Good." Ismae motions one of the numerous pages over and sends him with a message to the Brigantian convent.

Once he has scampered away, Sybella asks, "How *is* Isabeau?"

Ismae closes her eyes briefly and shakes her head. "Not good. Between my own small knowledge and the sisters of Brigantia, everything is being done, but it is not anywhere near enough. Even so, I'm sure she will be glad of some younger girls for company, so your sisters may visit whenever you wish them to."

I feel as if I have stepped onto the shores of some mysterious foreign land where everything is unfamiliar. As if fate wishes to make this even more apparent, the nobleman Duval approaches with the lumbering standing stone of a charbonnerie beside him. He must easily be the ugliest man I have ever seen. He is as tall as a tree, and twice as wide, with muscles that look like boulders. His nose looks like a mashed turnip, and his eyes gleam in a disturbingly feral manner. Much to my surprise, Ismae—who has only ever viewed men as targets for her assassin skills —turns and throws her arms around him. *Merde.* I have never seen such hugging from these two.

"Thank you," she says fiercely. When she pulls back, Sybella is staring at her with narrowed eyes. "Did you put him up to that . . . stunt?" But there is little heat in her words.

Ismae steps away from the man and shrugs. "I told him what you had been assigned to do and that you were leaving—that is all."

Sybella opens her mouth to say something, but Ismae ignores her and decides to pull out her manners like a long-forgotten handkerchief. "Annith, allow me to present to you Sir Benebic de Waroch, otherwise known as Beast. You may have heard of his exploits."

"I believe I have," I say as I drop a curtsy. "It is an honor, Sir Waroch."

"Beast." His deep voice rumbles across the space between us. Then he surprises me by taking my hand and bowing as prettily as any courtier. "The honor is all mine, my lady."

Ismae puts her hand on my shoulder and turns me slightly toward the other nobleman. "And this is Lord Gavriel Duval, half brother to the duchess and one of her closest advisors."

"And Ismae's lover." Sybella's whisper in my ear just as I sink into a curtsy causes my head to snap up. So that is why she wrote to me asking whether or not the convent allowed initiates to have lovers.

"This is Annith," Ismae continues. "One of Sybella's and my sisters from the convent."

"Good," Duval says with a firm nod. "We can always use another assassin as this hornets' nest thickens."

I am warmed by his quick easy acceptance of me as well as by his obvious pleasure at having another assassin at court. I will need to gather as much support as possible to avoid being summarily sent packing by the abbess.

A small tempest erupts behind me. It is not movement or even noise —it is more as if a windstorm of violent displeasure has arrived. I am not at all surprised when I turn around and see the abbess. Her face is bone-white and her brows drawn down into two furious slashes. "Sybella."

Sybella's face goes eerily still, then she slowly turns to the other woman. "Reverend Mother." Her voice is as flat as a blade of trampled grass.

The abbess waits for a moment, expecting Sybella to come to her. When Sybella does not, the abbess's jaw twitches, but she lifts her skirts and descends the stairs so that whatever she is about to say will not be heard by the entire courtyard full of people. It does not work, however, for all of them can sense the storm brewing in their midst, and they all stop to watch.

Her eyes are as frigid as ice. "You disobeyed me?" Her voice is terrible in its softness, as if she has slipped velvet over a hammer just before she intends to use it.

Keeping her gaze fixed on the abbess's, Sybella grips either side of her shabby gown and dips into a perfect, reverent curtsy. When she rises, she lifts her chin, ever so slightly. "Count d'Albret is dead. My duty to the convent is fulfilled, and I will no longer serve you."

I gasp; I cannot help it. Beside me, Ismae stiffens, but the abbess does not so much as blink. Indeed, I think I discern a small glint of triumph in her gaze. "You no longer wish to serve as Death's handmaiden, then? You no longer wish to be a daughter of Mortain?"

"Oh, I am His daughter, and I plan to serve Him all the rest of my days. I simply do not need you or the convent in order to do so." And with that, she loops one of her arms through Ismae's and the other one through my own and pulls us away from the abbess. I can feel the roar of victory thrumming through her as she leads us toward the palace door.

Chapter Twenty-Seven

ONCE WE ARE INSIDE, Ismae leads us toward a different part of the palace than I have been in before. She stops in the hall to order a servant to have a bath prepared in the room. As the maid hurries away, Sybella gives me a sly, knowing smile. "Has she told you of her lover?"

I spear Ismae with an accusing look. "No, she has not."

Greatly discomfited, Ismae blushes and glances around to see if anyone overheard, but we are alone. "He is *not* my lover."

Sybella raises one perfectly arched eyebrow. "So, you have not lain with him and —"

"He is my betrothed."

Sybella and I both stop walking, our linked arms forcing Ismae to stop as well. "Your what?" I ask at the same time that Sybella says, "Praise the Nine! He's convinced you, then?"

"Shh!" Ismae glances around once more, then lengthens her stride, pulling us along behind her like a farmer dragging stubborn sheep to market. Finally, she reaches for one of the closed doors, opens it, and fair shoves us inside. "Yes." She blows out a breath. "He's convinced me. We've agreed that if — when — the duchess has this French threat well behind her, we will marry."

So many questions crowd my tongue that they become entangled and all I can manage is a sputtered "You? Married?" I cannot believe this of Ismae, Ismae who hated men so much that it was the very promise of killing them that had her embracing her role at the convent.

She turns to me. "I told you we have much to catch up on."

"But wait." I put my hand on her arm. "Aren't you already married? I mean, to the pig farmer?"

"No. The abbess had that annulled my first year at the convent."

"B-but . . ." I still cannot wrap my mind around this. "You said you would never—"

Ismae huffs out a sigh. "You do not need to remind me what I said. I have had plenty of occasions to eat those words."

"But what of your other concerns?" Sybella asks quietly as she begins unwinding the linen coif from her head. "Your worry of giving someone so much power over you?"

Ismae crosses to the fireplace, takes up the poker leaning against the wall, and stirs the embers to life. "I trust him," she says. "It is that simple."

Sybella barks out a laugh, but it is not as sharp as it once would have been. "Trust is never simple."

"Do you trust Beast?"

Sybella pauses in her undressing. "With my life," she says.

Ismae had warned me, but seeing Sybella's face soften with love as she speaks of Beast drives home the force of her feelings for him in a visceral way.

Ismae glances at me in sorrow and then looks down. "I am sorry, but like Sybella, I cannot in good conscience serve the convent any longer. Not after what the abbess has put her through, and not after what you have told me. I will continue to serve Mortain all the rest of my days, but I am not beholden to the convent, only to my god and myself."

"As His mercy," Sybella murmurs.

Ismae's head snaps up. "What did you say?"

Sybella looks over to meet her gaze. "You will serve as His mercy, and I His justice. Those are the roles He has chosen for us."

"How do you know this?"

Sybella shrugs. "I too came face to face with our Father, and it was exactly as you said. He loves us with a love beyond our imagining, a love of such acceptance and grace that nothing we do—not even turning away from Him—can destroy it."

The world tilts dizzily as I am assailed by an entire host of conflicting emotions. Joy, that Sybella has clearly found such peace and happiness. Relief, that yet another one of His handmaidens has seen Him, thus removing the possible significance of my own brief sighting years ago. But I am also filled with a nearly unbearable sense of loss. My seeing Him is no longer a sign of any uniqueness on my part. Not only that, but my two friends have been given roles as His instruments here on earth, whereas I have yet to receive a single order from Him.

The knock at the door pulls me from my self-pity, and a bevy of maidservants enter, carrying a tub and kettles full of steaming water. As they bustle about their duties, I turn my mind to the puzzle of the convent. It is a relief to see that Ismae and Sybella are plagued by the same doubts and concerns that I have, but they are willing to walk away from it. I do not see how I can abandon Florette and Lisabet and Aveline and Loisse to the abbess's machinations. Besides, Ismae and Sybella each have something—*someone*—to walk to.

A sudden pang of loss twists sharply in my side, and an image of Balthazaar's dark, brooding eyes fills my mind. I should not miss him so. Not only is he likely hunting me, but his long penance hints at crimes too terrible to speak of. He is a creature of the Underworld, trapped on his path to redemption for who knows how long. There is no future for us, and even the present puts me in jeopardy. And yet I do miss him. He fits so comfortably into the contours of my own silences and doubts.

When the tub is finally full, Ismae dismisses the maids and the room is once again silent. She turns to Sybella. "Enough of such small talk. I want to know how your mission went."

A cloud passes over Sybella's face, then she slips her arms out of her gown and lets it fall to the floor. She pulls her shift over her head then walks to the tub. I marvel at how easily she moves in her nakedness; she always has.

"Tell us," Ismae says once she has settled in the water.

Sybella's eyes grow bleak and she busies herself with the soap and sponge. "It is done," she says. "Count d'Albret is as good as dead— would be dead, but Mortain Himself refused to accept him into the Underworld, a promise He made to my mother and others whom d'Albret has killed. D'Albret's black soul has been sundered from his body, which will wither and rot like a corpse for Mortain Himself only knows how long. So the duchess is safe from him."

"And you?"

I do not understand the gentleness in Ismae's voice, for Sybella has never been squeamish and I cannot imagine why she would be racked with regret. But Sybella's smile looks so fragile that I fear she might shatter.

"I will be fine. I got to my sisters in time, so they are safe. But Pierre is still alive and will no doubt take up the d'Albret mantle."

Ismae frowns in puzzlement. "I thought Julian was the next eldest?"

"He was, but he too is dead." For a moment, she looks like the old Sybella, brittle and damaged, but then her face settles into a determined look. "However, the d'Albret plans will not stop with their death. They have been negotiating with the French camped but a few leagues from Nantes for some time. I do not know the full extent of their plans, but if they are allying themselves with the French in any way, it cannot be good for the duchess."

Ismae purses her lips in thought while Sybella dunks her head under the water to rinse the soap from her hair. "Could they simply have been playing both sides against the middle, or perhaps using false promises to hold the French at bay?"

"Anything is possible, but we should prepare for the worst just the same. Now, enough talk of my grim duty. I want to hear of Annith's adventures and how she comes to be in Rennes in spite of the abbess's wishes." She rises up out of the water, reaches for the linen towel, and begins to dry herself off.

And so I find myself telling my story for Sybella while she dresses. By the time I am done, she is smiling at me with pride, as if she herself had been responsible for my daring. Which—I realize with a jolt of understanding—she partially is. In giving me love, Ismae and Sybella have given me strength.

"And what did our fair abbess say when she found you here, under her very nose?"

"She was as furious as you'd expect, but it seemed that there was more than just anger there. I want to say fear, except that emotion is not one I would ever ascribe to her."

"Nor I." Ismae gives a firm shake of her head. "But when I told her of my meeting with Mortain, told her that I believe the convent, at least some of the time, misunderstands His wishes, she grew furious with me, and I too thought there was fear lying at the heart of it."

"What?" I stare at her in alarm. "The convent misunderstands Mortain's will? Why do you think such a thing?"

Her gaze softens. "After seeing so very much death in this world, death not directed by the convent, I have come to learn that everyone who dies bears His marque, and that the marque alone does not indicate that someone must die at one of our hands. Every man who died on the field in front of Nantes bore a marque, and of a certainty, I was not meant to kill them all."

Her words strike the very breath from my lungs and all I can do is stare at her as my mind struggles to make sense of this, to find a way to make it fit in with the precepts that I hold so dear. "Maybe that is why the seeress is so important?" I finally suggest. "Because that is the only way to tell which of those marqued are meant to die at the convent's command?"

"That is what I had hoped as well, but I received orders after you informed me that Sister Vereda had fallen ill, and if those orders did not come from one of her visions, then whose visions did they come from? Yours?"

I shake my head. "It was not mine, for I have not yet Seen a thing. Certainly nothing I would be willing to stake a man's life upon."

There is another knock on the door—in truth, there is no end to the comings and goings here at court. Ismae hurries over to open it, then talks quietly to whoever is there.

I turn to where Sybella is drying her hair by the fire. "Why were you so angry when you first saw me?"

She closes her eyes briefly, then opens them. "I'm sorry for that. It wasn't that I was not happy to see you." She focuses intently on rubbing the wet strands of her hair with the towel. "The abbess said that if I would not return to d'Albret's household and feed her information as required, then she would send you in my stead." She looks up at me then, her entire face glowing with intensity. "I could not risk that. You are too good and pure. I could not have you tainted with the stain of my family. I could not bear that." It is as near to a declaration of love from Sybella as I have ever heard, and I hold it close, trying not to feel slighted that she doubted I could handle myself in such a situation, a situation I have trained for longer than she.

Although perhaps that is not true. From what Ismae has told me of Sybella's family, no manner of training could prepare one for their dark and twisted deeds. "Thank you," I say softly. "For caring enough to return to the lion's den yourself."

Uncomfortable as ever with my sincerity, she waves my words aside just as Ismae steps away from the door. "We have been summoned to the duchess's council chamber," she says, and for a moment, I once again feel outside the circle of our friendship. I turn away so they will not see my longing and disappointment, but Ismae reaches out and tweaks the sleeve of my gown.

"The duchess asked for you as well. The council wishes to hear not only Sybella's account of what happened at Nantes but your message from the Arduinnites." She winks, and I cannot help but smile back. With the duchess's help, Ismae has outmaneuvered the abbess.

At least for the moment.

Chapter Twenty-Eight

As SOON AS I STEP into the council chamber, I feel the abbess's cold gaze upon me. Were the meeting even slightly less formal, I feel certain she would take me aside and reprimand me for my presence here.

I pretend she does not exist. It is a trick Sybella used in the past to drive the abbess nearly mad with fury, and I hope to use it to similar effect.

As Sybella tells the Privy Council what she told Ismae and me of what transpired in Nantes, I study the councilors and try to get a sense of their characters.

Across from Lord Duval sits a barrel of a man who looks as stalwart as a thickly rooted tree. He is dressed in soldier's garb and I guess him to be Dunois, captain of the duchess's armies. Next to him is a tall, slender man with gray hair at his temples. His eyes are kind, his smile sad, and a chain of office glints around his neck that marks him as the duchess's new chancellor, Lord Montauban, and captain of Rennes, the city that has given her such needed refuge.

Across from him sits a bishop in scarlet robes with fat jeweled rings upon his fingers. I am somewhat startled to see Father Effram sitting beside him. He wears no trappings of high-church office, and I cannot help but wonder what his role is here. Next to him is a man whose sharp features put me in mind of the ospreys who hunt off the rocky shores near the convent, but I can glean no hint of his identity from his appearance.

More than once, my gaze is drawn to the Beast of Waroch. His sheer ugliness is nearly an affront in such polished company, not to mention shocking next to the beauty that Sybella possesses. And yet . . .

And yet the ferocity of his exterior matches the scarred ferocity of her soul, and I believe, against all appearances, that they will suit wonderfully. Any doubts I may have had are quickly dispelled by the quiet pride in the man's feral eyes as he watches and listens to Sybella give her account. I can almost feel the weight of his regard for her reach across the table and wrap itself around her like a protective arm.

I also slip occasional glances at this Duval fellow who has stolen Ismae's heart. I would never believe they had once fought like cats and dogs in the reverend mother's office if I had not seen it with my own eyes. Although Duval spends less time gazing at Ismae than Beast does at Sybella, I can still feel the bond between them, like steady, nurturing roots from some invisible tree.

When Sybella has finished her tale, the room falls into a stunned but respectful silence. After a moment, Duval turns to Beast. "Tell us of the battle for Morlaix."

Something in the way that Beast squares his massive shoulders makes me believe that he would prefer to be back on the battlefield rather than speaking before the council. "The abbess of Saint Mer was most helpful," he begins, his voice deep and graveled. "As were the people of Morlaix, and the charbonnerie." The bishop sniffs his disdain at the mention of the charcoal-burners, for they followed the Dark Matrona when the Church cast her out. Father Effram, however, folds his hands and smiles beatifically, as if especially pleased with beloved children.

"In truth," Beast says, somewhat sharply, "it was the charbonnerie and their way with fire that allowed us to take the town's cannon back from the French and use the weapons against them.

"We sent another group to the winch house where the great chain

ЉЉЉЉЉЉЉЉ

that guards the mouth of the bay was secured. They seized control of the winch and lowered the chain. Once the dual threats of the cannon fire and the barricade had been removed, the British ships were able to pass."

"And just in time." Sybella picks up the tale. "For our group was small and there were a great number of French troops in the city. Once again, the charbonnerie were crucial, as they devised a most clever scheme to smoke the bulk of the enemy's troops out of the barracks right over the city walls, which rendered their numbers manageable."

With the grace and timing an accomplished dancer would envy, Beast now resumes talking, as if he and Sybella had planned this. "Once the British troops disembarked, it was all but over." He falls silent for a moment before continuing. "Four brave charbonnerie lost their lives for the cause, as did six of our own men. But make no mistake, we would not have prevailed had it not been for the charbonnerie."

Father Effram smiles and spreads his hands wide. "It is almost as if it were willed by God and His Nine."

Beast appears to notice the old man for the first time and gives him a bemused look. "I do not believe we have met before . . ."

The bishop in red sniffs again, and Duval passes a hand across his mouth. I do not know him well enough to be sure that he is hiding a smile, but that is what I suspect. "Allow me to introduce Father Effram. He was once the bishop here in Rennes—"

"A long time ago," the current bishop mutters.

"—but is retired now. His wisdom has proved most helpful," Duval adds, pointedly not looking at the current bishop.

The duchess leans forward. "Sir Waroch, Lady Sybella. The charbonnerie have fulfilled their part of the bargain, and now I would fulfill mine. They were promised a place at our table, and I would honor that. Do you have suggestions?"

Beast and Sybella exchange a thoughtful look, considering. "I believe they simply wish to continue their way of life, Your Grace, but without being reviled."

"That is just as well, as our treasury is utterly depleted and we have nothing with which to pay them," Chancellor Montauban says dryly.

"It was never about money," Sybella says sharply.

Montauban bows his head. "I know that, my lady. It was but an attempt to lighten the mood of a grim situation."

Sybella blinks in surprise at his apology, then smiles prettily to let him know it has been accepted.

"What they need is to be treated with honor and respect," Beast says.

"What if," Duval muses, pulling on his chin, "what if we created a military order just for them, like an honor guard, but of the realm rather than of the duchess's person? That would both elevate their status and recognize their past deeds."

"Continuing deeds," Beast corrects. "They have no intention of withdrawing their assistance. They are, if anything, even more committed than before."

"An order." The old priest presses the tips of his fingers together. "I like that. May I suggest calling it the Order of the Flame?" He shrugs apologetically. "If no one has any other proposals."

Duval looks at Beast and Sybella, who turn to the duchess. She nods. "It is perfect. It speaks to their unique gifts and form of service. Lord Duval, see that it is so. And we will have a ceremony to honor them."

Poor Chancellor Montauban winces. "How extravagant a ceremony did you have in mind, Your Grace?"

"I take it by your dour look that our coffers do not hold even so much as crumbs?" Duval asks.

Montauban shakes his head. "I am afraid not. The funds received for the duchess's jewels have already been used to pay the mercenary troops *some* of what we owe them in order to prevent them from sacking the city from the inside."

"Our soldiers have not been paid in a long while either," Captain Dunois says. "It does not sit well with them that the mercenaries have been paid first. More than one fight has broken out because of it."

Duval spears the man with a look and gives a curt shake of his head. He does not wish to discuss this now, whether due to the duchess's presence or some other reason, I do not know.

For the first time the duchess looks over at the hawklike man. "Any word from my lord husband?" She stumbles over the word *husband*, and I realize the man she addresses must be the Holy Roman emperor's vassal Jean de Chalon.

"Your Grace, I am sorry, but he is most beset by increasing problems of his own — and not by chance. The French regent has increased the troops along his borders, thus necessitating he stay engaged there. That they have managed to make a barrier of themselves between you two is but an added benefit."

The duchess tries to keep her face impassive, but her color drains away at this news. As if to shore up her own hopes, she says, "There are others who will fight by our side." She looks to me. "Lady Annith, please tell what the Arduinnites have offered."

As I relay their offer of aid, all eyes in the room turn to me. "Surely they are mere legend!" Chalon exclaims when I have finished.

Beast raises one craggy eyebrow at him. "That is also what you claimed of the charbonnerie."

The bishop leans forward, the look on his face a mixture of outrage and disbelief. "But they are women!"

The abbess, who has been as still and silent as a statue this entire time, slowly turns her cold gaze on the bishop. "As, may I remind you, are we who serve Mortain."

The bishop swallows once, twice, and all but squirms in his chair. Captain Dunois casts a sympathetic glance at the man before speaking. "Surely their numbers are too small to be of great use to us."

Beast shifts in his seat so that he can see the man. "I think the charbonnerie would disagree with that assessment."

"As would the Arduinnites," I say. "Though their numbers are small, they did great damage to the French at Vannes."

"We will accept whatever aid our countrymen are willing to give." The duchess's voice is loud and firm. Then she turns to Duval. "Will the defeats at Morlaix, Vannes, and Guingamp deter the French regent?"

"If that doesn't, your marriage should," Chalon mutters.

Duval addresses the duchess. "We can hope it deters them," he says. "And at least we do not have d'Albret and his troops to worry about any longer."

Sybella shifts in her seat. "Do not be so certain of that, Lord Duval."

His gaze moves to her. "What do you mean?"

"I mean that whatever d'Albret was planning will not necessarily end with his death. He had been negotiating with the French, who are camped only a short way down the Loire from Nantes. I was not able to learn what he had planned, but if his men are working with the French, I am sure it will not benefit the duchess in any way."

"Do you think they have learned of the marriage by proxy to the Holy Roman emperor?" Chalon asks.

"Of a certainty, d'Albret knew. Whether he — or someone else — got that information to the French regent is anyone's guess."

"With as many spies as they have at court, I have no doubt they've learned it by now," Duval mutters.

"More importantly," Captain Dunois says to no one in particular, "will it cause them to take action?"

Chapter Twenty-Nine

WHEN THE COUNCIL DISPERSES, THE duchess requests that Ismae attend her, and Sybella excuses herself so she can check on her sisters at Saint Brigantia's convent to see that they are comfortably settled in. As I watch them all go, my heart aches with the all too familiar sensation of being passed by. Only this time, it is not some thrilling assignment I am being left out of but life itself, and I feel as lonely and trapped as I did back at the convent.

Ismae now has someone with whom to build a life outside the convent walls. So does Sybella, and while I do not know much about the Beast of Waroch, I can see the great joy and peace he brings her, and that alone is enough to make me love him greatly.

But what of me? What role is it my destiny to play? For the only thing that would have made being seeress bearable was seeing Sybella and Ismae when I had visions of their assignments and hearing the tales of their adventures. I could at least have lived vicariously through them.

But now—now it does not look like they will ever set foot on that small island again.

Even though I am a hundred leagues away from the convent, I can suddenly feel the walls pressing in on me as surely as if I were in the seeress's chamber itself. Or perhaps after several weeks on the open road I have simply grown accustomed to being outdoors. Either way, if I do not get some fresh air, I fear I will suffocate.

I go to my room to grab a cloak, wrap it around my shoulders, and return to the palace corridors.

Even though I have no idea where I am going, I stride off purposefully, ignoring the few curious gazes directed my way. Surely if I just keep walking, I will get to a door of some kind.

However, there is no doorway at the end of this hall. Instead, it ends in another hall, forcing me to choose right or left. I go left, assuming that will lead to the outer edges of the palace. However, I do not find a doorway, but a staircase. I follow the narrow stone steps up and up and up again until, at last, there is a door. But it is guarded by sentries.

Remembering Ismae's claim that as one of Mortain's own, I can go where I please, I give the men-at-arms a serene nod and motion for them to open the door. Much to my surprise, they do. When I walk through, I find that I am at last outside. I take a deep breath of fresh air and try to get my bearings. I am not in the front of the palace, as I had hoped, but instead have come out the back, where the palace abuts the city wall. There is another set of stairs, which I climb until I gain the ramparts.

As I stand on the battlements looking out over the valley beyond the city wall, something deep inside me uncoils. I lift my face to the cool night breeze that whips at my hair and my cloak. I think of the Arduinnites, their camp hidden out there among the trees. I think of the hellequin and their desolate existence brightened only by the distant promise of redemption and the individual gifts they bring to their duties. I marvel at all I have learned, which hardens my resolve. I will not let the abbess, or self pity, defeat me.

The awareness that I am not alone comes to me slowly, like waking from a particularly deep sleep. Someone is nearby, in the shadows where the wall meets the rampart. I can feel him watching me. It cannot be a sentry, for he would not have stood so still for so long without making himself known. Uncertain whether my lack of fear is a sign of wisdom or folly, I fold my arms in front of me so that the daggers at my wrists are within easy reach, then turn around to face the shadows, pressing against the stone wall behind me. "Show yourself."

A darkness within the shadows begins to move slightly, causing me to catch my breath until I see that it is only a black cloak rippling as a man steps forward.

Recognition slams into me, causing my heart to clatter against my ribs and all the blood to drain from my face.

Balthazaar.

Even as joy—silver and bright—skips lightly through my veins, I reach for the knife at my wrist, for that joy is overlaid with a dark, heavy thrum of apprehension. "What are you doing here?" How I manage to sound so calm with so many emotions coursing through me, I do not know, but I am grateful all the same.

Instead of grabbing me or attacking me, Balthazaar barks out a laugh, the sound cutting through the darkness like a blade. "I have asked myself that a thousand times, calling myself a fool for every one of them, and yet, here I am."

And though we stand in the shadows, it is not too dark for me to see the pain that this admission of his own desire causes him. Good, I think, for if I must flounder and flail with whatever it is that lies between us, as least I do not suffer alone.

"So the hellequin do not hunt me?"

He grows so still it seems as if even his cloak has stopped moving. "Why would you think we were hunting you?"

Did he not carry my own arrow in his saddlebag? What if I had been mistaken? What if it simply looked like one of my own? Perhaps it was my guilt and uncertainty that led me to believe it was mine. Or perhaps it was truly mine and I am too cowardly to force the issue. I turn and look out over the valley. "You told me they would if I were to leave. You said I would only be safe in their midst."

There is a faint clank of chain mail as he folds his arms across his chest and leans back against the wall. "If their blood was up and they were in the throes of a hunt, they might not stop to consider long enough to realize that they *weren't* hunting you." He tilts his head, considering me. "Have you done something that would cause us to hunt you?" There is a faint thread of amusement in his voice, which pricks my temper.

"No, but neither am I who you think I am. I am Mortain's daughter, one of His handmaidens." I watch his face closely, looking for any glint of recognition that would show he has been hunting me and has now found what he seeks.

Even though he is still mostly in shadow, the weight of his regard presses down on me. "Why are you telling me this now?"

Why, indeed? Because I no longer believe he is hunting me? Because I feel inexplicably safe with him? Or is it simply because I am three times a fool? "For the same reason you followed me to Rennes, most likely," I mutter.

He clenches his fists, his eyes darkening into twin pools of blackness as all traces of amusement disappear. "Why did you run away?" It is hard to tell if that is a note of anguish I detect in his voice or if it is merely my own longings reflected back at me.

Briefly, I consider telling him of the arrow I saw, but for some reason it feels like admitting that I was doing something wrong, although I was not. "I had business elsewhere. I told you that many times, and many times you promised we were drawing closer. And yet, we never reached Guérande. My business could not wait any longer."

He takes a step toward me and my heart begins to beat faster. "If you were traveling to Guérande, why are you now in Rennes?"

"I was so long on the road that the person I needed to see had traveled here, and so I followed." I tell myself he is only studying me so intently to see if I am lying, but that is not what I feel in his gaze. What

I feel is his need and desire and longing, crashing against me like waves against the shore, calling to those same unwanted feelings I hold for him. And always that inexplicable connection that draws me to him.

Sister Arnette once showed us a special rock that had the power to draw iron shavings to it. I remember how the dust and splinters of metal moved inexorably toward the rock. Even though I know he is dangerous, I am drawn to Balthazaar just as those shavings were to the lodestone. "Is it allowed for you to be here?" I force my voice to lightness, determined to hide my own traitorous emotions from him. "I thought cities were barred to your kind."

"We cannot hunt or ride through the cities, but as you can see, I am able to enter them."

There are so very many reasons why I should not trust him. Why I should tell him to leave, order him away. He has done things—horrible things—that have earned him this relentless penance. He and his hellequin are naught but outlaws and thugs, barely cobbling together a shred of decency among them as they desperately try to atone for their worldly sins. Truly, the midden heap of Mortain's grace. While I, I am sworn to a life in service to Mortain. Surely our being together is like the daughter of the gaoler courting the prisoner.

But none of those arguments amount to anything when weighed against the pain and despair that sits so heavily upon him, and the knowledge that I, in some way, am able to ease that, just as his presence fills some dark lonely need of my own.

He moves nearer then until all I can see is him—his mail-covered chest, his dark eyes boring into mine as if he could read the depths of my soul. His gaze is too overwhelming, so I focus on the dark stubble along his jaw and wonder what it would feel like against my hand, my fingers clenching into a fist so that I do not reach out and run them along his cheek.

The night breeze shifts, bringing a gust of cool air with it, and I shiver. Balthazaar raises his hands slowly, places them on my arms, and draws me into the shelter of his body. And still I cannot bring myself to meet his gaze, for it moves across my face like a caress. I fear if I look up, naked hunger will sit as plainly on my face as it does on his. I am content to simply stand in his arms, letting them act as a buffer between me and the rest of the world for these few stolen moments.

And then he moves, lowering his head to mine. With a sharp thrill, I realize he is going to kiss me. I tilt my head up to meet his lips and wonder if they will be cool like the night air or warm like his eyes when he thinks I am not watching.

But before our lips meet, there is a crunch of a boot heel on the catwalk behind us. I leap away guiltily, but he reaches out and grabs my arm. "Say you will return," he says. "Tomorrow night."

I pull my arm from his grip and glance over my shoulder. Two guards are making their rounds. Surely they will see the hellequin, and no good can come of that. "I will. If not tomorrow, then the night after." But when I turn to tell the hellequin he must leave now, he is already gone.

After bidding the guards good night, I slowly make my way down the steps to the palace. My heart does a most inappropriate and ill-advised jig as I walk back to my chambers. Balthazaar has followed me here. It is not like Ismae's new life with the noble Duval, or even Sybella's new place at the heroic Beast's side. But it is a green shoot of a life beyond the convent, and it is wholly mine. For tonight, that is enough.

Chapter Thirty

THE NEXT MORNING, BEFORE THE sun is even up, there is a knock on my chamber door. It is a page, who informs me that the abbess insists that I attend upon her right away. The summons jolts me fully awake. As I hurry to dress, my mind runs over all the arguments I did not have a chance to make during our first meeting. I will explain to her that I know how seeresses are chosen — it does not have to be me. That it is her decision, not Mortain's.

Then I will force her to tell me what flaw or lack she sees in me that prevents her from sending me out, and I will insist I be given a chance to fix it. If she denies there is any such thing behind her decision, then I will ask if it was she who tore the page with my name from the convent register, and if so, why?

When I am ushered into the abbess's chambers, a sort of calm settles over me. Now that I am out from behind the convent walls, the power she has held over me for so long has dissipated, like smoke in a room once the door is opened.

"Annith." Her cool voice reaches out across the room.

I dip a curtsy. "Yes, Reverend Mother?"

She lets the silence between us build. Whether that is because she is choosing her words carefully or because she hopes to unnerve me with her silence, I do not know or care.

To show her I am not unnerved, I glance to the crows on their perches behind her desk. There are three perches but only two crows, and I wonder if she has sent one to the convent with news of my arrival.

"You may sit." The abbess's voice is tinged with a hint of warmth, which I do not trust at all.

"Thank you, Reverend Mother, but I prefer to stand." That way she will have to strain her neck to look up at me.

Her mouth tightens slightly in annoyance before she forces all emotion from her face. "It is your choice." She leans back in her chair and studies me. "What do you want from me, Annith? To know that I am sorry—heartbroken—about young Matelaine's death? For of course I am. Her death pains me as does the death of any of our handmaidens. I grieve much as a mother does over her children." Her face is soft, a look of gentle understanding in her eyes, and her brows are drawn together in an imitation of concern.

"And what of Sybella's death? Would you have grieved for her if she had died on that mission you sent her on? A mission no seeress had countenanced?"

"Sybella is no concern of yours—"

"You are wrong." The words fly from my mouth like small, sharp rocks. "She is one of my greatest concerns. As is Ismae and Florette and all the girls that I have been raised with. And you sent Sybella back to that . . . that monster."

"What makes you think it wasn't Mortain's will that she be sent there? How can you be so certain that is not expressly why Mortain put her on this earth—to bring d'Albret down? No one else could have gotten close to him—no one else would ever have been able to gain a position of such trust."

"But what of her trust in you? She came to us half mad with despair and grief, and she had barely healed before you sent her back into that lion's den. And Matelaine, she had been there less than two years, not nearly enough time to have learned half of what she needed to know. And Ismae? You sent her out blind, not even telling her who she was being assigned to."

"I did not want his identity to prejudice any conclusions she might draw."

"And what of Ismae's letters?"

The abbess blinks. "What letters?"

"The ones she sent to me that I never received. The one asking if I knew the antidote to a poison."

Our gazes hold for a long moment before I lean forward and plant my hands on her desk. "You never even told her of the entirety of her gift. How she was able to draw poison from others' skin, just like Sister Serafina."

"I had to be certain she was able to fulfill her duties for Mortain without remorse or second thoughts. I feared that her kind heart would cause her to use it without permission, and those fears proved founded when she wrote to you."

"You had no right to take my letters—"

"No right? What rights do you think you have but those that are granted to you by me? All that you have, the clothes on your back, the food that has filled your belly, and any rights, are at my discretion. You seem to have forgotten that."

"I forget nothing."

"And so I ask again, what do you want from me?"

"I want to know that you have the novitiates' best interests at heart. That you are not picking and choosing who to send based on some whim or personal favorite."

The abbess snorts. "Do not flatter yourself. I do not care for you *that* much. I have been kind to you, that is all."

While the words she speaks have the weight of truth to them, I do not believe them all the same. She has cared more for me than for the others, for all that she wishes to deny it now. "I want an explanation for why I have not been sent out, then."

"Must I carve it upon the skin of your arm? You have been chosen to be the convent's seeress. Where did you think they came from if not from the ranks of our initiates? We plucked them from a magical tree?"

"Except I have had a chance to research this matter and now know that there are many others qualified to be the convent's seeress. Anyone who is a virgin, or who is past childbearing years and swears celibacy. I am not the only one who can serve in this manner. Why are you so set on me?"

"How do you know that I am? Is not the first mission a novitiate is given one meant to prove her absolute obedience and loyalty? A task designed to demonstrate she can be trusted to carry out her duties?"

Ignoring the sudden uncertainty that twists in my belly, I tilt my head and allow a bitter smile to play about my lips. "That is most odd, because I distinctly remember you telling Sister Thomine it was precisely because I was so biddable and obedient that I would excel as seeress."

Her eyes widen at the recognition of just how often I must have listened at her door, and the blood drains from her face. She turns to look at the papers on her desk to hide it, but it is too late. I have seen it and know that she is afraid of what I may have overheard.

"Perhaps it is not what you have, but what you lack," she says at last. Her words are like a slap. "What do you mean?"

"I mean, you have no gifts, no special skills, *nothing* that would be of any use to Mortain in the execution of His wishes. Augury can be taught. The sorts of gifts the other novitiates possess cannot. However"— she leans back in her chair again and lifts a folded message from her desk—"this latest turn of events should please you greatly. In spite of your lack of true gifts, I will have to send you out on assignment after all. It will give you a chance to prove yourself. To convince me I was wrong to waste you as seeress."

And there it is: everything I have ever wanted, everything I have trained and fought for, only now I do not trust it. "You will have to forgive me if I seem less than grateful, for I find it hard to have confidence in such an order—now, at this time."

"You have asked me for an explanation, and I have given you one. I use the tools Mortain gives me in the manner best suited to their gifts. Matelaine, for all her youth, had inherent gifts that made her more valuable in her service to Mortain than you. But she is gone now and all the others are too young, as you have so movingly pointed out, so there is no one left but you." She tilts her head. "I thought you were willing to do anything to prove your ability to serve Him in just such a manner?"

Her faintly mocking tone sets my teeth on edge. "It is too late to catch me with that trap. Besides, the duchess has requested I assist her in caring for Isabeau, and I cannot turn my back on a command from my sovereign."

Her face tightens in annoyance. "That was a request, not a command, and likely made just as a favor to Ismae to give you something to do. And as Sybella is back, she can assist Isabeau in your stead." Then she arches her brows at me in such a way that causes all the muscles along my neck and shoulders to clench in apprehension. "Besides, the man to be killed is not only a proven traitor to the crown but also the man responsible for Matelaine's death."

And just like that, I am hooked like a fish. And she knows it. Even so, I try to feign indifference. "And who is this proven traitor to the crown?"

"Chancellor Crunard. Or, I should say, the former chancellor Crunard."

I glance at the empty perch behind her desk. "Has Sister Vereda Seen this?"

"Yes." Our gazes meet, and I think of all the times I thought she was telling the truth only to learn later that she had lied. There is no way I can take her word on this.

"Why? According to Ismae, he has been sitting in a prison for months. What possible threat could he pose now?"

"Someone is communicating our movements, positions, and strategies to the French. We know that Crunard has close ties with them and can only assume he is using some bribed guard in Guérande to get word to them of our activities."

"Yes, but how is he getting word of the duchess's plans? He is no longer in her confidence."

"Perhaps there is yet another traitor. I do not know, I know only that we are to make every effort to halt the French. Are you willing to do this?"

"What if I do not see a marque? What then?"

"I told you. Sister Vereda has Seen it. Kill him anyway."

Back in our chambers, Ismae looks at me with worried eyes. "I think it is a bad idea."

I glance away and begin folding some of the clothes I will take. "Not if I am aware that the abbess is up to something," I point out.

Sybella moves away from the window. "You do not fully understand her motives."

"I understand enough to know she does not have my best interests at heart."

"But why?" Ismae asks. As if she is unable to keep still, she reaches out and begins helping me fold. "Why would you go, knowing that?"

I look over at Sybella. "Why did you ride out to meet d'Albret?" I ask softly.

She stares at me a long moment, then gives a curt nod. "Well and so. It is something you have to do."

"Precisely. I must do it for Matelaine's sake." And my own, although I do not tell them that. The abbess has all but taunted me with my own deficiencies, and I feel poised for a battle of wills. I am fully prepared for that. I am not prepared to stand down or walk away or turn my back on the only destiny I have ever wanted.

Ismae stops folding my extra gown. "Have you acquired the ability to see marques since I left? For if not, how will you know if he is intended to die?"

I shrug and avoid answering her question by asking one of my own. "Did you search Crunard thoroughly? Mayhap he bore one that was hidden beneath his clothing."

"It is too bad we do not have the Tears of Mortain here with us," Sybella says. "For surely that would solve our problem."

I open my mouth to tell her that we *do* have the Tears, but something keeps me from uttering the words. I don't want them to know that I am small enough to have stolen something so precious from the convent. "Do you think the duchess will mind my absence? I tried to tell the abbess that those duties would prevent me from going, but she dismissed it."

Ismae shakes her head. "The duchess and Isabeau will be fine. It is you I am worried about." She sets the folded gown down in my bag, then crosses her arms across her chest, clearly uneasy. "Crunard is as wily as an old fox and cares nothing for his honor or any cause. Everything he has done has been for love of his sole remaining son."

"Do we know if this son is still alive?" Sybella asks. "Crunard failed in the task the French regent set for him and has been imprisoned. Have we any reason to think the French regent has not killed him as she said she would?"

Ismae opens her mouth, then closes it again. "I do not know," she finally admits, "but I would like to think she would not kill an innocent man."

Sybella rolls her eyes. "There is a reason you are Mortain's mercy and I am not."

"It is one thing to hold him for ransom," Ismae says. "Quite another to execute him outright." Then she grimaces. "Let us hope she has been too busy plotting her other moves against Brittany."

Chapter Thirty-One

ON MY WAY OUT OF the city, I see small groups of Arduinnites patrolling the surrounding countryside. One of the women waves, but she is too far away for me to tell if it is Tola or Floris. I know it is not Aeva, for she would never condescend to be so friendly to me. I pretend I do not see the woman waving, for I do not wish to stop and talk with her, not with my duties to Mortain sitting so uneasily upon my shoulders. Especially if Aeva is with them.

It is twenty-six leagues to Guérande, a two days' hard ride, and I see no reason not to push. Even though I do not trust the abbess, a small part of me is thrilled to finally be doing what I was trained for. This will be no simple fight such as with the French soldiers in Vannes, for I will be acting as Mortain's true handmaiden.

There are few villages or towns on the road between Rennes and Guérande, and it is sparsely traveled, especially with the threat of French invasion hanging over the country. Fortuna is well rested from her time in the stables and we do not need to stop often. The distance flies by. Luckily, the days have grown longer, if not warmer. I pull my cloak more tightly around me and glance overhead at the threatening storm clouds, hoping the rain will hold off one more day.

I do not know what to expect in Guérande. It is likely that the abbess is setting some trap—but if so, is it for me or Crunard?

If it is for me, then at least I am not going into it unaware. Not only do I have more training than Matelaine, but thanks to the events of recent weeks, I have far more experience as well. Experience in the falseness of the human heart and the many ways it can lie.

The burning question is, why would the abbess now give me that which she has withheld so long? There is a possibility, although a remote one, that it is precisely as she claims: there is no one else, I am at hand, and Sister Vereda has Seen it.

Or, more likely, is it because I now have something to hold over her and she thinks I will quietly forget about Matelaine's death if she gives me what I have always wished for.

If so, she will be sorely disappointed.

It is my fervent hope that I am being sent now simply because I have passed whatever test Mortain set before me. Mortain—not the convent. I have stood nose to nose with the hellequin and held my own; I have fought beside those who serve Arduinna and done our convent proud, in spite of the history and animosity that lays between our two orders; and, perhaps most importantly, I have a much broader view of Mortain's gifts and how they affect us all.

Surely my actions have proven beyond all doubt how fully committed I am to Him. Not to the current abbess, who was so kind to me years ago, and not to the Dragonette, who offered me a warped bargain in exchange for a home, safety, a sense of *belonging*. But to Him.

Tired of these weighty thoughts, I turn my mind to all the weapons I carry and entertain myself by reviewing the many ways I know how to kill. I wonder which one I shall use on Crunard.

I have a supply of poison that I can use in small doses to disable any guards. I wear a braided silver cuff that doubles as a garrote and carry five knives, which are concealed within my skirts and sleeves, as well as my beloved bow. I feel certain that if this is a kill sanctioned by Mortain, then I will feel none of the uncertainty or hesitation I have felt in the past, for I will be engaged in my own god's work.

If Crunard is truly the one to have killed Matelaine, avenging her death seems justifiable, at least to me, but I realize I do not know how Mortain Himself feels about vengeance. It never came up in our lessons.

Certainly if Matelaine had realized her life was in danger, she would have been well within her rights to defend herself, but this cold, calculated desire for revenge I hold in my heart feels much more human than divine. The whole issue is made even more complex by all that I have learned from Ismae and Sybella; so many guilty have not been marqued, and so many innocent have been. Surely that suggests that Mortain's will is not easily discernible, or even recognizable.

Who should pay for Matelaine's death, Crunard or the abbess?

And then I remember I will not be going into this blind. I have the Tears of Mortain with me. I smile, realizing I will be able to discern Mortain's will after all. It is all I can do not to stop right there and administer the Tears in the middle of the road, but I force myself to keep going. There will be time enough when I stop for the night.

When the sun begins to dip below the horizon, I realize I must either come upon a village soon or pitch camp. I travel another half a league, hoping for a lone inn or farmhouse where I can pass the night, but there is nothing. I glance up at the sky once more, relieved to see that the gray clouds have blown to the north. As I turn my gaze back to the road, a flock of crows launches from one of the nearby trees, a hundred black wings rising into the sky, flapping their wings in unison like the folds of a single cloak.

At the sight of them, I am suddenly reminded of Balthazaar, and a wave of remorse washes over me. I was so eager to ride out that I completely forgot my promise to meet him again on the ramparts.

On the heels of my remorse comes a surge of ire. I did not invite him to follow me to Rennes, and surely I do not owe him an accounting of my whereabouts. It was his choice to come, and it is not my responsibility to look to his comfort. Besides, I had thought we were done with each other, that I would never see him again.

And yet, I cannot argue away the small thrill of joy I felt when I did see him again. And while it saddens me to think that my thoughtlessness might add to the despair that already haunts him, it is not my concern, no matter how often I see his face when I close my eyes at night or how much I miss his silent, brooding presence skulking nearby. Mortain's work and the abbess's plotting are what I must focus on now.

A short while later, I spy a small copse of trees near a scattering of large, moss-covered boulders. The trees are thickly canopied and would afford some shelter if the clouds return, while the boulders will help shield me from view of the road. There is even a small streamlet on the far side of the copse. Thus decided, I dismount and lead Fortuna to the water and let her drink. I am pleased to see there are some fresh green shoots of grass nearby that she can graze upon.

Once I have removed her saddle and tack, I rub her down thoroughly and settle her near the grazing area. Then I must look to my own needs before the light fails altogether. By the time I have a small fire built, darkness has settled. My stomach rumbles with hunger, but when I pull my saddlebags closer, it is not the food that my fingers search for. They dig deep, down into the very bottom, where the small vial of Tears is cushioned by the calfskin-bound journal.

I pull out the heavy bottle, unwrap the cloth around it, and find myself staring into the dark black crystal, the reflected flames of the fire leaping and dancing in its faceted depths.

I think of all the handmaidens who have gone before me, who have had their senses opened to Mortain's will so they could see the world more as He saw it. Surely, few of them could have needed to see His will as desperately as I do now, with not only Crunard's life hanging in the balance, but my own future with the convent as well.

I carefully lift the stopper, revealing a long, thin wand of crystal. I dip it into the Tears, then slowly pull it all the way out. I set the vial down on one of the rocks surrounding the fire and bring the crystal wand up to my eye. I pause to say a small prayer. *Please, Mortain, let Your will be clear to me so that I may better serve You.* I hold my eyelid open with my free hand, then tap the dropper once.

The Tear falls in, heavy and cold. Even as I fumble to dip the wand in the vial again, a burning begins. Forcing my right eye open, I repeat the procedure, shuddering at the cold heavy feel of it.

The burning is stronger now, growing instead of receding. It burns so brightly that it turns the inside of my eyelids red, as if I am staring at the sun through closed eyes. I bite my lip and wait for it to pass.

But it does not. I feel the first trickle of panic as the sensation moves from my eyes to my forehead, then creeps along my skull and works its way down my neck so that even my throat throbs.

I lift my hands to rub the pain away, then stop, not knowing if that will make it better or worse. Instead, I clench my hands into fists and pray that the feeling will cease.

I do not know how long it takes — when one is in pain, every second feels like an hour — but eventually the sensation begins to lessen and I risk opening my eyes.

I blink, and blink again. I lift my hand and bring it close to my face, then hold my breath and blink a third time.

I cannot see a thing.

No. That cannot *be.* I lift my hands and press them gently against my closed lids, as if I can rub the blackness away. But when I open my eyes, I still see nothing but more blackness. My heart begins to race, thudding loudly in my chest. Perhaps it is only temporary, a strong reaction to the sacred Tears. For all I know, every novitiate who has been administered the Tears has felt this.

Except . . . if that were true, surely there would have been some rumor of it. Besides, Ismae was administered the Tears only a short while before she left with Chancellor Crunard on her second assignment. If it affected her sight thusly, it cannot have been for long.

Before I can take any comfort from that, a new thought occurs to me, one so galling that my limbs begin to tremble.

What if this is the wrong bottle?

It is entirely possible, for there is no label on it, and Sister Vereda's room was a mad jumble of odds and ends. It looked like the bottle I had heard so much about, but there was nothing except my own willful defiance to lead me to that conclusion.

Or could it be yet another test? I wonder. Please, Mortain, no. I have passed enough tests to choke an ox; surely there is no need for further proof of my dedication.

Or perhaps . . . My thoughts stumble and stutter, rearranging themselves in an entirely new formation. Could the abbess have gotten hold of the Tears and altered them in some way? I have rarely been in my chambers, and she has free access at the palace. Likely no one would even note her coming or going as she pretended to meet with her handmaidens in their room.

She is plainly dead set against my serving Mortain as an assassin, but would she have resorted to such brutal tactics?

I snort, answering my own question. Of course she would. We have crossed a new line in our relationship.

Afraid I will be sick, I plant my hands on my knees and bend over, fighting to take in great big gulps of air. I wish, desperately, to move, to stand up, to pace, to *do something*, but I am afraid of losing my bearings. I close my eyes and the panic ebbs somewhat, as if my body is comfortable with being sightless as long as my eyes are closed.

What now? What does this mean for my journey to Guérande?

Indeed, what does it mean for my very life? Now I will have no choice but to sit behind the stone walls of the convent in that dark tomblike chamber for all the rest of my days.

No.

The word swims up from inside me like some ancient fish from the bottom of the deepest part of the sea. No. I will not sit here like a bump in the road, waiting for the abbess to come fetch me and escort me back to the convent, an obedient brood mare for her precious, endless visions.

I have tasted freedom and can never relinquish control of my life to others again.

But how can I go forward if I cannot see?

One step at a time. The words seep into my awareness like rain into parched ground, calming me somewhat.

Instead of allowing myself to despair, I will simply have to pray that my sight returns in the morning.

I grope along the boulder on my right until my hand comes into contact with my saddlebag. I walk my fingers along its bulk until they touch the thin leather straps and the cold metal of the buckles that hold my bedroll in place. It is easy enough to remove it from rest of the pack. I close my eyes again so I may concentrate on remembering my surroundings. I had secured Fortuna just beyond the northernmost tree. The other trees spread out in a half circle from there. Clutching the bedroll in front of me like a softly padded shield so I do not break my nose if I miscalculate, I begin counting out the steps to the next tree, pleased when I feel the rough bark under my palms only two steps farther than I thought.

My sense of smell is stronger, whether from the Tears themselves or simply because I cannot see, I do not know, but I find that helps me as well, the sharp pungent scent of the sap guiding me to the next tree, a mere four steps ahead. Good. I am far enough away from Fortuna that she will not accidentally stomp on my head as I sleep.

Keeping the tree at my back, and the heat of the fire in front of me, I lower myself to the ground. With all the grace and precision of a performing bear, I clear away rocks and branches before unrolling the woolen blanket. When that is done, I sit back on my heels. Although the night is cold, perspiration trickles along my body from my efforts.

I am back from the road and hidden enough from view, and there is no moon tonight. Even so, I pray to Mortain, asking Him to let the darkness conceal me.

Chapter Thirty-Two

I AWAKEN WITH THE GROUND beneath me rumbling like thunder in the far distance. I glance up at the sky to see if storm clouds have formed, cursing when only black nothingness greets me.

Slowly, I stand up. Fortuna snorts and stomps her foot. Another noise follows the first, the screech of an owl perhaps, or the cry of some small creature whose life has just been cut short.

The thundering grows louder and I hear Fortuna tossing her head and whinnying. That is not thunder, but horses. My heart slams against my ribs — the hunt.

I cock my ear, straining to hear better. No. Just one horse. A lone traveler, then. Although why anyone would be galloping so hard in the dead of night, I do not know. But if he is in such a hurry, he will likely pass by without seeing my camp. Especially now that the fire is dying.

I wait, poised in the darkness, listening carefully, surprised when the rider does not pass but instead turns off the road and heads in my direction. Quickly, I grope with my right hand until it closes around an arrow, then I snag my bow with my left. Slowly, I rise to my feet, keeping all my senses pinned on the approaching rider.

The hooves grow even louder as they draw near and I cannot help but wonder if it is my fear that makes them seem so loud or simply my hearing compensating for my lack of sight. Either way, I nock an arrow to my bow and wait.

When the horse explodes into the copse, it is all I can do not to release the arrow, but I will have only one shot — I'd best wait until I am certain I can make it count.

With a great blowing of breath and heaving of lungs, the horse barrels to a stop just outside the ring of boulders that surrounds my campsite. I hear the creak of a saddle and the swish of leather as someone dismounts. I consider calling out for him to identify himself, then realize I do not wish to give away my position or the element of surprise.

There is a crunch of heavy boots on the forest floor, and my skin draws tight across my bones as I wait.

His scent reaches me first: the rich clean scent of earth and spring leaves accompanied by the faint whiff of leather and horse. *"Balthazaar?"* His name comes out part whisper and part prayer.

He does not answer me with so much as a grunt. I have never felt so vulnerable, so wary of where I am to place my feet. It is as if the world itself is now some huge trap I must carefully navigate. Because that so infuriates me, I lift my loaded bow and point it in his direction. His footsteps stop.

"What?" he asks. "What is wrong?"

The sound and timbre of his voice wraps itself around me and I give in to the sweet relief that flows through my limbs.

Do I tell him? No, not until I know why he is here. "I am just surprised to see you. That is all. Why are you here?"

"You said you would return. That you would meet me on the battlements. And instead, you ran away. Again."

Though his voice thrums with his anger, it does not quite hide the faint note of pain that resides there as well. "And so you *hunted me down?*"

"No." He sounds vaguely outraged. "I had business nearby."

I cannot decide if my heart quickens with joy or apprehension. "You followed me."

"I do *not* follow; I hunt."

The sound of his voice is closer, but as I listen for the rustle of his boots upon the forest floor or the crunch of a twig under his boot heel, there is nothing. The man moves as quietly as a wraith, with no clank of weapon or creak of armor to help me pinpoint his location.

It is hard to pretend to keep my eyes focused on him when he moves so quietly, but I do not wish him to know that I am blind. I feel foolish and silly and would rather keep this secret from him. "I do not understand you. Sometimes I cannot tell if you hate me or wish to devour me."

"Both," he whispers, and I can feel the heat of him draw closer.

I open my mouth to tell him he is standing too close, but instead I find myself saying, "I am glad you are here."

He grasps my arms with his hands—hard—and pulls me even closer so that our bodies touch and I can feel the swish of my skirts as they tangle around his legs.

"What spell have you cast over me that I have no choice but to gallop after you across the countryside like some lovesick hound?"

My heart tumbles excitedly at his words. "I thought you said you were not hunting me?"

"Hunting. Following." Disgust at himself is thick in his voice. "Either way, I will have none of it." He gives me a little shake with each word, as if he can throw off the hold he claims that I have over him. And then, without any warning at all, he presses his lips against mine.

As his mouth covers my own, I find myself reeling, as if I have been tipped backward and am falling, falling, so that even the stars in the sky are spinning. His lips are warm and soft, the unrelenting pull of his desire for me as strong as the pull of the waves against the sand.

It is not like practicing with Ismae, or even Sybella. It is not like any of the first kisses I have imagined over the years. It is far, far better and more wondrous, and yet terrifying as well, like one of the raging storms that pound against the convent walls in the winter, threatening to breach its defenses. So too does this kiss threaten something deep within me that I cannot even name.

Then, just as suddenly, he sets me away from him, leaving the entire front of my body cold and bereft and wanting *more*. There is a faint rustle of his cloak as he steps back from me. I long to put my fingers to my lips. To see if they feel as different on the outside as I do on the inside. Then I remember who — and what — he is. "Will you pay for that?" I ask, recalling the hellequin and their talk of the price of temptation.

"You would charge me for a kiss?"

I long to reach out and smack him — but I would have to be able to see him first. Instead, I turn toward the faint heat of the dying fire and hold my hands out over it. "No, you dolt. I was worried that giving in to temptation would extend your penance."

There is a moment of silence before he finally speaks. "I follow you for twelve leagues, accost you in the dead of night, and you are worried about my penance?"

I sniff. "You did not accost me; I *let* you kiss me, make no mistake."

For some reason, I feel certain that he smiles, although I cannot hear such a thing. I wonder briefly if it is quick and sharp or slow and easy. "Thank you for that clarification, my lady."

His eyes linger on me — I can feel it just as surely as I could his touch mere moments ago — and I wish to hide myself from them. But any move I make would give away my situation.

"What is wrong with you?" he asks softly.

"Nothing." I turn my back to him then, not caring how childish it might seem.

"But there is. Come here." He reaches out and snags my chin with his fingers, and he gently pulls my face back around. I look up at where I desperately hope his eyes are.

"You are blind."

It is all I can do to keep from reaching up and feeling my face. "How can you tell? Are my eyes scarred?" I ask, dreading the answer.

"No, they are fine." The warmth and softness in his voice sends a shiver down my spine.

He leans in and I expect a kiss, but instead, he sniffs. Then sniffs again. Just when I think he will sniff a third time, he leans down and captures my lips again in an all too brief kiss. "Tell me."

And so I do. Leaving out the part about the Tears being stolen.

As I tell my tale, I realize he listens to me in a way that few others do. I can *feel* him listening, and I fear he hears things I do not even know I am saying.

When I am done, he does not speak for a long while. The night is so quiet I imagine I can hear the stars passing across the sky. "Were you so very hungry to experience the world as Mortain does?" he finally asks.

And even though I fear it will hurt him, I cannot lie. "Yes."

There is the whisper of thick wool as he shifts, and I feel his hand take mine, the cool leather of his glove smooth against my palm. "Most in your situation would simply give up, turn back." He tugs gently on my hand, and there is a faint rustle of leaves as he sits down on the forest floor.

Since he will not release my hand, I lower myself to the ground. "I have always been willful and stubborn. It is one of my greatest sins."

"But is it a sin? If it allows you to survive? Endure? Prevail?"

I am absurdly warmed by his words. So he will not see this, I snort derisively. "I do not know that this"—I gesture to my blind self sitting in my camp in the middle of nowhere—"qualifies as *prevailing*."

He kisses my brow, and for some reason it makes me want to weep.

"For now, tonight, it is prevailing. We do not know what tomorrow will bring, but that is always the case, is it not?" He puts his arm around me and draws me against his chest.

I hold very still. "Are you going to seduce me?" I ask, although in truth, it would not be much of a seduction, as I need little convincing.

He leans in and rubs his cheek against my hair. "Would you like me to?"

Yes, I think, but do not — quite — manage to say.

He plants a kiss behind my ear, then sighs. "Alas, no." I hear the smile in his voice. "Not when you must spend the entire day tomorrow on horseback. I am not that selfish. Not quite."

When the full meaning of his words sink in, I blush so furiously I give off more heat than the fire, and Balthazaar laughs. Because it is only the second time I have ever heard him do so, I do not even mind — much — that it was at my expense.

"Sleep," he whispers softly. "I will watch over you till morning, and then we can decide what to do."

We. Not *you,* but *we.* I know I should resent that he presumes so much, but instead, I hold it close, like a promise.

"Be safe, my love," a voice murmurs. Then I feel the press of cool lips upon my eyelids.

At the shock of his touch, I wrench my eyes open. The sun is just beginning to shine through the trees, and I swear that I can still feel the hellequin's body against my own, the bite of the chain mail he wears sharp against my back. But when I turn to look at him, he is gone.

That is when I realize I can see. Relief surges through me, so overpowering that I am nearly dizzy with it.

In the distance, I hear the sound of galloping hooves. When I look up, I see that he has left. Confusion and hurt swell up inside, tightening my throat.

No. I will not feel any of those things for him. I will not let myself get waylaid by emotions. Not for him or for the abbess. My god's will is my sole purpose right now. And I'm embarrassed that Balthazaar could make me forget that. I have an assignment. An assignment my very future hangs on, and I will not let Balthazaar cloud my mind.

It occurs to me that he too could have been a test, sent by Mortain. I reach down and begin collecting my bedroll. If he was, then I am getting heartily sick of these tests. If Mortain does not understand my dedication by now, then surely there is nothing more I can do that will prove it to Him.

Chapter Thirty-Three

ALONE, I APPROACH THE GATE to Guérande, the looming height of the two towers on either side of it making me feel small and insignificant. The guard manning the gate eyes me as I pass, and I take a coin from my purse and toss it to him. "Which is the best inn for the night?" I ask.

"The Hammer and Cross, if they're not full up."

I glance around to the nearly empty streets. "Would they be?"

He shakes his head. "Few enough travelers right now. There should be rooms available."

"Thank you."

Guérande is a smaller town than Rennes, with fewer people and less bustle — at least, at this time of night. A lone woman hurries down the street with her market basket. Two merchants walk side by side with their heads bent close in conversation.

The inn is a sturdy stone building set back slightly from the street. A wooden sign painted with a picture of a blacksmith's hammer and Saint Cissonius's cross hangs above it. As I steer Fortuna into the courtyard, a stable boy no older than Florette hurries forward to take the reins. "Take especially good care of her," I tell him as I dismount. "She has ridden hard these last two days."

When I enter the inn, I am engulfed by the scents of roasting meat, smoke, wine, and the fresh rushes on the floor. The innkeeper, a thick man built like a bear and nearly as furry, looks up at my arrival. His head and face are covered in coarse brown hair, and his cheeks are reddened from his work. His eyes are wary, but not unkind. He wipes his hands on his leather apron and comes to greet me. "May I help you?"

"I'm looking for a place to pass the night. Possibly two. Have you room?"

"Aye. If you've coin."

"I do." I pull two from the purse at my waist and hold them out to him.

The wariness leaves his eyes as he plucks the coins from my fingers. "Would you like some supper as well?"

"I would, thank you."

After a satisfying meal in the common room, I retire to my chamber, fully expecting to drop into sleep like a stone into a river. But instead, I toss and turn restlessly.

It is not, I tell myself, because I miss the hellequin.

The next morning I am up early, grab some bread and cheese from the common room, then venture out into the streets of Guérande. They are much busier now, with people scurrying everywhere about their business. It is easy enough to blend in with the crowd. I pause and admire a ribbon seller's wares, pretend to consider purchasing one of the scrawny chickens at the market, but all the while I am forming a map of the city in my mind. The cathedral acts as my true north as I get a feel for the streets of the city and the gates that they lead to. When all of that is firmly fixed in my mind, I make my way to the palace and spend the rest of the day committing the entrances, the exits, and the comings and goings of the sentries to memory. I will return tonight, under the cloak of darkness, and do what must be done.

* * *

Back at the inn, I have an early supper, then retire to my room and wait. When it is three hours after nightfall, I carefully arm myself with every weapon I possess, slip the vials of poison into the pouch at my waist, and sling my quiver over my shoulder. I carry it lower than is comfortable, but this way it will be hidden by my cloak.

As I make my way down the narrow staircase, I realize that the common room is quiet — unnaturally quiet. I lighten my footsteps on the stairs to make as little noise as possible and draw one of the knives from its sheath. When I reach the landing, I slowly ease into the main room.

The innkeeper is holding a blacksmith's hammer and scowling at the front door. Following his gaze, I see a tall, darkly cloaked figure glaring back, the reek of the Underworld rolling off him like a mist from the sea and filling the entire room with darkness and foreboding.

I blink, wondering briefly if hellequin can be summoned merely by allowing oneself to think of them.

"Let me through." Balthazaar's voice is deep and low and altogether threatening.

"You're not coming into my establishment." The innkeeper makes the sign of the cross with his right hand. He holds the handle of the hammer in a loose grip with his other hand and hefts it over his shoulder.

Muttering an oath, I shove my knife back in its sheath and hurry forward, my mind scrambling for some way I can pour oil on these troubled waters. "My lord?" I make my voice young and light and breathless. "I told you I would come to you." I am hardly even aware of what I am babbling, I know only that I must create some distraction that will keep these two from coming to blows.

Slowly taking his gaze from the bristling innkeeper, Balthazaar looks at me, an entire thunderstorm of emotion roiling in his eyes. I glance nervously around us, then lower my voice, as if ashamed. "I . . . I did not wish to meet you here. In front of others, my lord," I whisper. As I drop my gaze and pick at my skirt, I see a look of understanding — and disgust—flare in the innkeeper's face, but the tension across his shoulders lessens somewhat and he lowers the hammer a fraction of an inch.

"You know this man?"

"Oh, yes!" I step forward to subtly insert myself between the two men. Giddy—I would be giddy if I were meeting a lover. I stare up at Balthazaar with open admiration. If I did not think that the blacksmith's life hung in the balance, I'm fairly certain I would sicken myself. "I am ready to leave, my lord."

He stares down and blinks, his dark eyes unreadable. He nods once, grabs my arm, then hauls me toward the door.

I link my arm through his and snuggle up against him so that it will look more like he is escorting me and less like he is hauling me off to be ravished or dragged to the Underworld. "I will be back shortly," I call to the innkeeper.

"We lock the doors at the third bell and do not open them again till morning. If you're not back by then, do not bother."

"Thank you! I will be back before the third bell rings." And then we are at the door. Balthazaar flings it open, shoves me out into the night, and shuts it behind us. Before I can berate him for creating such a scene, he presses me up against the wall, lowers his head, and captures my lips with his.

The force of it fair steals my breath and for a moment, I can do nothing but stand there and reel. Taking advantage of my inaction, he wraps his arm around me, pulling me closer, as if even the small space between us is too much. Luckily, the movement brings me back to my senses, and I—less forcefully than I should—shove him away. "What are you doing here?"

He stares down at me, and I must force myself to look away for fear I will lose myself in that gaze once again. "Were you not acting my lover just then?"

I glance around to see if anyone has witnessed our display. Luckily, we are alone in the courtyard, most likely because his enormous black stallion is tossing his head and pawing at the ground like the creature from the Underworld he is. "Yes, you lummox, but only so you and the innkeeper would not come to blows. Now, get off me. I have work to do." I want to ask him why he left me and where he went, but refuse to let those questions pass my lips. Lips that still feel the press of his upon them.

"I finished my work in Nantes," he says.

My head snaps up and I half fear he has read my mind.

"That is what I am doing here."

I push away from the wall. "What business did you have in Nantes?"

"A new hellequin has been sworn to our service."

"Truly?"

"Truly."

Because lies fall as easily from his lips as ripe fruit from a tree, I press further. "What sins is he seeking redemption from?"

"He was overcome with lust for his own sister, and yet died trying to protect her. In his moment of death, he begged for a chance to redeem himself, and so it has been granted."

"So that is why you left with not so much as a by-your-leave."

His voice softens. "I said goodbye."

So. That was no dream, then. I study him suspiciously. "You left not even knowing if my sight had returned."

"But it had."

And how could he know that? *"Be safe, my love,"* a voice murmurs. *Then I feel the press of cool lips upon my eyelids.* I scoff at my suspicions. Hellequin have no such powers. It was but a coincidence. My body finally adjusted to the power of the Tears, that is all. "Well, I am fine now, as you can see. And I have work to do."

"I will accompany you."

Merde, that is all I need, him looking over my shoulder. "You will not! My work is meant to be done in private."

"As is mine, and yet you witnessed it for nearly three weeks."

"At *your* invitation."

"Besides, what if you go blind again? Or lose your hearing? Or power of speech? Then you will need my help." There is a faint note of smug satisfaction in his voice.

I nearly shove him again in frustration, but then I see how the spark of humor lights up his eyes, lifting the despair and making them nearly human. And just like that, my anger dissipates. "Very well. But you must do as I tell you."

He places a hand on his chest. "Always."

I roll my eyes.

Crunard is being held in the northeast gate tower. As we head through the nearly deserted streets of Guérande, I keep a careful eye out for the city watch. Beside me, the hellequin moves as quietly as a wraith. Indeed, the shadows of the night seem to pool around him, as if his very presence attracts them. It is most unsettling and it takes every ounce of training I have to push it out of my mind and concentrate on the task at hand.

I am ready for this. I have spent my entire life preparing for this moment, this chance to serve Mortain. Instead of sitting walled up in some suffocating tomb using nothing of who I am to serve Him, now every skill I possess, every bit of intellect, every moment of training, will be brought to bear on this task, and in doing this, I will dedicate my life to His service.

If He will have me.

I do not know what I will do if the life I want is denied me, but the thought is less bleak now than it once was. I tell myself that has nothing to do with the hellequin at my side. Or if it does, it is only because I have learned through him just how far Mortain's grace and mercy can extend.

I ignore his dark brooding presence at my elbow and review everything I have learned about marques—about how and where they appear and the different ways in which Mortain's daughters see them. I know that Ismae has seen marques since she was young and that they appear to her in ways that suggest the method of death. Sybella only sees them on the victim's forehead, and she did not see that until after she was administered the Tears.

There are initiates who never see marques at all, although those are rare. That is why we rely so heavily on the seeress, and it is no small part of why I am so terrified of having that rest on my shoulders—I cannot believe that I am to be His voice in this world.

When we reach the gate tower, I put my hand out to stop the hellequin. Just as I do, two guards emerge from the door. Before I can react, the hellequin grabs me by the shoulders and spins me around so that my back is against the wall. Leaning over me, he presses our bodies together, his cloak swirling forward with the movement and wrapping itself around my legs. Then he brings his hooded head down toward mine, so close I think he plans to kiss me again, and while I am annoyed with his actions, my traitorous heart gives a small, eager leap. Just as I prepare to wrench away from him, he whispers in my ear, "Hold still."

I curse my own loss of focus. He is right. It is one of the first lessons we learn at the convent, how to meld with the shadows. And I would have remembered it if I hadn't been so distracted by the idea of him kissing me again. There is a good chance the sentries will not see us, and if they do, they will likely think it is merely some soldier's dalliance.

I feel Balthazaar's heart beating against my own as the two soldiers pass by. They are close enough that the hellequin could reach out and

touch them if he wished, but they do not so much as look in our direction. When they have passed and their footsteps no longer echo on the
cobblestones, Balthazaar steps away.

"I told you you would have need of me."

I avoid his eyes as I adjust my skirts. "I could have escaped their
notice equally well on my own. I have been sneaking and skulking since
I was a child, and am very good at it. Now, are you ready to play your
part?" It was the price I demanded if he insisted on coming with me.

"I still say you would make a better distraction than I."

I give him a grin that is all teeth and little humor. "Yes, but I have the
sleeping draft and you do not." I give him a push, which is like pushing
a stone wall. He makes certain I know this by resisting a long moment
before finally choosing to step back.

I squelch the urge to reach out and kick him.

As he slips away, I keep myself from asking him what he plans to do
to distract the guards. Instead, I slide along the gate-tower wall, ease
myself toward the guard room, then slip inside. Torches flicker lazily
in their iron sconces, causing long shadows to dance in the dim light. I
move quickly to the table where the men had been sitting, their dice still
lying upon its surface. Quickly, I remove the small paper of fine white
powder from the cuff of my sleeve, tap a sprinkle into each cup, then
pour the rest into the jug. Before I can do more than that, I hear the
footsteps of the returning men.

I step back into the shadows near the corner of the room, grateful for
the sputtering torch light that is barely enough to see the dice by.

And then I wait.

The men take their seats. One of them says something, laughs, then
lifts his cup and takes a swig of wine. As he lifts the jug to pour himself
more, his companion drains his cup and holds it out to be filled as well.
Some of the tension in my shoulders relaxes and I lean back against the
wall, waiting for the draft to do its work.

I do not know if it takes longer than it should or if it is just very hard to wait while crouching in the shadows. At last, their heads nod, and first one, then the other, slumps over the table, the movement causing the dice to fall to the floor.

Victory wells up within me. Now I may face Crunard.

Slowly, I turn and walk from the antechamber to the short narrow hallway beyond, then pause. There are no doors here, only grilles of ironwork, much like the portcullis. A lone man sits behind one of them. For all that he is in need of a haircut and his beard a trim, I recognize him immediately from his visits to the convent.

Feeling my eyes upon him, he looks up. Slowly, he leans back against the wall, one side of his mouth lifting in a bitter smile. "I wondered when she would send someone after me. It is not like her to waste an opportunity when one of her opponents has been weakened."

"I am not sent by the duchess," I tell him as I search his face for any hint of the dark smudge that I am so desperately praying for.

"I know. You are sent by the abbess of Saint Mortain."

Chapter Thirty-Four

AT HIS WORDS, everything inside me grows still. "You know why I am here?"

"Perhaps even better than you do."

His words prick at something uncomfortable in me. "What do you mean?" That I must ask this question rankles me, but my need to know what hidden web is being woven is greater than my pride.

He shrugs, a surprisingly elegant gesture. "It means that I understand better than you why you have been sent. You think you are on Mortain's business, but you are not. You are here on hers."

I force out a laugh and hope it does not sound as false to his ears as it does to mine. "You are facing death, my lord. It is not surprising that you would say anything you can think of to stay my hand."

He shifts then, rises to his feet. Good! If he comes closer to the light, mayhap I will see a cursed marque. I silently raise my bow.

He ignores the arrow pointed straight at his chest and stands just on the other side of the iron bars. "Did she tell you why I must die?"

"You betrayed the duchess, did everything in your power to hand our kingdom over to the French regent. I do not think there is much to explain."

"Your fellow handmaiden chose not to kill me once. Perhaps she knew something you did not?"

My heart twists painfully. "Matelaine?"

He frowns slightly. "No, Ismae. When she first discovered I was the one behind the plots here at court, she chose not to exact justice. Have you asked yourself why?"

Even though there is hardly any room, I take a step closer. "No. I was too busy trying to puzzle out why you had killed the second handmaiden sent after you. Surely you recognize that now, in addition to your crimes against the kingdom, you have committed crimes against Mortain."

His frowns deepens and he appears genuinely puzzled. "A second handmaiden?"

I laugh again. "Playing dumb will not help you, not when I stand here with an arrow pointed at your black heart."

He spreads his hands wide, as if giving me a clear shot at his chest. "If you think I am eager to cling to this life when all I have ever cared for is gone—my family, my lands, my honor—then you are sadly mistaken." Crunard grips the bars with his hands. "I welcome death," he whispers.

"Then you shall have it," I whisper back. But even though every fiber of my being wishes to see this man dead for what he did to Matelaine —and to the duchess—I find I cannot release the arrow.

He leans forward. "Do you see one of your precious marques on me?"

Shock travels along my bones that he would know of such things. "It is probably hidden by your clothing." I motion with the bow. "Strip." While I am eager to see if he bears a marque, I am equally eager to wipe the smug certainty from his face.

There is a whisper of movement to my left as I feel Balthazaar unfold himself from the shadows, and I wonder how long he has been there. He leans close enough to whisper in my ear. "Let me have him."

Scowling, I turn my arrow on him. "He is mine."

Balthazaar holds his hands up in a placating gesture and slips back into the shadows. I return my attention to Crunard and watch as he pulls off his doublet, then unlaces his linen shirt and pulls it over his head. His chest is still broad with muscle, even though the hair upon it has gone white. But there is no marque.

Before I can respond to that stark fact, the hellequin grabs my arm and pulls me aside, out of Crunard's hearing. "*Do* you see a marque on him?"

"No," I admit, making no effort to hide my disgust. Hopefully, his accursedly sharp hearing will not pick up on the despair I feel — that even with the Tears, I do not possess this most basic of skills.

"Have you seen all you need to see?" Crunard's dry voice cuts through my thoughts. "For it is cold and damp and I would rather not catch a fever and die that way. Better for you to simply kill me with your arrow now. It would be a far more merciful death."

"You assume that you deserve mercy," I snap, "when I am sure of no such thing. And yes, you may put your clothes back on."

While he dresses, I ponder my options.

I cannot say with utter certainty that Crunard is meant to die. If Mortain Himself or the duchess's justice demands it, that would be one thing, but I do not trust the abbess's word that he must die. Especially with the unsubtle insinuations Crunard is throwing around.

I huff out a sigh. "Very well." At Balthazaar's eager look, I give him a shove, releasing some of that frustration on him. "No, you will *not* hunt him," I say. "But I will take him back to Rennes to face the duchess's justice, and she can decide his fate. Unless Mortain marques him on the way. Then I will kill him."

The hellequin studies me a moment and then gives a single nod. "So be it," he says.

My mind spins furiously, devising a plan. It will be easy enough to get Crunard free of his prison. Harder to get him out of the city. I turn to Crunard, who is watching us both with hungry eyes. "As you heard, you will be coming with us. But if you make one noise when you should not, make any attempt to escape, I will cheerfully kill you, then drag your body back to the abbess and the duchess. Is that clear?"

He nods. "Most clear, demoiselle."

In the end, I decide that moving quickly is better than sitting around devising the perfect plan. I slip back out to the antechamber and the two drugged guards, remove the key from the jailor's belt, then return to Crunard's cell. As I fit the key into the lock, I pause, for some reason reminded of the old tale of the girl whose curiosity drove her to open a box that let loose all sorts of evils upon the world. I too feel as if I am on the brink of answers, answers that have the power to move through my life like a storm surge. I cannot help but wonder what will be left when I am on the other side.

"Come along," I tell him, slipping one of my knives into my hand where he can see it. "And quietly."

He nods, then steps out of his prison slowly, as if unable to believe I will not slam the door in his face. I turn to Balthazaar. "Tie his hands behind his back."

After a moment's hesitation, Crunard reluctantly turns around. As the hellequin tends to that, I close the door, lock it, then toss the keys inside. At his raised eyebrow, I shrug. "It will give them something to puzzle over." Then I grab Crunard's arm and shove him in front of me. Balthazaar falls into step behind us like a sinister shadow.

Crunard spares one glance at the two guards slumped over the table, their dice on the floor. "Did you kill them?" he asks.

"Yes," I lie, hoping he will think me ruthless and therefore be less inclined to attempt escape. "Now, hush and act the contrite prisoner, or I will kill you as well."

My plan, such as it is, is to pretend we have been charged with transferring the prisoner to Rennes, where he is to stand trial for his crimes.

All the lessons on subterfuge and lying that have served me so well at the convent will serve me equally well here. Or so I hope.

As we reach the landing, I pause, listening for the sentries. Still only two, I think. Very well. I glance over at the hellequin. "You are my escort, provided to me by the duchess herself."

He raises one darkly arched brow, then nods. I draw a deep breath, straighten my shoulders, lift my chin, then step outside.

At once, the two sentries spring to attention, raising their weapons in spite of their surprise. "Halt!" the taller one cries, his eyes widening when he recognizes Crunard.

I scowl at them, letting the men know just how much they annoy me. "Delay us at your own risk," I warn.

They glance at each other.

"We are sent to bring the prisoner to Rennes to stand trial for his crimes. If you detain us, you are delaying the duchess's own business."

Finally, unable to help himself, the taller one asks, "How did you get in there?"

I meet his gaze, unflinching. "We walked right past you, and you can be certain your lack of attention to your duties will not go unmentioned."

The shorter one glances down at my hand—the one that does not hold the knife. "Do you have orders of some kind?" It may be my imagination, but I think I detect a new note of respect in his voice.

I shove Crunard a short distance from me so they can see my attire. "Do you dare to question one of Mortain's own?"

The taller guard crosses himself, the superstitious gesture grating on me, but the shorter guard gives a small bow.

"Besides, the guards below had no problem letting us through. Perhaps you should consult with them."

They pause a long moment, then finally relent. "Very well, demoiselle," the taller one says. "You may be on your way. I have no wish to keep this traitor from his rightful punishment."

I nod regally. "In the name of Mortain, I thank you."

As we step out of earshot of the guards, I feel the hellequin lean in close. "You take great pleasure in throwing that name around, don't you?"

I swat at him, disappointed when I miss hitting his long nose. "You may go now. I have no more need of your services."

"Not a chance," he says, and I fear I can hear amusement in his voice. "Besides, you will need assistance getting him back to Rennes. In truth, you will need assistance getting him out of the city, no?"

And though I wish to argue and tell him he is wrong, I am not willing to jeopardize my prisoner for my pride. "I could manage on my own, but if you insist on hanging about, then you'd best make yourself useful. Return to the inn and collect my saddlebag from my room and then get our horses. If you could find a third horse, that would be most beneficial."

"And you? What will you do?"

"I am going to get him out of the city gates. We will meet on the outside, near the copse of trees just in sight of the bridge."

Balthazaar does not even hesitate, simply nods his agreement, and I am reluctantly impressed. Getting two horses, much less three, through the city gates at this hour will be no small feat. I have the far easier task with Crunard.

Once the hellequin has disappeared down the street, I turn to Crunard. "What is the easiest way to get out of the city when the main gate is closed?"

"There is a sally port near the north tower. It is usually only guarded by one man and will be our best chance."

I stare into his face, trying to determine if he is telling the truth or sending me into a trap.

"It is no lie I tell you, demoiselle. You are my only hope for freedom, and I will not jeopardize it."

In the end, I have no choice but to trust him, and I am rewarded by the truth of his words. There is but one lone guard on duty. Even better, he is dozing. I glance at Crunard. "Truly, this city's security is lacking."

He shrugs. "The duchess is not here. There is no one worth guarding. And they have never particularly cared who got out. It was always preventing someone from getting in that they focused on."

"Are they not worried that the French will attempt to take the town?"

"I do not know," he says, his eyes glittering with something sharp. "They no longer include me in their counsel."

We are fortunate that there is enough moonlight from the crescent moon for us to make our way to the copse of trees without stumbling or breaking an ankle. As we walk, I try to assess Crunard's movement and determine how old he is and how much his imprisonment has sapped his strength. He does not appear to be ill treated or half starved, which is a relief, as he will not hinder our travel that way.

When we reach the agreed-upon meeting place, I am unsurprised to find Balthazaar already there astride his demon spawn of a horse, holding Fortuna's reins as well as those of another horse I have never seen. It even sports a fine saddle. I almost ask how he acquired it, then think better of it. "I do not expect to be pursued — at least, not until the guards learn that I was not officially sent, but we should be well behind the gates of Rennes by then, so I am not overly concerned. Even so, I think it best if we put a few hours' ride between us and the city immediately." I glance over at Crunard. He is old, but he has also had weeks of rest in his prison and surely he is as eager as I to put some distance between himself and the city. He gives a nod of assent, then turns and motions with his arms that I should untie him.

"Surely a seasoned soldier such as yourself is able to ride a horse with your hands tied."

He glances at me over his shoulder. "Ride, yes. Mount one, no."

Unfortunately, he is right. I glance at Balthazaar. "Draw your sword."

He gives a mock bow in his saddle. "With pleasure, my lady." The ring of steel being unsheathed sounds loud in the quiet darkness. "What would you have me do with it?"

"Be certain he does not try to escape once I untie him."

"You do not mean to give him free rein?"

"Only long enough to get on his horse." Drawing my knife, I step forward and use the tip of it to loosen the knots of the rope that binds Crunard's wrists, careful to avoid nicking his flesh. When I am done, I keep the knife pointed at him. "Get up. Then once you are settled, bring your wrists in front of you and lean down so that I may reach them."

He stares at me a long moment. "What if I gave you my word that I will not attempt to escape? I am just as eager to be gone from this city as you are."

"Gone from this city, yes, but I am not at all convinced you wish to face the duchess's justice. Besides, why would I trust the word of a confirmed traitor?"

After another moment of hesitation, he does what I ask. I hope he will not argue every step of the way, else it will be a most tedious journey. Perhaps I shall have to gag him.

Once he is settled and retied, I mount Fortuna, glad to have her solid, friendly bulk beneath me once more. I hold out my hand to the hellequin so that I may take my own reins and Crunard's as well. He hands me mine but does not release Crunard's. "Let me lead him," he says, sounding surprisingly like Aveline when she is eager for some task that she knows will be denied her.

I bark out a laugh. "I think not."

"I would not toy with him. Much," the hellequin grumbles.

"No." I hold my hand out, and with great reluctance, he gives the reins to me.

I secure Crunard's reins to my saddle, then nudge Fortuna to the open road.

"So how do you know of the marques?" I finally ask when we have been traveling a while. "That is a well-guarded secret of Mortain's."

"As the liaison between the convent and the Breton court, I have worked closely with the abbess for many years. Of a necessity, we have had to share information with each other so that we could ensure no mistakes were made."

"And yet, not only were mistakes made, but you betrayed the duchess and every measure of trust the abbess has put in you." I make no effort to hide the censure in my voice, and I wonder again at how the abbess came to judge this man so wrongly. "So, now that I have decided to spare your miserable life, tell me of how Matelaine died."

"Who?"

I study his face for the signs of lying we have been taught to look for, but there are none. Or else he is an exceptionally accomplished liar. "The first assassin sent to kill you."

"Other than Ismae, you are the first."

"You are wrong," I say firmly, hoping it is not I who am wrong, steered down a false path by the scheming abbess.

"What did she look like?" he asks softly.

"She was young. All of fifteen. Skin as pale as milk and bright red hair."

"Ah," he says, and I pounce.

"Tell me."

There is a long moment of silence before he speaks. "Since you are hungry for information, as I am, I propose an exchange. A trade, if you will. I will answer one of your questions, and you will answer one of mine."

Before I can respond, Balthazaar butts in. "Or we could play the game my way: If you do not simply answer her question, I will run you through with my sword."

Crunard does not so much spare him a glance. "Have we a deal?"

"Be careful," Balthazaar warns me. "He is toying with you, lulling you into a false sense of security."

"Not that I do not agree, but what makes you think so?"

The hellequin glances over at Crunard, his face growing dark. "Let us just say that one hunter is easily able to recognize the tactics of another."

I follow the direction of his scowl. "You're jealous!" I am so surprised I scarce remember to keep my voice low.

He flinches at the word, then looks sorely affronted. "Jealous? Of that old man? Nay, it is just that if anyone is to hunt you, it should be me."

A flutter of something both terrifying and thrilling moves low in my belly. I know him well enough now to recognize that when he appears to be disgusted with me, it is actually himself he is unhappy with. Before I can say anything, he puts his heels to his horse and, with a flapping of his dark cloak, draws to the front of our group.

I turn my thoughts back to Crunard's proposal. I have no secrets to hide, and he appears to know nearly as much as I do as to how the convent operates. "Very well. We will trade. What do you know of Matelaine?"

"The truth is, I never met her," Crunard says. When I open my mouth to protest, he raises his bound hands in an appeasing gesture. "However, one of the kitchen maids used to carry on a flirtation with one of my guards. She fits your description of this Matelaine."

Matelaine. Flirting with a guard. Most likely so she could get close to Crunard.

"But I have not seen her in weeks," Crunard adds.

"Because you recognized she was from the convent and killed her."

"I have already said that I have not. I have nothing to gain from lying at this point."

"Nevertheless, she is dead." I stare at him, willing myself to see past the flesh and bone to his soul and discern whether or not he is telling the truth.

"How did she die?" he asks.

I look away. "I do not know. There were no marks on her body, no bruises, cuts, or injuries."

"Surely the convent has ways of determining the cause of death."

"True, but we cannot discern it from a glimpse of the body in a bone cart on the side of the road."

Crunard's eyes are narrowed in thought. "And she had nothing on her?"

"Only her gown." She was wearing a plain gown, maid attire, now that I think about it. "And she was holding a white chess piece in her left hand."

The skin around his eyes tightens imperceptibly, as does his mouth. "I do know how she died, then, and I fear it was naught but an accident," he says gently. "She was merely caught in a trap set for someone else."

"An accident," I repeat hollowly. It was terrible enough that Matelaine had died on a mission she was not qualified to undertake. But to have her death be an accident makes it not only tragic but a waste.

Sensing my hesitation, Crunard continues. "If it is the truth you are after, perhaps you should ask yourself why I had access to Arduinna's snare, the convent's own poison. If it is the truth you are after, perhaps you should ask yourself why the abbess has sent you here now. Is there to be a trial? Does the duchess know? Duval? Do you truly know whose orders you are carrying out as you stand there and hand out death like God on Judgment Day?"

"You are guilty."

"No," he says dryly. "The man I sought to poison is very much alive." He frowns, as if still unable to understand how that happened, and I think of Ismae and her gift and her love for Duval.

"Perhaps you do not know quite as many convent secrets as you think you do," I tell him. "Now, what is your question? I would be done with you, at least for now, but I will not go back on my promise."

"What has the abbess told you of me?"

I am puzzled by the question, but even more so by his manner, which is almost tentative and seems out of character for him. "Nothing," I say truthfully. "I know only that you were her liaison at court, but she never spoke of you. Not until she explained you were responsible for Matelaine's death."

He is quiet for a long moment before he speaks again. "Have you another question, demoiselle?" While Crunard's words are most polite, there is an underlying tightness in his tone that perplexes me.

"No more for now," I tell him. "Only a warning. If you annoy me too much, I *will* kill you, the abbess and Mortain's justice be damned."

At the sound of the god's name, the hellequin quirks one eyebrow and holds up three fingers. It is the third time I have mentioned the god tonight. I glare at him, until he too falls silent.

Two leagues later, I call a halt for the night. Our horses need rest, even if we do not. It is a tedious camp, with Crunard making exaggerated, stilted movements, as if his bindings are cutting off his very life force, and the hellequin's moroseness filling the small clearing like smoke from the stuttering fire. I do my best to ignore them both, get Fortuna settled, and locate a soft spot on which to pass the rest of the night.

In an attempt to give Balthazaar something to do beside glare at Crunard, I hand him a length of rope. "Here. Tie Crunard up so that he cannot escape during the night."

Balthazaar visibly cheers at this, snapping the rope against his hands and carefully considering Crunard as he stalks toward him.

"I will not try to escape," Crunard says. "There is no need to tie me up."

"There is every need, as I do not trust you any more than I would a fox who has caught scent of a hen house. Your freedom calls to you so loudly that *I* can hear it singing in my ears. So, yes, we will tie you up."

With a sigh, Crunard settles on the ground where the hellequin has pointed. "I have no bedroll," Crunard observes.

I give a short laugh of disbelief. "I am not some maid to do your bidding and see to your comfort. You are a prisoner being escorted to a trial, a trial where you will very likely be sentenced to death. I care not how comfortable you are." I glance around us. "It is warm enough that you won't freeze, and there are no rain clouds nearby. Besides, surely a seasoned soldier such as yourself is well accustomed to a little hardship."

Crunard's mouth draws into a tight, firm line. My words have displeased him, and I can see the wheels of his mind turning as he tries to determine how to make me pay for this slight.

I turn to Balthazaar. "Shall I take first watch, or shall you?"

He pauses in his tying. "Hark! What sound is that? Does the fair maid ask for my help?"

I fold my arms. "If I did not plan on using you, I would not have allowed you to accompany us. Now, shall I take first watch, or shall you?"

"I will, as my need for sleep is less than yours."

"Do I have your promise that you will not somehow manage to kill the prisoner while I sleep?"

He glances at me, his eyes widening slightly in surprise. "Do you trust me so little, then?"

"Let us just say that it is easy to recognize the tactics of one who is as eager to do Mortain's work as I am. Your word."

After a pause, he nods. "You have it."

Crunard protests. "I cannot believe you will take his word but not mine."

I shake out my bedroll with a loud snap. "He has had occasion to prove his worth to me—more than once. You have not. Now, hold your tongue, else I will have him gag you."

After that, there is blessed silence. But even once I have made myself as comfortable as the forest floor will allow, I cannot settle my mind. It is as restless as a horse who has scented a pack of wolves, and I would do well to heed its warning.

Chapter Thirty-Five

TWO DAYS LATER, WE REACH Rennes in the early afternoon. I do not wish to announce to all and sundry that I have brought a traitor into the city — at least, not until I better understand the nature of the orders I have been given. I glance over at Crunard. "Pull your hood as far forward as you can."

He shoots me a questioning look, as if challenging me. "Don't tell me your courage has failed you, demoiselle?"

I lean over so he can hear me more clearly. "Lest the townsfolk recognize you, pull you from your horse, and decide to administer the duchess's justice on their own."

He does as instructed.

We are not stopped at the gate, although one of the sentries gives Balthazaar a long hard look, but then he sees me and recognizes that I serve Mortain.

Our journey through the streets of the city is similarly unimpeded and people almost seem to make way before us — whether because of the faint sense of darkness that clings to Balthazaar as firmly as his cloak, his pawing, prancing stallion, or the fact that Crunard's hands are tied, I cannot tell. Whatever the reason, by the time we reach the palace courtyard, a small crowd has gathered and follows us at a distance.

I angle my horse to block the sight of Crunard somewhat, then dismount. A groom hurries forward to take the reins, looking nervously at

Balthazaar's horse. The hellequin ignores him and speaks directly to me. "I do not think you will be needing my help anymore."

"No. I do not think that I will." I long to ask when—if—I will see him again. On the ramparts—perhaps even later tonight? But I do not.

He bows in his saddle, then turns his mount and canters out of the courtyard, causing grooms and the overly curious bystanders to scatter like ashes before the wind.

When I look away from Balthazaar's departing figure, I find Crunard watching me. Before I can tell him to keep his bedamned eyes to himself, there is a small flurry of movement at the entrance to the palace, and a slim, black silhouette emerges from the door. It is the abbess, her hands clutched tightly in front of her, her gaze searching the courtyard. Seeing me, she relaxes somewhat and a welcoming smile touches her lips. As if she believes I have done precisely what she asked and now everything will be as it once was between us.

I smile back, but there is no warmth in it. Then I step out of the way to show her who I brought with me. When she sees Monsieur Crunard, a mask of anger slams into place.

But not before I see the glimmer of fear. She is not simply angry that Crunard is here—she is terrified.

Ismae comes running out of the palace just then and spots me immediately. If she is relieved that I have returned, she does not show it as plainly as the abbess. Or mayhap she simply had more faith in my abilities.

At the sight of Monsieur Crunard, her eyes widen in surprise. She lifts her skirts and hurries down the steps to join me in the courtyard. As she draws closer, her gaze goes again to Crunard, narrowing this time, and the heat of her glare reminds me of all that this man has done to betray his country and our convent. Unable to help myself, I search out the abbess once more, only to find she is no longer waiting upon the steps, but has returned inside.

I take Ismae's arm and pull her a short way from Crunard so he cannot hear us. "Is he marqued?"

She glances at him again, her eyes raking over him in open disdain. "No. And why that is the case, I do not know. What will you do with him now that he is here?"

"Ismae, he knows things about the convent and the abbess. Things that may help us determine what game she is playing. He seems to think I was sent to kill him because the abbess wished to be rid of him rather than because of his actual crimes. And while it is not surprising that he would claim such a thing, if you see no marque on him, then that bears him out somewhat."

She nods reluctantly. "It at least warrants careful consideration."

"Can we put him in the dungeons here? It should not make any difference as to where he is imprisoned, should it?"

She pats my arm reassuringly. "If it does, we will find a way to turn it to our advantage. Let me escort you and help get him settled."

I look at her in surprise, and she laughs. "Oh, I do not mean to see to his comfort, only to be certain the guards know he is a prisoner and that he is to be well guarded."

I gratefully accept Ismae's offer, for I do not know where the dungeons are, nor do I know if the men would take an order from me. But mostly, I do not wish to appear a bumbling green fool under Crunard's sharp gaze that misses nothing. Every time I hesitate or fumble, I fear I have unwittingly given him some new weapon to use against me.

Once Crunard is safely locked behind a wood and iron door, Ismae and I make our way back to the palace proper, my mind churning like a water wheel.

"What are you thinking on so furiously?" Ismae asks.

"How to get the abbess to tell me the truth."

Ismae laughs. "You may as well ask how to keep an ass from braying or a bird from flying. I am beginning to think she has lost the ability to tell a plain truth."

"I fear you have the right of it. Perhaps I will simply claim that Crunard has told me everything and demand to know if it is true. As if I am giving her a chance to clear her name before I condemn her in my own mind."

Ismae smiles. "You are frighteningly good at playing these games with her."

"Only because I have done so my entire life," I mutter. Just then, a page comes racing toward us, breathless as he skids to a stop.

"My lady," he huffs out to Ismae. "You are to report to the duchess's chambers immediately."

Ismae grabs the boy's shoulders. "Is it Princess Isabeau?" she asks, her fear for the young girl plain in her voice.

The page replies, "Oh no, my lady! It is Marshal Rieux. He is here and requesting an audience with the duchess."

"Go," I tell her. "I can find my own way to the abbess's chambers."

In answer, Ismae reaches out and grabs my hand. "No, come with me. Best you hear what is said as well. Besides, the abbess will no doubt already have been summoned."

The duchess's privy chamber is nearly full by the time we arrive. All of her councilors — Duval, Captain Dunois, Chancellor Montauban, Jean de Chalon, the bishop, and even Father Effram — are there. Ismae and I slip in unnoticed by most except for Duval, who appears to be attuned to Ismae's presence like a bee to a flower, and the abbess, who notes my arrival with a look of dour disapproval.

Once the duchess is seated, the rest of her councilors take their seats. Ismae, Sybella, and I remain standing. Duval has us positioned just behind the duchess's chair and motions us to expose our weapons. As I step into place beside Sybella, she reaches out and gives my arm a squeeze of greeting.

Then Marshal Rieux is announced and brought into the chamber. He is a tall man with an imposing manner and is dressed in an elegant doublet and cloak. "Your Grace," he says with a deep bow. For all that he has come to worm his way back into the duchess's good graces, it looks as if it pains him to bend his knee to her.

"Marshal Rieux." The duchess tilts her head in greeting, her voice cool and distant.

"I am pleased to see you are well, Your Grace." His words are awkwardly delivered but seem sincere nonetheless.

"With no thanks to you." Duval throws the words down like a gauntlet.

Marshal Rieux shakes his head. "I had nothing to do with the trap d'Albret sprang before Nantes. We argued fiercely over it, and it is one of the many reasons he and I have parted ways."

Duval glances at Sybella, who gives a tiny nod of confirmation. Rieux's gaze follows the movement, his eyes growing wide when he sees who Duval is communicating with. "What is she doing here?"

"You have no authority to question those who serve me." The duchess's reprimand is swift and sharp and I wish to hug her for her staunch support of Sybella.

With some difficulty, Rieux swallows whatever further arguments he had been planning on making. "That is true, Your Grace, but she can also vouch for me. She was there and saw me arguing with d'Albret. We nearly came to blows over it. Tell them," he demands.

All of us turn to look at Sybella, who studies him much as a cat deciding whether a skinny mouse is worth the effort. "It is true that you argued with him over that trap. But it is also true that you were at his side when he took Nantes, that you stood idly by while his men slaughtered innocent palace retainers and city folk."

The room is as quiet as a tomb, and Rieux himself has gone pale as Sybella throws his crimes at his feet. "Yes, but what you cannot know —since you did not ride out on those sorties yourself—is that neither I nor my men participated. We had no idea his methods would be so brutal, else I would never have supported him in the first place."

"You mean, else you never would have betrayed the duchess in the first place." Duval's voice is harder than stone.

Rieux turns to the duchess and speaks directly to her. "Your Grace, your father assigned me to guard over you, as both your tutor and your advisor."

"A sacred duty that you not only abandoned, but betrayed."

He takes a step forward, and as one, Sybella, Ismae, and I place our hands on our weapons. He stops. "Your Grace, it was but a play to force you to do what I thought best for you and the country. In my own way, I was being loyal to the duty your father had entrusted to me."

"But you were not loyal to *me.*"

"I have never stopped being on your side," he insists. "Which is why I left d'Albret once I understood the full scope of his plans. My troops and I have chased the French from three towns."

"But how do we know you speak the truth?" Lord Duval asks. "How do we know you are not here simply because d'Albret is dead and you wish to throw your lot in with the stronger side now that the tide has turned?"

Marshal Rieux's head snaps back to Duval. "D'Albret is dead?"

"As good as."

The marshal looks over at Sybella, who gives a brief nod, confirming

Duval's words. He looks stunned for a moment, then shakes his head. "Though it pains me to say it of any man, that is probably a good thing, I fear."

At his words, Lord Duval and Captain Dunois exchange a look. "So why are you here?" the captain asks.

Marshal Rieux looks up again, as if surprised they need ask. "Why, to offer my fealty to the duchess and serve her as marshal once more. This is no time for internal differences to divide us."

"It was no time to be divided four months ago either."

"And I have seen the error of my ways. I am asking for a second chance and offering you the not insignificant resources I have at my disposal."

"How could we trust you again?" the duchess asks, and this time, her voice sounds young to my ears, as if there is as much heartbreak beneath her question as political calculation.

"I know that I will have to earn that trust back slowly, piece by agonizing piece, but I am asking for a chance to do so."

It is the right answer, and Duval and Dunois exchange glances once more. "You cannot expect Her Grace to decide this immediately. She will need to think on it."

"Of course. I await your pleasure, Your Grace. But do not wait too long, for of a certainty, the French regent will not."

"Wait!" It is Sybella who speaks, drawing all eyes toward her. "Does that mean you know what plot d'Albret was hatching with the French regent?"

Rieux stares at her, surprise etched clearly on his face, as if he realizes he has just been granted an opportunity to make himself valuable. "And you do not?"

Sybella gives a sharp shake of her head, and Rieux turns back to the duchess. "D'Albret always claimed that if he could not have the duchy as his own, he would hand it over to the French regent. When he received word that Your Grace had been married by proxy to the Holy Roman emperor, he began negotiations with the French. He plans to hand over the city of Nantes to them."

A collective gasp goes up around the room, and the duchess's small hands grow white as she grips the arms of her chair.

"That is the reason I am here, Your Grace. If we do not join forces, we shall surely fall."

The shocked silence that fills the room is louder than a hundred murmuring voices. Then, almost as one, all turn to look at Sybella, myself included. Although she holds her head high and proud, I sense the tangle of feelings in her: anger, embarrassment, defiance, and shame. Instead of acknowledging any of those, she meets Duval's questioning gaze. "Well, now we know," she says.

"Are you certain — very certain, my lady — that you did not know this earlier?" It is Chalon who asks the question.

Before she can answer him, Beast turns on Chalon, who visibly blanches at the anger and heat he sees there. "I know you are not questioning the lady's loyalty, my lord, for she has done more than any of us here to ensure the duchess's and our kingdom's safety." Beast's voice is soft, polite even, but there is no mistaking the threat that underlies his every word.

The entire room watches silently as Chalon splutters out an apology. When he has finished, Sybella answers the question he posed.

"I did not," she says. "But I cannot say it surprises me, for it became clear that he was like an enraged child who would break a toy completely before allowing another to play with it."

I cannot help but think it is a frighteningly apt description of what Count d'Albret has done to our country.

Chapter Thirty-Six

CONTEMPLATING THE FULL WEIGHT OF what Rieux has told us, Duval begins stroking his chin. "We will need to know if the city is resisting, or if its citizens have accepted French rule as easily as they did d'Albret's."

Marshal Rieux shifts on his feet. "There are rumored to be small pockets of resistance, my lord, for while few understood that d'Albret was not acting with the full blessing of the duchess, most everyone knows that the French assuredly have no such blessing."

"Do we know what they plan to do? Simply hold the town? Use it to launch their offensive?"

"No," Rieux says. "D'Albret did not trust me with the full details of his plan."

"Do we know if he made the deal with the French regent or the king himself?"

"Does it matter?" Chalon asks.

"It could, possibly. The regent, the king's sister, has been in charge since their father's death, and even though the king reached his majority two years ago, she still appears to be holding the reins. If they are not in agreement, or if the king is champing at the bit to take control on his own, perhaps we can use that to create some sort of wedge between them."

"To what purpose?" the bishop asks.

Duval shrugs, then glances pointedly at Marshal Rieux. "To weaken them, as our wedges have weakened us. And perhaps to buy us enough time for an opportunity to present itself."

"Buy us a miracle, you mean."

Duval nods. "That is precisely what I mean. Opportunity, miracle —I welcome them all."

"How do you propose to determine who is in charge?" Captain Dunois asks.

Beast's voice rumbles through the room. "Do not even think of sending the Lady Sybella."

Duval glances over at his friend. "It never crossed my mind," he assures him.

Chancellor Montauban speaks for the first time. "But the information could prove most beneficial, as you have stated."

"I will go." Ismae's quiet words cause the room to fall silent.

Duval looks at her as if she is mad. "No, you will not. We have others we can send. Besides, what of your duties to the duchess?"

Ismae nods at me. "Annith is here now, and she is more than capable of serving the duchess in my stead. Indeed, she is far better suited for it than I."

The two of them stare at each other a long moment before Ismae speaks. "This is what I am trained for," she reminds him softly. "You cannot turn a wolf into a lap dog."

Duval opens his mouth, then closes it, then opens it again. "We will speak of this later," he finally says.

Ismae smiles. "We will, my lord." And I have no doubt that she will be going to Nantes.

The meeting winds down quickly after that, in no small part because it is clear from the dark glances Duval keeps sending Ismae that he wishes to dissuade her from going. As for me, my thoughts are taken up with the abbess and what I will say to her once we are alone.

The duchess formally dismisses us with thanks for our counsel. As she stands, her eyes seek out mine and she smiles. "I look forward to having you as one of my ladies," she says.

I drop a curtsy. "The honor is all mine, Your Grace."

She smiles again and shifts her attention to her brother, releasing me from her presence. I turn to find the abbess has already quit the room so that I must hurry to catch up with her. There are enough other courtiers in the hallway that I do not wish to gallop after her, so instead I call out softly, "Reverend Mother! If it please you, I would have a word." She halts her progress but does not turn to greet me.

When I reach her, I dip another curtsy. "I would speak with you of my trip to Guérande and what I learned there. I think you will find it as enlightening as I did."

"I know everything I need to know about your trip." The barely controlled fury in her voice fair blisters my skin. "You have failed in the duties Mortain set before you."

I open my mouth to explain that Crunard was not marqued, but she does not let me so much as speak. "Clearly," she continues, her voice low and heated, "I was correct in not sending you out on assignment earlier. Now leave me. I do not have time to discuss your mistakes in depth." She glances over my shoulder, then gives me a sour smile. "Besides, I believe the duchess has need of you."

Then she continues walking down the hall, her head held high, and I am left standing in her wake, all my questions and accusations rolling around like stones in a barrel with nowhere to go.

"Lady Annith?"

The duchess's voice pulls me out of my thoughts, and I whirl around and sink into a deep curtsy. "Your Grace."

"I would request you attend upon me and Isabeau, as Ismae wishes to argue with my brother over whether or not she will be going to Nantes."

"But of course, Your Grace. It would be my honor." I hope for Ismae's sake that her arguments will prove more fruitful than mine have.

As I walk with the duchess back to her solar, she gives me an apologetic glance. "I am sorry if you have other pressing duties you wish to attend to." I detect a faint note of curiosity in her voice and realize she is intrigued by my role at the convent. If only she knew how little I've truly done.

"Not at all, Your Grace. The reverend mother and I were just making arrangements to meet later."

"Good." She smiles, showing a charming dimple. "Isabeau has been begging for stories, and I have none. Perhaps you will have one or two."

"But of course, Your Grace. I know a number of stories. How is her health, by the way?" I feel a sharp pang of guilt for having done nothing to help the young princess.

The dimple disappears. "She is holding steady and has grown no worse. Neither does she grow any better, however."

We have arrived at the solar, and I follow the duchess into the room. Isabeau is snuggled deep in her bed, her skin nearly as pale as the snowy linen sheets, her eyes too large in her small, pointed face. She may not be any worse, but one does not need to serve Mortain to know that this child will never get any better. Her days are truly numbered.

The duchess motions me toward Isabeau, then goes to speak with the girl's attendants. I sit myself down on a nearby stool and pull it close to the bed. We have not spent much time together, Isabeau and I, but I am immediately drawn to her fragility coupled with her valiant spirit. "I hear you are wishing for more stories. What story is your favorite?"

"My favorite is the one about how Amourna went to the Underworld to become its queen."

Ah, how very clever of Ismae to tell her that story. What story should

I tell? The younger girls at the convent love the story of the time Salonius, the god of mistakes, tricked Death, but I do not wish to give
Isabeau false hope. Instead, I tell her the story of how Saint Brigantia
outsmarted Camulos, the god of war and battle.

When I am done, she asks, "Did you know my sister is dedicated to
Saint Brigantia?"

"No, but I am not surprised, for she is very smart."

"Maybe she can outfox France, just as Saint Brigantia did."

"If anyone can find a way," I assure her, "it will be she." Then I think
of the tale I have not told her yet, one I'm sure she would dearly love to
hear. "Have you heard the story of Saint Arduinna? Of how she came to
a young ruler's aid?"

Isabeau grows absolutely still, her eyes huge. "No," she whispers.

"Well, once upon a time, a young woman ruled over our fair land.
She was wise and kind and much loved by her people, but she was beset
by enemies on all sides. Enemies in the north, enemies in the south, and
especially enemies just across her eastern border.

"The young ruler had many resources at her disposal — a valiant
army, a skilled navy, and many, many wise counselors to advise her.

"She also had something that no other ruler had ever had before, and
that was a young sister who loved her with a love that was stronger than
all those armies put together." She ducks her head, but not before I see
a small, pleased smile.

"The poor ruler's enemies were great, and her problems many, so
one night her young sister decided to take matters into her own hands.
She snuck out of bed when no one was looking and crept down flights
of stairs and long dark hallways to the small chapel."

"Was she frightened?"

"She was terrified, but she was determined to do this for her sister. It
was the only way she could think of to help. Finally, she arrived at the

chapel. Once there, she placed an offering on the niche of Saint Arduinna and said the sacred prayer to invoke her protection.

"Then she crept back to bed, exhausted and made ill because of her
nighttime journey."

Isabeau coughs just then and looks faintly guilty.

"The stories do not say what sort of protection the sister wished for
the young ruler. What do you imagine she prayed for?" I ask.

"Well." Isabeau makes a great show of thinking upon the question,
her face scrunched up and one small finger placed under her chin. "She
had armies and knights to help with the fighting, so that probably was
not it."

Good, I think. They have been able to protect this child from knowing how dire our situation is.

"My guess would be that the girl was worried about her sister's
heart."

"Her heart?"

"Yes. For the young ruler had no one to love, save for the little sister,
and the sister wished for the young ruler to have someone to love in
case . . . in case anything ever happened to her."

I stare into Isabeau's eyes and see that she knows full well that she is
not long for this world. That she worries about her sister at a time like
this is a testament to her remarkable character.

"Well." Unable to help myself, I reach out and smooth the silky
strands of hair away from her face. "The ways of Arduinna are mysterious, but the goddess of love heard the young girl and accepted her offering. Shortly thereafter, she sent a handful of her best warriors to see
what they could do to assist the young ruler."

Isabeau settles back against the pillow, a small, satisfied smile upon
her lips. "I know," she says, surprising me, for I have made up the entire
story on the spot as a way to tell her that the Arduinnites have come.

"How do you know?" I ask, in mock outrage. "How can you know the end to my story?"

She giggles, a truly delightful sound. "Because Father Effram told me."

"He did?"

"Yes." She looks around the room to see where her sister is. When she is certain we cannot be overheard, she leans forward slightly. "And he told me that you are who they sent."

When the child has fallen asleep, I leave her side and cross the room to attend the duchess. At my approach, she looks up from her embroidery. "You are good with children, demoiselle."

"I was raised in a convent full of motherless girls, many of them younger than me. I am used to their ways and their needs."

"Did you know that is one of the options the French regent has offered me? To have me sealed away in a convent for the rest of my life?"

I raise my brows. "I had not heard that, Your Grace."

"Oh, it is not their official position, of course. Officially, they have located several suitable husbands for me, nearly all of them over sixty and in possession of no more than half their original wits. It is either wed one of them or be sent to their convent, and I assure you, the convent the regent has in mind is not nearly as interesting as the one you serve." She looks up at me suddenly. "Have you been satisfied with your life? Spending your days in prayer and devotion and service to your saint?"

Ah, and what do I tell her? That I thought I was until I learned that the abbess is corrupt and no longer trust anything she says? But, I remind myself, that is not the whole of it. "I have always wished to serve the Divine, Your Grace."

"When did you first realize that was your life's wish?"

That is harder to answer. Especially now when I must work to separate my own desires from those the convent has planted in me. But —no. Actually, it is not hard, for I remember the moment so clearly: it was when Mortain came to me, sat beside me, His gentle presence an inspiration, a comfort, and a source of strength, and I realized that I wanted to be worthy of that presence, to be in that presence as much as possible. "Ever since I was old enough to have desires, that is what I wished to do. Serve Him with all my heart." And now the abbess has torn everything asunder with her conniving, calculating plots and lies.

"I too have only ever wanted one thing since I was young—to serve my people as their leader. I too have loved my Church, and surely it is my faith that has seen me through these hard years. But more than my love of the Church, my love of Brittany has shaped my life, molded me. I have loved my people, been buoyed by their cheering, found strength in their faith in me, and been comforted by their warm regard. It is what I have been trained for, raised for, to be their leader and to see to their interests. But now—now I fear that their trust has been misplaced. I fear that I will not be worthy of the honor they have done me. Here I sit with war at our doorstep and the conviction that no matter what I do, I will have failed them."

The despair in her voice pierces my heart, and I kneel beside her. "Your Grace, you have been left with very few choices, and none of them good. I am sure your people understand you are doing the best you can."

"But will it be good enough?" she whispers.

And as I stare at her, this young girl whose father left her with an unstable kingdom, an empty treasury, and a surfeit of suitors, none of whom cared one fig for her beyond the riches she could bring to their coffers, I become angry. Just as I am angry on Matelaine's behalf, I am suddenly furious for this girl—for that is all she is, a thirteen-year-old girl—whose guardians have abandoned her in pursuit of their own

ambitions. "Your Grace, it is not you who have failed, but your father."
The moment the words are out of my mouth, I regret them, for surely
I am taking an egregious liberty.

But then she looks up at me with a faint glimmer of . . . hope? Relief? I do not know her well enough to understand what she is feeling.
She stops stitching and closes her eyes for a moment. At first, I think she
is struggling not to cry. But when she opens them again, I see that she is
angry, furious, in fact, and struggling to rein it in. When she speaks, her
voice is so soft I must lean in close to catch the words. "There are times
when I am alone in my bed at night and cannot sleep for the fear and
worry trying to claw their way out of my belly. On those nights I am so
angry with my father." She whispers, as if even now that he is dead, he
might somehow hear her.

And suddenly, she is no longer my duchess or sovereign, but a young
wounded thing, like those who arrive at the convent every year, and it
is that girl that I try to speak to. "As you should be, Your Grace. We are
given no choices in life—we must rely on our fathers or guardians to
make them for us. And when they choose poorly or make weak decisions, they risk destroying our entire lives with their folly. How can
we not be angry?" By the time I finish talking, I am no longer certain
whom I am talking about: the duchess or myself.

Chapter Thirty-Seven

ONCE I HAVE BEEN DISMISSED, I return to my chambers. My conversation with the duchess has stirred up all my simmering anger and frustration, like muck at the bottom of a pond. Alone in the room, my breath comes fast, my fists clenching at my sides. Between Crunard's insinuations and my own confrontations with the abbess, I am drawing close — so close — to finally understanding what is at the heart of the abbess's plots and intrigues. Crunard knows more than he is telling. I do not know if this is some strange game being played between him and the abbess or if he knows even more about the convent than she does.

Of course, the simplest answer is the most painful one, that she is lying — has been lying — to me since the beginning.

Frustration bubbles up from deep inside, so hot and urgent I fear I will scream. Instead, I stride over to the clothes chest, lift the lid, and root through my meager belongings there. When my hand closes around the satin-smooth finish of lacquered wood, I pull the black box from the depths of the chest and carry it over to the window. Even in the bright light of the afternoon sun, I can find no seam, no joint, nothing to indicate how it can be opened. Other than by breaking it.

I take the box over to fireplace, place it on the hard stone hearth, and grab an iron poker from where it leans against the wall. I raise it up over my shoulder, then bring it down against the smooth unmarred surface.

It sinks in with a splintering crack. I place my foot on the box to hold it steady, then pull the poker back up and strike again. And again and again, until I am certain the noise will bring someone running. I toss the poker to the floor, then pick up the box and begin yanking the splintered wood away from the hole that I have made.

When there is an opening big enough, I shove my hand inside, ignoring the sting of splinters biting into my flesh. My fingers search, but I feel no parchment or vellum, only a slim rod of some sort. Slowly, I maneuver the thing around until I can extract it from the hole I have made.

It is long and thin, with a piece of chipped stone at one end. An arrow shaft, I realize, with some ancient arrowhead still attached. Not answers, then, but some musty relic. With a growl of frustration, I hurl the arrow onto the bed, then slam the box onto the floor, relishing the cracking sound it makes. It is all I can do to resist grinding the wretched thing under my heel until it is naught but sawdust and ash.

Instead, I take a deep breath and force myself to a state of calm. The abbess refused to see me this afternoon, but she cannot put me off forever. I do not care with whom she is sequestered or what duties she is performing, I will force a meeting with her and find out what rotten core is at the heart of the twisted web she weaves. I am so close to *knowing*. It is as if I can put my hand out and feel the shape and contours of the lies, but I am unable to discern the whole of it.

I will meet with the abbess tomorrow, and this time, I will not be put off.

I am not able to get in to see her until the afternoon. It is late, and most people have retired to make ready for dinner, but not the abbess. She is still at work in her office. I rap once on the door. "Come in," she calls out. Her invitation to enter surprises me — I had expected some resistance — but I step into her office, then shut the door firmly behind me.

At the loud click, she looks up, scowling when she sees it is me. "I did not send for you."

"You also told me to kill Crunard, and I did not, so clearly my desire to follow your every order has waned somewhat."

"You are making a grave mistake. Do you think I favor you so much that I will not punish you?"

"Do you honestly think that I care any longer? My need for answers —for the truth—has grown far greater than my need to please you. Now tell me," I demand, "what lies between Crunard and yourself. Tell me why you have not sent me out until now. Tell me why you ordered him killed when he bears no marque at all."

"You can see marques?" She studies me closely and I consider demanding to know what she put in the Tears that caused me to go blind. Except I am not certain enough that she is behind it to risk sharing that information with her. It would be too easy for her to use it against me.

"No. I cannot. But Ismae can, and once Crunard was here in Rennes, I had her look for me. What happened to Matelaine? Why was she gone so long if she was only to kill Crunard?"

Her mouth pinches in annoyance, but she answers me all the same. "It was a complex assignment. Everyone in Guérande was on edge, and the man was in prison. It took her a while to get into position to make her move."

"You never saw a vision for her to kill Crunard, did you? She hesitated because she couldn't see a marque on him either, and yet you ordered her to remain there."

The abbess's nostrils flare. At first I think it is in irritation, but then I see how wide her pupils are, how rapidly the pulse in her neck is beating, and I realize it is fear. I take a step toward her. "Why are you so afraid of him?"

She turns and carefully folds the letter she's been reading. "I am not afraid of him; he has just become a liability to the convent. He has betrayed his country and shamed us by association. I truly believed him to be marqued."

"Believed? You told me Sister Vereda had Seen it, but if so, Ismae would have seen a marque."

She whips her gaze up from the letter and narrows her eyes. "And I told you that Vereda was too old, too enfeebled, to be relied on for such things any longer. Do not throw her vision in my face when you are the one who has defied my order to replace her."

"How can you take His will into your own hands like that? What gives you the right to break the rules that lies at the heart of our service to Him?"

She does not answer, and as she sits there, saying nothing, my frustration continues to simmer until it boils over. "Tell me precisely what is going on and why I should not report it to the others. Then, once you have told me that, you will explain why you sent Matelaine out instead of me."

"You have been chosen to be the next seer—"

"No! *You* have chosen me to be the next seeress—not Mortain, not Vereda, *you*. And for no reason that anyone could determine. There are plenty of other virgin novitiates or nuns beyond childbearing years who could easily, perhaps even happily, step into that role. Sister Claude would welcome an opportunity to come in from the rookery."

The abbess gives a snort of derision. "You would put such weighty decisions in the hands of a tired old woman who reeks of bird droppings?"

"No," I say quietly. "I would put them in the hands of Mortain, where they belong." But it is too late. I understand now why she so desperately wants me to fill this role. "You want me to be seeress because you think you can control me. You think you will only have to make a suggestion here or nudge me a bit there to have me 'Seeing' precisely what you want me to." After all, not only have I had exceptional training in the assassin's arts, but in blind obedience and biddability as well. The thought of how much of my own will I have handed over to her and the Dragonette throughout the years causes a hot, painful wave of mortification to course through me.

"How can you threaten me?" The abbess rises to her feet, fists clenched. "I, who have spent my entire life at the convent protecting you, shielding you, saving you from that wretched woman?"

"The Dragonette?" I snort. "You did not shield me, or even save me —you were simply there once in a while to offer me comfort."

She stands as still as any statue as my words echo in the silence between us. Then she turns, as if she cannot bear to look upon me a second longer, but not before I see the pain that twists her mouth. "You do not wish to know the answers to your questions, not really."

"Oh, but I do. That is why I have left the convent and ridden one hundred and twenty leagues across the country. I have come in search of answers as well as my destiny."

"Your destiny? You think to find your destiny here? You will find nothing, nothing but heartache and things you do not want to know." She turns around then, her hands clasped before her and anguish in her eyes. "Annith, I beg you, leave off these questions. Return to the convent and assume the duties of seeress, and you will have a destiny to be proud of, one that few can claim as their own."

"What you do not seem able to grasp is that I will not return to the convent — not if I am forced to be seeress."

She draws herself up, and, to my surprise, her lips curl in a half smile. "You will change your mind when you hear the truth, for any sin that falls upon my head will also fall upon yours."

"Why? I was never a party to your scheming. I had no knowledge of your plans."

"That will not matter, for our close ties will speak far louder than any words you can say." She takes a step toward me, then another, until we are close enough that I can see the faint lines that have begun to appear at the corners of her eyes. Abruptly, she turns away. "Would you like to hear the story of your birth? I know it has plagued you for years, not knowing how you came into this world."

I blink in surprise and everything inside me grows still. "What do you mean?" My voice does not sound like my own. "No one knows anything about my birth." I am not at all certain I wish to hear, for I am suddenly terrified of this story I have hungered for my entire life.

Unaware of my inner turmoil, the abbess begins to speak, her voice soft, as if she is peering down the corridor of time. "It was raining that night. They had traveled far, and the lady had only an old castoff maid from her father's household, for he declared her dead to him once he learned of her plight. She was exhausted, and well beyond the point where she should have been traveling, but it was as if her shame and her heartache were some location on a map and she had to get as far away from them as she could.

"And then the pains began, leagues from a city of any size, and the lady and her maid both panicked. They stopped at the next house they passed and asked for the nearest midwife. There was none. The closest thing was the herbwife who lived at the edge of the mill road. It would have to do.

"It took them forever to reach it, with the rain and the mud, and the lady having to stop every few minutes and wait for the pain to pass. It was like someone had wrapped iron bands around her stomach and was squeezing. She dropped to her knees in the mud twice due to the pain.

"But she refused to have her baby—even a bastard babe—in the mud, so she pressed on, using her poor, near hysterical maid as a crutch.

"The herbwife—" Here the abbess pauses, a faint smile playing on her lips. "She seemed to be expecting them and opened her door as they drew near. The fire had already been built up, and clean sheets put on the single narrow bed in the one-room cottage. Drying herbs hung from the ceiling, so low the lady had to duck in places.

"The pains were coming much more quickly then, so quick she could scarce catch her breath. Before she could even lie down, there was a great gushing and water ran down her leg. She thought she would die from embarrassment, but that feeling quickly dissolved in the next squeeze that gripped her belly.

"The herbwife and the maid helped the lady onto the bed, and the next hours narrowed into an endless blur of pain and sweat. She could not help but scream, as she feared the pains would rend her in two—punishment, no doubt, for the sins she had committed.

"You arrived in the world after one last anguished push." She smiles again and glances up at me with such fondness, such tenderness, that I am struck dumb. "As the herbwife wrapped you tightly in swaddling, the lady's maid cleaned up her mistress as best she could, and then you were placed in her arms. You were perfect even then."

"How can you know all this?" I whisper.

She lifts her gaze to meet mine. "Have you not yet guessed, Annith? You are my own flesh and blood, born of my body. Every sin I have committed, every rule I have broken, every girl you feel I have betrayed in some way—it has all been done out of my love for you, for you are my own daughter."

The sheer audacity of her claim presses down on my chest, making it hard to draw breath. My mind scrambles to fit this new revelation into all that I know of the world. If I am sired by Mortain, can the abbess also be sired by Him? Surely He would not lie with His own daughter? "So you lied to the convent? You are not sired by Mortain?" The enormity of this is such that I can scarce wrap my mind around it.

The abbess stares at me, her eyes more human than I have ever seen them, and there is genuine sympathy there. It is all I can do not to place my hands over my ears, and something cold and slippery slithers in my belly.

"No, Annith. I am not." She takes a step closer, and although I long to back away from her, the wall is already behind me and I have nowhere to go. "And neither are you."

Chapter Thirty-Eight

MY WORLD SHATTERS into a thousand pieces, each one of them as sharp as glass. Each one of them slicing me from the mooring that has anchored me my entire life.

I am not one of Mortain's own, not His daughter, not His handmaiden. I am nothing to Him. Nothing. My chest grows tighter and tighter, as if the god Himself is wringing the very air from my lungs until I can scarcely breathe. "You are lying," I say, but my voice is weak, my words a feeble attempt to fend off an opponent's mortal blow. "You are simply saying that to taint me with your sins, in the hope that I will fear whatever punishment heaped on you will also fall upon me. You, not me, have deceived everyone into believing you were sired by Mortain." A hot bitterness fills my belly and I fear I will be sick.

She ignores my outburst and continues with her story. "All my anger and outrage at my circumstances disappeared in that moment, for whatever else I had endured, it had brought me you. My feeling of euphoria lasted but an hour before worries of what we would do, how we would survive in this world on our own with no family to support us and no friends willing to take us in. I even asked if I could apprentice to the herbwife in exchange for my keep — and yours — but she laughed and said she could scarce scratch out a living on her own.

"So all that long night, as I held you and you dozed and suckled at my breast, I tried to think of a way we could be together and have some life that did not involve begging or selling ourselves to the highest bidder. Since you were a bastard—a mistake—I could have taken you to one of Saint Salonius's orphanages, but they would not have allowed me to stay, so I would never have seen you again. Or I could have found work at a brothel or tavern, but who would hire a woman with a babe for such work?

"And then I remembered my youngest sister, who had been sent away to a convent when she was thirteen, a convent that took in young girls and trained them for service. So in the morning, when some sleep had returned my wits, the herbwife asked me who the father was, and I told her Mortain, and began to lay the foundation for my great lie."

"And she believed you?"

"She did, for as she explained, Mortain brought many daughters into this world, and I must be especially favored if I was allowed to live to raise mine.

"But while that meant the convent would take you in, it would not gain me entrance, except mayhap as a wet nurse for the first few months of your life. So I plotted some more, and by the end of the week, I had a plan firmly in place. It was not without its costs, and they were high, but it was the best I could salvage from the wreckage of my life, and so I committed to it with every fiber of my being and vowed to make it work.

"I told the herbwife I would accompany her to the hedge priest who would see that you were delivered to the convent, which I did. That was the hardest part, being separated from you for the first few months, but it was so we could be together for the rest of our lives.

"As I stood in the shadow of the church and watched the night rower row you out to the convent, I cried so much I thought I would die from it. The pain of that was far worse than any of the birthing pains."

"Then what did you do?"

"And then I went to Brest, found work in a respectable tavern for three months, and came up with a convincing story that I could present at the convent when I arrived, a story that I had been sired by Mortain and come late to His service." She spreads her hands wide in supplication, desperation shining clearly on her face. "Surely now you understand why you cannot speak of this to anyone. While my sins might be the greater, you will suffer as well."

I cannot think. I cannot even feel. I am empty as a barrel. "What is the punishment for such deceit?" I ask.

The abbess shrugs. "I do not know. I have never heard of anyone who has done it, but perhaps that simply means it was dealt with in silence."

"And my father? Who is he really?"

"He was charming, and well-titled. His family's holding bordered ours, so I had known him since I was a young child. I loved him. Or thought I loved him, and I was sure that he loved me too. He came to visit often, either to hunt with my father and his men or to pay court to the ladies of our house.

"I knew that at first he came for my older sister, Marie, but it soon grew obvious—at least to me—that in her fickleness, her attentions turned to another. But he did not see it, or would not accept it. Even now I do not know which it was. But my fair sister had higher ambitions than the neighbor baron. And even still, he thought he had a chance—thought that she was being forced by our parents into a different match.

"He and I talked frequently, either in person or by note. I thought this meant he had turned his attention—and his affection—to me, but he was merely gathering information on the one he truly desired."

"So he played you false." I harden my heart against her and what must have seemed a shocking betrayal to her. "What is his name? My family's name?"

She turns away from me then. "Is it not enough to know that he is not Mortain? What lies between us is old history that I do not wish to resurrect."

"Tell me."

She sighs, the sound coming from some great well of despair deep within her. "Crunard," she says at last. "Your real father is Crunard."

Chapter Thirty-Nine

As I leave the abbess's chambers, I feel as if I have been shrouded in a thick mist that prevents my thoughts from taking shape. It is as if someone has reached inside my chest and yanked my very self from my body. Or as if, with her words, the abbess created one loose thread, which she then used to unravel my entire soul.

I was not fathered by Mortain.

I bear not a single drop of His blood.

I was not born to serve Him, have received none of His gifts. Have, in fact, been an impostor on such a massive scale it is hard, even now, to grasp the fullness of it.

My mother never lay with Death, never welcomed Him into her life, except when she needed a refuge, a safe place to hide from the world. And she has pulled me, unwitting and unwilling, into the duplicity with her.

Even worse, she tried to have me commit patricide. For of all the crimes she has committed, surely that one is the most vile. I could have killed my own father and never even known it.

Of course, that was the abbess's intent. It is easy enough to see that now, with the benefit of hindsight. One quick strike, and the only person from her past who could expose her secrets would be silenced forever.

Without thinking about it, I find my feet leading me toward the back of the palace, then outside and down two long, winding flights of stairs until I find myself at the door behind which my true father sits, awaiting his judgment.

The lone guard considers asking me what my business is, but when he takes one look at my face, his mouth snaps shut. He, at least, does not yet know I was not sired by Mortain.

There is a single torch outside Crunard's cell, the light cast by its oily flames feeble against the thick darkness of the dungeon. I move as silently as a shadow to him, then lean back against the wall to watch him unobserved. Although I make no sound, he lifts his head and sees me. Slowly, he straightens, his eyes meeting mine.

"You knew, didn't you?" I ask.

He tilts his head. "I suspected, which is very different from knowing."

"Did you suspect from the very beginning, when I first showed up in Guérande?"

"No. Then I knew only that you had been sent to silence me. It wasn't until we were on the road the next day and I saw you in broad daylight that I noticed the similarities between you and the abbess."

I hold his gaze, unflinching. "And did you also know then that you were my sire?" I cannot call this stranger father.

His entire body stills. Indeed, it does not look as if he is even breathing. And then something in his face shifts and he smiles, surprising me. "You are my daughter. Well, I had wondered. Your abbess was a virgin when she and I knew each other, and your age seemed about right."

He stares at me with such a painful mixture of warmth and hope that I cross my arms, as if by that gesture I can ward off his affection. "You will forgive me if I do not greet the news quite as warmly. All my life I have been laboring under the assumption that I was sired by a god. To learn instead that I was sired by one of the kingdom's greatest traitors brings me little joy."

He shrugs. "And you will forgive me if I seem overzealous, but I have sat in the dungeons of Guérande for over three months now under the assumption that the very last of my children had been killed. To find that I have another is an unexpected mercy I never dared dream of. Even if she did try to kill me."

And then it hits me. Not only do I now have a human father—but I once had an entire family. The thought brings a surprising twist of pain with it—that I learned this only after they were all dead is yet one more thing the abbess has stolen from me. "Why did she want you dead?"

The sly look is back on his face before I have finished my question. Clearly, any affection he may feel for his daughter will not be at the expense of his own hide. "To cover up her crimes, of course."

"And what crimes would those be?"

"The crimes of not being a daughter of Mortain. Of having deceived not only the convent, but the crown. It is fraud. Surely you realize that. One can only imagine the punishment for such crimes."

And though his words do nothing more than echo my own thoughts, I know in my heart there is more to it than that. I do not ask the question that hovers on my lips: *How come you abandoned her and your unborn child to fend for themselves?* Instead, I ask, "How did you come to reconnect with her after all that time had passed?"

His faint chuckle surprised me. "That was purely by accident. As much a shock to me as to her, I assure you. In my position as chancellor to the late duke, I was also his unofficial spymaster and liaison with the convent. Imagine my surprise when I paid them a visit and found my ex-lover posing as abbess."

His mockery of her—when he had so callously abandoned her—rankles. "She was not posing as abbess. She came by that position through her own efforts and skill."

"Ah, I admire loyalty in my children. That speaks well of you, Annith."

I do not care for the sound of my name coming from his lips, nor do

I care for the tenderness with which he infuses it. "It is too bad that you were not as loyal to those whose lives you so carelessly used and then discarded," I say quietly. "Any loyalty I have learned has not come from you."

My heart heavier than it has ever been, I turn and leave the dungeon. I have a father. And brothers, though they are all most likely dead. Family.

The realization worms into me as I move through the palace corridors, trying to find my way back to my chamber, a place where I can be alone with my thoughts as the full weight of the abbess's treachery begins to settle over me.

She stole so much from me. With the choices she made, she took one life and gave me instead . . . an imprisonment. Memories of my early years in the convent fly through my head like a flock of disturbed crows, each one dark and unsettling. All those special sessions with the Dragonette. All those harsh punishments when I failed her tests. And the abbess—Sister Etienne—stood idly by.

No. Honesty forces me to admit that is not precisely true. She often *did* intervene, when she could. Slipped me bread or cheese when I had been denied supper. Snuck a candle to me so I could light the darkness of my punishment. She was often the one to unlock the door when it was over so she could fuss over me a bit and be certain I was all right.

Oh, how surprised she must have been when her imagined refuge turned into such a series of labors and trials! Her well-laid plans for the two of us collapsing under the weight of the Dragonette's spiritual ambition.

That thought causes my steps to falter as I realize—fully realize— how very hard that must have been for her. To have the haven she'd sought turn into such a grim reality. One she was just as powerless to alter as she would have been had she remained outside the convent.

Her sanctuary where the two of us need never be parted turned into a nightmare.

Is that why she wished me to be seeress? So we would still never need to be parted? How did she envision that future? Did she honestly think she could nudge and shape my visions to suit herself?

Or . . . another motive occurs to me. Perhaps it was her fear for my safety that controlled her actions. Her fear that, since I was not sired by Mortain, I would be vulnerable as I enacted His will in the world. Or mayhap she was concerned for my immortal soul.

But it matters not, for what she did was wrong. Doubly so when she sacrificed others such as Sybella and Matelaine to keep me safe. *She* is not the injured one here, no matter how she might try to present herself thus.

The closer I get to my chambers, the more I realize that I am unable to face Ismae and Sybella in my current state, and my feet change course, taking the next passageway out of the main corridor. Because I am tempted to hang my head in shame at the lie I have been a part of, I force myself to hold it high and squarely meet the glances of any of the passing nobles or courtiers who look at me. They do not know. Not yet.

But they will soon enough.

I cannot fathom how I am to exist in this world without my role as Death's handmaiden to give shape and purpose to my life. I feel as useless and unformed as wine without a cup.

And when it is learned who my father is? I may well be tossed into the dungeon beside him.

No. Ismae would not let that happen. She would tell them that I had no knowledge of any of this. But will they believe her?

The pain of it all twists inside me so that I must stop and grip the wall for support. And yet, even through the mists of the pain, I have to look down to be certain my legs are still attached to my body, for I can scarcely feel them any longer.

I force myself to resume walking—faster—as if I can escape the awareness the abbess has handed me. Before long, I find myself standing at the foot of the stairs that lead to the battlements, drawn there, just as those metal shavings found themselves drawn to the lodestone.

Yes, the pain inside me howls. Go to Balthazaar. He has lived with a similar pain for hundreds of years. Surely he will know what to do with it.

With no one to see, I lift my skirts and take the stairs two at a time, welcoming the strain it causes in my legs. When I reach the top, I am breathless and trembling, but that has nothing to do with my climb. I step outside into the cold, not surprised to see that night has fallen. Indeed, it feels as if entire lifetimes have passed in the space of the last hour.

Every single thing I have ever believed about my life is naught but a lie. That thought writhes through my mind—through my entire body—like a serpent. Nothing, not one thing is true. The girls I have called sisters all my life are not of my blood. Not even Ismae and Sybella. I am not the first and most skilled among a special cadre of His chosen handmaidens, but some blatant impostor slipped into His nest while He was not looking.

Every prayer I have ever uttered to Him rears up in my mind, filling me with mortification. Shying away from the pain of that, I search the shadows that pool along the stone walls. Anger begins to simmer through me when I do not see him, and I focus on that rather than my despair. The one time I wish him to be here, he is not. I want to put my head back and roar out a demand that he appear, but even in my current state, I cannot bring myself to be that bold. Instead, I begin walking along the length of the battlement in the opposite direction of the sentries. "Balthazaar?" I whisper into the darkness.

When there is no answer, I continue down to the farthest corner, where the catwalk disappears into a guard tower. I turn and look out over the battlements to the city below. I long to pray, but I no longer even know to whom I should direct my prayers. Salonius, the god of mistakes, perhaps?

There is a faint whisper of sound behind me. My heart lifts in hope as I whirl around, and there he is. "You came."

"I have always been here," he says. "Waiting."

My spirits rise at the faint goading in his voice. I fold my arms and take three steps toward him. "Well, you need wait no longer. Here I am." Then I reach out, put my hands against his chest, and shove. Caught off-guard, he stumbles. I push again, and again, until he is up against the wall. He looks down at me, his face a mask of confusion.

"You've wanted me since the night when you first happened upon me. Well, now I am giving myself to you." I have denied myself so much in the belief that I owed my life to others, but that belief is gone now. If I am nothing other than the most ordinary of mortals, then I may as well roll in the full slop of life.

I want Balthazaar's arms around me, his lips upon mine. I want to feel something other than this howling nothingness that screams through my soul.

I reach up and wrap my arms around Balthazaar's neck, rise up on my toes, then plant my lips on his. Or try to.

"Wait." He pulls away, staring down at me as if I have sprouted antlers. "What is it you want?"

I stare at him steadily. "You. Me. Entwined." I want him to make me forget. Make me remember. Make me feel extraordinary in this new, mortal way that is all that is left to me.

When he continues to hesitate, I grow incensed. How dare he change his mind now, when I have decided this is what I want? "But if you are not man enough, there are thousands of soldiers wandering the city. I'm

311

sure one of them will oblige." I turn to leave, holding my breath to see if he will let me go, exalting when he reaches out and grabs my arm. He spins me around so that my back is against the wall. He is angry now. I respond by leaning into it, by letting his fury ignite my own and using it to warm the chill at the very heart of my being.

"Something's changed you."

"Yes." Something has changed me, but it has also freed me. I feel a frantic bubble of laughter rising in my throat. I have always felt torn in two by my opposing desires—to live my own life, or to serve Mortain as He wills it. Well, I have only my own life to live now. And what I want—in this moment—is to *feel*. I want to feel something new and forbidden. I want to feel powerful in some way—as I do when Balthazaar looks at me with heat in his eyes. I want to feel the full force of that heat on my lips, my hands, my entire body. I reach for him again and this time he does not stop me. Slowly, I bring my lips up to his.

"I do not want to take you against the wall." His lips brush against mine with each word, his gaze boring into me as if plumbing my depths to see what is hidden there.

"But I *want* to be taken against the wall." I nibble at his lips in the same way I would a sweetmeat. I welcome the bite and chafe of the rough stone against my back.

"You're angry . . ."

"It's nothing to do with you."

"But what if you regret this?"

I pull far enough away that I can glare at him. "For a spawn of the Underworld, you have far too much honor."

He does not look away but instead waits patiently for my answer.

I sigh. "Trust me, on the long list of regrets I might have, this would be near the bottom." To convince him, I begin unlacing my gown.

He grabs my hands to still them, but this time he pulls me away from the wall. With my hands still wrapped in his, he leads me down the battlement.

As we draw out of the shadows, I am tempted to keep my head down in case one of the sentries should see us. Except my action shames no one but me, and I am not ashamed of what I am doing. It is perhaps the only thing I am not ashamed of right now. It feels as if it is one of the most honest things I have ever done.

It is comforting, this new knowing where my boundaries lie. Before, it was as if I were still forming, waiting for the edges of my self to fill in. But now I know that this is it. The sum and total of who I am and who I will ever be is already contained within me.

Balthazaar pauses outside a narrow door, listens, then opens it. It is a storage room of sorts, full of extra weapons and unused armor. It is, I think, the perfect place.

He swiftly shuts the door, then pulls me closer. He lifts his hands to my face and cups it, his eyes searching mine. "Are you certain?"

In answer, I put my arms around his neck again and press my entire body along the length of his. "Yes." The word rings as clear and sharp as a bell, for I am certain of nothing but this. My waiting is over; it is now time to claim the life that I want, even if I must drag it kicking and screaming to a garrison closet.

Then—finally!—he leans down to place his lips on mine.

It is everything I remember. At first, they are surprisingly cool, but within seconds it is as if the heat of my own desire flows into him as he takes what I offer, moving his own mouth so that it completely captures my own. I fall into the kiss, like a stone into a deep pond, sinking deeper and deeper until I am not sure I will ever leave. I let go of everything, everything but the sensations that engulf me.

He has beautiful lips, I realize, running my tongue along the fullness of them. They are shapely and full enough to invite kissing. Best of all, they chase away the taste of bitterness and despair that have threatened to drown me.

The faint rasp of his whiskers. The silky spot of skin my fingers find, just below his ear. His hands, sure and strong, caressing my waist, moving up along my rib cage and then down again to my hip, as if he would memorize the shape of me.

The feel of his heart echoing mine as they both beat too fast.

I step back—just a bit—to give myself room to finish unlacing my gown. I meet his eyes and am thrilled to see no sign of bleakness or despair or grim duty there. They are warm and glowing like sun-warmed stones, and the heat in them causes my heart to race faster and my fingers to falter.

"Here," he whispers. "Let me."

And I do.

Afterward, as I lie in his arms, savoring the feel of them around me, savoring the feel of his heart hammering under my hand where it lies upon his chest, I realize that I cannot even pretend our time together was enough. I am more drawn to him than ever, drawn to this meeting of not just our bodies and hearts, but our souls. It is an intimacy that I have hungered for my entire life yet have never been able to name. If I think this is all I will ever have of him, I fear I will weep.

I saw hope in his eyes, and an easing of his bleakness, just as I felt hope in my own heart and no longer felt alone. I promise myself that this is just the beginning. Now that I have no obligation to the convent or the abbess, I can begin to shape the future I want for myself.

Chapter Forty

As I make my way to my chamber, I send out a silent plea to let it be empty. Please let Sybella be visiting her sisters and Ismae be attending to the duchess. Or locked in some private chamber with Duval. With all that has happened in the past few hours, I am feeling far too confused and raw to explain anything to anyone, even my dearest friends.

But my prayers are not answered. When I open the door, both Ismae and Sybella are there. Sybella's gaze sharpens as her eyes rake over me, her nostrils flaring. If anyone could detect such activity as I have just been engaged in, it would be she. But to my immense relief, she says nothing about her suspicions. "Here." She shoves a garment at Ismae. "Go put that on." As Ismae disappears behind the screen, Sybella pours me a cup of wine and hands it to me. I am surprised at the thoughtfulness—just one more way in which she has changed. "Thank you."

"Are you all right?" she asks under her breath, dispelling any notion I might have had that I fooled her.

I stare at my goblet as if it is the most fascinating thing in the world. "I am fine," I assure her, then take a gulp of wine. The room is quiet except for the sound of Ismae slipping into her gown.

When she is done changing, Ismae steps out from behind the screen and hurries toward me, a look of concern on her face. I wonder how on earth I am to tell her—tell them both—that that we are not sisters.

That we do not share a father and that, indeed, I have no right to the title I have claimed all my life.

When she reaches me, she grabs my arms and squeezes. "How did it go?" she asks. "How furious was the abbess?"

I laugh. "*Furious* does not even begin to do her reaction justice."

Sybella frowns. "Is she going to punish you?"

That, at least, I can answer honestly. "I do not know; she has not yet said."

Ismae goes over to Sybella and motions for her to lace up her gown. "What will she do with Crunard?"

At her question, one of Crunard's assertions comes back to me. "He said that before, when you were in Guérande, you had a chance to kill him and you did not. May I ask why? Was he not marqued then either?"

She glances down at her hands, then back up at me. "He was marqued. However, I had just come from a battlefield where scores were marqued for death, deaths I had no hand in, so my uncertainty of how the convent was interpreting these marques had already begun to form. And now he is no longer marqued."

Despair fills me as the knowledge that I will never see marques settles over me. "What do you think should be done with him?" I ask Ismae. "You are more familiar with his crimes than either the abbess or I am."

Sybella smirks. "Notice she does not ask *me*."

Ismae is silent for a long moment while she puts on her shoes. "I think it should be left to the duchess's justice. Put him on trial. Have him answer for his crimes. Then, if he is to die, have it be for those crimes he has been convicted of, not some shadow that falls across his forehead that I do not trust the convent to correctly interpret."

Her honesty has created a safe, almost holy space around us. It is the perfect opportunity to tell her of what I have learned. I take a deep breath, meaning to do precisely that, but find I cannot bend my tongue to my will. Besides, I do not yet know what I will do with my new knowledge.

Leave the convent? Report the abbess—but to whom? The sheer enormity of this revelation and its reverberations forces me to tread cautiously.

More importantly, as I stare into their dear faces, I realize that as strong as I have been, as much as I have endured, I am not strong enough to sever this bond. If I lose that, I fear I will unravel into a pile of tattered threads. "She still has not told me all." While it is not the whole truth, it does not feel like too great a lie. That is when I notice they are both dressed most strangely. "Why are you wearing servant gowns?"

"Do you like it?" Sybella lifts her skirt and twirls prettily, as if it is some magnificent dress that she wears and not merely sewn-together rags. "I am sneaking out with Beast tonight when he and his men patrol the city. All the various troops and mercenary factions are teeming with pent-up energy and frustration, and they have nothing to fight. Except each other."

Ismae arches an eyebrow. "I can't believe he agreed to let you come with him."

Sybella flashes a cheerful smile. "Oh, he did not. He does not even know that is what I intend. But I shall go mad if I must sit here one more day, twiddling my thumbs with embroidery."

"And you, Ismae?" I ask. "Are you going out to rein in the mercenaries as well?"

Sybella's face sobers. "No, she is leaving for Nantes in a few hours."

"You convinced Duval, then?"

Ismae snorts. "Let us just say that all his arguments were to no avail."

"Which means," Sybella says, plucking the wine goblet from my hands, "that you are to attend upon the duchess while we are busy. But not until we get you freshened up."

"Isn't that where you've been, with the duchess?" Ismae asks.

"No. I . . . needed some time to think, to cool my temper after my meeting with the abbess."

Sybella begins combing my hair, her fingers gentle and light. I close my eyes and let the sheer comfort of the touch lull me into calmness. Now, I think. Now I will tell them. As I open my mouth to do that, there is a knock on the door. We all stiffen. "If it is the abbess, I've not returned," I warn them.

But when Ismae opens the door, it is Duval's deep voice that we hear. "I'm not going to argue any more about this," she tells him.

"Good. I am not here to argue, but would like to see you before you leave."

"Of course." Before following him out into the hall, she comes and gives Sybella and me a hug. "Be safe, you two."

"And you," Sybella says. "And remember, the abbess at Brigantia will grant you sanctuary if it comes to that."

"It won't." Then it is my turn to hug her before she is gone.

Chapter Forty-One

FOUR DAYS LATER, THE FRENCH ambassador arrives. With the mud of his journey still clinging to his boots, he comes striding into the hall where the duchess is holding court. As he steps through the door, Duval's head snaps up, and he grows still, like a wolf who has just sensed another predator.

Sybella and I stand just behind the duchess's chair. We exchange a glance, and, almost as if we have rehearsed it, our hands go to our weapons. Not that we will kill him on sight, but we will simply remind him to step carefully.

The ambassador is tall and leanly muscled, with a great beak of a nose and piercing green eyes. As he draws toward the dais, Duval motions subtly with his hands for the soldiers to begin clearing the others out.

As the people make their way to the door, the duchess looks up from the stolid burgher whose claim she has been adjudicating and sees what is happening. Although she keeps her face serene and composed, I can see the faint trembling in her fingers before she tightens her grip on the arms of her chair.

"Gisors." Duval's voice is pleasant, for all that his body is fairly humming with tension. "I did not expect to see you again. Ever."

Gisors ignores him and executes a flawless bow, his attention never wavering from the duchess. "My lady." There are small gasps from around the room, as he pointedly does not use the respectful form of address her title demands. Sybella's hand closes around the hilt of her knife, her eyes narrowing in anticipation. The ambassador catches her movement and becomes slightly more circumspect. "I pray my visit finds you in good health."

"It does, Lord Gisors. And I hope you have had a pleasant journey." The duchess clings to the protocol and courtesies required by her position.

"I apologize for appearing before you in such an unworthy state, but the message I bring cannot be delayed."

"By all means, then, let us hear it," Duval says. Gisors continues to ignore him and waits for the duchess to nod her agreement.

"I have been sent by His Majesty to accept your unconditional surrender of Brittany, her offices and estates and lands and armies. Once you have surrendered these, I am authorized to offer you safe passage to the court of your new . . . *husband.*" He manages to imbue the word with utter contempt.

The entire room is as quiet as a crypt, with not even the sound of breathing to disturb the utter silence his words have effected.

Duval leans forward. "And this message comes from His Majesty the king or from the French regent?"

"It matters not, for they speak as one. My lady? May I report to His Majesty that you agree to the terms?"

By the tense line in the duchess's jaw, I can tell she wishes to tell him that no, he may not, but even now, under such circumstances, her grace and bearing hold. "I fear I cannot make such an enormous decision without careful consideration, my lord. I would give you and *your king*"—she manages to infuse *your king* with as much acid as Gisors did the word *husband* only moments ago—"in a few days' time."

"Time is the one thing we do not have much of, my lady."

"Nevertheless, I must insist. I have my people to consider and their interests must come first."

Gisors opens his mouth to argue, but Duval motions for sentries to step forward and escort him away. Unless the man wishes to be dragged from the room, he has no choice but to comply. "I will expect an answer by tomorrow, my lady."

"You may expect all you want, but you will not get it," she mutters under her breath.

When he is gone, she turns shakily to Duval. "I think I will return to my chambers now," the duchess says.

"But of course." Duval leaps up and helps her to her feet. He glances at Sybella. "Find Beast for me, would you?" She nods and hurries off. Together, Duval and I escort the duchess to her chambers.

Once she and I are alone in her room, I slip the heavy headdress off her head and place it on the bureau.

"Have you ever been in love?"

Her question surprises me so much that I nearly drop the brush I hold in my hand.

Without waiting for an answer, she says softly, almost to herself, "I have. Once." I begin brushing her hair. "I was very young." She closes her eyes. "Do you think you can fall in love with someone when you're that young?"

An image of Mortain sitting beside me in the wine cellar fills my mind. "Yes, Your Grace. I do."

Her eyes flash open and she turns to look at me, surprised. She smiles. "You are the first to agree with me," she confides. "I knew we would get along." She turns back around so I may finish her hair. "His name was Louis, Louis d'Orléans, and he came to my father's court when I was but five years old. He was so charming and gallant, but mostly kind, kind and gentle with the child I was then. And of course, I had heard plenty of stories of how bravely he fought beside my father as they tried to restrain France's encroachment on her surrounding duchies."

My mind scrambles to the tapestry back at the convent, but Louis d'Orléans was a French noble, not a Breton one, so I knew little about him other than that he is a cousin of Charles VIII, and that he fought in the Mad War beside the duchess's father.

"Why did your father not betroth you to him? Surely it would have been a good match."

The duchess sighs in sorrow. "Louis was forced to marry Joan, the daughter of the late king, when he was only fourteen years old. It was especially hard because his wife's physical infirmities left her sterile, so he would have no hope of producing an heir."

"And thus there would be no threat to the French crown," I murmur.

"Precisely. There was talk, during that visit, of having his marriage annulled so that we could marry, but the plan was vehemently blocked by France, which held much sway with the pope.

"And then he was captured last year and has been kept as a prisoner ever since." There are tears in her eyes. Whether because he is imprisoned or due to her lost dreams, I cannot tell.

Chapter Forty-Two

IT IS LATE, FAR TOO close to dawn. I should grab a few hours' sleep before morning, but I am filled with a need to see Balthazaar, even as an unwelcome sense of shyness and uncertainty settles over me at the memory of the things we did together four nights ago. I wonder if that is all he will think of now when he sees me.

I wonder if he will want to do it again.

And how soon.

When I reach the ramparts, I step quietly onto the catwalk. The sentries are so familiar with my habit of haunting their domain that they barely acknowledge my presence except to stand a little more alertly and shake themselves awake. I turn and walk in the opposite direction. Usually by the time I reach the far corner, Balthazaar is there waiting for me. But tonight as I peer into the shadows and whisper his name, I can see that they are empty.

My heart twists uncomfortably in my chest, then I scold myself for being foolish. He does have other things to do — hellequin duties he must attend to. It is unreasonable to expect him always to be here when I need him. And yet, he is, and I do.

I whisper his name again, then wait a few moments. I lean on the battlements so that if the sentries should look my way, they will think me pensive or in prayer.

The minutes drag into a quarter of an hour and still he does not come. A most disturbing thought fills me. Does he feel he has gotten what he wanted and so sees no reason to return? He is a hunter, after all, and I his prey. Now that I have been duly lured into his trap, has his interest faded? My hands grip the stone wall in front of me. No. Our connection is more than simple lust, although that is part of it, no question. But it wasn't only my body he was after.

I glance at the sky. Nearly an hour has passed and I have run out of arguments and justifications as to why he is not here. I put my hand on my chest, over the tender place there, and tell myself it is not pain I am feeling. As I turn to leave, I detect movement in the shadows. "Balthazaar?"

After a moment's hesitation, he steps forward.

"How long have you been there?" I ask.

"Not long. It is late. Surely you should be sleeping."

"I will, but I wished to see you."

"Why?"

I frown. "Because I am daft, clearly."

He sighs, then steps over to the battlements, puts his hands on the wall, and leans out, staring at the city below, careful to keep a goodly distance between us. "Do they not miss you when you come up here?" His voice is gruff, guarded, and he does not look at me.

"I am careful not to come that often." I do not slip away nearly as often as I would like.

"You should not come here anymore."

I hold very still, trying to study his face, but he keeps it turned toward the city. "What are you saying?" I keep my voice very low. "Are you *rejecting* me?" Outrage mingles with mortification.

"No." The word is harsh. He turns to face me, and I recoil at the intensity of the emotions in his eyes. He takes a step closer, looming over me. "I am not *rejecting* you—I am trying to save you. To save you from being pulled any further into my bleak existence."

"It is not *I* who need saving, but *you.*"

He blinks in surprise, his mouth parting slightly, but no words emerge and I realize I have hit the mark far more accurately than I dreamed.

He turns to look back over the city. "Do not be ridiculous." His voice is ripe with scorn and mockery. "It is others, including you, who must find safety from me."

"Truly?" I take a step closer to him and he cringes. It is a mere tightening of muscle and skin, but I see it and suddenly I know he is not cringing in revulsion or rejection but because he is fighting a fierce battle with his own desires and his own heart. "What must I fear from you?" My voice is as soft and gentle as the caress I long to give him. "That you will touch me?"

I reach out and put my hand on his neck, feel his flesh twitch and flutter beneath my fingers. I draw even nearer, pressing myself close against his unyielding side. "That you would do this?" I put my fingers in his hair and force him to look at me. The anguish and conflict in his eyes nearly break my heart anew. If ever anyone needed saving, it is this tortured man. "Or this?" I rise up on my toes and softly place my lips against his. He resists at first, and then it is as if a floodgate opens and all his need pours out.

He turns from the battlements and pulls me into his arms as if he could pull me into his very chest so I might reside against his heart. His manner shifts, changing from resistant to possessive, and he cups my head in his hands and devours my mouth as if he would pull all that I am into him. Breathless, he stops and rests his forehead against mine, our hearts beating in a joint frantic rhythm.

"How can you expect me to walk away from this?" I whisper.

"But there is no freedom for me, only death."

"Even now? After all that you have done and all the years you have ridden with the hunt?"

He shrugs, a sharp frustrated jerk of the shoulders. "It is the nature of my existence. And what I wish to save you from—giving your heart to someone who cannot be with you in the way you deserve. Who cannot be the man you deserve."

But his warning comes far too late. My heart is already his.

I do not sleep much that night, not with thoughts of Balthazaar rolling around in my head like an uneven cart wheel. When I am not thinking about him, I worry about the duchess and the corner the French have backed her into. And when my thoughts finally turn from that, then it is young Isabeau who comes to mind, and I wonder just how much longer she will live and how the duchess will bear it when she dies.

But when morning comes, I am determined to do something, anything. And that is when I remember Crunard, languishing in the dungeon, a traitor who once had the ear of the French crown and who may well still be in contact with the regent.

I find Crunard in his cell, stretched out on the small pallet there. When he hears my footsteps, he sits up. Seeing it is me, he quickly runs a hand over his hair and straightens his shirt. I cannot decide if I find his gesture humorous or touching. He nods in greeting. I say nothing but simply stare at him, giving the whirlwind of emotions I feel every time I look at him a chance to subside.

"What do you know of Marshal Rieux and his alliance with d'Albret?"

"It was too much to hope for a pleasant father-and-daughter chat, wasn't it?"

"It was. What do you know of their alliance?"

He leans back against the stone wall and shrugs. "That Rieux believed allying with d'Albret would be our best chance to gain enough force to repel France's aggression."

"Did he not know of the rumors surrounding d'Albret's earlier marriages, or did he simply not care?" For that, far more than the political betrayal, is what rankles me.

"We had all heard rumors, but Rieux believed them to be just that, rumors that followed a brutish leader who was not loved by his people. I think he also believed that the duchess's position would keep her safe, for it is one thing to have so many accidents befall one's wives, when they are far from their homes and the people who would avenge them, but a far different thing to openly attack the beloved ruler of a nation."

"And you?"

He meets my gaze steadily. "I feared them more than simply rumors. Whatever other treachery I may have committed, I was not willing to consign the duchess to d'Albret's tender care."

"Duly noted." I fold my arms across my chest and begin to pace in front of his door. "The question is, can the duchess trust Rieux's offer to become her loyal subject once more?"

"I do not see that she has any choice. Rieux is a brilliant military tactician, and he brings many troops with him, troops the duchess will no doubt need."

"But how can she be certain he will not betray her again?"

"She cannot. But she can be certain he will not betray her with d'Albret again, and can take precautions in case his loyalty shifts with the winds of opportunity." He rises to his feet and comes to stand nearer the door. "You have to understand, for years the French crown has bribed many in the Breton court to report all the duchy's activity and options and counsel. A person was of little importance if the French did not try to recruit him. Most took the money. Some gave them useful information in exchange. Others gave them meaningless crumbs.

"Madame Hivern, François, Madame Dinan, Marshal Rieux, fully half the nobles of Brittany took bribes or payments of some kind."

"And you."

He glances sharply at me. "No. I never took the bribes. Not until the duke lay dead and the promised payment was my last remaining son."

I shake my head. "No wonder the poor duke could never win a damned war," I mutter.

"Precisely. Oddly, some of his most loyal men were actually French —Captain Dunois, Louis d'Orléans."

That is the second time I have heard that name mentioned. "How many sons did you have, all told?" I ask softly, for we are speaking of my brothers.

"Four."

"What were their names?"

"Phillipe was the eldest, then Rogier, followed by Ives, then Anton."

"And Anton was the one the French held captive?"

"Yes. He and Duval were great friends. They grew up together, trained together."

"And how would he feel about your betrayal of Brittany?"

That arrow strikes home. Crunard's nostrils flare in irritation and he looks away, but not before I see a brief twinge of shame. "He would not understand because he is young and full of noble ideals and has no idea what it is like to watch your children crumple before you like so many trampled weeds."

I do not know what to say to that, for part of me agrees. How can any of us know the heartache such a loss would create? How can any of us know how we would live—or try to live—with such pain?

But I am unwilling to stay here and sympathize with him. I lift my skirts and turn to leave, but one last thought occurs to me. "Would any of the duchess's suitors have helped her stave off the French invasion?"

"Does it matter? She is now married to the Holy Roman emperor."

"Who has helped her very little. I want to know if she would have stood a chance with any of the others."

He thinks for a long moment, then shakes his head. "No."

"So all this has been for naught? The outcome was fixed from the start?"

"Yes." He laughs, a painful, defeated sound. "Her only hope of avoiding the war would have been a betrothal to the heir to the French throne himself."

"Why wasn't she?"

"Because at the time, the dauphin was betrothed to another, and the old king held too much animosity for the duke to award him such a prize as making his daughter queen. Once he died, the French regent was just as rigid in her thinking as her father."

"One last question. Does the French regent intend to allow the duchess to join the Holy Roman emperor in Austria? Or will some mysterious harm befall her along the way?"

He meets my eyes and shakes his head. "That, I do not know. We can always hope that she will be true to her word."

And while he might be willing to pin the duchess's future on such thin hopes, I am not.

Chapter Forty-Three

TWO DAYS LATER, THERE IS yet another Privy Council meeting. As they debate Marshal Rieux's true intentions and his trustworthiness to lead troops who will actually fight for the duchess and not turn against her when he snaps his fingers, I feel someone's gaze on me. It is the abbess, looking at me like a hungry vulture watching a dying fox and wondering if the fox is worth the effort or if the vulture herself will be taken down in the struggle. I consider smiling coolly at her, but it takes more energy than I wish to expend on her behalf. Instead, I simply ignore her. Which has the added benefit of inflaming her further.

I still do not know what I wish to do with the knowledge of her treachery. Whom I will tell. As I pointedly turn away from her, I glance at Father Effram, his lively blue eyes intent upon my face. When our gazes meet, he does not even have the grace to look away. Not knowing what to do, I bow my head in his direction, acknowledging him. He smiles broadly, so much so that it catches the abbess's attention, who in turn scowls at the both of us. I nearly laugh, that she thinks she can silence us like two restless children in church when we are respected peers in this elevated company.

I study the wooden cross that hangs around Father Effram's neck and the hempen prayer cord with the nine beads. He is old. Older than anyone I have ever seen, and he clearly follows and respects the old ways. And from what I gathered from our conversation in the chapel, he seems wise and knowledgable. I glance once more at the abbess, who has returned her frigid gaze to the conversation going on. If anyone would know what sort of court or church council oversees the convent, it is he.

"Very well, we will trust him." Duval's voice breaks into my thoughts. "But with caution, and we will appoint his second in command and make certain that person is someone loyal to us."

Everyone at the table agrees, except for Captain Dunois, who cannot find it in his heart to forgive the man.

Chancellor Montauban clears his throat. "The French ambassador visits my chamber nearly every hour, demanding an audience with the duchess—and her answer." The older man looks at the duchess with fondness and deep sympathy.

"Is there no word from François?" she asks worriedly.

"No, Your Grace. Which we must assume means there will be no more help from the Holy Roman emperor."

"I told you there wouldn't be," Chalon points out. "He is already spread too thin."

Duval turns his steely gaze upon Chalon, who tries not to flinch under it. "Oh, that is not why he cannot come."

"No?" Chalon sounds surprised.

"No. He cannot come because the French regent has brokered a truce with him."

"My own husband betrayed me?" The duchess tries to sound strong, but it is hard not to hear the distress in her voice.

"He did not betray you, Your Grace." Chalon comes to his liege's defense. "He has been fighting this war for years, and it has cost him untold resources in material and lives. He needed that truce for his own people and the security of his kingdom."

"At the expense of ours," she murmurs.

Duval nods. "Yes, for it has the undeniable effect of essentially tying his hands where Brittany is concerned, because if he makes a move to aid us, he finds himself embroiled in war with France once again." In spite of Duval's ire, there is also a note of begrudging admiration at how neatly the French regent has boxed us in and cut us off from our own allies.

"What of the English forces? Have any more of their troops arrived in Rennes?"

Captain Dunois shakes his head, looking almost ill. "No, Your Grace. The rest of the English troops will not be joining us here in the city."

Her brow creases in puzzlement. "Why not?"

Dunois takes a deep breath. "They will be staying in Morlaix." He and Montauban exchange a glance. "They are holding it as surety against payment for their aid," he says softly.

"And so the net tightens," mutters Duval in disgust.

When the council meeting is over, the abbess rises and heads my way. I pretend I do not see her and mutter into Sybella's ear, "Distract her for a moment, would you?"

She smiles wickedly. "But of course." I do not linger to see how she does it, although part of me would like to, because I am certain it will be entertaining. Instead, I slip away to the old chapel. I do not know if I will find Father Effram there, but other than the council meetings, the chapel is the only place I have ever seen him.

I walk slowly, hoping he will see where I am headed and that his curiosity will compel him to follow.

Even if he does not, I could certainly do with some quiet contemplation and prayer right now. I have no earthly idea what to do. With the duchess and her council — nay, the very country — so beset by enemies and turmoil, I can hardly bear to add to it by telling them of the newest in a long line of betrayals. And yet . . .

And yet surely those who have been wronged by the abbess's choices and actions deserve justice, if not vengeance.

The chapel is empty but for the nine flickering candles in front of the nine niches. As I stare at the Nine, an emptiness opens up inside me. Even the comfort of prayer has been taken from me, for I am no longer certain whom to pray to. I ball my hands into fists and force myself to take a deep breath.

"Lady Annith? Is that you scowling at my altar?"

I whirl around. "Father Effram! No, I wasn't scowling. Well, not at your altar, at least. Only at all the weighty problems that bedevil us."

He cocks his head to the side. "And by *us,* you mean the duchess and Brittany? Or is there some other *us?*"

The man may be older than time itself, but he is nobody's fool. "Father, I would have you hear my confession."

He blinks in surprise, but he is not half as surprised as I am. "I did not know that followers of Mortain must needs confess their sins."

"That is part of what I must confess to you."

His curiosity is as pungent as the incense burning in the chapel's censers. He motions for me to follow him to a small corner. "I cannot imagine you have anything to confess, my child. Surely you move within your god's grace —"

"But that is what I must tell you." Tell someone. The secret presses against me, so heavy and full that I fear it will burst from me like an overripe plum from its skin.

But once we are seated and his kind, curious eyes are on me, all the words that were crowding to get out flee before the immenseness of my confession.

"What is it, my child? What troubles you?"

"How great a sin is it to spend your entire life pretending you are one thing, only to find out that you were not that thing at all?"

"I assume you are talking of yourself?"

"Yes."

"What thing did you pretend to be?"

"A daughter of Mortain, sired by Him to be His handmaiden."

"And you are not His daughter?"

"No. I have learned that I am not."

"Ah." He leans back in his seat. "And now you feel as if you've tricked everyone?" When I nod, he tilts his head and studies me. "How old were you when you came to the convent?"

"A babe."

"Well, then." He spread his hands wide. "It cannot be your fault at all. If the convent made that assumption and had no methods for confirming such claims . . ."

"But they were tricked. Someone knew. My mother, the abbess, for one."

His eyes widen in surprise, and I proceed to tell him the whole sordid story. It rushes out of me in one enormous surge of relief.

When I have finished, he looks at me with a gentle expression. "Surely you must know that you are innocent in all this?"

While I wish to believe this, I cannot. I look down at my hands, which are tangled in my lap. "Not so innocent, Father, for I have killed men."

He takes my hands in his own, forcing me to look up at him. "I believe He will understand, for even Mortain has been known to make mistakes."

I recoil in surprise. "Surely He has not!"

"Ah, have you not heard the tale of how He took Amourna by mistake when it was really her sister He was after?"

"Well, yes, but that is just a story those who follow Salonius tell. It is not what actually happened."

"Isn't it?"

"No! We at the convent know what truly happened."

"So say the followers of each of the Nine."

I sigh in exasperation, and he holds up his hand. "I did not say your version was wrong. But think on it: Why would they tell a story about a god as feared and revered as Mortain making a mistake?"

I shrug. "I don't know." In truth, I am in no mood for theological puzzles.

He leans forward. "To show that even someone such as Mortain is capable of making a mistake."

"But He is a god!"

"He is *a* god, but not *God*." He points heavenward.

I do not know what to say that. Instead, I change the subject. "One more thing, Father, and then I will leave you to your duties. Whom do those who worship the Nine answer to?"

"Their gods, of course."

"Yes, but in matters of more earthly jurisdiction. I know there is a council of bishops who oversee the new church's matters, but surely they do not hold authority over the Nine, do they?"

"Authority? In what way?"

"If someone must be brought to account, much like a Catholic priest might be stripped of his office, who would address such matters?"

"Are you speaking of your mother?"

"Yes."

He leans back, sighing. "That sort of thing has not come up in a very, very long time, but when it has happened in the past, a convocation of the Nine was called to preside over and judge such things."

"And that is?"

"A council, a convocation, attended by the heads of each of the Nine, where the matter is brought before them and they decide what punishment, if any, is to be meted out."

"And how does one call a convocation of the Nine?"

"A message is sent to the high priest or priestess or abbess of each of the Nine, and they in turn each send a representative to attend. But again, it has not been done in years. Certainly not in my lifetime."

"What—what would the punishment be for such crimes?" For all that I want her to be held to account, I do not think I wish for her to be put to death.

His eyes soften with understanding. "No one is beyond God's forgiveness." The certainty in his voice astounds me.

"How can you know that?"

He shrugs, somewhat sheepishly. "When one has made as many mistakes as I have, one becomes very familiar with the fullness of God's grace and mercy."

Chapter Forty-Four

As I make my way from the chapel to my chambers, I am accosted by a somewhat frantic page. "Lady Annith! Lady Annith!"

His alarm is nearly infectious and I find I must hold on to my composure. "What?"

"The duchess says you're to come at once. It's the princess Isabeau. I've been looking for you everywhere," he says accusingly.

"I was praying," I explain, then lift up my skirts and hurry after him.

When I reach the duchess's chambers, I am shown in immediately. The duchess sits beside Isabeau. Sybella and one of the Brigantian sisters are on the other side. The girl's skin is nearly translucent, and her breath comes in great rasping heaves. "What happened?" I ask softly.

The Brigantian nun rises and hurries to my side. "She just took a turn for the worse while everyone was in the council meeting." Her face softens in sympathy. "It is not unexpected. It is amazing she has held on this long."

My eyes are fixed on Isabeau as she struggles for breath. "Is there anything that can be done to ease her breathing?"

"I have used all the knowledge our convent possesses. The duchess thought—hoped—you might know of some remedy that we did not." If the nun resents this in any way, she gives no sign. My thoughts go back to nursing Sister Vereda and what we did then. "We have more experience with poisons and wounds than with illness," I murmur. "But I do know of one poultice that might help."

I give her the short list of ingredients, but before she can leave the room, Sybella rises and hurries forward. "I will help her," she says. At my questioning glance, she leans in close. "I cannot watch this," she murmurs, her face stark white. I am taken aback for a moment until I remember her younger sister Louise suffers from a similar ailment. Once they have left, I approach the bedside.

"I am so sorry, Your Grace. I was in the chapel, praying."

"There is no need to apologize. I am just glad they found you." She looks up. When she sees that the Brigantian nun has left the room, she turns to me. "Ismae discovered that one of her"—she lowers her voice —"poisons eased Isabeau's symptoms, and she often gave her a drop or two when her breathing grew painful like this. Do you know what she used? Might you have any? It does seem to ease her suffering."

My mind scrambles for a moment, carefully going over all the poisons we use at the convent, until it lands on Mortain's caress—a poison that is made from the milk of the poppy. "I do! I will be right back." I hurry from the room, and once in the hallway, I break into a run. When I reach my chamber, I rifle though my saddlebag until I find the carefully wrapped brightly colored bottles. I snag Mortain's caress, return the rest to the saddlebag, then race back to the sickroom.

I am cautious with the amount of poison I give Isabeau, perhaps more cautious than I need to be, but I do not have Ismae's skill with it —or her ability to correct fatal mistakes.

However, even the small amount does seem to work. Isabeau's breathing grows less painful, although the fluid that fills her lungs does not diminish.

She is dying. For all that I am not a daughter of Mortain, I can still feel His presence heavy in the room. I want to shout at Him to hurry up and ease her suffering, except that I know it will cause the duchess great pain.

The next four days are consumed with tending to Isabeau, doing everything we can to restore a fragile balance to her body. We try poultices and tisanes, simples and salves, and none of them manage to turn the inexorable tide of her death. The only relief any of us can find is in the few precious drops of Mortain's caress.

When the French ambassador sends word that he is still waiting, the duchess nearly grabs Duval's sword from his hip and goes after him, so desperate is she for something—or someone—to strike out at.

Duval and the duchess and I consider trying to get word to Ismae, but in the end, there is little she could do, and trying to contact her would risk exposing her to even more danger. So, instead, we wait. We take turns by Isabeau's side, sitting with her so she will not be alone should she wake. Or should she die.

On the fourth day, the bishop comes to administer the last rites. The young princess rouses enough to say that she wants Father Effram to be the one to perform that duty for her. After a moment of stunned silence, Father Effram is quickly sent for. The duchess stays by Isabeau's side, holding her hand the entire time, tears flowing down her face.

And still, Death does not come.

That night, when the duchess has fallen asleep on the floor beside Isabeau's bed, and I am sitting with the young princess, bathing her fevered brow with lavender water, her eyes flutter open. I am so startled, I nearly drop the linen cloth I am holding.

"Where is Anne?" she asks.

"Right here. Asleep. Shall I wake her?"

Isabeau shakes her head. "No, she has been at my side for days; she needs the rest." She falls silent for a while and simply tries to take air into her lungs. "What is it like?" she finally whispers to me.

"What is what like?"

"Death. What is death like?"

Although she meets my eyes bravely, there is a faint tremble to her lips that tells me how hard she is trying to be brave.

I do not let myself think of graves or crypts or cold plots of earth but instead fill my mind with thoughts of Mortain Himself when He came to me that first time when I was a prisoner in the wine cellar. "He is quiet and still, and oh, so peaceful," I tell her. "Fear will no longer hold any sway over you, nor will worry or sadness." I pause for a moment, trying to think how to best help her young mind grasp such things. "Can you think of a time when you were especially tired? Perhaps after a long day of travel?"

She does not bother to try and speak, but simply nods.

"Do you remember how lovely it was to climb into your feather bed that night? How grateful your tired limbs were? How welcoming it felt? How delicious to close your eyes and finally rest?"

"Yes," she whispers, her eyes aglow.

"It is just like that," I tell her.

"Oh," she breathes, and the faint crease between her eyebrows smoothes away. "I just wish I did not have to go alone," she whispers. "I do not like being alone."

At her words, I am filled with the memory of the terror I felt all those times I was shut alone in the cellar, that dark prison I feared I would never be released from. That is when it occurs to me that Isabeau need not make this journey alone.

Balthazaar could take her. He could escort her to the Underworld. There is little comfort I can offer her, but this would surely help.

As soon as Isabeau drifts off to sleep, I excuse myself from her bedside to search out the hellequin. When I am in the corridor, I lift my skirts and run, ignoring those who pause to watch me in surprise.

When I reach the battlements, dusk has only just begun to fall, and I worry it might be too early for him. Even so, I must try. *Please, Mortain, even though I am not Your daughter, please let him be here.* I hurry to the shadows where he always waits for me. At first, I think it is empty, and disappointment nearly chokes me. Then the shadows move and he steps forward.

I throw myself into his arms. For one brief moment I shut out all the complications and tragedies that surround us and allow myself to draw on the comfort he offers me. Then, reluctantly, I pull away. "I must ask a favor of you."

"Anything," he says.

Such a simple word, but it takes me utterly aback. "There is a young girl in the palace, the duchess's sister, and she even now hovers at Death's door."

He glances to the palace behind us as if he could peer through the walls. "I know."

"She is so young and so afraid of being alone on that dark journey into death. And then it occurred to me, she doesn't have to be alone. You could take her."

Balthazaar raises his eyebrows in surprise. "Would my presence not simply frighten her even more?"

I study his noble, fierce face. "Mayhap if you tried smiling," I suggest, "it would help. Besides, she is used to soldiers and men-at-arms —and you are not so very much more terrifying than they."

"It is not my role to play, you know that. She is not a wicked soul or a lost one."

"No, but she is a terrified young girl, trying to be brave. Surely Mortain's grace extends to her as well."

His dark brows draw together as he stares down at me. "You place much faith in Mortain's grace."

"I do, for I have known it firsthand."

He looks away then, out over the city, his face heavy with a sense of resignation and regret that I do not understand. His eyes soften and his hand reaches up to caress my cheek, a cool slide of sensation that touches something deep inside me. "Is that what you wish for, Annith? If Death could grant you a wish, you would use it for someone else? Trade your happiness for someone else's?"

I frown, confused. "Why must I trade my happiness? I do not understand."

He reaches up with his other hand so that he cups my face. I allow myself to lean into it, savoring the comfort and promise that he offers. Then he bends down and places a gentle kiss upon my lips, a kiss that is tender and achingly sad.

"What? What are you not telling me?"

Instead of answering me, he smiles. The smile is so full of sorrow and loneliness that it pierces my heart. "I am sorry," he whispers. He pulls his cloak tightly around him, steps out of the shadows, and heads for the door into the palace. Still puzzled, but relieved that he will do this, I follow.

Needing no direction, he makes his way unerringly to Isabeau's room. I briefly wonder if he has been there before, perhaps when waiting for me. He walks slowly toward the princess's bed, past the Brigantian nuns and the princess's attendants, but no one in the room appears to notice him. Indeed, it is as if they cannot see him at all.

He kneels beside the bed, his manner so gentle it makes me want to weep. As his hood slips away from his face, the light from the candles in the room casts his profile in harsh relief, plucking at a buried string of memory.

Isabeau looks up at him with enormous eyes, and he reaches for her small, thin hand. "Be not afraid," he says, and she nods her head, her eyes never leaving his.

"It is not so very scary a place, where we are going. And you will not be alone. I will take you there myself."

I stare at that noble brow, at the hood puddled around his neck, and recognition begins to seep into me.

Young Isabeau turns to Anne and gives her a brave little smile. "Do not be sad, Anne. I will not be alone. Besides," she adds shyly, "you have always gone first. This time, it will be my turn to go first, and *I* will wait for *you*." The duchess grabs Isabeau's hand, silent tears streaming down her face. She still does not look at the stranger kneeling beside her.

And then—even though Isabeau is not yet dead—my lover leans forward, gathers Isabeau up in his arms, and cradles her against his chest.

Except it is not *her*, but her soul, for her body still lies on the bed, as empty as a husk.

No, I think. It is not possible. A hellequin cannot call a soul from its body.

Isabeau peeks over his broad shoulder and gives me a tiny wave. Then, together, the two of them step through the door, and none but the living remain.

That is when I realize that I have not fallen in love with a mere hellequin, but with Death Himself.

Chapter Forty-Five

I SINK TO MY KNEES beside the duchess and she remains by the bed, gripping Isabeau's hand.

Balthazaar is Death.

How could I not have known? Not have recognized it? For of course, looking back, I see all the signs are there. That deep sense of recognition. Him leading the hunt. Possessing my arrow. How could I have been so blind?

But my heart — my heart was not, for it knew Him even if my eyes were too clouded to see it.

My face flames anew when I remember the manner in which I threw His name around, and I nearly writhe in embarrassment.

And what does this mean? For me? For us? Surely there can be no future with Death?

It is too much, too huge a thing to wrap my mind around. Instead, I turn my attention to the duchess. She will need my help to begin to deal with her grief.

In the morning, before the duchess can even stir from her tears, we learn that the French army has arrived and is just outside the city.

"Where is Gisors? Bring him to me at once!" Duval is so agitated he cannot sit still and is pacing the privy chamber.

Chancellor Montauban's brow is furrowed. "What of our scouts? Surely they should have warned us of the approaching army."

Duval whirls upon him, jaw clenched tight, but Captain Dunois hurries to answer. "It can only mean the French erected checkpoints along the road and intercepted our scouts so they could not bring us the news."

I look at Duval, the reason for his distress suddenly clear. What of Ismae? Will they have intercepted her?

The messenger returns just then, his face white. "Ambassador Gisors is no longer in the palace, my lord. He and his retinue left last night."

Duval clenches his fist, clearly wishing to smash it into something. However, he politely dismisses the messenger before swearing a black oath. "It was a trap. A setup. They knew we would not surrender, but they thought to divert us with such talk."

"And it worked," Chalon points out.

Duval's head whips up. "Only because they stopped our scouts and left us blind." But it is clear that he blames himself.

The duchess tries to remain brave in the face of this setback. "What must we do to combat the siege?" Her voice is small, and she sounds painfully like the child she is.

All eyes turn to her, and Duval's voice is gentle. "There is not much to be done but play out our hand. We knew this was coming, Your Grace."

"Although we had hoped we'd have more time," Captain Dunois says.

"But we do not." Marshal Rieux's voice is curt and abrupt.

"So what do we do now?" asks the bishop, trying not to wring his hands.

"Fight," Dunois says grimly. "Or surrender."

"Surely that is not an option," Chalon says. "Not after we have turned down every chance they have given us to make peace. They will grant us no quarter, nor will we be able to negotiate favorable terms of surrender."

"We can withstand a siege for months," Chancellor Montauban points out.

"Yes, but to what end? There is no more aid coming. Whatever victory we will wrest from this thing must done with what we have on hand. All our aid and supplies will be cut off. Before long, they will starve us out. And again, to what end? Simply to surrender later rather than sooner?"

"Enough!" Duval cuts off Chalon.

Marshal Rieux shifts in his seat. "It will take days before the supply trains arrive, let alone their siege engines. We have a little time. Best to have the men ride out immediately and secure all the food supplies and livestock that can be found. No point in leaving it for our enemies, and we will have need of it soon enough."

Duval nods. "Agreed. We must also find out their numbers, their plans. What siege engines they will bring." He glances up at Captain Dunois. "Whom shall we send?"

Sybella steps away from her place behind the duchess. "I will go," she says, and I am immediately filled with shame that I did not think to make such an offer.

"What?" she asks, seeing the councilors' horrified looks. "Do you think if you ride out on your chargers with shield and banner flying, they will simply confess to you their strategy?" She snorts. "Do not be absurd. But they will never expect a woman, for who is more invisible than a camp follower or laundress? No one notices a woman's comings and goings."

Beast looks as if he wishes to put his head down on the table and weep. Or perhaps lock Sybella up in her chamber for the next few weeks.

Duval sends an apologetic glance Beast's way. "Very well. But be careful, and if there is any sign of trouble, get back here immediately. Find out how many troops they have, what engines of war they bring,

346

how many cannon, if any. We need to know precisely what we are up against."

Sybella curtsies, then quits the room, grateful, I think, to have some action to perform. Unlike the rest of us, who must wait and wonder.

"Should I go as well?" I offer belatedly.

"No." Duval gives a decisive shake of his head. "I want one of you to stay with the duchess."

"You think France will make an attempt on her life?" Captain Dunois asks.

"No, but I am not willing to stake her safety on that." Duval turns to the window and rubs a hand over his face. Between Isabeau's death and this, he appears to have aged ten years in a single night. "There has been no word from Ismae?"

It is not clear whom he is asking, so I glance at the abbess. She gives a curt shake of her head, then realizes he cannot see it. "No, my lord. There has been no word. But as it was not a convent-sanctioned escapade, I do not expect she would be in contact with me."

He sends her a searing glare that would shrivel a lesser woman, then turns to me, his face more gentle. "Have you heard anything?"

"No, my lord."

"Very well. But if you do, send word to me immediately. I have promised my sister I will help with the funeral arrangements." At the words, a fresh wave of grief passes across his face. He is such a good tactician, so great a strategist, that it is easy to forget he is also an older brother who has just lost a sibling.

There are a hundred small details to be seen to in order make certain that Isabeau is laid to rest with all the honor and respect due her as a princess of Brittany. She was beloved not only by Anne and her family but by the people as well.

The duchess is so pale as she works with her ladies to prepare Isabeau's body that I fear she will fall ill too. The young princess is dressed in her favorite gown of crimson velvet, and Anne herself braids the pearls into her long brown hair. On the day of Isabeau's funeral, the cortege carries her to the great cathedral in Rennes, where she is buried beneath the choir.

I have not talked to Balthazaar. It is too hard to think of him as Death since the night He — no, he — carried Isabeau away. It is nearly impossible to reconcile my roguish, moody hellequin with Death. I climb the stairs, moving slowly. I am still uncertain of what to say, how to be with him. I cannot treat him as if he were still simply Balthazaar. And yet, the idea of treating him as formally as I would Mortain feels equally wrong, for we have been much more to each other than that.

The thought has me blushing. To have lain with a god and not even known! Truly, I am three kinds of fool. But looking back, I feel as if my heart has always known. How else to explain that sense of recognition, of connection, that I felt at our first meeting? Is that even possible? For our hearts to know things that our minds do not?

Would he ever have told me if I had not asked him to escort Isabeau? That is one of the questions that has been tumbling around in my mind for the past three days. Was he trying to trick me? And why does he carry my arrow with him?

My fear is that I somehow called him to me, much as Arduinna binds hearts with her arrows, and that feels like another sort of trickery all its own. One that I never intended.

And how will we ever be together again? It was bad enough to have fallen in love with a hellequin, but to fall in love with Death? Surely there can be no happy ending to *that* story.

When I reach the battlements, I take a deep breath, then step outside, grasping my skirts firmly so that I will not feel the trembling in my hands. As I make my way to the shadowed corner, all the clever things I have thought of to say, all the burning questions I have wrestled with coalesce into one: Why me?

Unable to help myself, I slow my steps before I reach the corner. As I take another deep breath to fortify myself, Balthazaar's low deep voice rumbles out into the night. "I wondered if you would ever return." While his voice is teasing, I can hear the thread of true worry that underlies it. Then he steps out of the shadows, onto the catwalk.

"My lord." Without conscious thought, I start to drop to my knees.

"Stop." The feel of his hand grasping my arm startles me into silence.

I long to look up, to see his face, to try to discern if he is angry or amused or any of a hundred possibilities. But I am too embarrassed and feel far too foolish.

"Do not treat me differently now. Please." The annoyance and frustration in his voice sound so much like Balthazaar that it is almost possible to forget all that has transpired.

I sigh. "I do not know whether to rail at you in anger or beg your forgiveness."

He lets go of my arm. "Most likely there will be both before we are done, but know this: You have nothing to ask forgiveness for. It is I who tricked you, although I did not intend it to be a trick."

I do look up at him then. "What was your intent?"

His dark, depthless eyes study me a moment, as if he himself is perplexed by the question. Then he goes to lean against the parapet and stares out into the night. He runs his hand through his hair, and in that moment, he is so much a man rather than a god that the tight iron band around my lungs loosens somewhat.

"Once, I was so much a part of both life and death that time had no meaning for me. My existence was as much about beginnings as it was endings. People recognized that death was part of the journey, not some grim punishment meted out for one's sins. But over time, and with the help of the new church, my existence narrowed so that all I was and would ever be was Death. Oblivion, at best, and at worst, eternal hell-fire and damnation. Everything that gave purpose and meaning to my existence was stripped from me."

I grow very still.

"I had been reduced from a god who brought death with one hand and used it to create life with the other to a demonic specter of the night used to frighten people into complying with the new church's beliefs. I found myself the ruler of only half a kingdom, and it was the terrifying, feared half."

"Except for the convent," I whisper.

He nods. "The convent remembered me as I was, as well as small pockets of people here and there. Enough to sustain me, albeit in a reduced existence. To ease my loneliness, I sought a wife—"

"Amourna."

"No. Not Amourna. Arduinna."

I suck in a breath. "So it *was* a mistake."

"Yes. A horrible, tragic mistake that ended so disastrously, I resolved to simply be with those mortal women who invited me into their beds. But those moments were always fleeting and did little to ease the loneliness that grew inside me. If not for my daughters, who maintained a faint thread of connection with me through their worship, I think I would have gone mad.

"Then, into this grim existence, a new heart opened up to me, as unexpected and surprising as a rose blooming in the dead of winter. This heart was not praying for deliverance or offering herself to me rather than her loutish husband. This heart simply belonged to a small, pure soul, one who brought a glimmer of joy to me once more.

"One day, this soul cried out in terror, and she was so open to me that I heard her. I, who had not been invited into anyone's life in centuries, had a purpose. And so I went to her, and being with her eased that great loneliness in my soul in a way that lying with all those other women had not. So even as I comforted her, she comforted me. Even as she was nourished by our connection, I was fed as well. For a short span of time—months? Years? I do not know—I was not lonely.

"And then, it stopped. As if a door had been slammed in my face. And once again, I knew despair."

"I was that soul," I whisper.

He turns to face me, his eyes bleak with his painful memories. "Yes. You filled a hole that I had all but forgotten about."

"But I was only five years old."

He shrugs. "In the world of spirit, where I most often reside, a soul —and the light it shines—is utterly removed from such things as age. I did not know you were a child until I came upon you in the cellar, and then it was too late. I was caught. You prayed and chatted with me constantly, and I did not have the strength to let go of the gift that you offered. It was like bread to a starving man.

"Then later, when that barrier came up between us, it was as if the sun had fallen from the sky, and my existence became even more miserable than before because you had reminded me of all that I missed."

"And yet," I say, remembering those long hard years, "you never abandoned me. Even when you thought I had turned my back on you, you did not turn your back on me."

He turns away, as if embarrassed. "But then you sent me your arrow, and I could not understand why you would do such a thing. It felt like a taunt, and it enraged me, filling me with equal parts hope and fury, and I could not tell what you truly wished from me.

"I had not decided what I would do about it, but I carried the arrow with me. I carry it still," he says.

"I know. I saw it. That's why I ran away from the hunt. I thought the hellequin had been sent to punish me for having left the convent without your permission."

He looks taken aback—almost affronted—that I would think such a thing.

"I am sorry. It was a threat the nuns used with us when we were young, and I believed them."

"You never needed my permission. You were always free to come and go as you pleased."

"But that is not what they teach us," I murmur.

He frowns, distracted by my words, but continues his tale. "And then one night, while I was leading the hunt, there you were. Standing with your back to a tree, making ready to take on the entire hunt if need be. Looking at you opened old wounds." He clenches his hands into fists. "I hated that I could be made to want again." He lifts his face to the stars, as if he is too embarrassed to look at me. "I wished to understand the nature of you, the *why* of you. And so I decided to take you with me."

"If I recall, I came willingly."

He tilts his head. "Somewhat. Although I would have insisted either way. I had lost you for long years and was not about to do so again, not until I was ready to set you aside."

My stomach drops all the way to my toes at his words. "And are you?" I whisper. "Ready to set me aside?"

His eyes burn into me. "No." After a long moment in which I must look away under the intensity of that gaze, he whispers, "So, what happened? Why did you shut the door and stop letting me in like that?"

"I told someone I had seen you. And I was punished for it, told I was lying, making things up. And so it became my secret, something that I shared with no one. But I was eventually caught out—and punished." Brutally, but I do not tell him that, nor do I tell him the nature of the punishment, for it shames me still. "Shortly after that, the abbess who made my life so harsh died, and fear was no longer my constant companion. I did not feel as if I constantly walked the razor's edge between life and death, and so my need for you lessened." But also, the cost of opening myself to him had proved too great. "With the new abbess, I had been given a new chance, and I did not wish to risk making the same mistake."

He reaches out and takes my hand in his own, gripping it firmly, as if he could pull me out of the dark confines of my memory. "And thus at a young age you became acquainted with the limits of Death and His power." He closes his eyes, but not before I glimpse the anger and regret that fills them.

When he opens them again, he looks to the sky. "Dawn is coming."

I am not ready to leave. There is still so much we must talk about. "When will I see you again?"

He holds very still, as if hope is some fragile thing he must coax forth bit by bit. "Would you like to?"

"I would. I am not done with trying to understand what is between us."

He smiles then, and bows, then disappears into the shadows.

Chapter Forty-Six

"THE NEWS IS NOT GOOD." Captain Dunois's face is gray—with exhaustion or worry, I cannot tell. Perhaps both.

Duval glances at the duchess. "You do not need to be here, you know. We can handle this for you, at least for a little while longer."

"No." She gives a firm shake of her head. "I will not abandon my responsibility and let the hard decisions be made by others."

Duval motions to Sybella. "Tell us."

"There are fifteen thousand troops outside Rennes." A gasp goes up around the room; no one expected that many. "It looks as if the bulk of them will be camped south of the city, with maybe a third of their forces in the north."

"So we are surrounded," Duval muses. "Even if someone were to send help, they would have to fight their way through the French to reach us."

"Exactly so." Sybella glances at the duchess as if she is loath for her to hear what she has to say next. "They have also brought the engines of war with them. Catapults, scaling towers. Cannon."

The duchess looks like she might faint. "They would destroy the city itself."

Captain Dunois tries to offer her some small comfort. "It is possible — probable even — that they are to be used as a threat only, for it would bring the king little joy to take possession of a ruined city."

Duval turns to Marshal Rieux. "And what do you have to report?"

"Equally unwelcome news, I am afraid. Four more cities have fallen to the French, and they have retaken Vannes. The entire south of Brittany is now in their hands. Parts of the west as well."

We are all of us stunned into silence at this sobering turn of events.

"Which means we have lost," the duchess whispers.

No one contradicts her. Dunois says, "The British captain has sent word that if you leave now, before the French cut off all the routes, he can get you to the coast and take you to the Netherlands. From there he can get you safely to your husband, the Holy Roman emperor."

"And abandon my people? What sort of craven do they take me for?"

Beast clears his throat, and Duval motions for him to speak. "It might be the only way we can keep you safe, Your Grace."

"What do you mean?"

"I mean, the conditions in the city have deteriorated greatly. With the coffers empty once more, the mercenaries now loot and raid the city, treating the townspeople's homes and businesses like their own personal larders. Unfortunately, the foreign troops here in the city greatly outnumber our own Breton troops, and it is all we can do to keep them in check."

"What of the Arduinnites?" At my question, everyone turns and looks at me.

"They offered their help weeks ago, and we have yet to take them up on it. Would they not be put to good use protecting the citizens of Rennes? It is their calling, you know, protecting the innocent."

"Yes." The duchess's voice comes swift and firm, cutting off any possible argument. "Let us accept what generous aid these women offer us. You will arrange it?" she asks me.

"Of course, Your Grace."

* * *

I grab my cloak and hurry from the palace. The French troops' circle around the city is drawing tighter, but it has not closed yet. It is easy enough to go into the stables, saddle Fortuna, then slip out the postern gate without being noticed. It is harder to avoid the sentries at the Arduinnites' encampment. Before I have spotted them, I hear a command to halt. I look up into a tree, where an Arduinnite I do not know is straddling the branch, her arrow aimed directly at me. "I have come to see Floris," I say. "Please tell her that Annith requests an audience."

She stares at me a moment, then nods her head. Another woman separates herself from her hiding place in the tree and disappears toward the camp. All I can do now is wait. Although it is hard with the sentry's eyes on me and her arrow at the ready, I ignore her and turn my attention to the sparse woods around me. The night is cool rather than cold, with the breath of late springtime upon us at last. I let my mind flow once more over the words I must say to Floris and think how best to say them, for Arduinna's followers have proven themselves a prickly bunch and I do not wish to risk raising old angers or feuds when I wish to bring the duchess some solutions.

That is my answer. The duchess, for it is she whom the Arduinnites have agreed to help. I will tell them of Isabeau's small offering to them on behalf of her sister. Perhaps that will soften their hearts.

Besides, I must know the truth of what lies between Arduinna and Mortain so that I may better understand the man — the god — who has captured my heart. For it comes to me then that beyond all that is reasonable or sensible or even explicable, I am in love with Balthazaar.

It does not come like a thunderbolt from the sky, nor does it clout me alongside my head like a hammer, but seeps slowly into my consciousness, like a tendril of mist or a trickle of water from an underground stream.

But why? He is stubborn and close-mouthed and half drowning in despair.

And yet . . . something about him fits so comfortably against my own heart.

And though I wish I could have scraped together enough common sense to avoid falling in love with a bedamned god, apparently it does not matter to my heart one whit whether he is a hellequin or the god the hellequin serve—for other than a faint sense of awe and incredulity, my feelings for him have not changed.

There is a whisper of movement, then the sentry who was sent with my request appears before me. "Floris will see you," she says, doing a poor job of keeping the surprise out of her voice. "You are to follow me."

She leads me, still on Fortuna, from the trees toward the scattering of campfires and the small dark mounds that I recognize as tents. Someone at the nearest fire lifts a hand in a cheerful wave, and I recognize Tola. She rises to her feet and lopes toward me, still holding the joint of meat she was having for supper. "What brings Mortain's own out of her mighty palace?" she asks, but there is no sting to her words, only a friendly teasing.

"I find I miss the smell of wood smoke and grew tired of eating off plates."

She grins back at me, quick and easy. "By all means, join us."

I look down at the haunch she is gnawing on and realize how very long it has been since I have eaten. "I am actually here to see Floris. I bring word from the duchess."

The woman leading me stops suddenly, and I must rein in Fortuna so she does not trample her. "You may tie your horse up here," she says, indicating a slender tree.

I dismount, then secure the reins to one of the branches. Tola takes one last bite of her dinner, then tosses the bone into the nearest campfire. "I'll take her," she says to the other woman, who shrugs, as if it makes no difference to her, then steps away.

I smile. "I have missed you."

She grins, then leads the way to the largest of the tents, set up toward the back. When we reach it, she holds up her hand to stop me, then slips inside. Two seconds later she is back, holding the flap aside and motioning me in.

Inside the tent, Floris sits near the fire, flanked by two older women whom I vaguely recognize from my time with them.

"Annith," she says softly, her face calm and serious.

Even though it is not their way, I curtsy before her, wanting to demonstrate the respect I have for her. "Thank you for seeing me on such short notice and at such a late hour.

"The duchess has sent me to accept your offer of help. Inside the city, we are much beset by the very mercenaries she needs to defend us against the French. They grow bored and restless with the waiting. Even worse, with the French troops encircling the city, the mercenaries are demanding their pay, but her coffers are empty. They have taken to terrorizing the citizens of Rennes as their pastime, and I told her that protecting the innocent was the nature of your service to the goddess. Will you help?"

"But of course we will help." Floris looks out toward the twinkling campfires of the French. "They will have the city fully surrounded in another day or two."

"I know. There has been a steady flood of refugees ever since their banners were first spotted."

"They'd best hurry, for once the French are in position, no one will be able to get in or out of the city."

In the silence that follows, I wish to ask her if she will tell me her story of Arduinna and Mortain, to see if it is the same as the one Father Effram and Mortain have told me. But as closely as they hold their secrets, I dare not ask. Especially not in front of so many.

* * *

The following day, Duval, Dunois, and Beast spend their time poring over maps, trying to mark the French encampments. The duchess excuses herself and retires to her solar. Or tries to. She is exhausted but too ill at ease to be able to rest. In the end, she takes herself and her ladies off to the cathedral to pray beside Isabeau's tomb.

I have little enough to do except worry about Ismae and miss Sybella, who awoke late while we were in the council meeting and has now taken herself to the convent of Brigantia to spend time with her sisters. Isabeau's passing has made them all the more precious to her.

As I pace in front of the fireplace, my eyes fall on the black box, now splintered and broken, and I remember the arrow. I hurry over and dig through the wreckage. The moment my fingers touch the slim, dark wood, a deep knowing runs through my fingers. I pull the arrow out and carry it over to study it in the light from the window.

I think of the story both Father Effram and Mortain told me, how Death's capturing Amourna was naught but a mistake, a wretched, human mistake, and how it was Arduinna whom he had loved all those centuries.

I think of the Arduinnites, who have refused to share their story with anyone and let us all assume it was because they did not wish to contradict either Dea Matrona or Amourna and prove either of them wrong. But of a certainty, pride goes hand in hand with ferocity. What if they simply could not bear for the world to know that Arduinna had been rejected for her younger, fairer sister? Floris as much as admitted that Mortain had played her goddess false.

The fragment of the arrow I hold is older than anything I have ever seen except for the standing stones and cromlechs that litter the countryside like discarded playthings of the gods. The wood is so hard as to almost be stone, and the arrowhead is of some metal—bronze, I think—gone black with age.

The implications send me reeling, for they are almost too incredible to believe. And yet . . .

And yet, why else would an ancient arrow be kept in the heart of the convent, concealed in a box with no means of opening it, as if Mortain himself were hoarding some small keepsake of his lost love?

What if I am holding the last of Arduinna's arrows in the palm of my hand, a true relic of the gods?

My mind gallops over everything I have ever heard said of Arduinna and her arrows. That they fly straight and sure, that they never miss, and that they bring the pain of true love to those that they strike.

My pulse starts to race. What if we could take this relic, the ancient weapon, and find a way to use it to the duchess's advantage?

As I turn the arrow over and over in my hand, an idea of how to not only avert war but turn this defeat into a triumph for our duchess begins to form. A triumph of not just politics, but the heart.

Chapter Forty-Seven

"WELL?" I ASK IMPATIENTLY. "Do you think it could work?"

Father Effram studies the arrow, his hands tucked into his sleeves as if he is afraid to touch it. "It is *possible* . . ." He looks up at me, his eyes alight with excitement. "Probable, even, for as you say, why else would the convent of Mortain have held on to such a thing for so long?" He reaches out, his fingers hovering just above the arrow. "How very old it must be," he muses.

"But what if I am wrong?" I clasp my hands together and begin to pace. "I do not wish to kill the king of France."

"Don't you?" He cocks his head, truly curious.

"No."

He nods. "Well, then, I suppose there is one way to be certain. You will need to ask your abbess—"

"She does not know."

"Well, someone should have the answers you seek. I admit, it is a most appealing idea."

"I know the duchess does not wish all those deaths on her conscience," I tell him. "And I know she is worried sick for all the countrymen who must die if we go to war. It is the only way I can think of to avert bloodshed."

"Perhaps it is even worth the king's life," he suggests.

"No," I say sharply. "It is not. Besides, the French regent would only seek retaliation, which would be swift and far more brutal than a simple war."

"If a war can ever be called simple," he murmurs. We stare at the arrow a moment longer.

"How do I ensure that if the king is struck with it, he will fall in love with the duchess rather than the one who has shot the arrow?"

His answer is swift and sure. "By putting the duchess's blood on it."

I look up at him in surprise, and he gives a sheepish shrug. "It is the only option that makes sense."

I gently pick up the arrow, lay it on the length of velvet, and roll the fabric back up, my movements slow and reluctant. "I suppose it is time for me to have a talk with someone who knows."

Because of my duties for the duchess, I am unable to slip away to the battlements for three days. The entire city is preparing for both a war and a siege, and the duchess's presence and authority are in much demand, as she is forced to make hard decision after hard decision. How many of the hundreds of people fleeing the threat of war can she allow into the city before our resources and supplies are stretched so thin that we assure only our own deaths by starvation or our quick surrender? Which of the many foreign troops that are garrisoned in the city can be trusted not to abandon their posts? Or worse, switch sides, given that they have been paid only a small portion of their fees and have little hope of receiving anything more than sad little coins made of leather, essentially worthless? It is one long endless heartbreak for her, and I do not envy her the task.

"You returned."

Balthazaar's voice unfurls from the darkness in the corner, and I whirl around to face him. "I did not mean to stay away so long," I say.

"The duchess is beset by problems and we are busier than I would have imagined. She also misses Isabeau and hates being alone, and so she keeps me nearly constantly at her side."

"And you, Annith? Have you been eager to see me? Or are you still discomfited by my presence?" He says the words lightly, but something in his voice draws my gaze up to meet his. That is when I see him —Balthazaar is there in the bleakness and sorrow that lurks in Death's eyes, and I realize that whatever skin or body he wears, his heart spoke the truth to me, and my own heart responded. Even more telling, when I was most in pain, most in need of comfort, it was him I went to. Not Ismae, not Sybella, but him.

"I am growing accustomed to it all." I will him to see that I am telling the truth. Something in my face must convince him, because the pain in his expression eases somewhat. He glances down at the parcel I carry.

"What is that?"

"It is something I must ask you about. I . . . I found it at the convent, before I left, and took it not understanding what it was." I place the parcel on the flat surface of the crenellation and carefully unroll the velvet to reveal the arrow. I feel him stiffen beside me.

He stares at the arrow a long time, saying nothing. After a while, he reaches out and—almost tenderly—runs his finger along its surface. "It is mine, yes."

"And is it also Arduinna's?"

He looks at me. "Yes. It is the arrow she used to pierce my heart."

"So that part of the tale is true, then?"

"That she pierced my heart? Yes. But it is also true that it was pierced with love for her, not her sister. Nor do the tales mention that my hellequin—my damned hellequin—went out and captured the wrong sister, believing they were doing me a great service, for they thought her lovelier than Arduinna, and more biddable besides. They did not realize it was her ferocity and defiance that drew me to her. I knew she was one of the few who might be strong enough to survive in my kingdom."

"Those that follow Salonius always claimed it was a mistake."

Balthazaar snorts. "They should know, as I believe he had a hand in it." He shakes his head as if still unable to believe it. "How could I reject Amourna and tell her it was not she I desired, but her sister? She was soft and lovely and she was much taken with the idea of being queen of the Underworld."

"But you loved Arduinna."

"Yes. And she thought I had played her false."

"What happened to Amourna? For she seems to have faded from the world even more than the other gods."

"As I said, she was soft and somewhat flighty. At first, she loved being queen, but soon it no longer entertained her—it wasn't the pageant and festivity she had been longing for, and the pain of loving the damned became too much for her. Slowly, over the centuries, she simply faded away, as the first flush of easy love often does."

"And you were left alone, with neither sister."

He looks at me, and I feel the force of his gaze like a blow as he takes a step closer. "Until you opened your heart to me." I fear I will drown in that gaze, but I cannot look away. Giving me time to pull back or turn my head or do any number of things to let him know he is no longer wanted, he slowly lowers his lips to mine.

They are cool. Cooler than I remember. But the shape of them is the same, and the taste of him. But even more importantly—the need and longing his lips awaken in me has not changed. Slowly, we draw apart. "If you loved Arduinna, then why have you slept with so many women throughout the centuries?" I did not intend to ask such an artless question, but now it hangs in the air between us.

It is hard to tell in the dark, but I think his lips twitch with a hint of amusement. However, that is quickly chased away by the bleakness that is all too familiar. "It was the only way left for me to partake of life. All the other ways that I, that Death, had been a part of life were absorbed by the new church or forgotten and no longer celebrated."

"Oh." I do not know what to say to that, but it goes a long way toward relieving me of any jealousy that I had been harboring.

"Come." He holds out his hand, and for a moment I panic, thinking he is going to ask me to lie with him again. I can't. Not now. Or at least, not *yet*, for it is all still too new and strange and . . . overwhelming. "Sit with me," he says, then lowers himself gracefully onto the ground.

I hesitate only a moment before allowing myself to be coaxed into joining him. We sit, stiffly, side by side. "You are one of her line, you know."

"Whose?"

"Arduinna's."

I pull away from his shoulder and stare at him. "What do you mean?"

"You even bear her mark." He slowly reaches out and places his finger just below my ear, then runs it along the sensitive skin at my throat to the back of my neck, making me shiver. "Here," he says. "A small red starburst, Arduinna's bite, they call it, although I do not know why, for she has never bitten anyone as far as I know."

"How can that be? They told me that Arduinnites were made, not born." I reach up to feel it, but my fingers discern nothing. This does, however, awaken the memory of Tola asking about a mark I had there. She *knew.*

He settles back against the wall. "Just because she marks you does not mean she has given you special skills or talents. But those who are conceived under the cloud of jealousy or through deceitful means are hers, for hers is the domain of those who feel love's sharp bite and the pain of rejection. Whether or not they choose to act upon it is up to them."

My mind goes immediately to the story the abbess—my mother —told me of her desperate attempt to win Crunard's heart, although it had already been given to another.

"If you decided to wield that arrow, it would strike with love as permanent as if it flew from Arduinna's own bow." He reaches up and places his cool fingers against my cheek, turning my face toward him. "If you doubt me or my constancy, you have only to pierce me with it and you can be certain I will be yours for eternity."

"But what of Arduinna? She pierced you once and you have not remained faithful to her."

He drops his hand and turns away, but not before I see the old pain in his eyes. "That was because our ties became severed by the twin blades of pride and anger. Each of us had a hand in that. Even her gift can be eroded by those things. Eroded, but not destroyed." His voice grows soft. "I do still love her, in a way. It is rarely a lack of love that forces two hearts apart, but other obstacles."

It is all too easy to conjure up all the obstacles that face us, and it is tempting, oh, so tempting, to tie his love to me for all eternity so that I am the final one he will ever love. But it is too close to what the abbess tried to do to me: to bind me so tightly to her that I could not love or live on my own, could not make my own choices. "No," I say firmly. "I do not want a love if I must bind it to me in such a manner, for does not the very binding of it make it less like love?"

He smiles at me, one of his rare, dazzling smiles, as if I have pleased him beyond measure. He lifts my hand and brings it up to his lips, which graze against it tenderly.

"Besides," I say, "there is something else I must do with it."

Chapter Forty-Eight

AT THIS LATE HOUR, I find the duchess in her chambers. Duval is sitting with her, which causes me a moment of guilt—she must have sent for him because I was gone for so long. I sink into a deep curtsy. "I beg your pardon, Your Grace. I did not intend my errand to be such a lengthy one."

She smiles, but it is a pale, watery thing that hurts to look at. "It is no matter. Come in, come in."

Duval rises to his feet and excuses himself. Once he has left, I turn to the duchess. "I have something I would speak with you about."

The duchess's interest is piqued. "Pray continue."

And so I lay out my plan before her, explaining the old power contained in the arrow and how it could be wielded for the country's advantage. The duchess's eyes grow brighter and brighter as I explain my plan, for she has struggled mightily to find some way out of this mess.

When I am finished, hope teeters in her face, then slowly seeps away. "It is a fine idea," she says at last. "Except that I am already married."

A situation that is all too easy to forget, with as little help as her lord husband has provided her.

"Only by proxy," I point out. "And it is not consummated. You agreed to the marriage in the belief that it would help you hold on to Brittany, but instead, it has had precisely the opposite effect, driving France to move more openly against us. It has proved a poor bargain."

The duchess rises to her feet, her hands clasped tightly together. "That is true, and I am sorry for it. But we are still bound before the eyes of God and the Church. We had a ceremony," she says. "Presided over by the bishop and feted with a celebration. How can we just put that aside now? Besides"—her voice grows stronger and more laced with pride—"how can I consider marrying the man who has caused my kingdom so much woe?"

"Your Grace, we know that it was his sister the French regent who was behind much of what has transpired, as she held the kingdom for him." It is so easy to forget that he is just a few years older than the duchess. "We do not know how much he was consulted in her plans and strategies."

She presses her fingertips against her eyes. "This is all making my head spin."

I am immediately contrite. "I am sorry, Your Grace. I did not wish to push so hard."

"No, you are right to push for solutions." The duchess gives me a grim smile. "Even though I am not certain I can do what you suggest, I thank you for at least bringing me a new option to consider. Odd, is it not, that those who have been the most helpful to me are my bastard brother and the ones who serve the old saints the Church would just as soon deny.

"Every one of my allies has failed to assist in any meaningful way. Especially my lord husband." Her words are bitter and laced with pain. "Unless God or His saints send me a miracle . . ."

"Could not this ancient magic at the heart of the old gods be a sort of miracle?" I ask softly.

"It could, but I fear breaking my vows. Besides, how can I marry King Charles? His family has been behind every grief that has befallen mine in the past fifteen years."

"His *family*, Your Grace. Not him." I think of the abbess and all that she has done in my name. "We cannot be held responsible for what our families do, especially when we have no way to control them."

She nods, conceding the point, reluctantly. "But it will be delivering Brittany right into the hands of the French—something my father fought all his life to avoid, something I have sworn to prevent at all costs."

"And yet," I remind her, "you said yourself the costs might be too high. War is ugly and lives will be lost. Not only that, but in wedding the king of France, you would be setting Brittany's true heir upon the French throne—you would bear that country's future kings. Not an altogether bad way to maintain control of your duchy. Besides, I am not sure you are required to sacrifice your life—your chance at happiness —for your father's goals."

"No! It is my wish as well. It has been ever since I can remember."

"But only because you have been raised to wish it," I say gently. "It was trained into you just as surely as dancing or embroidery. But just as those are not truly you, neither is this desire for independence at any cost."

She whirls on me. "Why are you so quick to surrender? To give up?" The moment she asks the question, I realize I will have to tell her who my father is, else, when she finds out, she will feel sorely betrayed and will doubt my loyalty.

Am I being quick to surrender? Is there some weakness, some traitor blood that flows in my veins? I consider a moment. "It is not that I am so very quick to give up," I finally say, "but rather that I do not wish to spend my life pursuing goals that others have chosen for me. If I must perish, if I must stumble and fail, then let it be in pursuit of the ideals and dreams that I hold in my own heart."

She stares at me a long moment. "I do not want all those deaths on my conscience," she whispers. "Indeed, it haunts my dreams, and I fear that I will not be able to live with myself."

"I would have a hard time with that decision as well, Your Grace." I take a deep breath. "In truth, killing holds little appeal for me."

Her head jerks up in surprise.

"Oh, have no fear, I can fight better than most, for I am well trained, but I have never enjoyed taking life. And that was something I thought was a weakness of mine, something to be ashamed of and do penance for. I have spent my entire life praying for the strength to embrace killing."

"And have you received it?"

"No. But I have learned something that I must share with you, something I have shared with few others." I take a deep breath. "As it turns out, I was not sired by Mortain after all. I am not his daughter. My entire life has been a lie." A bemused laugh escapes my throat. It still stuns me to say those words. "I have spent my life pursuing dreams and goals that were never mine to pursue. And one of the reasons I tell you this is that before you make a decision on the option that I have given you, you need to know the truth about not only me, but my true father."

"Who is he?"

"Crunard, Your Grace. My father is Chancellor Crunard." It is the first time I have ever spoken those words, and the sound of them echoing in the room is like a death knell for the person I have been all my life. Saying them, and to my duchess, no less, is akin to stepping out of an old skin and standing naked before the world. "There must be truth between us so you can make the best, most informed decision available to you. If I had hid my identity from you now, when you found out, you would always question my loyalty, and that would wound me greatly, for serving you has been an unexpected grace."

She stares at me a long moment, her eyes wide and deep with thoughts. She shakes her head with a rueful smile. "I thank you for your honesty, Lady Annith, but be assured, I trust the counsel you have given me. As you say, I understand well how we can serve in spite of our parentage."

Now it is my turn to give her a bemused look.

She smiles tightly and folds her arms across her chest. "Do you know how much Breton blood I possess?"

"No, Your Grace."

"None. Not one drop. My father was a French noble who inherited Brittany from his wife."

"Your mother."

"No." She gives a quick, firm shake of her head. "Not my mother. His first wife, the heir to Brittany, died years before I was born. My mother was also named Marguerite, but she was Marguerite of Foix, not Brittany. So you see, the whole of my life has been a lie as well.

"But," she continues, "the cause of Breton independence has defined my entire life, and in that I am more Breton that most of the Breton nobles, who have been receiving bribes and payments from the French regent for years.

"So instead, I will think of Brittany's true people, those who have lived here since time out of mind and who have worked the land and built the castles and cathedrals and roads. Those are the lives I must weigh."

And just like that, I know that it is time for me to meet with the abbess once more, for we still have much that lies unspoken and unsettled between us. But it is not her, or even the convent, that I must worry about. Like the duchess, my true concern is those whose lives will be most affected — all the girls that I have loved as sisters.

Chapter Forty-Nine

THE NEXT DAY, THE ABBESS forces me to wait for a full hour before she will see me. It is a rank display of power, and all the more pitiful for it. Luckily, it serves me well, for it allows me to run through a number of different ways the conversation can go. By the time I am finally admitted to her office, I am calm and sure of what I wish to say to her.

"Annith."

She gives no greeting, but merely says my name, so I do the same. "Reverend Mother."

I add a shallow curtsy to maintain the pretense of respect, but it is shallow enough that she knows that's all it is—a mere formality and devoid of the former esteem and admiration I once felt for her.

"I am hoping you are here to tell me that you have come to your senses and will be returning to the convent immediately."

"On the contrary, I am here to tell you that this cannot go on. You cannot keep serving as reverend mother. It corrupts the very nature of what we do and whom we serve."

Her nostrils flare with irritation. "We have no choice, don't you understand? Besides, no one except you knows or even suspects."

I think back to the probing glances Sister Serafina often gave me and to the openly hostile manner of Sister Eonette. "I am not sure that is true."

"How do you propose that we go about this?" She spreads her arms wide as if it is too big a thought to put her arms around. "How do we tell them?"

"I do not know; it is not my sin to confess." I meet her gaze steadily.

She leans back in her chair, a smile playing about her lips, a smile that sends a whisper of unease down my spine. "You are every bit as culpable as I am, make no mistake."

I frown in confusion. "What do you mean? I was a mere infant; I did not ask to be brought there."

She picks up a quill from her desk and examines the tip. "Do you remember the great tragedy?"

The sinking feeling in my gut reminds me of why I have been so reluctant to confront her again. "Yes," I say quietly. "Of course I do. We lost four beloved nuns."

She picks up a knife and begins sharpening the point of the quill. I want to shake her and scream at her to stop. Instead, I clasp my hands tightly together and wait for whatever is coming. "Do you also remember how, a few days before that, you and I went out for a walk and carried a small luncheon with us?"

The sinking feeling now turns into a sick churning. "Of course I remember." It was one of the rare special outings Sister Etienne and I were allowed.

She finally looks up from the quill, piercing me with her cold blue eyes. "Do you remember what else we did that day, besides walk the island and picnic?"

"We picked mushrooms," I whisper.

She sets the knife and quill down and folds her hands in front of her. "Exactly."

Dread begins to seep into my bones. "But you said they were the safe ones!"

She tilts her head to the side. "Did I?"

"Of course you did, or else I would never have touched them!"

"Odd. I don't remember that conversation." She leans forward, face triumphant with victory. "It was you, Annith, you who picked the mushrooms that killed the nuns that day."

Awareness slams into me like a battering ram. "But, but if you knew, why didn't you throw them away?"

"I had to do something to save you from that woman. She was going to kill you. And you—obedient, besotted sheep that you were—you were just going to let her."

My mind reels. I had thought that learning I was not sired by Mortain was surely the worst shock of my life, but even it pales when compared to this. "And you let Sister Magdelena take the blame for it?"

"Sister Magdelena was old, well past her time, and she had begun to suspect, I think."

A fresh wave of insight crashes over me. "It was you who made Sister Vereda ill as well, wasn't it!"

For a moment, she simply stares at me, then inclines her head. "Yes." Her voice softens. "But I had learned much and was more subtle. I made certain only to sicken her, not kill her. But she too had begun to question things that she Saw. Things that she did not understand. And I had orders, orders that could not come from her."

"Crunard was blackmailing you."

"Yes." Her voice is as flat and hard as her eyes. "If I did not help him, he was going to expose me to the world. He did not know about you. I made certain to keep that from him." She drops her head into her hands for a long moment. When she looks up again, her face is soft, pleading. "Don't you see, sweeting? That is why I was going to have you be seeress. Together we could decide what would be best for the convent and the country and we could steer the others to fulfill those plans."

"Were you ever going to tell me all this?" The force of this second betrayal nearly brings me to my knees, for I had come to understand why a desperate young mother might need to take shelter. But this . . . this

374

committing murder—and now, years later, laying it at my feet—has turned my entire world upside down. "How were you going to force me to See what you wanted?"

"You were always biddable and obedient. At least, before Sybella arrived. You seemed to sense what others wanted or needed from you and were only too happy to provide it. I was simply going to let you continue on that course. That and help you interpret your visions and read the signs of augury."

"That is why you sent Sybella away so soon!"

"She was ruining you. Corrupting your innocence and your cooperativeness. She was ruining Ismae as well," she adds as an afterthought.

"She was my friend. And your *sacred* charge, and you betrayed her for your own ends."

The abbess lifts her shoulders in a cold, unfeeling gesture. "She was not you, and you were all that I cared about. All that I still care about."

I feel sick, tainted with the stain of her sins.

The abbess stands up and comes around to my side of the desk. She reaches out to take my hand, but I jerk it away from her. Pain flares in her eyes. "You were to be my sacrifice to Mortain," she says. "My penance. My atonement. By dedicating you to His service, I was certain He would grant us forgiveness."

"But it was not *your* life to sacrifice to him."

"If not for me, you would not have had life in the first place. If not for me, that wretched Dragonette would have killed or maimed you."

I clench my fists in frustration. She is right. In some ways, I owe her much. But not my life. My gratitude, perhaps. And my loyalty?

It feels as if she lost her right to that when she murdered people and tried to blame it on me. Slowly, I look up and meet her gaze. "I owe you nothing." My voice is quiet but sure. "Any loyalty or respect I might have felt for you was lost the day you killed others and risked young girls' safety to try and shelter me."

She reels back, as if my words have the force of a blow. After a moment, she puts her hands into her sleeves and returns to the other side of the desk. "Very well." When she looks at me again, she is all business, any signs of the pleading mother gone. "Then I will give you what you have always wanted. If you say nothing of this to anyone, you can be an assassin. I will not make you seeress. I had hoped to protect you, not only your physical self, but your immortal soul as well. But if you do not care, so be it. You have only to hold your tongue."

I nearly laugh at how little she offers me and how far too late it comes. "No. I will never serve under you, nor carry out your wishes. I will not even maintain this charade of yours much longer."

Then I turn and leave the room, every belief I have ever held, about myself, the abbess, even the world, crushed beneath her crimes.

It is time to have Father Effram call a convocation of the Nine.

Chapter Fifty

THREE DAYS LATER, I am in the solar with the duchess and her ladies in waiting. They are stitching, but I find I cannot sit still. I feel as if every bone in my body has been taken out and put back in in the wrong place, and I must relearn how to move, to think, to act. I try to be subtle about it, but the duchess keeps glancing in my direction, looking as if she is about to say something then changing her mind. I am supposed to offer her protection and comfort, not disturb her with my restlessness. I have just decided that, propriety be damned, I will tie myself to one of the chairs in order to keep still when there is a commotion just outside the door. The duchess and I exchange glances, then I move in that direction, my hands reaching for my weapons. Just as my blades clear their sheaths, Duval comes through the door. His eyes are bright and tension runs through his body like a bow that has just been drawn. He glances at my knives, nods in approval, then turns to the duchess. "Ismae has returned," he says, and it is impossible not to love him a little for the relief that colors his voice. "She wishes to speak with you immediately."

The duchess has already risen to her feet and is handing her embroidery to one of her attendants. "Shall we call the other councilors?"

"Yes."

Duval sends a swarm of pages off to collect the others, then together, the three of us make our way to the council chambers. When we arrive, we find Ismae already there. She has not taken the time to change from her traveling gown. "Your Grace." She sinks into a low curtsy.

The duchess puts out her hand and helps her rise. "I am glad you are safely returned to us," she says.

"As am I. I only wish I had better news to bring you." Before she can elaborate further, the rest of the councilors begin filing into the chamber. The bishop and the abbess arrive together, a most disconcerting sight, and I cannot help but wonder if she has decided to try to curry his favor in preparation for the accusations I will soon be making.

When Sybella arrives and sees that Ismae is safe, her lips curve in pleasure, but she says nothing as she comes to stand beside me at our post behind the duchess's chair. She nudges my elbow with her own, whether in joy at Ismae's return or simply to annoy the abbess, I do not know. One never knows with Sybella.

When everyone is seated, Duval motions to Ismae. "Tell us what you have learned." His face is tense and grim and I wonder if she has already told him what transpired in private.

"The French hold the city of Nantes easily enough — there is no resistance." She glances apologetically at the duchess as she says this. "I was not able to get into the palace proper. They have double guards posted at every entrance, and everyone who comes through the doors must be vouched for by at least two others. They are taking no chances. They closed the gates to the city shortly after I got there and are not letting anyone out. There were also reports that they were going to post checkpoints along the northern roads."

"They did," Duval says. "They were able to intercept our scouts so that the army's arrival caught us by surprise."

"Just as I arrived in Rennes this morning, the French troops showed up in front of the city gate. I was one of the last they let through, and the gates were shut and bolted behind me."

"And so it is official, then," Duval mutters. "We are besieged."

"With no help is on the way," Chalon adds. Duval looks as if he wishes to kick him.

Slowly, the duchess turns to me. Her dark eyes are haunted and in them I can see that she has turned over and over my suggestion. Winning the heart of the king of France is the only way to wrest some victory from defeat and save her people. "I think I would like you all to hear what Lady Annith has to say."

There is a moment of stunned silence and the councilors exchange surprised glances, as if they are trying to remember who Lady Annith is.

The duchess continues. "We have one last option, one that Annith brought to my attention only a short while ago. It is . . . far-fetched, to put it mildly, and I do not know if it can be done, but I would have her tell you, so we may at least discuss it. Lady Annith?"

I take a deep breath and tell the Privy Council of the last of Arduinna's arrows that I possess and what I believe we may use it for. I direct most of my tale to Ismae and Duval, for they will be the easiest to convince.

As I had presumed, the rest of the council is skeptical of the plan. The bishop in particular looks both scornful and indignant. "But she has already married the Holy Roman emperor," he protests.

"By proxy," Duval points out.

Father Effram places a hand on the bishop's arm, reining in his protests. "And it is not uncommon for the pope to grant annulments when the need for political expediency is great."

"That is true," the bishop reluctantly concedes.

Montauban and Captain Dunois are more polite in expressing their doubts over the plan. It is only Duval who seems truly heartened. He has learned of the old gods through Ismae, so he understands their power more than the most. Only then, when I know I have his support, do I allow myself to look at the abbess. Her gaze is fixed on me, her rage etched in grim lines on either side of her mouth. If it were not for the presence of the council, I am certain she would fly across the table and strike me.

In the end, all on the council agree that it is worth trying, although the only reason the abbess does so is so that her lone objection will not be noted.

The rest of the council meeting turns into a planning session, for it is no small thing to work one's way into the heart of fifteen thousand French troops, locate their king, then shoot him with an arrow. Not to mention get back out again.

"She cannot go on foot." Duval gives a firm shake of his head. "It could take her days to walk through the encampment, allowing them far too much time to detect her. But more importantly, she would have no means of escape, for once the king has been hit, his guard will swarm her like flies."

"It is not impossible," Ismae points out with a glance in Sybella's direction. "She could easily post as a laundress or camp follower and go unnoticed."

"Not and make her way through thousands of French soldiers."

"Sybella did it."

"Briefly, and only to collect information. And while the army was just arriving and in disarray."

"We are trained to stealth and cunning." Ismae's voice holds a note of gentle reproach. "You do Annith a disservice by not trusting in her abilities."

Duval turns to me. "My apologies, Lady Annith, for it is not you I do not trust, but the fifteen thousand French soldiers. With that many men, there is just too great a chance you would be noticed, and your disguise will afford you little protection if you draw enough soldiers' interest."

"Sybella and I could go with her."

Duval snorts. "So you can gut every soldier who propositions you and leave a trail of dead bodies in your wake? I do not think that will help her go unnoticed."

Beast clears his throat—somewhat delicately, given his size. "Must it be her that shoots the arrow?"

Duval glances at me in question. My hand slowly drifts up to the back of my neck, my fingers seeking out the small mark that I have never seen. "Yes," I say. "It must."

"Why not one of the Arduinnites?" The abbess's voice is pitched high, shrill even.

I turn and look at her coldly. "To what purpose? I can ride as well as they can, shoot as accurately as any of them. What do we gain by asking them?"

"Your life," Duval says gently.

I know he means well, that he has only my safety in mind, so I work to keep my voice level. "I am done sending others out to risk their lives while I sit safely behind. I will do this." Besides, of all the great dreams I once had, of serving the gods, of making some contribution, this is now the only way I can do that.

"Very well. So Annith going by foot is out, as is sending others. No, Ismae." Duval puts his hand up to forestall further argument. "The trick will be getting mounted riders through the encampment. Even a small group would be immediately noticed."

"What if we just sent a full mounted guard and punched through the camp like a battering ram, clearing her a path to the king?" Beast says, and Sybella looks as if she will stride across the room and clout his thick head. "If we sent enough men, there should be some left to get her safely back."

"Except," Captain Dunois points out, "how will you get any mounted men out of this city without their being noticed? For once they are seen, the French archers will pick them off. Or send a matching force to fight them."

We all grow silent, for that is indeed the biggest problem. Getting enough of a force—getting anyone—out undetected.

Duval sighs and scrubs his hand over his face. "Well, this will not be decided tonight. Is there anything else we need to discuss?"

"Aye." Captain Dunois's voice is heavy with disgust. His face is nearly gray with fatigue, and my heart goes out to him. "There is a problem with the mercenaries."

"What now?" Duval says in disbelief. "Dare I hope that they are killing one another?"

"No, but their numbers have dwindled all the same. It is the French, my lord. They have been in contact with the mercenaries."

"How? All the entrances to the city are well guarded."

"With this." Beast dumps something heavy on the council table. It is a rolled-up ladder made of leather. "The French threw this up and over the wall, then climbed in."

Duval looks as if he would like to strike something. "And to what purpose?"

"Aware of our empty treasury, the French have offered the mercenaries their back pay, as well as a bonus if they agree to leave the city."

Duval looks as if he will be ill. "Double—no, triple—the perimeter watch." He grimaces. "How many of the mercenaries have taken them up on their offer?"

"Nearly a third."

There is a long moment of silence as that number sinks in. "Well, at least when the food stores get low, there will be that many fewer mouths to feed."

But for all the bright polish he tries to put on it, it is a grim blow indeed.

Chapter Fifty-One

WHEN THE COUNCIL MEETING is dismissed, Sybella and I are granted permission by the duchess to excuse ourselves from her service long enough to attend to Ismae as she refreshes herself from her travel. Upon reaching our chambers, we find that a tub has already been set up, and the water is still steaming. I help Ismae undress while Sybella pours three goblets of wine. She waits until Ismae has stepped into the tub, then hands me one. Over the rim of her goblet, she looks at me with her probing gaze. "How do you come to know so very much about Arduinna's arrows?"

I quickly down half the wine. "I have learned some things. About the abbess and the convent. And myself."

Sybella and Ismae exchange a glance, then Ismae motions for Sybella to hand her the soap. "Do go on," Sybella says. "We are listening."

How do I begin? What part of this tale will lead the most cleanly into the full story? "I found out why the abbess has refused to send me out on assignments and why I have been picked as seeress."

Unable to meet their curious faces, I look down at the goblet I hold in my hand and rub my fingers over the finely chased silver etchings. The faint splashing of the water in the tub grows silent. Afraid my courage will fail me, I say the words in a rush. "It is because I am not sired by Mortain."

"Sweet Jésu," Sybella mutters.

"There is more," I warn them, then take a deep breath. "The abbess is my mother." I do not stop there, but keep going, much like one takes bitter medicine quickly so that it may be over with as soon as possible. "Crunard, my father. He had been blackmailing her with exposure in order to bend the convent's will to his own wishes."

There is a faint splash as Ismae rises from the tub and grabs a towel. "Oh, Annith!" she whispers.

"And even that is not all," I say ruefully. "The abbess had been poisoning Sister Vereda to make her too sick to See what was afoot. Seven years ago"—my voice falters—"seven years ago, she poisoned three nuns, including the old seeress and the former abbess, in order to stage a silent rebellion."

"She is even more ambitious than I gave her credit for." There is a note of begrudging admiration in Sybella's voice.

I shake my head, feeling sick all over again. "It was not ambition. It was protection. She was trying to protect me." I look over at Ismae. "Do you remember I told you about the former abbess making my life more difficult than that of most of the other novitiates?"

"I remember you wouldn't say much about it."

But now, now the words come pouring out of me, like ill humors from a festering wound that has been lanced. "They called her the Dragonette. She was beautiful in the way that a venomous spider is beautiful. She caught your eye with her sharp edges and distinct markings." I glance up at Ismae. "Do you remember the test the reverend mother gave you the first day you arrived at the convent?"

Dressed in her shift now, Ismae slowly lowers herself onto the bed. "With the poisoned wine. Of course, I could never forget."

Sybella sets down her goblet quickly. "What poisoned wine?"

"It was a way for her to test whether I was immune to poison or not," Ismae explains.

"I was given that test when I was but four years old," I say.

Ismae nearly comes up off the bed in her indignation. "Four?"

I nod. "I learned later that the test is never administered without some indication that the novitiate might be immune to poison. I had never demonstrated any such potential, but it did not matter. The Dragonette was determined to find all my hidden strengths and talents, then mold them to perfection in order to glorify both Mortain and herself."

"Sweet Jésu," Sybella mutters again.

I try to smile, but my lips will not obey. "Precisely. The first ten years of my life were one long test, a never-ending trial during which I had to be ever sharp and ever vigilant.

"That's when I first began listening at doors—in the hopes that I could catch some hint or warning of what I was to be subjected to, and thus prepare myself. It is also, I suspect, why I became so very good at reading people, then doing what they wanted before they even asked. I had so few tools for survival. I had to use everything at my disposal." The abbess's words—*obedient and biddable*—still sting. "They are not traits I am proud of, but they did allow me to survive.

"Sister Etienne—for that was what she was called before she became the abbess—was the one bright spot in my life. She was my champion when I was young. Always saving me a bit of bread when I had been forced to go without supper. Letting me out of the wine cellar earlier than my punishments called for. Only now, with the knowledge that she was—is—my mother, can I understand how she must have suffered along with me."

"No." Sybella shoves to her feet and begins pacing the room. Her face is so fierce and holds such rage that I fear she would strike the abbess dead if she were in the room with us. "She did not suffer like you did—not even close, for there was nothing preventing her from taking you and fleeing in the middle of the night, which is what she should have done."

"Perhaps she was afraid they would come after us? We have all heard stories of how they send the hellequin to punish disobedient novitiates. Mayhap she simply thought those tales were true."

"So what brought this all to a boil?" Ismae's voice is gentle, a calming counterweight to Sybella's anger.

"It was a new punishment the Dragonette devised." I do not tell them I was punished because she caught me one day leaving small offerings for Mortain at the doorway to his realm or that she heard me chatting with him in spite of my continued promises to her that I no longer believed I had really seen him.

"It was a cilice, a small silver chain into which sharp thorns had been affixed, meant to be worn around the skin at my waist." I still remember the shame I felt as she lifted the skirt of my gown, exposing my lower body, and slipped the chain around my waist. Remember the bite of pain of each thorn as it pierced my flesh.

Ismae's hand flies up to her lips. My own hand drifts to my stomach, and the scars that still encircle it. "It festered and grew foul, so that I was sent to the infirmary. Sister Serafina was the one who tended to me, her hands gentle and her manner calm. But I think she must have told Sister Etienne, for she found out, and soon after that, she and I had one of our special outings. We were to have a picnic and collect wildflowers. While we were out, we also gathered some mushrooms for the convent stew pot.

"Only, they were poisonous. She had told me they were safe, which is the only reason I picked them. But they were poisonous, and she let me pick them, and somehow she got them past the cook and slipped them into the pot. Three nuns died that evening, then Sister Magdelena, the old poisons mistress, killed herself, thinking it was she who had made the error.

"She used me to poison them." Even now, the enormity of that betrayal forces all the air from my lungs and I feel as if I will never be able to draw a full breath again.

Suddenly, Ismae is at my side, taking my hands in hers, chafing them. Sybella's arm snakes around my shoulders and she pulls me close to her. "No," she whispers fiercely. "Don't you dare think you had anything to do with that. It was not you, not even a little bit, it was all her."

I close my eyes and bask in the solace they offer. "I know it with my mind, but my heart—my heart is still bruised and sick with it."

Sybella gives my shoulders once last squeeze—so hard it is almost painful—then begins pacing again. "I shall kill her," she says at last. "Clearly, she does not deserve to live. Clearly, she is not serving Mortain or even the convent—"

"But is she marqued?" Ismae asks quietly. "For unless a marque has appeared in the last hour, or exists under her gown, I have not seen it."

Sybella's face grows white with frustration, then she tosses her head. "It doesn't matter. I shall kill her anyway." And though she does not mean it—at least, I do not think she does—her saying it brings me great comfort. I take a deep breath and let myself feel the absence of the weight of all the secrets I have been carrying.

Well, not *all* the secrets. "There is more," I offer shyly.

Sybella gapes at me, looking so comical that I must tamp down a desire to laugh. *"More?"* she says.

"I also have a lover."

Sybella stares at me a long moment, then whoops out a laugh while Ismae has a turn at gaping at me. "I thought so, but then you said nothing, so I was uncertain."

A smile catches at my lips. "I knew that if anyone could guess, it would be you."

"But when have you had time to take a lover?" Ismae asks. "And where?" She looks around the room we have shared as if searching for signs of our stolen moments.

"You have not asked me who," I point out.

"I'm not sure we can bear to learn of it," Ismae says faintly.

"He is a hellequin." They both stare at me, struck beyond speech. "Or so I thought. Until I learned that he was only masquerading as one. It is actually Death Himself whom I have taken to my bed."

Chapter Fifty-Two

BOTH ARE SPEECHLESS for a long moment. Then Sybella huffs out a sigh and runs her hand through her hair. Ismae simply continues to stare. "Is this a jest of some sort?" she asks weakly.

"No, it is the truth." Then I tell them of the night Isabeau died and the small boon I asked of the hellequin, and how that in turn led to me learning his true identity.

"But—but he is *our father,*" Ismae says.

My heart sinks as I realize I was right; this has the power to cause a divide between us, a divide that the revelation of my parentage did not. "Your father," I point out. "Not mine."

"The duchess came within a handbreadth of marrying *my* father," Sybella reminds Ismae. "And I did not think any less of her for it." Sybella's voice is calm and free of any judgment. Of course, with her own family's twisted past, she would have the easiest time understanding.

A new wave of horror crosses Ismae's face. "Are you going to marry Death?"

"Marry him?" My laughter is tinged with mania.

Sybella's face softens with sympathy. "Do you carry his child?"

"No!" My hands drift to my stomach. "At least, I do not *think* so." Indeed, I had not even considered that, although clearly that is at the heart of his relationship with women.

"I'm sorry, Annith." Ismae gets up from the bed to stand in front of the fire. She puts her hands out toward the flames, as if they have grown cold suddenly. "It just feels so . . ."

"Overwhelming?" I offer.

"Yes, but also unbelievable. Twisted. Like some cautionary tale of long ago. I feel like a snake must when he has accidentally swallowed a goat and is struggling to digest it."

Sybella stares past Ismae into the flames. "I am beginning to think that love itself is never wrong. It is what love can drive people to do that is the problem. And this particular love is far less misplaced than some," she says dryly. "Besides"—her voice turns thoughtful, as if she is considering all the complex knots that must be untangled—"I am certain that the rules governing human hearts do not govern how the gods may love. We have only to think of the old tales to know that. Even better," she adds with a twinkle, "consider how furious the abbess will be."

That surprises a laugh out of me, and she joins in. Ismae does not, but she does smile, which gives me hope. Sybella reaches out and pinches her cheek. "Do not be such an old wart. Does it not make perfect sense that our beloved Saint Annith has captured Death's heart? Who else among us could have done so?"

I roll my eyes. "After all that I have told you, you should realize just how poor a fit the title of saint is when applied to me."

Her face grows serious once more, filling with sincerity. "I think you deserve it now more than ever," she says.

I let her words wash over me, as healing as one of Sister Serafina's balms. "Thank you," I whisper, unable to stop the tears that spring to my eyes.

"Oh no. Do not start leaking. Ismae, come over here and hug her so we can all pretend it never happened and get on with our lives."

Ismae's gaze meets mine as she moves away from the fire. "Of course I am amazed and admiring of all that you have been through." When she reaches me she wraps her arms around me and holds me close. "As you say, it is all just a little overwhelming."

"Thank you," I whisper. As long as I know they are still my friends, as long as I know that our connection cannot be broken, I shall be fine.

Once they leave to see to their other duties, I go to stand before the fire, feeling once again as if I have been completely upended and remade anew, when in truth, I have barely caught my breath from the first time my life shattered before my eyes.

But this—this is different. This is no shattering, but rather some great knitting together of the broken pieces into a stronger whole.

I feel cleansed, not only of sin—but of artifice. I am stripped down to nothing but my raw self. As uncomfortable as it makes me feel, there is freedom in it as well, for there is no place left for others' expectations and desires of me to hide. The worst things that I could have ever imagined have happened.

I turn and stare at my saddlebag, tossed carelessly in the corner. Slowly, I cross the room and kneel beside it. I reach in, down to the very bottom of the pack with the crumbs of hardened cheese, and retrieve the small calfskin-bound journal that I took from the abbess's office: the Dragonette's accounting of me, my childhood, of all the things she did to me, and all the ways I failed and showed my weakness. I have not read all of it, but I do not have to. I lived it. I remember. But I am not that child anymore. My younger self served me well, as well as any child in her circumstances could have. But I have new strengths and skills that I can rely on.

I feel the weight of the pages in my hand, the heft of the secrets and shame written there, the complexity of the ties that bind me to the convent. Then I turn and hurl the journal into the fireplace. As I watch, the orange and gold flames lick at the pages, making them curl in on themselves and shrink like a dying creature. I close my eyes, feel the heat of the fire against my face, my arms, my heart, and let those same flames burn away the last vestiges of shame and humiliation and mortification. They are simply scars now, like the silvery white marks around my waist, a path to show how far I have traveled in order to get where I am. But they are no longer who I am, if ever they were.

And with that new realization comes another—I have always loved Death. Not as a father, but as a true champion, for that is how he first came to me. He showed me a capacity for love—for acceptance—that was greater than that of any human heart I had encountered.

Even Sister Etienne, as much as she was fond of me, or perhaps even loved me, our time together was always interwoven with her need to see that I was happy. She needed me to be happy like a fish needs water to swim—and so I quickly learned to be happy when I was with her.

Mortain's was the only love that placed no demands upon me, the only one who loved me for simply being. His love was as unwavering and constant as the sun. It was what gave me the strength to keep going. The faith to keep trying. The hope I needed to persevere. That was him all along—whether I called him Mortain or Balthazaar, my heart knew him, recognized him.

Filled with this new awareness, I leave the room and begin making my way to the battlements. He never saw my love as a flaw or a weakness, but instead accepted it, letting it flow into him like a stream tumbling across parched earth.

I eased his dreadful aloneness as much as he eased mine, and I welcomed that feeling, that I had something to give him in return.

Is that not as good a reason to love someone as any? Is that not, in fact, at the very root of why anyone loves another?

As I reach the landing and shove open the heavy door, I have another flash of understanding. On some level, the Dragonette saw all this. She saw the special connection I shared with our god and that was why she punished and shamed me. Not because she did not believe me, but because my seeing him set me apart from her made me special in my own way rather than by her efforts.

I walk to the far end of the catwalk, my head so full of this jumble of thoughts that I do not even see Mortain standing against the battlement until I nearly plow into him. He puts his hand out to steady me.

"My lord! I am sorry. I did not see you. Normally, you are lurking in the corners or skulking in the shadows, not standing in plain sight."

His mouth quirks, ever so slightly. "I never skulk, and lurk only sometimes."

I shoot him a disbelieving glance, then join him at the parapet, looking out over the eastern part of the city, past the wall to the fields below. "The French army will be here tomorrow," I tell him. "The day after, at the latest."

He pulls his gaze from the darkened streets and fields and turns it upon me. "I know. I can feel it, all those souls loosening from their bodies in preparation for their imminent deaths, like so much wheat making ready to loosen from the sheath. She has lost already, you know. Your duchess."

Although he says nothing I do not already know, it is hard to hear it from the lips of a god. "I know. She knows. We *all* know." I look up and study his profile, which is as still and calm as the stone beneath my hand. "Can you see what will come to pass? Do you know what will happen?"

He gives a single shake of his head. "No, for I am not all-seeing. Only Death is my realm, and I know well enough when it is near."

"Do you know who among us will live and who will die?" I cannot help but think of Duval and Beast, of stalwart Captain Dunois, trying to turn a fractious, undisciplined group of mercenaries into a cadre of men who can withstand a siege. I think of the duchess and wonder if they will let her live. And what of us? Those who serve the old gods, the convent? Will we be punished for our role in helping her?

"Not yet. It is too soon. And even once the marque is upon someone, it is not a guarantee of death. There are too many variables, many of which I do not control. It is only when one of my daughters serves within my grace that I am able to exert some small portion of control on things."

Suddenly, he turns to me, his eyes burning. "You could come with me," he says. "Come to the Underworld and be my queen." Even as I gape in shock at this invitation, he shakes his head and turns away to look back out over the countryside. "No." His voice is heavy with despair. "It would only force you to share my prison with me, and I will not subject you to that."

I can see in his eyes, even though they are averted from me, and feel from the timbre of his voice just how sorely his entrapment chafes at him. Just how thoroughly it has corroded not only his view of the world, but his view of himself.

And that has been my gift to him. Not just now, or in the last few months, but since I was young, I have always seen him as a man and honored the gifts he brings to the world. I have loved him for those things long before I understood the nature of who he was.

I reach out and take his hand in mine. "I would gladly share your prison, but I am not worthy of such an honor. I am bastard-born, and mortal through and through, as I have surely proven to you over and over again throughout the time we have known each other."

He throws back his head and laughs, surprising me. "And I am Death. Unwelcome, the thief in the night, destroyer of lives." And that is when I see that he is in danger as well, in danger of believing all that is said of him, of forgetting his own true essence. He turns to face me, pulling me close. "Don't you see? Your mortal heart shines like a candle flame and I, like one of those hapless black moths you used to leave as an offering, am helpless before its lure."

I step fully into his arms, and place my head against his chest, his words wrapping themselves around me. To him, my brokenness, my muddied birth, my scars—none of that defines me, it is all encompassed within the entirety of who I am, just as Death encompasses sorrow and joy, justice and mercy, and the beginnings of new life. We are all of us, gods and mortals, made up of many pieces, some of them broken, some of them scarred, but none of them the sum and total of who we are.

I feel his heart beating against my ear, marvel that a god even has such a human thing as a heart. "It does not matter," I say. "For there is something else I must do."

"What is that?"

I take a deep breath, for I know he will not like what is coming. "Our country is beset from all sides and there is a chance that I have the power to help. So I must."

He pulls back and stares down at me, brow furrowed. "How?"

"I will use the arrow—your arrow—on the French king and see if it will compel him to turn his affections toward our duchess rather than his armies."

He gestures to the thousands of tents stretched out before the city walls. "You will have to ride through thousands of French to do it— surely that is madness. Impossible!"

"I think it can be done. At the very least, I have to try." As I draw back to look at him, the sorrow and desolation I see is almost more than I can bear. I raise my hand and place it against his cheek. "Would that you could join me in my world, rather than me in yours."

He grows utterly still, except for his eyes, which shine with intensity. "But I have no place there, not once my unwelcome duties have been seen to."

I slip my arms up around his neck. "You have a place with me, in my heart, at my side."

He laughs, a sour, distressing sound. "You would upend the very nature of Death so that we could be together?"

"I would, for I will no longer sit and wait patiently for my happiness to grow like some budding fruit on the limbs of a tree, but will mold it and shape it with my own hands."

I find Father Effram in the chapel. He has just lit fresh candles and is placing them under the nine niches. "Father."

He turns around, pleased to see me. "Annith. What brings you here so late at night?"

"I have a question I would ask you."

"Another one?"

I wince at his words, until I see that he is teasing. Even so, I can only imagine what a trial I am making of myself.

"Oh, do not look so! I was only jesting. In truth, it is refreshing having someone to discuss these esoteric theological issues with."

Feeling somewhat mollified, I approach the nave. "This will be my most far-fetched question yet," I assure him.

He sets down the last candle and rubs his hands in anticipation, but I do not know how to frame the question. "If a god grows tired of his duties or is no longer believed in or worshiped, what paths does he have open to him?"

Father Effram holds very, very still. "Do you know such a god as this?" he finally asks.

Unwilling to lie to him, I shrug. "It is a question I have been thinking much upon lately, that is all."

His face furrows in thought, his long bony fingers reaching up to pluck at his chin. He comes to some silent decision, then takes a seat on the prayer bench and motions for me to join him. "If a god should grow weary of his burden—and some do—there is a way to set aside their godhood, if they so choose."

"Truly?"

"Dear child, when Christ died on the cross, He was not only creating a way for man to become immortal and live forever in God's kingdom, but also showing those few immortals left in the world how they could become mortal if they chose. Thus they would be able to access the kingdom of heaven if they wished. God is the maker of all things, and He would never abandon any of His creatures."

"So they—and those of us who worship them—are not outside His grace?"

Father Effram gives a firm shake of his head. "No. They were always part of His plans for this mortal world."

"Do the gods themselves know this?"

He nods. "Yes." There is an ocean of sympathy and compassion in his face. "Child." He reaches out and takes my hand in his. "Your love cannot change a man—or a god. All it can do is open a door, create a new path for him to choose. One that has not been open to him before. That is what the power of your love can offer him—all of that, and no more."

I look away. "I have no desire to change him, only to see him happy."

"I am certain your love does make him happy. Whether it will give him the courage to step through that door remains to be seen."

Chapter Fifty-Three

TWO DAYS LATER, the planning begins in earnest. The duchess insists on being a part of it, claiming if I can make the sacrifice, the least she can do is stay informed. Ismae and Sybella are there as well, but more as moral support, I suspect, than in any official capacity. The abbess too has somehow managed to worm her way into the proceedings, and it is all I can do not to ask the duchess to order her from the room.

Beast has invited both the Arduinnites and the charbonnerie to attend, arguing that they have skills and knowledge that may prove useful to us. The Arduinnites have only been helping with maintaining order in the city for a matter of days, and already he is impressed with them.

It is odd, seeing them in the same room as the duchess's formal councilors, yet it feels right that all of the country's forces, both the old and the new, should come together to find a way to turn the tides of war from our land. In spite of the Arduinnites' unusual dress and unrefined manner, their presence and bearing is as regal as the duchess's, and I am proud to be one of Arduinna's line.

We have just sat down — the bishop as far away from the Arduinnites as he can manage, as if he is afraid they will taint his own faith just by their proximity — when the door opens. Duval whirls around to face the interloper. "I told you we were not to be disturbed."

Before the white-faced page can speak, a dark brooding figure fills the doorway. Without waiting for an invitation, he steps inside. Ismae gasps, her hand flying to her mouth, and Sybella's lips part in surprise, but no sound emerges.

Balthazaar walks slowly forward. "For too long I have kept to the shadows, and I will do so no longer. I would be a part of this."

The bishop crosses himself, and beside him Father Effram bows low, his cowl falling over his head as he does. No one else says anything or ventures into the awkward silence growing larger by the moment. I rise to my feet and clear my throat. "Your Grace, Lord Duval, may I present my lord, Mortain."

The duchess's eyes widen, but with curiosity and wonder rather than fear. She motions him forward. "Pray, join us."

Duval grows distinctly pale, and even Beast looks caught somewhere between awe and discomfiture. But it is the abbess's reaction that is most satisfying. Her entire body stiffens in surprise. Mortain turns to look at her a long moment, until she finally looks away, her guilt and shame burning inside her like a candle.

Duval clears his throat. "My lord. We were just discussing a way to get Annith into the French camp so she can fire Arduinna's arrow at their king."

"I know." Mortain comes to stand next to Duval and looks down at the map the others have made. "Please continue."

Duval tugs briefly at the collar of his doublet, then resumes. "I have been thinking, perhaps it would be best if Annith disguised herself as a camp follow — um, a laundress — as Ismae suggested, and insinuated herself into the camp. Then she could choose the right time to make her move. In the confusion that follows, there is a good chance she could easily slip into the nearby woods to hide for a few days."

Mortain stares down at the map, one white finger tracing a line from the center pavilion off to the side of the camp where it meets the forest. "That is a lot of occupied ground to cover with no escort."

Marshal Rieux gives a sharp shake of his head. "In any case, I'm afraid that it is no longer a possibility."

"Why not?"

"Because this morning, scouts and sentries reported that the French are moving their scaling towers and cannon into range, even as we speak."

"How soon until they will be ready to fire?"

Rieux shrugs. "It could be as little as two days from now."

Duval swears a black oath. "So, even time is no longer on our side." He runs his hand through his hair. "That reduces our options to an outright assault or a sortie of some kind."

Captain Dunois furrows his brow. "Neither of which creates a clear path for getting the girl back to safety."

"What if we created a diversion? Sent out a sortie to distract them, then sent out a second, smaller contingent to punch through to the pavilion during the ensuing scramble?"

"In addition to the second sortie," Beast muses, "we could use our own cannon. Remind the French that we have them and maybe even take out a few of theirs while we're at it."

Mortain's voice fills the room. "But that still leaves Annith's safe return to chance."

The room falls silent. "We could mount a full-scale charge," says Marshal Rieux. "Use what remaining mercenaries we have left to us."

"If they will even fight. Many of them will not until they are paid what is owed them."

Captain Dunois rubs his face with his hand. "That reminds me. There is another contingent of mercenaries demanding to leave the city."

Mortain looks quizzically at him, and Duval attempts to explain. "The French king is buying off our mercenaries, hiring them out from under us." He turns to Dunois. "Let them go, and good riddance."

MORTAL HEART

"Wait!" Beast's eyes grow distant, as if he is studying some invisible map that only he can see. "How many mercenaries are attempting to leave?"

"Three or four hundred."

A grin spreads across Beast's face, lighting it with a nearly unholy glee. "We have just found our way out of the city."

Duval grins back, discerning his meaning at once. "Our forces can slip out with the mercenaries."

Mortain plants his hands on the table and leans forward. "While it is an excellent plan for getting to the French king, it does not address how Annith will get safely back into the city."

"We will have to plan two diversions and utilize our cannon. We could send a sortie out this sally port." Duval points to the map. "The French would think we were taking advantage of the departing mercenaries when, in truth, we would be creating a diversion of our own. It is common enough for the besieged to make forays into enemy camp hoping to find food or loot of some kind.

"Then, even if the first group posing as mercenaries can't get her back, the second group can clear a path for her."

"But who will clear a path for them?" My question gives all of them pause. "We are trying to avoid countless deaths, not hasten them." The duchess and I exchange glances, and suddenly, I have no idea how she has borne the weight of these decisions. I do not think I could bear it. "You are asking them all to sacrifice their lives simply to give me a chance to shoot the arrow. An arrow we do not even know will work—"

"It will work," Mortain says.

"Even so, we cannot ask so many men to ride to what will certainly be their death."

There is a long moment of silence. "That is what they are trained for," Captain Dunois explains gently. "And they well understand the

401

need for some to die in order that a great many more can live. It is the very nature of a soldier's life."

Mortain looks at me. "What if," he asks softly, "we do not ask your men to ride to their death? Instead, we will ask those that are already dead."

"The hellequin," I whisper.

"The hellequin. They wish to atone for their sins and find redemption. I believe sparing thousands of lives will grant them that."

The bishop clears his throat. "Can they be trusted to ride on such a mission without you leading them?"

Slowly, Mortain turns to face the bishop, causing the other man to flinch. The grim acceptance in his eyes causes a dark ribbon of unease to unfurl inside me, even before he speaks. "I will be leading them."

Father Effram steps forward, his hands clasped together and his head bowed in deep obeisance. "My lord, you do know what will happen if you choose to involve yourself in mortal affairs, do you not?"

Mortain looks at the old priest, almost as if he is surprised by his question. "I do," he says.

When no one says anything further, I cannot contain myself. "What? What will happen if you involve yourself in the affairs of mortals?"

Mortain looks back down at the map, avoiding my eyes. "Then I will die as one."

The duchess offers to prepare a chamber for Mortain, but he politely declines. We now stand up on the ramparts with the warm summer wind buffeting at our hair. "You cannot do it!" I tell him.

"You can give your life for your country but I cannot give my life for yours?"

"The weight of your life is far different from that of mine, measured out in centuries rather than simply years."

He turns away from me. "I have learned that the quality of life is not determined by its longevity. And I would argue that your life is worth more than mine. At least to me. Besides, the world is changing and the age of gods coming to an end. Just as smaller kingdoms are being devoured by larger ones, so too are we gods being assimilated by the One God. Our time is drawing to a close." Almost as an afterthought, he swivels his head around and scowls down at me. "Do you think so very poorly of my military skills that you are certain we will fail?"

"No! But the whole reason you and the hellequin will be riding out is to save others from certain death. The nature of the mission hasn't changed—it is most likely a one-way ride. The only thing that has changed is that you will be going, and I am not certain if I can bear it if you don't return." Saying such things makes me feel slightly foolish, for we have not talked of a future together. Well, except for the suggestion that I join him in the Underworld.

However, if he is gone, I will be utterly alone, without even Mortain's presence to sustain me with his strength and courage as he did when I was a child, for the god will have stepped fully into the mortal world.

But, I remind myself, that is his choice to make, just as being the one to fire the arrow is my choice to make, and so I keep silent.

"What will you do?" he asks. "After." He does not say after he has died, but the words sit heavy in the night air.

I stop and think. What *will* I do? I have given no thought beyond our goal. The answer comes to me, unexpected and surprising. "I shall return to the convent." I pull his hand into mine and squeeze it. "I will return to the convent and tell the others of their father, and what sort of man—and god—he was."

I have surprised him. After a moment's silence, he smiles. It is white and dazzling and rips my soul fair in two.

"And then?"

"And then? I do not know."

He looks down at our entwined hands. "I will wait for you. Before passing on to whatever is next, I will wait for you in the realm of death so we may travel there together."

My eyes burn with the unexpectedness of his gift. "No," I say fiercely. "I do not want you to suffer any longer than you must. You have already been stuck there an eternity."

He smiles. "I will not be suffering." He reaches out and places his palm upon my chest, over my heart. "You will always open to me. Through you, I will watch my daughters grow, feel the life flowing through your veins, bask in the love that fills your heart. It will pass like no time at all."

He pulls me into his arms then, our time for talking over. He lowers his lips to mine, placing them over my mouth gently, our kiss bearing the weight of a thousand we may never have.

Chapter Fifty-Four

THE FOLLOWING AFTERNOON, in a distant corner of the city, just as the sun begins to drop low in the sky, the hellequin begin trickling over the city walls, using the very same ladder that the French used to breach our defenses. They come spilling over, a shadowed, rippling darkness that makes no noise. The air itself seems to recoil at their presence, and the few soldiers who witness it cross themselves, the utter paleness of their faces giving voice to their fear even though they do not.

My eyes go immediately to Balthazaar. He is at his most human, wearing black leather and chain mail. His cheeks are covered in dark stubble, disguising somewhat his otherworldly pallor.

Fifty of them have volunteered for this mission, including many that I know: Begard, Malestroit, Sauvage, and Miserere, who is the last to scale the wall. I try to assure myself that their presence has nothing to do with their knowing or caring about me—they are hellequin and have assured me dozens of times that they care for no mortal; they are intent only on redemption. Half will be escorting me, and the other half—led by Miserere—will be raiding on the French supply wagons, the diversion they have settled upon.

They will not be coming back. Their only role is to provide us an escape route to allow us to get from the king's tent back to the postern gate and the safety of the city walls.

Beast has found four charbonnerie to accompany us, their mission to get to the cannon and use them against our enemy and buy us time.

The Arduinnites too have joined us and have offered their archers to act as cover when needed. As they are the best archers in the land, we gladly take them up on it.

Marshal Rieux has secured the strongest, fastest, and most skilled horses to be found in the city, but Aeva surprises me by dismounting and leading her horse to me. "Here," she says. "Ride this one."

While it is kind of her—and she is rarely kind—I politely decline. "I wish to ride Fortuna, for she has been with me since the beginning of my journey."

"My offer is not a slight against Fortuna, who is a fine horse. But my horse has been trained in the ways that Arduinna does battle and has some skills that even the noble Fortuna does not."

"What sorts of skills?" I ask, intrigued in spite of myself.

"If you whistle, like this"—she puts two fingers in her mouth and lets loose a piercing note—"she will come to you. And if you press your knees and twitch the reins just so"—she demonstrates—"she will stumble and appear to fall, putting your opponent off-guard." She goes on to show me a half a dozen tricks the horse knows, and in the end, I realize I cannot refuse her offer. Too much depends upon this mission's success.

Captain Dunois has amassed a small mountain of gear from the mercenaries—hauberks, helmets, gloves, and the like, although in truth, there is not much difference between them and what the helle-quin already wear.

It is I who have the most dressing up to do. They have refitted a special saddle for me, one that allows me to sit a little higher on the horse, giving me some much needed height. I am wearing two pad-ded hauberks, which give my shoulders and chest some additional girth and have the added advantage of hiding my breasts. Over that I wear a boiled-leather jerkin, vambraces, and riding leathers. I do not understand how any soldier is able to move once he has been suited up.

When it is time for me to don my helmet, my accursed hair will not cooperate. "Perhaps a linen cap would hold it in place," Sybella suggests.

"No. Just cut it off," I tell her.

She pauses a beat, and I turn to look at her. "It will grow back. And it is not worth risking it coming undone at the wrong moment, for how would I explain myself then?"

"True enough," she murmurs, then lifts her knife to my hair and chops it off.

As I try my helmet once more, there is a faint susurration of sound behind me. When I turn around, I see that the hellequin are pressing upon Sybella, requesting a lock of my hair to carry with them. For some reason, a lump forms in my throat; I do not understand why the hellequin would want such a thing, so I pretend I do not see and busy myself with the last step, smearing my face with charcoal dust to disguise the smoothness of my skin and my cleanliness. Then I take a few minutes to wave my arms back and forth and pretend to draw a bow, trying to adjust to the feel of the hauberks.

Finally, we are ready and mounted on our horses. "The French checkpoint at the main gate is expecting you," Captain Dunois informs us. "The terms have been set. You will be leaving with a group of nearly four hundred mercenaries, so your presence should not draw any undue attention."

"Will not the other mercenaries realize they have never seen us before?" Miserere asks.

Captain Dunois shakes his head. "There have been thousands of them in the city and there is no way any one man or contingent has met all of them."

Though Duval wanted to be here, there was no reason for someone in his position to involve himself with the mercenaries' departure, so he remains stuck in the palace. Ismae is attending the duchess. It was she who cut the duchess's hand and squeezed her blood onto the tip of the arrow, then bound the cut with a healing balm and bandaged it. She refused to say goodbye to me in the determined belief that I would be coming back.

In addition to Sybella, Beast is here, appearing right at home among the hellequin. Indeed, he looks as if he would seize a horse and ride with us if not for the death grip Sybella has on his arm. "Be safe," she tells me. "And may all the Nine bless your journey."

We begin moving to the main gate. In the northern part of town, far from our small group, fifteen hundred Breton forces wait, dressed for battle, chargers at the ready. If we fail, they will ride out to disable the cannon and destroy the siege towers before they can be used against us. It too will be a one-way mission. As they are not hellequin who welcome death, I pray they will not be needed.

Our plan is known to only a select few, so as we pass soldiers and men-at-arms in the city, they jeer at us and throw rotten food and rocks, thinking we are mercenaries leaving them to their fate. At least until Sauvage nearly rides a group of them down so that they must leap out of the way, after which they restrict their displeasure to slurs and taunts.

I ride in the center group, just behind Miserere, with Malestroit behind me. Balthazaar is in the lead. I am the weakest link in this chain we have constructed, for I am smaller than nearly all the others, except for Begard. With my padding and saddle platform, I am about the same size as he. Luckily, Captain Dunois has assured us that not all mercenaries are as enormous as the hellequin, so once we join the main group, we should be even less noticeable.

The throng of defecting mercenaries waits just inside the city gates. They believe the duchess and her councilors have no knowledge of their defections, and so they simply threaten the sentries with their lives. The sentries have been instructed not to resist or attempt to engage, so they give them no argument.

I am tense as we ride out under the stone arch, terrified that somehow someone has leaked word to the French of our plan and they are looking for us among the others. But the few French soldiers and officials who wait just outside the gate simply motion for us to pass on through. They are alert and on edge at first, and have a division of archers with bows drawn in case we are some warring sortie in disguise. But as the last of us rides out and no one charges, they lower their guard.

"Where do we get our gold?" one of the men shouts out.

The French captain does not try hard to hide his disdain. "Over there." He points toward the camp. "At the quartermaster's tent." Balthazaar and I exchange glances, pleased at this development, for it brings us even closer to our target without drawing any attention to ourselves.

As we wend our way through the camp, we can feel the French soldiers' regard upon us. Some stare in open disgust, others with mere curiosity. Mercenaries are not well loved by soldiers who fight for their liege.

As the minutes crawl by, we mill about with the others, waiting for our back pay. Each captain must dismount and sign for the purse, which he is then responsible for disbursing to his men. When it is Balthazaar's turn, I do not think I am the only one holding my breath. He still does not look wholly human to me, especially in the harsh, unforgiving light of day. But the soldiers do not notice. Or do not appear to. They all watch him warily—in truth, he looks far more dangerous than any of the others who have collected their purses. Once he has signed, he takes the purse, bounces it in his hand as if weighing the contents, then gives a grunt of approval. The quartermaster turns his attention to the next mercenary, but I do not breathe easy until Balthazaar is back on his horse.

HIS FAIR ASSASSIN

One of the hellequin, one of the ones I do not know well but recognize from my time with them, pounds his chest. "I am hungry! With nothing to eat but rats for the past week, I have a serious appetite."

I wince, fearing he may be overplaying this, for we in the city have not come to the eating of rats. Yet.

But someone points him toward the center of the camp and the supply wagons where, he tells him, there is food for sale. He winks. "And a woman?" The soldier grins and nods—that common need forging a link between them when their loyalties could not.

It was well done of him. With a purpose to our wanderings, we begin trickling through the camp, avoiding the tents, the hellequin talking amongst themselves, some even in German, which impresses me somewhat.

I scan the sea of tents, looking for the king's pavilion. It was so easy to see from the walls of the city, but here on the ground, it is harder to discern. "This way," Balthazaar mutters, drawing his horse nearer mine and shifting our direction. I keep my head down, as if I am sullen and ill-tempered.

We begin moving toward the center of camp, veering east slightly, so that when the diversions come, we will seem to be running toward them, like the rest of the encampment. Initially, no one pays us any heed. It is not until we have passed a dozen rows of tents that anyone hails us. "Hold there! What are you doing?" one of the patrolling soldiers asks.

It is Sauvage who answers. "The quartermaster told us that the food wagons and women were this way."

The soldier looks less than pleased but is no doubt put off by Sauvage's terrifying visage and intimidating manner and simply grumbles under his breath.

We have made our way past another dozen rows when the king's pavilion comes into sight. The tent is even larger up close, nearly as

410

large as one of the chambers in the palace. It is of purple- and gold-striped silk and has the king's banner flying atop, flapping cheerfully in the warm breeze. My entire body quivers with anticipation, but I try to keep my head down to avoid calling attention to myself. It is hard—so hard. I want to look and see, plot out my course and consider the hundred possible ways this could go, but I dare not risk drawing anyone's eyes for too long.

When we are but three rows away from the king's pavilion, I hear it: the shouts and scramble of soldiers accompanied by the distant thunder of riding horses. The soldiers near the king's tent crane their necks in curiosity as the sally port opens and the second group of hellequin ride out. Our diversion has arrived.

I look at Balthazaar, for now timing is everything. We have only a few moments to get to the tent, shoot the king, then retreat. If I take too long at any of those steps, the hellequin's chance of returning to the city with me will evaporate.

He nods, and I twitch my reins the way Aeva showed me. My horse whinnies and rears, throwing me to the ground. Since I am expecting it, I am able to roll off her somewhat gracefully and avoid too painful a landing. But now I am on the ground, on foot, and no one is paying any attention to me, except for two squires, who snicker. Then their knight barks at them and they hurry to help him into the armor so he may ride after the Breton raiders.

I make as if to kick at my horse in disgust, then grab her reins and begin limping behind the others. As we pass behind a large tent, I lift the bow from my saddle hook, then toss my reins to Balthazaar. He catches them neatly, then acts as if he is still making for the food wagons.

A quick glance shows me that no one is watching. Most of the surrounding French soldiers are scrambling toward the attacking Bretons, eager to engage after so many days of inactivity.

I sprint as if heading in the same direction, then veer around the back of the king's pavilion. Balthazaar raises his crossbow to offer cover should anyone spot me before I reach the tent.

For a moment, the sheer audacity of my plan steals my breath away. Because of me, Mortain has consigned himself to a mortal fate. If I fail, I will have robbed myself of not only a lover, but the god who has sustained me my entire life, and the father of all the girls at the convent. They will never know him, not as a man, not even as a god. This is what following my own desires has brought me to.

If the Dragonette or the abbess were here, how they would mock my pride, my willfulness, the sheer selfishness of my dreams.

But they are not here, only I am. For some reason, the gods have put this task in my hands. I grasp that thought and hold it tightly in my heart. Surely that is a sign of their belief in me.

Either that, or Salonius the god of mistakes has tricked us all.

With no one there to see, I throw myself to the ground and crawl toward the edge of the pavilion so I may slip under. But the tent is held firmly in place by a wooden peg. No matter how hard I pull, it will not budge. Swearing, I take a knife and begin stabbing at the dirt around the peg, trying to loosen it. Finally, after long painful seconds, I am able to wiggle it out. I pause to be certain my actions have not been noticed — either inside the tent or out — then slip under the heavy silk.

I pause, listening. There. Voices. Arguing. It is a man — the king? — and a woman.

"And I told you I did not want to use cannon." As he talks, I begin to creep forward on my belly, using the trunks by the royal bed to hide my movements. "The entire point of this exercise was to intimidate her, not to destroy the town and all its inhabitants. She is utterly surrounded; her country is in our hands. We have only to wait for her to recognize it."

"You are too soft." The woman's voice is thick with scorn. "She has given us no indication she is even considering surrendering." I slowly pull Arduinna's arrow from my quiver, then raise my head to peer over the thick leather chest in front of me.

"Her sister has just died." The king's voice is gentle, compassionate even. "She is likely clouded with grief, as I would be should you die, dear sister." There is a faint dry note in his voice that has me wondering if he would truly be as distraught as he claims.

"We must put an end to this farce."

"And we will. In good time. But we will not be using the cannon. Now, would you like to give the order? Because I know how much you dislike it when I countermand your orders in front of the men."

There is a long, tense moment before the regent says, "I will do it."

Boom! An earsplitting crack of thunder fills the camp, reverberating through the valley.

The king's head snaps up, and he glares at his sister. She shakes her head. "I did not order that," she says, then hurries from the tent. To my surprise, after a moment's hesitation, the king follows her.

I am frozen to the spot with shock as I watch my chance for averting this war stride out of the pavilion. What now?

I shove the arrow back in my quiver and rise to my knees. The king's tent is empty except for the two guards that stand just inside the tent flap. If I go back the way I came, I will run into Balthazaar, who will do everything he can to prevent me from burrowing deeper into the enemy's encampment.

Which means I will have to fight past the two guards.

I withdraw two regular arrows, clench one between my teeth, then nock the second one to the bowstring. Still crouching in the back of the tent, I release the first arrow, which catches the guard in the windpipe, ensuring his silence as he dies.

Before I can nock my second arrow, the other guard draws his sword and leaps toward me. He is faster than he looked, and I barely have time to drop my bow, grab the long dagger from my waist, and get it up in time to block the thrust of his sword. The force of the blow sends a shock all the way up my arm. As our blades lock together, I see in his eyes the moment he decides to call for reinforcements. As he opens his mouth, I reach up with my free hand as if to place it on the dagger handle for extra leverage. At the last minute, I grab at the second dagger hidden at my wrist, then spin inside his guard and bring it across his throat, cutting off his cry for help. Red blood spatters across my face like warm rain, but I hardly even notice.

Instead, I roll the smaller guard over, unbuckle his sword belt, and wrestle his French tabard over his head. The tabard marks him clearly as one of the royal guard, and wearing it may help me get closer to the king. I slip it on, then grab his helmet and sword as well.

I snag my bow from the ground, my heart hammering—not in fear, I realize, but with anticipation—and use the exhilaration to propel me to the door. Two more sentries wait outside, but with the king gone, their attention is focused on the smoke and noise coming from the northern part of the camp rather than on the empty tent behind them. Which makes it easy to slip up silently behind them and slit their throats, cutting through their vocal cords just as Sister Arnette taught me to do all those years ago.

Only this time, I do not throw up, or even feel a sickening lurch in my stomach. Instead, a grim satisfaction fills me, for I am that much closer to my goal.

Chapter Fifty-Five

MEN ARE SHOUTING, horses whinnying, and hooves thundering as hundreds of soldiers scramble toward a burning siege tower. Not wanting to risk standing out, I join them. The regent said she was going to rescind the order to fire the cannon and I can only hope that the king has followed her.

When I am well away from the tent, I lift my fingers to my mouth and whistle the way Aeva showed me. Because the air is already filled with the shouts of soldiers, the clash of swords, and the thud of galloping horses, I do not see my own horse drawing near until she is almost upon me. I launch myself onto her back and instantly feel more secure being upon a horse. My view is better as well, and I can now see over the heads of the foot soldiers.

The king is seated upon a horse, standing in the middle of a cluster of his cavalry, talking with his sister and the captain in charge of the remaining cannon. There is no way to worm my way through the scores of soldiers who now stand between me and my target.

I look around for the hellequin I rode out with. They linger half a bowshot away from the royal pavilion, waiting and looking. For me. Balthazaar in particular seems to scan the crowd more intensely than the others, his brooding gaze never straying far from the tent. Despair seeps into my bones, for every complication added to our simple plan diminishes his chances of returning to the city.

I look back at the king. Even though he is within range of my bow and we are both mounted, there are far too many other riders between us. I can barely see the top of his head. I do not know if my aim will be as true as Arduinna's, and it would be too easy to miss and waste the arrow on one of the people who surround him. Then our only chance would be lost.

I consider my options. One cannon is still billowing smoke, and one of the scaling towers is on fire, with hundreds of French troops scrambling with buckets so the flames will not spread. The second scaling tower sits abandoned. Our secondary diversion has already launched from the sally port. A hundred mounted French knights are bearing down hard on the escaping sortie—in truth, only a score of hellequin.

They will not last much longer, not when they are that outnumbered.

I glance over at the second scaling tower and calculate its distance from the king. If I were upon it, I could easily see him. It is even possible he would be in range of my bow. The arrow would have a far better chance of striking him if it came from above.

If I can reach the platform.

And if I can avoid drawing the attention of every French archer in the camp.

Deciding this is my best option, I lightly press my heels against my horse's sides and she leaps forward. I shut out all the noise and confusion on the field around me and focus on the platform that overhangs the wheels of the scaling tower. I grasp the front of the saddle to steady myself, pull my feet up beneath me, then—as I have a hundred times before—attune my body to every movement of the horse and begin to stand up. I have barely reached my full height when the platform is there, right in front of me, and I have no time to think but must simply react so that it does not knock me off the horse. I get my arms up just in time to grab on as my ribs connect solidly with the platform, and I give silent thanks for the two padded hauberks I wear. Then I scramble up on the platform, relieved when I feel the solidness of the wood beneath my feet. Afraid I have been spotted but not willing to stop and find out, I hurry to the beams and trellises of the scaling tower, step around one, and press myself close to it. Only then do I look back to check if I have been seen.

No one seems to have noticed. I glance over my shoulder at the city wall. From there I am in plain sight, but those on the field cannot see me. Or they have not bothered to look up. Either way, it is a small sliver of luck, and I will take it.

As I shrug my bow from my shoulder, I seek out the figure of the king. I can see him better now, and from this height, I should be able to shoot over the heads of his attendants and retainers. Except now that I am here and free from the press of bodies, I realize it is—just barely —too far, and the breeze is coming from the wrong direction. It blows toward me and away from the king, just enough to drag against the arrow, reducing its speed and range, making the shot impossible.

As I watch, his attendants step back. He is getting ready to dismount, and once he is off his horse and among the crowd, I will never be able to hit him.

There are only impossible options left to me. Even though I am not divine or even gifted by nature of my birth, it feels as if all I have struggled with my entire life, all that I have trained for, and all the skills I have practiced have brought me to this moment.

But I had also thought it impossible ever to leave the convent, or confront the abbess, or meet a god face to face, let alone fall in love with one. Impossible things do happen. But only if we make them.

I draw the arrow dipped in the duchess's blood, then fit it to the bowstring. I lift my bow, the black feathers of the fletching tickling my cheek. *Dear Arduinna,* I pray as I sight down the arrow. *Although I come newly to your service, please let me be your instrument in this. Guide this arrow, for the love you once bore him, for the love you might bear me as one marked by your own hand, but mostly to save all the innocents from the horror of war.*

As I pray, the breeze dies down, as if the hand of the goddess is holding it back. But I do not take the shot, for still air will only gain me ten feet, and I need at least thirty. Moments later, I feel a brush of wind against my neck, sending the strands of my hair forward to tickle at my cheeks.

But still, I do not take the shot.

I wait until the breeze sighs past my face and streams down along my shoulder, until I see the grass on the field below me begin to ripple as the gust dances its way downrange. Then, when it is in the best position to carry the arrow forward, I release the bowstring.

In that same moment, ready to dismount at last, the king stands up in his stirrups so that he is ever so slightly higher than those around him. The arrow strikes him in the fleshy part of the arm—praise the saints that he is not wearing full armor—then disintegrates, falling to the ground in a sprinkling of black dust.

I stare in dismay. Is the arrow too ancient to withstand the impact? Or is it part of the magic of the arrow itself?

The king frowns and swipes at his arm. Whatever happened, he has felt it, and that is a good sign. He leans close to examine a rip in his sleeve, his fingers coming away red with blood. I close my eyes, my body going slack with relief.

But my relief is short-lived, for I have been spotted. A small force of French archers has seen me. They drop to their knees in the field and raise their crossbows. I throw myself behind the thick wooden support beam of the siege tower, pray they are not excellent shots, and reload my own bow.

A rapid series of thuds, like hammer blows, descends upon me, the force of them causing the wood to tremble slightly. But no arrow finds me. While the archers are reloading their crossbows, I peer around the beam, raise my bow, and fire a shot. I pick off one, but there are easily a dozen more, and I duck back behind the safety of my beam. As I draw another arrow, I realize there is no way I will be able to take on all of them.

They fire again, one of the quarrels whistling past my ear as it misses the beam. As soon as the volley is over, I turn and take another shot, eliminating one more. Only ten left.

A third volley of arrows pins me behind the beam again, but there are far fewer than before, far fewer than could be accounted for by the two stricken archers.

There is a flash of movement off to my left. I turn and see that two of the archers have pulled out of formation and are approaching me, one on either side. I will be able to hit one, but not both. *Merde.* I lift my bow to the one on the right, for he is closer to being able to fire. When my arrow buries itself in his eye socket, I turn to face the other archer. But too late; his crossbow is raised, sighted on me.

Chapter Fifty-Six

A GREAT DARK SHAPE BARRELS down on the archer, sunlight glancing off the sword as it arcs toward his head. The archer's shot goes wide, then his headless body crumples to the ground.

Balthazaar.

There is a clash of steel as the rest of the hellequin fall upon the remaining bow men. I hurry over to the edge of the platform. "What took you so long?"

He steers his horse so that it is directly below me. "We were detained." Without giving myself time to think about it, I jump down. My breath leaves me in a dizzying rush and for one terrifying moment I fear I will miss, but the horse prances forward and then Balthazaar's arms are around me.

Infantry with lances and pikes are swarming toward us now. Sauvage and the rest of the hellequin wheel their horses around to engage. "Go!" Sauvage calls over his shoulder, lifting his sword. The weight of Balthazaar's despair at having to leave his men surrounded and outnumbered presses upon my heart like a stone.

Malestroit lifts his enormous hammer, then gives a nod — of farewell or relief or blessing, I cannot tell. Then he spurs his mount into the fray, his hammer swinging wildly.

I turn away, unable to watch when he should fall. Another contingent of pikesmen come running from the encampment, the sharp

points of their pikes gleaming silver in the sunlight. Balthazaar's arms
tighten around me. "Keep low," he says, then pulls me up close against
his chest and covers me with his body as he gallops for the postern gate.

But the French have figured out that is where we are headed, and
they know that I was the one who shot at their king. They too make for
the gate. Out of the corner of my eye I see rows of archers run forward,
then kneel and draw up their bows. I make myself as small as possible
and pray to every god in existence.

The twang of bowstrings fills the air, followed by the swish of arrows
in flight. I brace myself. Behind me, Balthazaar grunts, then jerks.

Before I can look to see if he has been hit, another volley of arrows
comes raining out of the sky, only these come from the city itself. I look
up at the ramparts, my heart swelling when I see the Arduinnites lined
up along the crenellations, already firing off another round.

We are almost at the gate now, almost to safety. Balthazaar hunkers
lower in the saddle and something wet begins to spread across my back.

A second volley of arrows come from the French behind us, but
a smaller volley, as the Arduinnites have reduced their numbers.
Balthazaar jerks again, his arms around me loosening their hold. When
we are half a bowshot from the gate, he starts to fall. I scramble to maintain my balance, to find a way to hang on to him and the horse both
and not topple over, but I cannot. As he falls, his weight pulls me from
the saddle, and we both go plummeting to the ground. His demonic
horse rears up, hooves flailing and nostrils flaring, before turning and
galloping directly for the attacking soldiers.

The impact drives all the air from my lungs and for a moment I fear
I have broken every bone in my body. But even as he fell, Balthazaar
maneuvered himself so he would land first, taking the brunt of it. As we
roll apart, I see he has easily a half a dozen arrows protruding from him.
Panic gnaws at my heart. I start to crawl toward him but must stop as a
fresh salvo of French arrows rain down around us, sending a final arrow

into his chest. There is a faint, almost silent twang as the Arduinnites answer with another volley of their own.

Using that as cover, I scramble to Balthazaar's side. Stark terror clutches at my heart at how white his face, how still his body. *No, no, no,* my heart screams. This was not how it was supposed to be. In the far distance, a lone hound begins to bray, the sound eerie and chilling even in the full light of day. More hounds take up the lament, and the earth itself seems to shudder, then stop, as if the very laws of its existence have been tested.

The entire field grows quiet as I stare down at Balthazaar's lifeless form. At the arms I will never again feel around me, the eyes that will never again peer so deeply into my soul, and the lips I will never again coax into a smile. "No," I whisper, then cup Balthazaar's pale cheek in my hand and lay my forehead against his. I know that his love does not die with him, that I will carry it with me always, but that is cold, empty comfort. My breath comes in short, ragged gasps and I am not sure I will ever draw a full breath again. This pain is worse than anything I have ever imagined—I, who have been familiar with pain my entire life.

A trumpet sounds just then—three shorts blasts. I do not know what it means, but the French soldiers do. Reluctantly, with mumbling and dark glances, they sheathe their weapons and point their spears down. A mounted knight comes riding before them and motions them back.

He is chasing them away.

Once they are out of arrow range, the knight turns and nods to me, and I want to shout at him that he is too late.

But others begin to reach us now, as soldiers from the city gate swarm forward, the Arduinnites covering them with their threat of another rain of arrows. Someone grabs me by the arms and tries to pull me back to the safety of the gates, but I refuse. The Brigantians come next, bringing a stretcher with which to carry Balthazaar back. Before they transfer him onto it, they stop to examine his wounds. Two arrows have gone straight through his chest, the arrowheads fashioned in such a way as to pierce even the mail that he wore.

Carefully, the Brigantians break the arrowheads from the shafts, then pull them slowly from his chest. As the shafts leave his body, Balthazaar arches up off his back. He gasps and draws in a huge gulp of air. His face spasms in pain, his hand going to his chest, and I stare down in disbelief.

"It hurts," he croaks, and I laugh, a giddy, frightened sound.

"Of course it hurts," I tell him, then bend down and begin raining kisses over his face. "You're alive."

He pulls his hand away from his chest and stares at the red blood that covers his palm. "I am alive." The marvel in his voice matches my own. A shadow falls across us just then, and when I look up, I see Father Effram. "He's alive," I whisper, afraid that if I say it too loudly, someone will hear and take it away.

Father Effram smiles. "He is alive."

"But how?"

He smiles gently at me, but before he can speak, Balthazaar begins to cough, clutching his chest. I start to panic, but Father Effram lays his hand on my shoulder. "This wound will not kill him. The first death makes him mortal; it is the second death that will carry him from this world."

"How do you know this?"

He looks from me to Balthazaar. I follow his gaze and see Balthazaar staring at him, recognition slowly filling his eyes. He gasps out a laugh, then clutches his chest again. "Salonius."

Father Effram bows his head. "At your service, my lord." Then he turns to my gaping self. "I know because I was once a god as well."

"You are—were—Saint Salonius?"

"Yes." He turns to Balthazaar once more, his face growing serious. "And this," he says to the man who was once Death. "Does this put right all that lies between us?"

Balthazaar stares at him a long moment, then nods. "It does." He puts out his hand. Father Effram grasps it and closes his eyes, almost as if receiving a benediction.

Balthazaar is taken to the Brigantian convent so they may tend his wounds, but it is hard — so hard — to let go of his hand. I wish to accompany him, to stay by his side forever if need be, to ensure that this is real and will not be snatched away.

But I have others I must see to.

A truce has been made, and the Breton forces have left the safety of the city walls in order to recover our dead. Every soldier seems to know that if not for the hellequin, it would be his own dead body being carried back on a litter.

Of the fifty hellequin that rode out, twenty-eight bodies are returned to us, among them Begard's, Malestroit's, and Sauvage's. Slowly, I drop to Malestroit's side. His face is no longer filled with sorrow but with serenity. I kiss the tips of my fingers, then press them to his lips. "Goodbye," I whisper. "And thank you. May you find peace at last."

Sauvage too is much transformed, his terrifying ferocity replaced by a peace so deep, he is hardly recognizable.

Begard looks even younger in death, relaxed, with no pinch of regret or guilt shadowing his face. I bid him goodbye as well. Father Effram joins me, and, together, we walk among the fallen hellequin. He gives them a final blessing and I bid them each farewell.

Some bodies are not recovered, and I do not know what that means. Most of those not recovered were on the sortie to the supply wagons, including Miserere. I think of his fierce, implacable face and mourn that he may not have found the redemption he so desperately wanted.

It is only when they have all been seen to and tended, and I confirm with my own eyes that the truce continues to hold, that I allow myself to return to the palace long enough to strip out of my blood-soaked clothes, scrub the worst of the filth from me, then head to the Brigantian convent.

I am not questioned at the convent but ushered immediately to Balthazaar's room. It is clean and smells of pungent herbs. At the door I pause, staring at the still figure on the bed, marveling that his chest rises and falls as he draws breath. Marveling that the pallor of death has left his face and he no longer appears to have been chiseled from the whitest marble.

He is, I realize, pulsing with life.

We have done it, he and I. We not only evoked one last gasp of magic from Arduinna's sacred arrow but managed to upend the order of the world and create a place for Balthazaar in it. At my side, hopefully, although we have not discussed that.

"It is a miracle, is it not?" I turn to find a grizzled nun standing beside me, her wrinkled face alight with wonder and awe.

"It is," I agree.

She looks up at me, tilting her head. "Are you the one he did it for?"

Her question makes me pause, uncertain of how to answer that. Did he do it for me? Or because he was finally offered a chance? Perhaps the two things cannot be separated from each other.

Seeing my discomfort, the nun smiles warmly, pats me on the arm, then goes about her business, leaving me alone with him.

"Quit lurking in the shadows." Balthazaar's voice rumbles up from the bed. "That is my role, not yours."

I cannot help it, I laugh and go to stand beside his bed. He has a most curious expression on his face. "Are you still in a lot of pain?" I ask.

"Yes," he says, but without bitterness or distress, merely wonder. He lifts one hand and stares down at it, then looks up at me. "But pleasure too. Everything"—he looks around the room, staring at the shafts of sunlight that play upon the shadows—"everything is so much *more*—more delineated, nuanced. And"—he turns his gaze back to me —"exquisite."

The warmth in his eyes almost unnerves me. I do not know what to do with a joyous Balthazaar. He takes my hand—wincing as he does so—then presses it to his lips. "I cannot believe that you have done it. Created a place for me in life."

"We did it," I remind him. "Not just me, but us. Together."

He stares at me a long moment, his dark gaze unreadable, and I long to know what he is thinking. He shakes his head, as if he is not quite able to grasp it all. "No one has ever invited me to share her life before." Then he tugs sharply on my hand, causing to me to stumble and fall onto the bed. I try to pull back, afraid to cause him more injury, but his other arm comes up around me and he shifts, making room for me beside him. Afraid I will cause him more agony if I fight him—and also because it's where I desperately wish to be—I allow myself to be tucked up against his side.

His hand runs down my back in a long, slow caress. "The helle-quin?" he asks.

I press myself closer against him, as if our closeness will diminish the sting of the words. "Most have found the peace they were looking for," I tell him. "We recovered over half of the bodies, including those of Malestroit and Begard."

His hand on my back stills. "And the others?"

"We found no trace of them."

I glance up at his face as a fresh wave of an entirely different sort of pain washes across his features. "I had hoped they would all end their journeys on that field."

"I know. What will happen to them now?"

He opens his mouth, then closes it and frowns. "I do not know. I am not sure what will happen to any of them now. Do we know yet if the arrow worked?"

I am relieved to have good news to share with him. "We know that they have called a truce and that the hostilities have ceased, at least for the moment. I would like to think that is at the command of the king as he decides how best to follow the direction his heart now points him in."

In the silence that follows, I can hear Balthazaar breathing, a faint, ragged sound. I long to ask him about us, what will happen with us now. We had spoken of how to live without each other but had not dared to dream of what we might do if our bold gamble worked. "Have you given any thought to what you will do now that you are free?" I say.

"As long as you are at my side, I care little. Except . . ."

"What?"

He shifts uncomfortably on the bed. "At some point, I would like to meet my daughters, to see them face to face and somehow be a part of their lives."

In that moment, I realize that if I was not already besotted with him, I would fall in love all over again. I rise up on my elbow and stare down at his face, losing myself in those eyes that now hold far more light and hope than bleakness. "Then that will be where we go first."

Chapter Fifty-Seven

TWO DAYS LATER, THE DUCHESS is holding court in the great hall. It is sparsely attended, for the entire city holds its breath, waiting to see what the French will do. Of course, the citizens do not know of the arrow and our hopes for it, but they did witness—or heard tell of—the skirmish, and they wonder what it portends.

It is the first time I have attended the duchess since we rode out into the French encampment, as she had given me leave to tend to Balthazaar and his injuries.

Sybella and Beast are at the Brigantian convent this morning, spending some well-deserved time with their families. Ismae and Duval are playing chess while the rest of us pretend not to watch, for he is trying to teach her and she is most impatient. She does not care for his being so much better than she is at the game, and she spends most of it glaring at him.

Just as Duval captures Ismae's second bishop and says, "Check," one of the sentries comes hurrying into the hall, his face pale, his eyes wide. I step closer to the duchess, my hands going to my knives. Their game forgotten, both Ismae and Duval rise to their feet. "What's happened?" Duval asks.

"We have a visitor." The messenger clears his throat. "It is the French king." The disbelief in his voice is mirrored on all our faces.

"How big is his party?"

"Only fifty archers, and he is bearing the flag of truce." The man clears his throat again. "And a rose."

Smiling, Duval turns to the duchess, who is smoothing her gown and straightening her headdress. "Your Grace?" For the first time since I have known him, his voice is filled with hope. It makes him sound younger than he normally does.

"If he is here to see us, then by all means, show him in." She and I exchange a glance.

The bemused sentry retreats, and we all wait, hope filling the room like birdsong.

The French king enters the hall with only a handful of his guard. My first impression is that he is smaller than I thought, and my next is that he is simply but elegantly dressed. He is not handsome in any sense of the word, but his eyes are kind. The duchess curtsies to him, for he is higher in rank. "Your Majesty."

He bows. "At last we meet face to face," he says. Then more gently: "I am sorry to hear of your recent loss." To my surprise, there is true sorrow in his eyes; this is no pretty courtier trick but genuine compassion.

"Isabeau is sorely missed, Your Majesty."

He glances around at the few courtiers in the hall. "I wonder if we could speak privately."

"But of course." She dismisses all her courtiers except Ismae and me, and the king in turn dismisses his guard. After that, he motions her to one of the window casements, and together they move to take a seat.

His voice is pitched low, but I have had much practice listening at doors.

"I would put these hostilities behind us if we can." He is perfectly still, except for his fingers, which fidget with his hat. That is when I realize that he is not speaking to her as a king, but rather as an equal, which does credit to his nature. "The truth is, I have come to admire the sharp mind and fierce spirit behind my noble opponent, and now that I am here, well"—he looks discomfited, as if flattery does not come easily to him—"I had not expected such a fierce and ardent defender of her people to be as lovely as yourself."

As he speaks, something inside me relaxes, for those are the words of a potential suitor rather than a conqueror. The duchess blushes prettily and bows her head, and something swells deep within me. She has been pursued by men and rulers of all sorts, and not one has approached her as a suitor rather than a political ally. Mayhap there will be love in her future after all.

I draw a little farther away to give them their privacy.

They talk for nearly an hour, and when they are finished, the duchess asks that I let the courtiers back in. As I do, I see that their numbers have doubled. News of the king's arrival has spread quickly. Duval is one of the first back in through the doors, with Captain Dunois and Chancellor Montauban following close behind.

When everyone has assembled, the duchess looks bashfully at the king, who nods kindly at her. She stands with her full regal bearing and surveys the nobles and attendants who have gathered. Briefly, her eyes rest on me, and she winks. It is all I can do not to whoop with relieved laughter.

"We have an announcement to make. His Majesty the king of France and I have discussed the future of our great countries and find that we have more in common than we have differences. We have decided to resolve those remaining differences through marriage."

A cheer goes up from everyone in the room: for having averted a disastrous conflict, for old differences put aside, and for the duchess having managed to thread this needle with love rather than war. As I look at both their faces, I realize it is indeed a triumph of the heart.

* * *

For the next three days, while the duchess and King Charles come to know each other, the duchess's councilors and a delegation from France sequester themselves in the privy chamber and wrestle over the details of the marriage contract. The king is of no help, for whatever point of contract the duchess's advisors insist on, he agrees to, until his own advisors throw up their hands in disgust. I think once more of Arduinna's last arrow and all that it has bought us.

Deep in the bowels of the castle, in a room tucked well away from observers, another series of meetings is held. The first of these is a private meeting between Crunard and me. In the rush of all that has happened, I had nearly forgotten about him, for he is still so new in my life, it is hard to remember I have a father.

I find him sitting in his cell, thinner than when I last saw him, and with the lines of fatigue etched more deeply in his face. When he sees me, he leaps to his feet and strides to the bars. "You are safe!"

"I am safe." I tilt my head. "Did you think I wouldn't be?"

"The guards—there have been rumors, stories flying about you riding out, but no one could give me any details." He appears to rein in his emotions somewhat. "I was worried for you, that is all."

"I appreciate your fatherly concern, but as you can see, I am fine. I do come bearing news, however. The duchess and the French king are to be married."

His eyes widen. "He agreed?"

"With a bit of persuasion, yes. But more importantly, she has agreed, and he appears to care for her, and there will be peace."

Crunard closes his eyes. "Peace," he says, the word bittersweet with all that he has lost.

I cannot help it then—I step forward, my voice gentling. "I come to bring you a boon. The duchess, as a sign of her appreciation for my help in this matter, has agreed to investigate the whereabouts of your son —my brother—herself. She will seek him out or learn what has happened to him, and if he is still alive, she will have him safely returned to Brittany. She has given her word."

Some of the grayness leaves his face, and his mouth twists in a sour smile. "And he can find me here, rotting in a prison for dishonoring us all."

"The duchess is in a forgiving mood," I tell him. "She has already pardoned many of those who crossed her. Perhaps she will pardon you as well."

His hands grip the iron bars. "And if so, what does that mean for us?"

I step back then. "Why should it mean anything? Why should I care at all for the man who abandoned my mother when she needed him most, who left me to be raised as an orphan, who betrayed his entire country? What makes you think there is any *us* to be considered?"

His gaze meets mine steadily. "Because I know the daughter to be a far better person than the father was, and I hope that she will see that the most recent of his crimes were committed out of love for his children."

I stare at him a moment longer, then leave without answering his question.

The second meeting is a convocation of the Nine, called in order to hold the abbess accountable for her crimes and to determine the rightful punishment.

On the first day, a delegate from each of the Nine arrives, called to the convocation by Father Effram's summons. The abbess from the Brigantian convent here in Rennes is the first to arrive, followed by Floris and the high priestess of Arduinna. Father Effram—I cannot quite manage to call him Salonius, for I am still not certain I believe that he is; it is just the sort of trick the gods like to play—presides over all.

The abbess of Saint Mer arrives, a wizened old woman with wild

432

gray hair and seashells strung around her neck like jewels. She is accompanied by two girls, one on either side, both followers of Saint Mer. I try not to stare, but I have never seen the sisters of Saint Mer before and they are startling to look at.

Beast is here, representing the followers of Saint Camulos, as their rank is closely tied with their order's hierarchy. A tall older man with dirty bare feet and a thick walking staff is introduced as the head of Saint Cissonius's order.

Mortain himself will take his place among the Nine. When he steps into the room, silence falls, as thick as a heavy snow. All eyes turn toward him, for these are people who have devoted their entire lives in the service of their gods, yet they have never met one face to face before. One by one, they sink into deep, reverent bows, their foreheads nearly touching the floor.

"Please, rise," he says, then makes his way to the seat that is for him. It is hard to tell in the torchlight, but it appears as if a faint tinge of pink has risen in his finely sculpted cheeks.

Two of the seats are empty. Amourna is no longer worshiped so much as her name is invoked when one is seeking true love. There is not any convent or abbey that serves her, and I cannot help but wonder if there ever was.

Dea Matrona too is not worshiped in a formal way, but instead finds her place in the homes and hearths and fields throughout our land.

Just as the Brigantian abbess calls the meeting to order, the door opens. An ancient, bent-back woman shuffles into the room, her long, gray hair nearly reaching the floor, her old homespun brown gown faded and closer to rags than a gown. She too has a staff, which she leans heavily upon. Slowly, she shuffles across the floor and takes the empty seat left for Dea Matrona.

Everyone stares in surprise, but she gestures impatiently for them to proceed.

The Brigantian nun begins speaking. "We are here for an accounting of the crimes of Sister Etienne de Froissard, who has posed as abbess of the convent of Saint Mortain for the past seven years, even though she bears none of his blood. She has wronged the gods by posing as a daughter of Mortain, and she has betrayed the trust placed in her with that position. She is also charged with endangering the girls put in her care, and has been accused of the murders of Sisters Druette, Appollonia, and Sabina."

And so it begins, the abbess's—my mother's—trial. Father Effram assured me that they never sentence anyone to death, else I am not certain I would be able to get through this. For all the anger I hold for her, for all the wrong that she has done, she did it out of love and a desire to protect me. I do not know if I will ever be able to resolve the two.

"Sister Etienne, what say you to these charges?"

The abbess looks almost naked without her distinctive headdress and habit, like a magnificent hawk who has lost all her feathers. She turns and looks at me, and even now, her head is not bowed in shame or remorse. I hold my breath, wondering if she will try to pull me into it, try to paint my actions with her own motives. She will not know that I have already told the members of the convocation that I too am not of Mortain's blood, although I did not learn of it until mere weeks ago.

But instead, she surprises me. "I accept responsibility for all that I am accused of. I would say only this in my defense: The previous abbess betrayed her duty to her young charges long before I did. I did not know of the existence of this convocation, else I might have tried to bring her before it. But I saw no other way to protect the girls. To protect my own daughter."

The Brigantian nun turns to Mortain, her manner becoming slightly nervous, as if she is not certain how this should all proceed in front of a true god. Or a former god. "Do you wish to handle this matter personally, as is your right?"

Mortain shakes his head. "No, I would leave it to the convocation to decide and will respect its decision." In truth, he is not nearly as angry at the abbess as I am, for he feels that without her, he would never have had me, and for that, he has told me, he will forgive her much.

"Very well. We shall withdraw to discuss sentencing—"

Her words are interrupted by a sharp, single rap on the floor. It is the old crone. Everyone turns to stare.

"I claim her as ours," she says. "She has proven herself such a devoted mother, let her serve the Great Mother awhile. Ten years."

Everyone glances around somewhat uncertainly, as no contact has been made with those who serve Dea Matrona in quite some time. Indeed, I think they all thought that she too had begun to fade from this world.

"Are there any objections?"

There are not. And so it is decided.

As the convocation breaks up, the various abbesses and priests pause long enough to greet one another and exchange a few words. It is not often they are all in the same room, and there is the sense that they have much they would like to discuss. A handful approach Balthazaar, wanting to see this miracle made flesh.

I stand off to the side, watching. Forgotten for the moment, the abbess makes her way over to me. We stare at each other. She has grown thin these last few days, and her face is drawn. "I am sorry," she whispers. As I stare into her hollow, gaunt face, it feels like the first true thing she has said to me in years. I nod, acknowledging her words. She looks down at her hands. Her nails are ragged and bitten to the quick. "I would ask one last indulgence, if I could."

I do not know that I have it in me to grant her anything, but I keep my voice level. "What is it?"

"May I hold you? Just once before I go, for I have not been able to do so since you were three years old. If I could have one wish before I die, it would be that."

Her request sneaks in under my guard and lands a painful blow, reminding me sharply that for many years, she was nothing but a young mother trying to be with her child. "Yes," I whisper. Slowly, as if unable to believe in it, she awkwardly wraps her arms around me, then pulls me close. I am not quite able to allow myself to relax into her embrace, but I do not resist, either. Some small, tentative thing passes between us. She gently kisses my brow, then reluctantly pulls away. "Will you ever forgive me?" she asks softly.

That small, tentative thing pulses inside me. "I will try. That is all I can promise. I will try."

She starts to leave, then stops. "May I come see you? When my sentence is served?"

I stare at her a long moment before I say, "Yes. But do not come back to the convent. Send word instead, and I will meet you."

Her eyes widen at my mention of the convent, and I see a hundred questions in them, questions about what I will do next, where I will go, and who I will be with. But our time is up. Dea Matrona's priestess is at her side, her ancient clawlike hand reaching out and pulling at the abbess's sleeve. "Come" is all she says. With one last look at me, the abbess leaves.

Chapter Fifty-Eight

THE DAY OF THE BETROTHAL CEREMONY dawns clear and sunny, as if God and His Nine are all as happy about this day as we are. A feeling of joy lies over the city, relief to be celebrating an impending marriage rather than a crushing defeat and untold deaths.

The cathedral is nearly empty as the duchess and the king of France pledge their vows. Only the privy councilors are in attendance, along with one French advisor and the French regent herself. I study this woman who was behind so much of the hostilities between our countries and wonder what drove her.

The duchess does her best to ignore the regent. I do not think they will ever be close.

Ismae, Sybella, and I are also in attendance. The duchess invited Mortain as well, but this made the poor bishop so nervous that Mortain declined.

Once the ceremony is concluded, the royal party turns their attention to signing the marriage contract and the peace treaty between Brittany and France. The three of us are not needed for that.

Just as she did when we were forced to attend chapel services back at the convent, Sybella begins whispering in church. "Ismae, are you still able to see marques?"

"I don't know," Ismae confesses, then looks around the few gathered in the cathedral. "No one here bears one, and I have not seen anyone marqued since . . . since three days ago, but perhaps it is simply because no one is ready to die just yet. And you? What of your gifts?"

Sybella nods. "I am still able to sense people's nearness, as always."

I smile. "Well, that is good, then, that your gifts did not disappear along with Mortain's godhood." I did not wish to be the reason they no longer had their abilities. "Which means the girls back at the convent will likely still have their gifts and abilities as well."

At my mention of the convent, Sybella pounces. "Is the rumor true? Will you be returning to the convent?" She does not sound surprised.

"Yes."

"But why?" Ismae asks. "You could not wait to leave."

How do I explain this to them? "I wanted to leave the suffocating restrictions and the painful memories that the convent held. But now, now that everything has changed, I want to go back and remake the convent into what it was originally intended to be—a place with life as well as death, with joy as well as solemn duty."

"But won't you be bored?"

I laugh. "No, for I am not like either of you. I do not relish killing. I am good at it, but I do not find any purpose in it."

"And you think you will find a purpose in returning to the convent?"

I shrug, embarrassed. "I want to show the others that they have choices, that their lives are theirs to live. I know it is not nearly as glamorous as what you two will be doing, but it is what I feel compelled to do—to put the convent back as it is supposed to be."

"What does all this mean for Mortain's daughters?" Ismae asks. "How will we be able to serve him?"

"I do not know," I admit. "Mayhap it will be no different from serving the duchess or any liege lord."

"And what of the convent and the duties it performs?"

"Again, I do not yet know. That is something we will figure out as we go."

Sybella smiles in her sly, wicked way. "Balthazaar will be going as well?"

"Yes, he wishes to meet his daughters. And put right what has gone off course."

"And with Mortain at your side, who will say you nay?"

My lips twitch into a smile. "True enough. Just because he is newly mortal does not mean that death will cease or that people will come to accept it or even that political events will not require intervention. But what about you?" I turn to Sybella. "I heard the duchess say that you are going to the French court with her?" I am still hoping I have heard that incorrectly.

Sybella smiles. "She will need someone to insinuate herself among all those long-faced French nobles that cling to her betrothed's robes like flies. Someone to report to her who can be trusted and who cannot. And she has agreed to foster my sisters at her court, which will afford them the best protection I can find against our brother."

"And what of Beast?"

"He is going as well, to serve as the captain of the queen's guard."

I am happy for her, and I try to smile, but she will be so far away.

"Oh, do not pull such a sad face! It will only be for a few years. I reckon I shall return right about the time Sister Beatriz will have to retire from her duties. I think I would make a most excellent womanly-arts teacher, don't you?"

I cannot help it, I laugh, as does Ismae. "The Nine save us," she says.

"The Eight, now."

"No, it is still the Nine. They did not change it when Amourna removed herself, and neither will they for Mort—Balthazaar. Bah! I cannot decide what to call him now."

"Just do not call him Father, and I will be happy," Ismae mutters.

"And you." I turn to her. "You will be close, so you must come visit once in a while." She and Duval will be staying in Rennes—Duval will be overseeing the duchy while his sister takes her place on the French throne.

"Oh, I shall. I may even let Duval come just so he can storm around the halls, for old times' sake." And thus everyone is accounted for, I think.

No, not everyone. My thoughts go again to the hellequin. Those who died on the field before Rennes that day have found both the redemption and peace that they so desperately sought. But what of the others? Those who did not ride out that day, or those whose bodies were not found? Did they too find their deserved reward? Or do they, even now, still ride on, trapped on some eternal hunt?

The next morning, Mortain and I set out on our own journey, one that will take us back to the convent. He has healed unnaturally fast.

As our horses prance and sidestep in the fresh morning air, I send him a glance. "I will not call you Mortain for all the rest of our lives. It will feel too much like being wedded to a god."

"Merely a former god. And you will only have to bow to me a little." His smile is as quick and welcome as a glimpse of sun in the dead of winter.

"Ah, you may be a former god, but you are only a newly made mortal, and I have had far more experience at being mortal than you."

He blinks in surprise. That I have had more experience than him in *anything* had not occurred to him. I cannot help it. I laugh as the wonder of the moment fills me. Our lives. They will — finally — be *ours* to live as we choose. Filled with our hopes and dreams and, yes, our heartaches as well. But they will be ours.

We will love freely. Laughter shall echo down the halls of the convent. And we will fight our enemies — fiercely — when needed, for as surely as winter follows summer, it will be needed.

But for now, I cannot wait to share with those whom I once called sisters all that I have learned. I will teach them how to think for themselves and not simply reflect back to the world what it wishes from them. They will be strong not only of body, but of mind and heart. And most important, I will teach them how to love, for in the end, that has been the greatest weapon of all. It has proven stronger even than Death.

AUTHOR'S NOTE

OVER THE CENTURIES, as the Church struggled to convert an entire population to Christianity, as a matter of policy they adopted pagan deities as saints, painting over the original myths with their own Christianized narrative. They also built churches on pagan holy sites and organized their own festivals and celebrations to coincide with earlier pagan celebrations to make them more palatable for the local populace. It has been said that Brittany in particular fought harder than other kingdoms against the loss of their own deities and form of worship.

Though the nine old gods of Brittany did not exist in the exact form in which they were portrayed in the His Fair Assassin books, they have been constructed from earlier Celtic gods and goddesses, about whom we know very little. I have added a few embellishments of my own.

As in the previous two books, many of the characters in *Mortal Heart* are actual historical figures, and I drew from the broad political events of the time for my story. As the second phase of the War of Breton Succession drew to a head, France did invade Brittany and held most of the duchy's cities and towns in its possession. The duchess was besieged at Rennes, surrounded by fifteen thousand French troops, trapped inside the city with thousands of mercenary soldiers who were better suited to fighting than waiting out a siege. The mercenaries roaming the city quickly became almost as much of a threat as the French troops, especially when the money to pay them ran out. That in turn created a weak link, which the French exploited by bribing the mercenaries to abandon the duchess. Even her supposed allies offered only minimal support—either holding her towns as surety to pay for the use of their troops or offering to escort her out of Brittany rather than helping her hold on to it. Maximilian, the Holy Roman emperor and her husband by proxy marriage, had his own wars with Hungary and France. France used that to their political advantage, effectively tying his hands and preventing him from being able to offer meaningful support to his wife. The situation was somewhat complicated by Maximilian's own daughter's betrothal to King Charles of France, which further bound him to that country and its ruling family.

As in *Dark Triumph,* one of the greatest liberties I have taken is compressing the timeline of the events in this book. In reality, these major events occurred over the course of two and a half years, with lots of fallow waiting periods in between. I pulled most of the major events of 1490 and 1491 into 1489, the year in which the story takes place. In reality, the betrothal that occurs at the end of *Mortal Heart* did not happen until the end of 1491.

Ultimately, the battle that had been brewing between France and Brittany did not culminate in full-scale war. Instead, Anne was convinced to abandon her proxy marriage to Maximilian and marry King Charles VIII of France. This marriage not only saved her beloved country and people from the horrors of yet another war, but gave her some political power with which to influence France's future policies toward Brittany. By many historical accounts, she and Charles held great fondness and affection for each other. After they had been together for seven years, Charles VIII died, leaving Anne once more in possession of an independent Brittany. She did go on to marry Louis d'Orleans and become Queen of France a second time, the only woman in history to do so.

But *that* is a story for another day . . .